D0042408

V WARS

A Chronicle of the Vampire Wars

Vwars : a chronicle of
vampire wars /
2012.
33305243707126
sa   05/09/19

A Chronicle of the Vampire Wars

Jonathan Maberry

Nancy Holder • John Everson • Yvonne Navarro

Scott Nicholson • James A. Moore

Keith R.A. DeCandido • Gregory Frost

Edited by Jonathan Maberry

Introduction by Dacre Stoker

San Diego 2012

DEDICATIONS

Gregory Frost: To the shapeshifters, transmogrifiers, and all the transitive vampires.

James A. Moore: This one is for my siblings, who always make my life interesting.

John Everson: This one's for my wife Geri, who's in big trouble if I turn *Wurdulac* because there's no one I could love more.

Jonathan Maberry: This is for Sara Jo and Sam.

Keith R.A. DeCandido: To my fellow jurors on People v. David Vega. A true Bronx story for my fellow residents of the Boogie-Down.

Nancy Holder: This story is for Scott Wolven.

Scott Nicholson: Dedicated to Gutenberg, Stoker, Romero, and King.

Yvonne Navarro: To Goblin, Ghost and Ghoulie, who help keep the monsters at bay when I'm home alone.

V-WARS

EDITOR: JONATHAN MABERRY

ASSOCIATE EDITOR / DESIGNER: JEFF CONNER
ASSOCIATE DESIGNER: ROBBIE ROBBINS
COVER DESIGN: TREVOR HUTCHISON

International Rights Representative, Christine Meyer: christine@gfloystudio.com   www.IDWPUBLISHING.com

Ted Adams, CEO & Publisher • Greg Goldstein, Chief Operating Officer • Robbie Robbins, EVP/Sr. Graphic Artist
Chris Ryall, Chief Creative Officer/Editor-in-Chief • Matthew Ruzicka, CPA, Chief Financial Officer • Alan Payne, VP of Sales

ISBN: 978-1-61377-151-8   15 14 13 12   1 2 3 4

Become our fan on Facebook **facebook.com/idwpublishing**
Follow us on Twitter **@idwpublishing**
Check us out on YouTube **youtube.com/idwpublishing**

V-WARS: CHRONICLE OF THE VAMPIRE WARS. APRIL 2012. FIRST PRINTING. © 2012 Idea and Design Works, LLC. All Rights Reserved. The IDW logo is registered in the U.S. Patent and Trademark Office. IDW Publishing, a division of Idea and Design Works, LLC. Editorial offices: 5080 Santa Fe St., San Diego, CA 92109. Any similarities to persons living, dead or other are purely coincidental. With the exception of artwork used for review purposes, none of the contents of this publication may be reprinted without the permission of Idea and Design Works, LLC. Printed in Korea.
IDW Publishing does not read or accept unsolicited submissions of ideas, stories, or artwork.

"Only the dead have seen the end of war."

— Plato

CONTENTS

INTRODUCTION

A s great grandnephew of Bram Stoker, I am frequently asked if the new variations of vampire characters in today's literature, plays, and movies are offensive to members of the Stoker family. Is great deviation from Count Dracula, long considered the "gold standard" of vampires, bordering on sacrilege? My answer is to the contrary; vampires have never been static, to survive they have adapted though the ages. Their very nature allows them to shape shift to affect camouflage and to adapt particular human characteristics in order to attract or horrify their victims. As the subjects of fiction, vampires have always willingly submitted to the vagaries of the pen, ensuring constant entertainment for readers and fans.

Although Count Dracula is the most famous vampire character of all time, Bram Stoker never implied the vampire was his invention or suggested the Count was the first vampire in literature. Years before Bram dreamed of *Dracula*, John Polidori wrote "The Vampyre" (1819) and J. Malcolm Rymer wrote *Varny the Vampire* (1847). It is logical to assume Bram was familiar with both, and that aspects of each influenced the writing of *Dracula* (1897).

This excerpt from the introduction to "The Vampyre" (1819) reveals significant detail about how folklore of Eastern Europe and beyond slowly gained credibility, so that when vampires appeared in English literature, readers were more likely to believe these bloodsuckers really existed.

The superstition upon which this tale is founded is very general in the East. Among the Arabians it appears to be common: it did not, however, extend itself to the Greeks until after the establishment of Christianity; and it has only assumed its present form since the division of the Latin and Greek churches; at which time, the idea becoming prevalent that a Latin body could not corrupt if buried in their territory, it gradually increased, and formed the subject of many wonderful stories, still extant, of the dead rising from their graves, and feeding upon the blood of the young and beautiful. In the West it spread, with some slight variation, all over Hungary, Poland, Austria, and Lorraine, where the belief existed that vampyres nightly imbibed a certain portion of the blood of their victims, who became emaciated, lost their strength, and speedily died of consumptions; whilst these human bloodsuckers fattened—and their veins became distended to such a state of repletion as to cause the blood to flow from all the passages of their bodies, and even from the very pores of their skins.

The one hundred and twenty-five pages of notes that Bram used to write *Dracula* show how he pieced together Count Dracula and his tale. They show how he blended commonly known folklore and mythology, with other historical information readily available to him in his own library, the British Museum, and most effectively with his own on site observations in London, Whitby, and Cruden Bay (Port Errol) The resulting creature, and the fear he incited is of course legendary.

Just a few months after *Dracula* was released in 1897, Bram explained to Jane Stoddard from the *British Weekly*, how he created his version of the vampire. He could never have imagined that his vampire would eclipse the original historical myths on which he based his story.

"He told me, in reply to a question, that the plot of the story had been a long time in his mind, and that he spent about three years in writing it. He had always been interested in the vampire legend."

"It is undoubtedly," he remarked, "a very fascinating theme, since it touches both on mystery and fact. In the Middle Ages the terror of the vampire depopulated whole villages."

"Is there any historical basis for the legend?"

"It rested, I imagine, on some such case as this. A person may have fallen into a death-like trance and been buried before the time. Afterwards the body may have been dug up and found alive, and from this a horror seized upon the people, and in their ignorance they imagined that a vampire was about. The more hysterical, through excess of fear, might themselves fall into trances in the same way; and so the story grew that one vampire might enslave many others and make them like himself. Even in the single villages it was believed that there might be many such creatures. When once the panic seized the population, their only thought was to escape."

"In what parts of Europe has this belief been most prevalent?"

"In certain parts of Styria it has survived longest and with most intensity, but the legend is common to many countries, to China, Iceland, Germany, Saxony, Turkey, the Chersonese, Russia, Poland, Italy, France, and England, besides all the Tartar communities."

"In order to understand the legend, I suppose it would be necessary to consult many authorities?"

Mr. Stoker told me that the knowledge of vampire superstitions shown in "Dracula" was gathered from a great deal of miscellaneous reading.

"No one book that I know of will give you all the facts. I learned a good deal from E. Gerard's 'Essays on Roumanian Superstitions,' [sic] which first appeared in The Nineteenth Century, and were afterwards published in a couple of volumes. I also learned something from Mr. Baring-Gould's 'Were-Wolves.' Mr. Gould has promised a book on vampires, but I do not know whether he has made any progress with it."

In *Bram Stoker's Notes for Dracula* (Rosenbach Museum) references include *The Book of Were-Wolves* (1865) by Rev. Sabine Baring-Gould. Bram's description of Count Dracula: canine teeth, pointed fingernails, hairy palms, and bushy eyebrows, illustrates that Bram associated the vampire with the were-wolf, just as many cultures, link the two creatures as allies with darkness and the supernatural.

Excerpt from *The Book of Were-Wolves:*

"Among the Bulgarians and Slovakians the were-wolf is called *vrkolak*, a name resembling that given it by the modern Greeks....The Greek were-wolf is closely related to the vampire. The lycanthropist falls into a cataleptic trance, during which his soul leaves his body, enters that of a wolf and ravens for blood. On the return of the soul, the body is exhausted and aches as though it had been put through violent exercise. After death lycanthropists become vampires. They are believed to frequent battlefields in wolf or hyena shapes, and to suck the breath from dying soldiers, or to enter houses and steal the infants from their cradles...."

Many characteristics of Dracula's precursors, were not applied by Bram to Count Dracula, but surfaced in subsequent effective vampiric personifications. But, it was without a doubt Bela Lugosi's Count Dracula who cemented the vision of a suave aristocratic vampire on stage (1927) then on screen (1931). Even today, around the world, the stereotypical vampire sports a black cape, dinner jacket, fangs, and eastern European accent, and is instantly recognizable by people of all ages.

Lugosi's Count Dracula has largely been retired to the costume shop. Vampires are no longer the aristocracy, today they are commonplace, living among the common man. Tolerance of the rebel, the bad boy, and the alien among us, has affected a divergence in the modern vampire genre. In contrast to the classic, evil, merciless vampire perfected by Bram, our world of inclusion welcomes vampires. Not only outcasts worthy of our pity and compassion, their sexual power and freedom are envied, certainly a far cry from the more solitary, grotesque, horrifying creatures of the past.

In the Introduction to *Blood Read* (1997) Joan Gordon and Veronica Hollinger comment on the work *Vampires, Burial and Death,* by cultural anthropologist Paul Barber: "How powerful the vampire's grip has been throughout history and across cultures and reminds us that the myths and legends surrounding the vampire do not describe an actual physical being, but something much more powerful, a creature who can take on the allegorical weight of the changing times and widely varying collective psyches."

The authors in V-WARS address the age-old issue: What would happen if vampires were real, and what would they be like if they adapted to our present world? What qualities would make the vampires more efficient predators, and at the same time keep them attractive and entertaining to the readers and fans of the modern vampire genre?

These stories explore the myth of the vampire from a variety of perspectives and incorporate the undead in new and intriguing situations. While their metaphorical roles remain consistent with historical vampire myth, in the mind and hand of each author the creatures have managed to adapt to the changing attitudes in our society. The vampires in V-WARS exemplify the evolution necessary for their survival.

V-WARS lets us glimpse into an older, darker world of vampires. There are no romantic heroes. Nothing sparkles. At the same time there is an exploration of the nature of the vampire. If they exist, are they merely monsters, or are they something far more complex? And, what does that mean for us? What does that mean when their *nature* drives them into conflict with ours?

The V-WARS stories are all different. As vampires are different. As we humans are different.

So...lock your doors and close the shutters. It's dark out there. Settle back and read on. You'll find it's dark in here, too.

—Dacre Stoker
April 2012

A Chronicle of the Vampire Wars

"JUNK" PT.1

Jonathan Maberry

–1–
NYPD 6th Precinct
October 12, 4:55 p.m.
One Day before the V-Event

"Was it your blood?"

The prisoner shook his head.

"Please speak up," asked the interviewer behind the glass. "Remember, we're taping this."

"No."

"No it—?"

"No, it wasn't my fucking blood. Christ, if I'd bled that much do you think I could run all that way? I'd have been passed out. I'd have been…"

"Go on."

The prisoner shook his head. *Dead* was not a word he wanted to use.

The interviewer said, "Do you remember running through the streets?"

"No." A pause. "I don't know. A little, maybe. I kind of remember it. Lot of shit's all tangled up in my head."

"Do you know why you were naked?"

"I'm…not sure."

"Do you remember where you left your clothes?"

"The cops asked me the same questions. I told them all this…"

"I'm not a cop," said the interviewer.

"You're working for them."

"*With* them."

"Whatever, man. I still told the cops. They have all of this."

"I would still like you to tell me."

"Why? They just want to lock me up and throw away the frigging key."

"They probably do."

The prisoner turned his head sharply and stared through the one-way glass. "What?"

"The police probably do want to lock you up," agreed the interviewer. "But as I said, I'm not the police."

"Then why are you asking me the same questions, man? What do *you* want?"

"I want to understand."

"Understand what?"

"You."

The prisoner laughed. It was short, bitter and ugly. "Me? What's to understand? *I* don't understand what happened. I don't *remember* what happened."

"I don't think that's true," said the interviewer. "I think you *do* remember. And I think you want to tell someone about it. You want to understand it, just as I want to understand it."

"No I don't."

"Yes," said the interviewer, "you do."

The prisoner looked at the mirrored surface of the reinforced window that separated him from the voice. "Then why don't you come in here and talk to me face-to-face."

"No," said the interviewer, "I don't think that would be a good idea."

"Why not?"

"Why do you think?"

The prisoner made a sound. Low and guttural. Possibly a grunt of anger or disgust, possibly a laugh. Possibly a sob.

"Why do you think I won't come in there?" prompted the interviewer.

"Because you're afraid of me."

"Yes," said the interviewer. "That's right."

After a pause, the prisoner said, "You should be."
"I know."

–**2**–

Starbucks -72 Grove St, West Village, NY
September 29, 12:25 p.m.
Fourteen Days before the V-Event

3

It was junk.

Pure goddamn junk.

Michael Fayne wanted to throw the script across the room. He wanted to pour lighter fluid on it and watch it burn.

Film that, he thought bitterly. *That would at least be entertainment.*

He glared at the script on the table. Couldn't really burn the frigging thing. Wouldn't be the best and most profitable use of the last five minutes of his break. The customers—those sheep—would freak. Even the regulars who were zombieing their way through the same kind of no-future, no-exit jobs as him. A flaming movie script sailing over the counter would push them dangerously close to actual reaction and interaction with the world, and you can't have that.

Fayne studied the line of caffeine addicts lined up at the counter, eyeing them with contempt. A little excitement would do them all good. Even a doctor would tell them that, but they would hate him for it.

And he needed the frigging tips.

Balls.

Besides, half of them probably had scripts like this one in their briefcases or backpacks. They were too busy ordering absurdly expensive and complicated coffee drinks because it made them feel better about reading the same kind of scripts for third-rate basic cable or direct-to-Netflix pieces of crap. No way they'd tear open a packet of compassion for anyone else. They'd think he was over-reacting and over-acting because *his* POS script was anywhere near as bad as *their* POS scripts.

He felt eyes on him and cut a sideways look to see two girls at the next table whispering to one another and stealing glances at him. They were cute. Early twenty-something, which was probably too young for him according to his driver's license but not according to his face. Fayne knew that he could still pass for twenty-six or -eight.

The girls were cute. The blonde had a few pounds on her, but most of it was grouped nicely. The brunette was borderline Goth. Thin, lots of eye makeup, too much weird jewelry, but Fayne knew the type. Emotionally damaged chicks like that were savages in the sack. Maybe a little clingy next day, but they could go at it all night.

He weighed his choices. He could give them the smile that he'd gotten by pretty much buying his dentist a new yacht. But that was overkill, and Fayne didn't think he needed to work that hard with either of these gals. Or he could give the half-smile that he wore on his head shot. Bit of Clint Eastwood from back when he used to be on the other side of the camera. Bit of Colin Farrell. A lot of Nathan Fillian. Chicks wanted to undress when they saw him do that.

So he did that one.

They both turned red and nearly collided heads as they instantly bent close to whisper.

Fayne turned away, but only enough to look like he wasn't looking.

The girls kept trying to catch a better look at the title of the script, which told him they were at least smart enough to know that it *was* a script.

Fayne set his coffee cup down on the top page of the script, obscuring the title.

Giant Ice Centipede vs. Slothtopus III.

Yeah, that would get him laid.

Not only was it a piece of crap, it was the third piece of crap in a series. They actually made two of these things already. The first one had enough of a pocket-change budget to get the guy who played the guy on that episode of *Stargate.* What was his frigging name? He was the one who went onto do that reality show about guys who used to play guys in shows like *Stargate.*

Fayne's phone did not so much as ring for that one. His agent didn't send an email for *Slothtopus* one. *Or* two. Which didn't even have that guy in it. No, for that one they used the guy who was on one episode of the soap that got canceled. He played a bartender and had something like two lines. Something like, "Last call, ladies." The kind of line Shakespeare got famous for writing. Stuff that gave David Mamet wood. That was the guy they got for the second flick. Fayne's phone didn't ring then, either.

No, his phone rang when they were getting ready to shoot number three. Three, which in any video series was a short step down from midget porn and a short step up from infomercials.

Welcome to Hollywood.

Welcome to bright lights, big cities, guest shots on Jon Stewart and all the first class ass you can handle.

Yeah, welcome to an economy plane ticket back to Newark and a day job spilling coffee in Manhattan. Welcome to crap roles that, sure, paid a bill, but at the same time dug his career a little deeper into a land-fill.

The two girls were giggling. He had to admit that they were hot. That was about the only perk there was to working a job like this. Hot chicks drank a lot of coffee. They drank fraps and lattes, and cappuccinos and mocha-god-damn-chinos, and anything else that sounded like it was something elegant people actually drank in Europe. Fayne had been to Europe. In Europe people drank fucking coffee, but you couldn't tell people that.

He eyed the girls who were still trying to read something off the top page of the script. Fayne casually tossed his cell phone atop the script to hide the name of the screenwriter. That clown was a hack anyway. Did mostly movie tie-in novels and stuff like *Slothtopus*, probably to feed a crack habit or pay alimony. Fayne couldn't believe that the writer did this kind of stuff out of artistic vision.

Giant Ice Centipede vs. Slothtopus III.

Three, for God's sake.

Four years ago he would have been the guy they called for the first one.

Seven years ago he would have been in a better movie because eight years ago he *was* in a better movie. Since then he should have been in a string of better movies. But his agent had sent him the wrong script, and to make it worse, Fayne had liked the script.

Frightbook.

Christ.

Frightbook sounded great. He got the script the same day *The Social Network* hit theaters. Shooting started the week before the Oscars. It was a can't-fail retro slasher flick that tapped the vein of social media. Even had some themes borrowed from the Craigslist Killer case. The tagline was "Facebook with Bite."

That was all over Twitter.

Good cast, too. Not great. No A or B listers, but serious character actors. The broad who used to be on CSI. The old fart from that John Carpenter flick. The kid who used to be a Mouseketeer before she grew tits and stopped bringing her common sense with her to parties. Classic—*classic*—ass. Eye-hurtingly perfect.

Except…

The Mouseketeer had too many key lines in the script; one too many pivotal scenes which absolutely depended on her to at least minimally—what was the word? Oh, yeah…*act*.

Which she could not frigging do.

She was so bad she couldn't even act like a bad actress.

Which no one expected. She was Disney trained, and say what you like about the Mouse House, they were the Gestapo when it came to training their talent. She had two Daytime Emmys for the love of Zeus. The girl should have been able to handle the part in her sleep. It wasn't Gertrude from *Hamlet*. All she had to do was act the part of a scared, pretty ingénue who showed her knockers and ran screaming from the guy with the knife.

But…nope.

The movie made about eight bucks in general release. Didn't even cruise high enough above the radar to qualify for a Razzie.

Thirty million dollar budget straight down the pooper. Made back about a mil, mostly from inbred mouth-breathers who rented the video because the cover art showed the Disney chick in a push-up bra. A last desperate attempt by the marketing department.

Fayne sipped his coffee and punched his phone to see the time. Three minutes and then he had to hoist his fake smile in place and fight the urge to serve spitters when no one was looking.

The blonde with the rack was trying to get the Goth chick to say something to him. Fayne gave them half a second of the half-a-smile. They both flushed bright crimson. Oh yeah, they might as well have bull's eye painted on them. Fayne would have bet his next paycheck that they both had tramp stamps on their lower backs. They were the type. Some Celtic knots or dolphin shit. Something like that.

He took a sip of coffee but hastily replaced the cup over the title. *Slothtopus* did not send a bang-me-blind vibe. Not even in Starbucks.

He thought about his second film. The one that was supposed to rescue his career from where it floated in the toilet next to anyone else who'd worked on *Frightbook*. That one was a science fiction thing by the guy who made one of the *Aliens* pictures. Pretty good director. Nice title, *Deep Ice*. Okay script, but it was FX driven, so no one was expecting Academy nods for acting. Fayne was second lead, the lantern-jawed good guy who turns out to be a villain in the third act and gets his ass handed to him by the plucky heroine. When Fayne agreed to it the producers were hinting at lead actresses like Mila Kunis or Emma Stone. When the cameras rolled they had the chick who did three guest spots on *Friends*, which was half a million years ago.

Deep Ice went direct to video. Didn't even nod at the multiplexes.

The thing that really torqued Fayne's ass was that he spent three months in some piss-hole place called Point Barrow, Alaska, the northernmost point of all the territory of the United States. Only twelve hundred miles from the actual North Pole. The producers wanted to use real footage of some archaeological site, something to do with the Thule people, ancestors of the Inuits, who pretty much no one cared about except on the Discovery Channel. Fayne froze his nads off for that flick. *And*, despite the expectations of the producers, he turned in a good performance. Layered and conflicted, a villain who was at odds with his own villainy. A performance that deserved to be seen.

He got sick as a dog, too; and even with a raging fever he managed to nail his lines, get his blocking right on every shot, and give them a death scene that would have had the audiences weeping in the aisles. But it never saw the inside of a movie house.

The virus he got up there—now that made a big debut. I1V1. The "ice virus." Some crap that was trapped in arctic ice a bazillion years ago and released by global warming, blah, blah, blah. Big deal. It nearly frigging killed him. By the time he got back to L.A. he had a fever of 104.7 and a stunning case of the shivering shits. Had to go to the hospital even though his medical coverage was long gone. He figured he'd still be paying that off when his grandkids were in college. And getting the studio to cover the flu when he couldn't prove he got it on their set was a complete waste of time, even with I1V1 making all the papers and scaring people worse than Swine Flu.

The flu didn't kill him, though, so put that in the win column. Actually, it didn't kill anyone, though there was all of the cliché panic, driven by hysterical news reports that were long on hype and short on facts. When Fayne got out of the hospital he went home and got sick again and again for the next month while his bills mounted and his bank account shrank smaller than his nutsack had up in Alaska.

That was almost two years ago now. The ice flu was as persistent as one of those CSRs from a credit card company. It kept coming back and never actually went away, and each time he went a little deeper into the hole because he lost work days. Twice it happened during film shoots. The producers were tolerant the first time; the second time he got replaced. Since then, all he got was voice-over crap for commercials and some background walk-by stuff on TV shows that he never watched.

If he took this new piece of crapola, then it meant two things. A paycheck that might at least get his nose above water, which was good, and it meant going back to the cold, which sucked. *Giant Ice Centipede vs. Slothtopus III* was scheduled to shoot in northern Canada. Not as far north as *Deep Ice*, but far enough. It was already October and those nutjobs wanted to begin shooting in early January. Ice flu be damned. Elk wouldn't go to northern Canada in the middle of winter, what the hell were they thinking? Did they actual believe that the boneheads who were going to watch the flick on SyFy were sober enough to care whether it was real snow or fake snow swirling around the set? After all, it was all about monsters, and they were CGI. So, what the hell did it—

"Yo, Mikey!"

Fayne looked up and saw the assistant shift manager waving at him. His break was up and although he longed to do it, Fayne had not held his lighter to the corners of the script. He hadn't thrown it out, either.

He cut another look at the girls. They were still staring at him.

"What the hell," he said and took a business card out of his wallet. It had his head shot–with the half smile—his email address, Facebook and Twitter links, and cell phone number. He turned it over, took a ballpoint pen from his pocket and made sure that they were looking at him when he wrote 'call me' on the back.

He stood up, pretending to ignore the manager, looking as cool as it was possible to look in a polyester three-button shirt and a green apron. He folded the script in half, tucked it under his arm, walked past the girls, bent and placed the card on the table exactly between them, giving them a last look at the half smile, and sauntered to the counter.

As it turned out, it was the blonde who texted him.

That was fine with him. When it came all the way down to the bottom line, he didn't give a shit who he nailed, as long as he nailed someone.

-3-

NYPD 6th Precinct
October 12, 5:06 p.m.
One Day before the V-Event

"They're going to fry me, aren't they?" asked the prisoner. "The cops, the D.A.....they're going to want me dead."

"They want to understand you," said the interviewer.

"Bullshit. *You* want to understand me. They're going to ask for the death penalty. The electric chair. Or—what's that other thing? Lethal injection? Isn't that what they use in this state?"

"We don't know what they are planning to do. Or want to do. Besides," said the interviewer, "there's no death penalty in New York. I don't think they even have a death row anymore."

"They want me dead," insisted the prisoner. He looked down at the floor for a moment, and then asked, "I bet they told you that they want to fry me."

"I'm a consultant. They don't discuss those kinds of things with people like me."

"What if they ask you?"

"They wouldn't."

"What if they did? Off the record. At the water cooler or over a beer. Do you think they should give me the death penalty?"

The prisoner was using the word "death" now. It was an encouraging sign. It showed that they were making a little progress.

"Even if there was a death penalty in this state," said the interviewer, "I wouldn't be in favor of it."

"That's a pussy answer. If you *did* believe in the death penalty, do you think they should do it? To me?"

"No," said the interviewer. "I don't think they should execute you, even if they had a legal right to do so."

The prisoner was silent for almost fifteen seconds.

"Okay," he said.

"Okay," said the interviewer.

"Thanks."

"Sure."

Another pause. Ten seconds.

The prisoner said, "I wasn't lying when I said I really don't remember everything."

The interviewer waited.

"There are chunks missing. Chunks of time, I mean. They're just… gone."

"Completely gone?"

"No…and that's what started to freak me out. I don't know if you'd call them blackouts or what."

"Have you ever had a blackout before?"

"Sure."

" 'Sure'?"

"Everyone loses some nights. You drink, you do a few lines…um, I mean, you…"

"You can say that you did some lines," said the interviewer. "I doubt the police are interested in filing drug charges against you."

The prisoner grunted again, and once more the interviewer could not tell if it was a laugh or a sob.

"Yeah," said the prisoner, "I guess so."

"The blackouts…," prompted the interviewer.

"I drink a bit. I'm not an alcoholic," the prisoner said quickly, "but I…yeah, I know how to knock 'em back. Later, when I moved to L.A., I started partying with the right crowd, and the right crowd always has some blow. Everybody does it."

"I've heard."

"Well, after some of those parties I'd wake up in some chick's pad, or in a chaise lounge by a pool at some rich fuck's house up in the hills. Woke up in my car a few times, too. Once all the way down in South Central and don't ask me how the fuck I wound up down there. I'm Whitey McWhiteboy. I don't even have many black friends."

"Okay."

"But this wasn't the same thing. These new blackouts, I mean. They were totally different."

"Different in what way?"

"They were…I don't know. You blackout after a party and you wake up feeling like a sick iguana pissed in your mouth. You feel really fucking bad. You want to die, that's how bad you feel."

"And these new blackouts?"

"Oh, shit, man…they're totally different."

−4−

Christopher Street, West Village, NY
September 30, 6:22 a.m.
Thirteen Days before the V-Event

It was the smell that woke Fayne up.

The stink.

"Christ," he growled and whipped back the sheet, certain that he'd accidentally shit the bed.

It wouldn't be the first time he'd been that drunk. Usually it was piss or vomit, but, yeah, he'd dropped his cargo once before. In college, the night he discovered that belly shots didn't mix with shotgunned Millers, Jägermeister doubles, and six lines of coke.

Ah, youth, right?

Fayne growled at his own memories—as crystal clear as digital film and accompanied by a wise-ass voice-over that was equal parts shoulder angel and devil. Both of them were assholes who used his life as the punch-line of tired jokes.

Fuck 'em and fuck this, Fayne thought as he sat up, wincing at the horrible stink.

There was no excrement on the sheet.

There was nothing on the sheet but an opened but unused condom and a smear of lipstick.

Fayne's eyes were filmed with sleep gunk and there was a taste in his mouth like a sick lizard took a whiz on his tongue.

The stink, though. Damn, that was everywhere. It was harsh.

It wasn't the only smell, though.

He looked around.

"Balls," he said. This wasn't his apartment. The bed had black sheets and comforter. Fayne would have figured the Goth chick for that color scheme, and figured it had been a Christmas gift from the blonde's friend. There was a pink scarf draped over the bedside lamp, but the lamp and the scarf were on the floor. So was the clock-radio, its plastic face cracked and screen dark.

There was no one else in the bedroom. Clearly a chick's place. Framed photographs on the walls—a girl on a horse, smiling people in family groups, a German shepherd. Who the hell frames a picture of a German shepherd, he wondered.

The dresser was littered with bottles and atomizers and tubes of cosmetic gunk. Not his shit; not anything he recognized.

But, damn, what the hell was that smell?

How awkward a scene would it be if whatever chick he'd banged last night was taking an evil dump right now? And how weird was it that she wasn't even giving him a courtesy flush. Smelled like something crawled up her ass and died.

Fayne swung his legs over the edge of the bed and pushed himself up.

Which is when things started to get really weird.

The motion of pushing himself off the bed shot him up and halfway across the floor. He crashed into the bureau and sent the perfumes and girl-junk flying everywhere. The impact sounded as loud as a car crash in the silence of the room.

Fayne froze—caught by the surprise of the sudden burst of energy and by the noise. He listened for sounds from the bathroom. A hasty flush. A timid enquiry.

But the place was quiet.

He slowly straightened.

His body felt strange. He vaguely remembered drinking a lot last night, so there should have been the trembling knees, the slosh of polluted sludge in his gut, and the throb of eyes that wanted to escape their sockets. None of that.

No pain at all, actually.

He felt bloated, though, like he'd eaten his way through the Hong Kong Buffet, and he wondered if he had. He always got hungry when he drank. It was one of the things his agent always got on him about. Five extra pounds didn't seem like much, except when a casting agent expected to see rock hard abs and no trace of love handles.

He touched his stomach. He was so full that his belly ached.

And yet he did not feel sick. Not really. Just…full.

His balance was for shit, though, but that was the only other thing askew. After everything he must have done last night, it was like getting off easy.

The smell was worse. Not like it was getting worse, but standing made it easier to take in a good lungful.

"Jesus Christ on roller-skates," he growled softly. The girl had to be in there with the shivering shits, locked into the fun and games of the epic hangover that he somehow avoided.

Better her than me, he thought.

He put the stuff back on the dresser, not bothering to arrange it. He had no idea what order it had been in. Before he turned away, he took a bottle of perfume and sprayed some on his fingers, then rubbed it on his upper lip. Best way in the world to kill the smell. It was a trick he learned when he was banging a Korean gal who worked at the Old Navy near the Starbucks. She was hotter than the surface of the sun but she reeked of garlic. Some cologne on the upper lip and *voila*—no sense of smell.

His clothes were on the floor, scattered between the closed door and the bed. He smiled. Although he could barely remember anything after that tenth shot of Jägermeister, he had a vague image of him and the blonde tearing at each other's clothes. She was about twenty pounds overweight, but a lot of it was butt and boobs, so he was totally down with it. Her clothes were on the rug, too. Matching bra and thong, so it was clear she was out hunting when he'd met her at Starbucks. Sometimes you pick up a chick and she's not only wearing granny-panties but she has one of those Batman utility-belt industrial bras. The kind they wore for function and which could probably stop a bullet better than Kevlar. When they were wearing that stuff, they usually excused themselves to the bathroom to do a quick-change before coming back in wearing something lacy and artfully losing all control.

Not this chick.

As Fayne bent to pick up his boxers he saw that her blouse was pretty badly torn. It made him smile. Real raw passion. You could never fake that in a film. When it happens like that, it's fast and furious and it's not pretty, but damn if it isn't fun.

He dressed quickly. No chance for a shower, not with whatever was going on in the bathroom. As he slipped his shirt on he felt a dull ache on his back, and he turned his back to the mirror and peered over his shoulder.

Christ.

His back was crisscrossed in scratch marks. Some of them had bled and now the blood was dry and caked. Drunk or not, he must have really screwed this chick's brains out last night.

Fayne grinned. "Groovy," he said quietly and winked at his reflection, and the horny bastard winked right back.

He debated writing a note, but decided against it. He had no idea what the girl's name was. He was moderately sure it began with a K. One of those trendy variations of Kathleen. Kaitlyn or Ketlen or Kettlecorn. Some shit like that.

Leave a note addressed to *K*?

He considered and decided what the hell. Can't be a total dick.

Fayne crossed to the dresser, found a Starbucks receipt among the junk and a pen from a bank. He wrote what he usually wrote.

> *K:*
>
> *You rock the universe!*
> *We really burned the town down, didn't we?*
>
> —*M*

Short and not too sweet. A player's note, not a promise of lifelong devotion.

He placed the note on the pillow and was just turning to go when his foot struck something heavy that was half buried by the black satin sheets.

Fayne plucked the sheet back and took a quick look.

And screamed.

He staggered backward and fell hard on his ass, and then kicked his whole body backward until his back struck the wall a yard from the bathroom door.

The thing he'd kicked lay half under the bed.

Fayne shoved a fist into his mouth to keep from screaming again.

The whole world collapsed down around him, freezing into place, choking him, wrapping bands of terror around his chest.

He heard a thin whine, a mewling voice calling on God over and over again. The voice was a broken version of his own, the sounded squeezing through the stricture in his throat and the fist that was pressed between his teeth.

"*Oh god oh god oh god oh god oh god oh god oh god oh god oh god oh god...*"

The contents of his stomach—all the food and booze he must have crammed down last night—suddenly felt like it wanted to come up and spew out. Except that he was too shocked even to vomit.

The moment stretched into impossibility. The thing under the bed refused to go away, refused to become part of some holdover of drunken fantasy.

It lay there, surrounded by the glistening black sheets.

It stared at him.

With big, blue eyes.

Fayne jerked his head around and stared at the closed bathroom
door. His fist dropped away from his mouth.

"Oh Christ no," he said hoarsely. "Please…no."

It took forever for him to climb to his feet. Every muscle trembled with the urge to simple go. To flip the sheet over the impossible thing on the floor and get the fuck out of this place.

But instead, against all sense, he reached for the bathroom doorknob.

Not wanting to. God, how he did not want to open that door.

His fingers closed around the handle and it turned with a faint click.

He released it and let it swing inward.

The blonde chick was there.

The rest of her was.

Suddenly Fayne dropped to his knees as his stomach gave a sickening lurch and everything he ate last night came surging up. It shot from his mouth in a torrent that splashed everything in the bathroom.

Not Chinese food from the Hong Kong Buffet.

No solid food at all.

The vomit painted the entire bathroom in dark red.

–5–

NYPD Emergency Services
September 30, 7:16 a.m.
Thirteen Days before the V-Event

Transcript of a 9-1-1 call received by New York Police Department Emergency Services at 7:16 a.m. on Tuesday, September 12.

DISPATCHER: 9-1-1, state your emergency.

MALE CALLER: Oh my God, she's dead. Oh, Jesus fuck she's dead and—

DISPATCHER: Slow down, sir. Tell me what happened.

MALE CALLER: She's all torn apart. Her head's on the floor…and the bathroom—oh, fuck me—

DISPATCHER: Sir, I need you to try and calm down. I need you to tell me where you are.

MALE CALLER: I–I don't know. Her place. Christ, I don't even know where I am.

DISPATCHER: Sir, are you hurt?

MALE CALLER: No, I found her like this and—

DISPATCHER: Are you in any immediate danger?

MALE CALLER: No.

DISPATCHER: What is the name of the injured person?

MALE CALLER: She's not injured—Christ, aren't you listening? She's torn apart and—

Call ends.

Serita Sanchez, emergency operator for the NYPD, looked at the screen. The software package used by emergency services displayed the street address and name of whoever pays the bill from any phone that calls in. The display read:

Kaitellyn Montgomery

The street address was a third floor walk-up in the West Village.

She contacted the dispatcher, who assigned the job to a patrol unit. It was rush hour on a New York Friday. It took thirty-six minutes for the cruiser to arrive. By then the unknown caller was gone.

There were bloody shoeprints on the landing, leading from the closed door to the stairs. The door was unlocked and ajar. The officers drew their guns, announced themselves, received no reply, and entered the apartment.

Detectives were called at once, along with the Crime Scene Unit.

"ROADKILL" PT.1

🦇

Nancy Holder

–1–

Buzzards have no borders. East of San Diego, west of Yuma, north of Mexico—as long as there was death, the scavengers had places to go, skulls to strip. With no shadows to signal day's end, they spiraled down in silence, about to land on suppertime.

The roar of seven motorcycles split the heavens like an atomic blast and the vultures shot back up into the sky. The president of the Ocotillo Militia, Bobby Morrisey, rode point; then his sergeant-at-arms, Fugly, and Johnny Rocket, his V.P. Little Sister and Manuel Mendoza made nine riders, but they occupied the bitch seats behind Monster and Bobby's younger brother, Walker. The O.M.s were on their way back from the post office two dusty towns over, where Bobby picked up something from their drop box—the mysterious nature of same being the red flag that had initiated covert governmental scrutiny. The club was headed back to Sonrisa, their town, and a misnamed hellhole if ever there was one—*sonrisa* meant "smile" in Spanish. No one was smiling in Sonrisa anymore.

Little Sister had on brand new black leather chaps—new to her, anyway. It was doubtful she knew Bobby had gotten them off a dead man. Manuel was a blip behind Monster; the eight-year-old's oversized helmet made him look like a comical action figure.

Bobby raised a gloved hand as he drew abreast of a blasted-out white panel van. It would have been easy to miss, stark as it was against the endless desert.

His brown beard was sun-streaked, and he wore a navy blue do-rag with a faded American flag silkscreened on the front. His face was leathery, with deep fissures between his heavy eyebrows and premature crow's feet tattooing his dark gray eyes. He had shiny white teeth, which he took very good care of, and he had that beefy, almost-fat appearance some bikers had—working out, maybe some steroids. Like Little Sister and half the men, he wore chaps over his jeans, and heavy boots. His wallet was attached to his belt with a large silver chain.

The other riders followed suit, climbing off, knocking their kickstands in place. Bobby pulled out his .38 short-barrel revolver. Fugly loosened his shotgun and Johnny Rocket unstrapped an Uzi, which was why he was called Johnny Rocket. Before the vampires, rifles and Uzi's were impractical carries on motorcycles. Above, the buzzards watched philosophically, as if confident there'd be more dead soon.

Second to the last in the line was Mark Thompson, about to move from six-month hang-around to recruit, a speedy time frame unheard of before the world went FUBAR. Bald and scarred, Poison was in the rear; he had been a hang-around for two years before he got his colors.

Thompson was red-headed, freckled, in a ripped-up denim jacket with lots of space for the full Ocotillo Militia patch if he made the grade. Six months before, he'd been mouthing off in the Shaft about wetbacks and bloodsuckers. Bodie, the bartender, nearly booted his ass for throwing an empty tequila bottle at the flat screen when Yuki Nitobe came on to report about the United Nations call for calm. He accidentally-on-purpose hit the mirror on the wall behind the bar, cracking it. Thompson lit into Bodie and told him no red-blooded American would blame him if he burned the Shaft to the ground for broadcasting that bullshit propaganda. Bobby intervened, explaining that the Shaft was owned by the Ocotillo Militia, and they did not appreciate vandalism nor harassment of their employees. Thompson apologized to Bodie after he sobered up and offered to buy the bar a new mirror, but Bobby took fifty dollars instead. Then Thompson and Bobby had a nice long talk about how the fucking illegals crossing the border now included fucking illegal vampires. Bobby invited him along. He could work in the bar for money. The O.M.s also cooked up a little meth in the back. Diversified sources of income.

The guys called Thompson Carrot Top, Gingersnatch, Lucille Balls. He kept up, did his patrols, acted like a square shooter. But he was a liar. He was not what he had told them, a one per-center who'd run a bike shop in Phoenix and shut it down to hit the road. He was not what they thought he was, a patriot like them, committed to the cause.

Thompson was the feds—D.E.A.—and he was undercover.

Behind his sunglasses, Thompson watched the militiamen with the same keen eye as the buzzards. He had seen someone lying in the sand. Bobby's glance in that direction said that Bobby had, too. Thompson thought about medical attention and water. But all he did was think about it.

Bobby's quiet brother Walker made sure Little Sister was off the bike before he got up. The slender fifteen-year-old girl stood beside the bike in a boy's denim jacket and beneath that, a black Oakland Raiders baseball jersey. Her long black hair was braided in a ponytail. Inexpertly applied eyeliner, and lots of cheap silver and gold bling, presents from the bikers. They got that off dead Mexicans, too, and maybe Little Sister didn't know that, either. Sunshine glinted off gangsta pendants and astrology signs; and her dead mother's cross and her father's medallion of the Virgin of Guadalupe. If religious symbols could have kept the vampires at bay, Little Sister would have been all set.

"Keep the kids away," Bobby called to Walker as he, Fug, and Johnny Rocket peered into the panel van with weapons drawn. Thompson maintained his respectful distance. It was a given that as the lowest rank, he stood guard, watching the highway, ready to sound the alarm if some kind of shit approached. He narrowed his eyes at the unmoving figure twenty yards from the van. He thought about water and medical attention.

Kept those thoughts to himself.

Reaching into the vehicle, Bobby handed a rusty dark green toolbox to Fug. As Fug cracked it open, Bobby rooted around some more, then re-emerged.

"Picked clean," Fug reported, holding out the tool box. "Clean as bones."

Bobby shrugged and holstered his .38 in the quick draw pocket of his jacket. He took off his black leather jacket, revealing muscular upper arms, one tattooed with the O.M.s insignia—American flags, twin

19

skulls, and "Ocotillo Militia." There were two long scars on the other bicep, from vampire fangs, he said. Wallet jangling, he crossed and joined the crowd of militiamen examining the body.

"Hey, there's someone lying in the sand," Manuel said in his accented English.

"I know," Bobby replied.

"Can I go see?" Manuel asked.

"No," Bobby said, heading for the dead man.

"But he might be dead. I want to see if he's dead," Manuel whined.

"Jesus, Manny," Fug said, throwing Manuel a look of disgust as he caught up with Bobby.

Bobby scowled at Fug. "Watch your language."

Bobby was thoughtful like that. He always kept the kids away from violence, death, and swearing, ever since he had executed their parents and the O.M.s became their band of uncles.

Walker opened the cooler strapped to his bike and pulled out two Horchata's he'd bought at the grocery store next to the post office. He had also bought Manuel a new coloring book and crayons. Manuel was eight. Walker handed a Horchata to Manuel and one to Little Sister. Thompson tracked their body language. She practically quivered when Walker's fingers brushed hers.

Then Walker led them over to the van, gesturing for them to sit in the dirt in a tiny patch of shade as he rolled his shoulders and cricked his neck. He smiled down at the last of the Mendozas. Little Sister's cheeks went pink and she fixedly studied the Horchata bottle.

"Do you want your new crayons?" Walker asked Manuel.

"Crayons are pussy. I want to see the guy," Manuel said, pouting.

"Don't speak like that. Drink your drink," Walker said. He looked at Little Sister. "You okay?"

She gave him a little nod, her cheeks getting redder. Walker didn't seem to notice as he sauntered away. He looked at Thompson and nodded. The word was given. The highway seemed safe enough.

Walker and Mark Thompson left the kids and joined the group around the dead man. The corpse looked like a contracted mummy, arms and knees drawn up, as if he'd been hiding in the van, died and stiffened, and got tossed out after the fact. The Bog Man of Mexico. The right side of his face was a varnished skull, bones deeply tanned, jagged teeth and a Jolly-Roger eye socket. The left half still had meat on it, leathery and desiccated. Streaks of blood mottled two deep cuts in the jerky with the deep, red-brown hue of manzanita.

The body smelled like rotten dog food. If it still had a smell, he hadn't died that long ago.

"Vampire?" Fug asked, looking at Bobby. Bobby, after all, had tangled with the vamps.

Thompson gazed from the scars on Bobby's shoulder to the fissures on the dead man's face. Did the vultures devour vampire flesh, too? Was it extra spicy? Did it have a special tang?

Bobby kicked at the body with the dusty toe of his boot. "Naw." Then, "Don't think so."

"He got left behind," Fug observed. "Where's everybody else?"

"Why'd he get left behind?" Johnny Rocket said.

"Because he died," Bobby said. He turned from the dead man and scanned the ground. "Maybe the van broke down so they dumped that, too. See any other tire marks?"

Thompson and Poison examined the melting blacktop, Thompson making a point of lifting his sunglasses so he could get a better look. He contributed to the club's well-being. He pulled his weight. Walking slowly, he followed the sprinkles of sand to the mirage beyond, where gooey blacktop shimmered like a waterfall. He had his private thoughts as he stood like a pinprick in the white-out. He hadn't made contact with his handler in a month. D.E.A. had been so wrong about the Ocotillo Militia. Whatever arrived in the post office box once or twice a month was not—or had not yet—distributed for profit. Thompson's instincts told him there were no drugs here, only overzealous vigilantes.

How far would you go, to protect your cover? Once the manuals and the badges were put away, that was what some guys on the job wanted to talk about. Over drinks. Over pool. Out of earshot of spouses and lovers.

Thompson never went there. He knew he would go as far as leaving someone cooking out in the sun. But that wasn't the issue anymore. He wasn't about D.E.A. These guys were into D.O.A. He was about that, now.

He looked at the kids. They couldn't have forgotten that these men had killed their parents. It had happened a year ago, six months before Thompson had faked his drunken scene at the Shaft. But what was a year to an eight-year-old boy? And if your mom got murdered by someone with a hot brother, did a teenage girl let time soften her rage? Did the two kids actually believe that their *papi* had been vampires? Had they been vampires?

Thompson didn't know that much about kids. But he did know that half of his own soul worked overtime to forget all the death, while the other half ripped incessantly at the scabs so the memories would always stay fresh. The memories had to bleed. Scars were a luxury he couldn't afford; what kept him in this game was the knowledge that before the vampires and other assorted mutants came, ("mutants" being a favorite term of Bobby's), life had been shitty and unfair, but it hadn't been like some page out of Revelation. Not like what was coming. In that respect, he saw the horizon with the same eyes as Bobby. It was the view up close that they disagreed on. Bobby saw vampires crossing the border. Thompson saw people as terrified of starving to death as they were of monsters.

Thompson knew what fear and hunger did to people. He had become D.E.A. because seven-year-old kids O.D.'ed, and honest cops got tortured and hung from freeway overpasses. Whoever said there was no war in the war on drugs was probably in favor of methadone, too.

But in that war, the field of battle was populated by normal people, no matter how low they sank. Horrible things happened because drugs equaled money equaled power, equaled being the ones who did the torturing and killing: human-on-human atrocities.

A new war was brewing, with a whole new brand of enemy. The scientist, Luther Swann, had his theories about what they were and how they had been created. These were normal people who had been victimized. A trigger had been pulled and the result was monsters. It was like they had disabilities. So during the discovery phase, there had been "dialogues" about cures. When no cures were forthcoming, the discussion turned to acceptance and peaceful coexistence, as if vampires and werewolves were just new ingredients in the complicated global-village melting pot. Sure, the "transformed" were aggressive and dangerous, but they didn't *want* to be. They needed resources to manage their "situation." They needed help. The words on the street became "considered tolerance" of the "misunderstood."

Turned out words were cheap. And meaningless. Which was why Thompson's temper tantrum at the Shaft attracted Bobby. As it was meant to.

22

Thompson stirred, aware that Bobby and the other O.M.s except for him and Walker were remounting their bikes. Walker was shaking his head at Manuel, who was throwing a fit of his own.

"I'm going!" Manuel bellowed. Thompson sauntered closer. Little Sister looked irritated as she gathered up his crayons, which were rolling every which-way in the blowback. "They're hunting!"

"You can hunt when you're older," Walker said. He ticked his glance over to Thompson and smiled at him grimly. "If there are any suckers left by then." Then he spat on the ground.

"We'll save you one," Thompson said to Manuel, and Walker chuckled.

"You're making fun of me. I'm not a little kid!" Manuel cried.

Little Sister snorted, rolling her eyes as she picked up the crayon box and started stuffing the crayons into it. With a roar of fury, Manuel balled his fists and lunged toward her. Sidewinder-quick, Walker shot between them, holding off the boy.

"We don't hit women," Walker said. That the O.M.s were so enlightened had been refreshing for Mark Thompson.

Manuel pushed at Walker. "She's not a woman. She's a snotty *puta*—"

"Hey," Walker said, giving him a light swat on the cheek. "Respect."

"She's stupid," Manuel shouted. Tears ran down his cheeks. "You let *her* make fun of *me*. Because you love her!"

"Shut up! He does not!" Little Sister yelled back. Her face was purple. She started to say something else, then darted a glance at Thompson. Throwing the crayons to the ground, she stomped away from the van, perhaps not realizing she was heading toward the corpse. She kept going, ignoring Walker as he ordered her to stop, and her brother as he launched into a barrage of filthy Spanish. Thompson had concealed the fact that he himself was fluent. Understanding every word, he knew then that no one had forgotten anything. Manuel told his sister that their parents were dead because of her, because she was a *puta* who had let vampires into the house to screw her and then let them bite their mother and father.

Then, as she kept going, Manuel started screaming her name, over and over, *Angela*, his voice keening and high and scared. It was as if a switch had been thrown. PTSD if Thomson had ever seen it.

Thompson watched her pretending to ignore his barrage. Her back was stiff, her shoulders hunched as if she were going to be sick. So the kids were not alright. He found that reassuring. The situation would be even more wrong if they were.

Aloof was how Thompson always played it about the biker gang. Quiet, standoffish. Just like lying, the simpler you kept your relationships, the easier they were to fake. He was no social worker; Angela and Manuel were not his problem. Still, he worried. Manuel was the only one who still called his sister Angela. She already had a biker name. Before the war, fifteen-year-old girls were old enough. Bobby had made it clear that Little Sister was off-limits, but for how long? Thompson was aware of the men circling, buzzards way out on her horizon, fresh kill or leftovers probably wouldn't matter that much. Sonrisa and its surrounding desert were so empty these days.

Before Thompson had arrived, there had been another gang, the Desert Kings, and they had old ladies they shared. The O.M.s used to party with them. But then the D.K.s moved on. Thompson wasn't sure exactly why. Bobby said they got bored, but the way he said it, Thompson knew something else had been involved. Maybe a woman. Maybe the corner on the meth market.

Manuel turned to Thompson. His narrowed his eyes. "Hey, Gingersnap," he said tartly, mispronouncing Thompson's nickname, "take me hunting."

"Respect," Walker said, pointing a finger at him, then walked off toward Little Sister.

She reached the corpse. Her back to Thompson and her brother, she covered her mouth with both hands, fell to her knees, and began to throw up.

Walker crouched protectively over her, not quite touching her. Thompson filed that away. Manuel bolted toward them, and Thompson considered his options. Choice made, he took off after Manuel, grabbing his wrist and yanking him back. Furious, Manuel started kicking at him. Thompson could have decked him, could have broken his arm or his leg or his spine like a little wax cylinder, but he kept him at bay while the boy thrashed and flailed, spittle flying everywhere.

"You let go of me, asshole! I want to see the dead guy!" he shouted.

He said, "Don't speak to me like that."

"I want to see him, *please*," Manuel said through his teeth, each syllable in admirable self-control.

Holding onto Manuel, Thompson looked over at Walker. "Oh what the hell," Walker said, shrugging.

"No. He shouldn't see it!" Little Sister shouted. But Thompson let go of Manuel, who raced over. He fell down onto his knees beside Little Sister as he stared at the dead man. Walker made four, a strange kind of family tableau. Thompson thought of Michelangelo's *La Pietà*, the sorrow and the pity. None was here. He kept his distance, peering inside the van for clues as to what had happened to the other travelers. Unless the man had been alone. Maybe the van had broken down and he'd tried to hoof it, curled up beneath the blazing sun, and died.

Am I close? Is that what happened? he asked the vultures as they wheeled above him in the bright blue sky.

They studied him as if to say, *Just die, already.*

–2–

The dead man had no I.D., no wallet, nothing in his pockets but sand. At Walker's request, Thompson helped him scoop out enough sand to give the body a half-assed burial. They managed to cover all the parts of his body, including his ass. Then Walker lowered his head and murmured a few words he explained were from a prayer for the souls in purgatory. Thompson wasn't Catholic but he had heard that purgatory had been taken off the menu. But he said nothing, just bowed his head along with Little Sister and Manuel.

Little Sister sang a sad song that Thompson had heard on the radio; she sang it through her nose like a pop star; and the buzzards seemed to ride invisible bouncing balls in the air above each high, whiny note. Little Sister's thighs were probably baking in the black leather chaps. She stole glances at Walker while Manuel blew air out of his cheeks and dug the tips of his tennis shoes into the sand, as if he wanted to take one more peek.

After she finished singing, Walker bent down, gathered up a handful of sand, and dribbled it onto the mound.

"Ashes to ashes, dust to dust," he intoned, despite the absence of both.

In another time and place, Walker would have been nicknamed "Preacher." He would have worn a flat, broad-brimmed hat and maybe a duster. He might have carried a Bible.

Walker and Thompson thoroughly searched the van, finding a handwritten note under the driver's seat that read *Moncho 12 Vieja*. There was a Vieja Street in Sonrisa, and a man named Ramón who lived in the unhappy town. "Moncho" was a nickname for Ramón. Neither Walker nor Thompson knew if Ramón lived at 12 Vieja.

When Bobby came back with the others, he was pissed off about the burial. It was clear to Thompson that he wasn't sure what to do about it. Before, when they'd been a simple motorcycle gang, they'd left all the patrolling to a local group of Minutemen. Those guys were long gone. Thompson wasn't sure what had happened to them. But when Bobby decided to take on the gig, the O.M.s had formed an alliance with the official Border Patrol, agreeing to return any live illegals they apprehended, and to report deaths like this one. As far as Thompson could tell, two factors had shattered that alliance: the execution of the Mendozas and the increased chaos in the world. Thompson wasn't even certain there were any Border Patrol agents in their territory anymore. The O.M.s were the law now.

Which could be bad luck for Moncho of 12 Vega.

As the club got on their bikes and resumed the ride back to Sonrisa, the buzzards spiraled down again and landed on the mound. Some broken-down mining equipment signaled the outskirts of the town, along with the ruins of a boxy, nondescript stucco building minus its roof and windows. About a thousand people still lived there, and about a hundred kids went to the elementary school. There was a bus for both the middle school and the high school—a forty-minute commute—but the number of students was dwindling as the world got scarier. The O.M.s escorted the bus every school day morning and afternoon. At first the gesture had generated enormous goodwill. Now folks were not so sure. Armed escort, armed guard? Were the kids passengers or hostages?

The insect buzz of the bikes reverberated off the ramshackle wood and stucco houses. No one had a lawn, but nearly everyone had an American flag. There were also a lot of statues of the Virgin of Guadalupe or Jesus or St. Francis in the sand beside porches and mailboxes. The Catholic Church was a busy place. The curly-haired black priest, Father Patrick, was nice to the O.M.s. He was grateful that they'd put a stop to the desecrations of the graveyard. He never said a word about the double grave where the Mendoza parents lay. There had been no witnesses except O.M.s when Bobby shot the Mendozas. There was a long, detailed police report describing how the tragedy had occurred—Bobby had thought they were home invaders, vampires—and no one ever said any different.

Shortly after that, the police department had already shuttered their storefront next to Sonrisa Liquor. They said they were being transferred to the storefront in Alameda del Sud, the next dusty town over. But that was crap. Their main street was even more boarded up than Sonrisa's.

Wind blew, sending a tumbleweed down the road. A few faces appeared in windows as the club roared into town. The O.M.s kept the townspeople safe while at the same time scaring the shit out of them. Thompson was sure they'd had discussions about which were worse, vampires or the O.M.s. The O.M.s had only killed two people. And maybe the cows and sheep, too. But maybe not.

The club lived in a compound of double-wides and one permanent building—Bobby and Walker's house, which was freshly painted a soft turquoise, with a large wrought iron cross on the front door and a painted shield of the O.M. colors hanging over the garage. Little Sister and Manuel had their own rooms. Thompson rented a nearby apartment, very ratty. Hang arounds didn't rate O.M. housing.

Walker and Monster took the kids inside the house. That left Bobby and four soldiers in the sandy front yard. Thompson knew they were headed for 12 Vega.

It took less than three minutes to reach the front door of 12. Bobby pulled out his .38, then surprised Thompson by pulling out another. All this time, Thompson hadn't detected the extra weapon on Bobby's person. Bobby held it out to Thompson.

"Time to earn your keep," Bobby said.

Sun and necessity had baked any vestiges of second-guessing out of Thompson. He took the gun with a steady hand.

"Maybe," he said, and Bobby scowled. "*Maybe* it's time."

"Ex-fucking 'scuse me?" Bobby said, narrowing his eyes.

"There may be nothing to do here," Thompson replied, cool, unfazed. Or at least acting that way. "It's 12 Vega, but we don't know what that means."

Bobby looked at him for a second or two. "I know that's bullshit," he said finally. Then he gestured at Thompson toward the door. "Kick it down."

"Better if I knock," Thompson said, "but I'll kick it down if you want me to."

"I don't give orders twice," Bobby said.

Then he looked past Thompson's shoulder with widening eyes. His mouth went slack. Looking at him, Thompson whirled around and dropped to one knee, aiming the .38 at whatever had startled his captain. The three remaining O.M.s stood behind Thompson, and they reacted, too, drawing weapons and turning, scanning for whatever was on Bobby's radar.

Sunshine, broken-down houses, the caw of a bird. "What?" Fugly said. "What's wrong, Bobby?"

Bobby spat on the porch, huffed out a deep breath and wiped sweat and grime from his forehead. "Fug, you and Johnny Rocket go around to the back. Just in case."

What the hell did he see? Thompson thought.

"Shit," Bobby muttered. "Screw it. Knock, Gingersnatch."

–3–

Turned out, yes, there were people inside who knew the dead man in the desert. Two men, two women. Moncho was their contact—someone's cousin—but Moncho was not there. They vagued it up about where he was, but Thompson understood their murmured Spanish, and knew Moncho had left to pick up another two folks who had been following the van in a Chevy.

In the living room, clean, loaded with religious statues and pictures of the Sacred Heart of Jesus, the four refugees sat on a worn blue velvet couch and a couple of dining room chairs—a girl about Little Sister's age, a teenaged boy, an old guy, and an older woman, all looking haggard, scared, and miserable. The four were holding big glasses of water and eating peanut butter sandwiches. They had come from some shithole border town Thompson had never heard of. Mexico was bad and getting worse—companies shutting down, stores closing, police officers joining the military. And vampires moving in.

"We see a *vampiro* yesterday," the girl said, through tears. The man in the desert had been her *novio*, her fiancé. But Thompson got the distinct impression that she was relieved that he was dead.

"So you brought your stink *here*?" Bobby shouted, grabbing her by her wrist and dragging her to her feet.

The two Mexican men jumped up, too. Thompson knew this was

his cue to let them see the .38. Poison did, too, but all they did was present arms. Thompson could see that Poison was troubled about the fact that Bobby was rapidly losing his cool again. He and Poison traded glances that said that something was wrong with him. Thompson wondered if the others had found something in the desert that they weren't telling him about. Or if the contents of the post office box had finally somehow come into play.

"We're killing you. We're killing you *now*," Bobby said, as he dragged the shrieking girl across the room.

The older woman flung herself at Bobby and Fugly pushed her back. She tottered backwards, then fell against the couch. Thompson learned more. The girl was named Maria. The woman hadn't known her until they'd met at the rendezvous point and paid the human trafficker, the *coyote* to drive them across. The dead man under the mound had been the *coyote*. The boy and the old man also were not related to Maria or the old woman, whose name Thompson did not yet know.

Thompson stayed steady as he, Poison, and Monster brandished weapons. The older woman was screaming. The two Mexican men got ready to rush the O.M.s, which would be suicidal.

"We shoot them, we may upset people," Thompson said.

"Who the fuck cares? This is our town," Bobby said. Then, "We should move anyway. This is a shit hole."

How far would you go, to save your own life?

This was not the world Thompson had signed up for.

The Mexican men started speaking in rapid Spanish, protesting that they were not vampires. Look, look, they couldn't turn their feet backwards. They could jump over spilled salt. Weird folklore, all of it. But with so many different kinds of vampires being discovered, who was to say what the right tests were to prove that these *muchachos* weren't fangholes?

Thompson knew Bobby couldn't understand what the Mexicans were saying, but he also knew none of their assurances would impress him. Moncho was going to drive them to Phoenix to find work. They were leaving soon.

The old man and the teenager also discussed the switchblades in their boots; there was a gun under one of the couch cushions and they were trying to formulate a plan to grab it and blow the bikers away. Thompson still didn't want Bobby to know he spoke Spanish, so he

29

gave the teenaged boy a hard look, dropped his gaze to the couch cushion, and very discreetly shook his head.

The boy blanched, told the older man that the gringo with the red hair understood Spanish; and the older man said loudly in Spanish, as if to make sure Thompson heard every syllable, "We're clean. I swear we're clean."

"You need to leave," Bobby said in English, the only language he knew. "If you don't leave, we'll kill you."

The old man started to glance at Thompson, but the teenager told him not to. So he kept his eyes on Bobby and said, "We'll leave when Moncho comes back. I swear it."

"They're planning something," Bobby said. "They're going to jump us."

"Then we'll have cause," Monster said. "Self-defense."

Bobby smirked as he kept hold of the girl, who was weeping. The older woman was telling her to stay calm.

"We don't need cause ever again." Bobby gestured with his gun. "Everyone sit down."

He propelled the girl in front of himself and pushed her down onto the couch. Thompson gazed at the teenager and gave his head another shake. When the boy sat down, he kept his hands on his knees, letting Thompson see them. The old man did the same. If Bobby thought they were acting strangely, he didn't indicate it.

Johnny Rocket and Fug stayed out back until Moncho drove up in a white panel van, followed by the other two men in a beat-up Ford Ranger. Moncho was young and tall. His passengers looked dried up, sunburned, eyes rheumy. After Monster and Poison searched them, Thompson and Fug herded them into the house. The living room was very crowded. Moncho lived there alone, and said he had inherited some money. More likely, he made a living ferrying folks across the desert.

"I will drive them to Phoenix, sir," Moncho said to Bobby. "They're looking for work. The girl is my cousin. We have more cousins in Phoenix."

"Thompson here is from Phoenix," Bobby said. "He owned a shop, what was it called? Sunbird Motorcycles?"

"Oh, maybe," Moncho said, cocking his head, then nodding. "Maybe I know it."

"You're a liar," Bobby shot back. "That wasn't what it was called."

"Phoenix is a big town," Moncho replied, which was exactly what Thompson was thinking. There probably was a chop shop called Sunbird. He cast a sidelong glance at Bobby. Things were not adding up with him today.

"I just want to take them to Phoenix, please," Moncho said.

"Illegally," Bobby replied.

Moncho hesitated. "There's no one left in México who can do the papers." He pointed at the older woman, who had been given permission to pour water and make sandwiches for the new people. "That lady, Amalia, her visa was granted, but there was no one at the office when she got there. Everyone was gone. Please, they all nearly died in the desert."

Thompson looked out the window. The sun was setting, casting washes of lavender and orange against the walls of the house next door. The colors transformed it, making it almost pretty. The loss of daylight was not an issue. According to Bobby, vampires could walk in full sun. They could walk into the Shaft and order a drink, and their reflection would show in the cracked mirror. They could go to the grocery store, attend Mass. Have sex. They couldn't turn into bats or rats or fly. Luther Swann had told the world that vampires didn't look any different from humans until it came time to feed. Then their canines extended so they could pierce an arterial wall. The victims died from blood loss.

Chickens, goats, cows and sheep had been dying from blood loss in Sonrisa for six months before Bobby executed the Mendozas. Folks kept livestock on their land and in common areas where some vegetation had managed to grow—the town was just too depressed to get excited over land rights, but they did get riled up when they found drained carcasses lying in the sand. A few of the browner persuasion did some Mexican witchcraft shit—nailed up pictures of the Virgin of Guadalupe, burned herbs, put eggs in jars of water inside stalls and pens. None of it did any good.

After the Mendozas were buried, the deaths had stopped for a while, then resumed. Walker thought it was *chupacabras*—"goat suckers." Winged, red- eyed monsters, lizard men, aliens—no one knew for sure what they looked like because the "facts" surrounding their existence were fodder for Coast to Coast, maybe, but nothing you'd learn in school.

The dude who ran the liquor store swore he'd seen one swooping down behind the church, but Father Patrick said he hadn't seen anything. Then there was a piece on the TV about vampires in Eastern Europe who recoiled from crosses and holy water. That was new information, and that freaked everyone out. There were some other vampires that *hopped*, and wasn't *that* weird shit? There were outbreaks all over the world, but each kind was different. So those morons on TV kept saying.

Thompson had thought about exhuming the Mendozas in secret to see if he could tell if they had been vampires, but there really wasn't any reason to. Besides, he didn't know what to look for. He was willing to bet the fangs gave it away. Bobby hadn't examined the bog man, which told Thompson that either Bobby didn't know how to pinpoint a vampire, either, or that there was some other way he'd known the Mendozas were the real thing.

"Please," Moncho said to Bobby. "Let them stay in America. Mexico isn't safe. It's going to hell."

"Go get two trucks," Bobby said to Thompson and Monster. "The Chevy and the Bronco. We'll have them ready to go by the time you get back." Ready to go, like they were processed cheese, or sheep.

"Ay, no," Moncho said in a hushed, despairing voice. The older woman crossed herself. The girl burst into fresh tears. The four illegal men stared at each other.

Thompson was the only one who knew about the gun in the couch. His D.E.A. mind ran down multiple scenarios that included shootouts, massacres, and miracles. He reminded himself that he was undercover, and that he was not a social worker. He was aware that he was reminding himself of that more and more often.

He and Poison went outside, got on their bikes, and went back to the compound. Walker was standing on the porch of his house, smoking a cigarette. He never smoked inside.

"We need two of the trucks," Poison said. "Bobby says."

"The keys are on the peg," Walker informed him. "Thompson, stay out here with me."

Poison went into the house. Thompson supposed that not being allowed inside was some kind of comment on his status—or lack thereof—so he stayed neutral, compliant. He wondered if Walker wanted to talk about something, open up.

Walker held out his pack of cigarettes. Thompson took one, and accepted a light off Walker's. The tips glowed in the looming darkness. The large cross on the turquoise door was like a shadow.

"Do you think any of those people are vampires?" Walker asked Thompson.

Thompson figured Walker wanted to place him in the middle between Bobby and himself. It was not a good spot to be.

"I don't know," Thompson said, taking a drag on his cigarette. It felt good. He had quit smoking two years before, but what the hell. "But they definitely are illegals."

Walker inhaled, held the smoke like it was weed, exhaled. His brow was furrowed. He took a second long draw and held it for a longer time, then blew it out. He picked some tobacco off his tongue. Nervous.

"Is Bobby going to kill them?" he asked Thompson.

"I don't know," Thompson repeated. "We're going to drive them out of here."

"Yeah. Good idea," Walker said. "They might be vampires. Or infected." He stared down at his cigarette. "I'm not sure I believe what they said about how somebody becomes a vampire."

"Yeah," Thompson said. "I still say *chupacabras*."

Walker nodded dubiously.

"We're driving them out in the trucks," Thompson added, "even though Moncho has a car and a van." That enraged him. Bobby was dumping them in the desert without a lifeboat, even.

"They're criminals," Walker said, but he sounded upset. "What they did is against the law."

"We should go the Shaft afterwards," Thompson said. "Blow off some steam." He had cell reception there. Maybe he could get through to his handler this time, figure out an exit strategy. He imagined the Phoenix office boarded up like the police storefront. Imagined his call going to voicemail inside the pocket of a dead man inside a coffin. With the way things were going, his cell phone was likely to wind up inside a coffin, too. Maybe he shouldn't leave. Maybe he could do something, stop something. He didn't know what he was supposed to do anymore. He thought about the dead man in the desert.

If I had thought he was still alive, would I have done something?

He thought about the girl and the other about to be dumped at the

33

border—if that was really Bobby's intention—at the mercy of whoever was still there—guard, *coyote*, pimp.

"The Shaft would be good," Walker said. "I'll talk to Bobby about it."

–4–

Thompson and Poison drove the trucks back to 12 Vega. The Mexican women were crying and there were two males lying down on the living room floor and two males on the floor in the kitchen. Moncho was sitting on the sofa with Bobby's .38 pressed against his temple. Moncho was crying, too. The smells of blood and gunpowder permeated the air like wet gauze.

The dumbass teenager had gone for the gun in the sofa. Bobby shot him through the shoulder and when the older woman tried to staunch the flow with her bare hands, Bobby wagged his gun in her face and told her to back off. The teenager was bleeding all over Moncho's linoleum kitchen floor, but that wasn't going to be a problem for Moncho anymore: Bobby was going to force him over the border as well, even though Moncho was a U.S. citizen. He had been born in Sonrisa twenty-three years ago. Went to the same high school all the bussed kids attended. His mother lived in Albuquerque, where she had been born.

Bobby didn't care. Moncho was part of the plague, the pestilence. If he loved the Mexicans so much, he could go live with them.

"I have no family there," Moncho protested, as he was herded into the truck beds, to be guarded by O.M.s. Bobby made Moncho walk with his palms against the back of his skull, like a POW. "No home. No job."

"Not my problem," Bobby said, watching as Thompson and Poison hoisted the unconscious teenager into the bed. All the men were going in one truck. Bobby had directed that the two women be put into the other truck bed, to cut down on the hysteria. Thompson was going to drive the bitch truck. Bobby would ride shotgun. Maybe Bobby sensed Thompson's wild hair: a crazy part of Thompson that wanted to careen into the darkness with his cargo of human misery and go someplace, anyplace, better.

If they had let Moncho take his car, his registration would be enough get him back across to America. Bobby was such a shit.

A few people came out of their houses as the two trucks trundled down the street. Most of them were Caucasians, but there were a few browner folks in the mix. The O.M.s had left their bikes at Moncho's house. Thompson assumed no one would dare to touch them. Or maybe today would be the day the revolution began.

Unless the Sonrisans were still too afraid of the vampires to do anything about the monsters already in their midst.

"They're fucking everywhere," Bobby said an hour later, as they bounced along a dry arroyo, having left the highway in their taillights. The trucks' headlights pierced the blackness, revealing figures scuttling into ravines, dodging behind the occasional boulder, trying to stay out of sight. Illegals, crossing the border. More now than there used to be. Maybe the D.K.s wouldn't have been so bored as before..

Bobby pulled out his .38. "Target practice," he said. But he didn't shoot.

Thompson held his breath and fought to keep his knuckles loose around the steering wheel. He did all the undercover tricks he'd been trained to do to give the impressions that he didn't give a damn one way or the other. But he could feel his adrenaline rising precipitously.

"Walker thought the Shaft might be good after this," Thompson said.

His .38 balanced against the base of the open passenger side window, Bobby stared into the darkness. Thompson stayed loose, kept his eyes on the road. "Huh," Bobby said, without firing, sounding disappointed.

"The Shaft. Yeah," Bobby said. They drove for another ten minutes or so. Then Bobby said, "Stop the truck."

Thompson obeyed. The other truck stopped, too. "Stay here." Bobby climbed out and walked over to the driver's side of the Bronco to parlay. The headlights of the Bronco went out. Overhead, the moon poured milky silver on the sand and scrub. Thompson pulled out his cell phone. No bars.

He unrolled his window. Something metallic groaned. Suddenly he heard shouting, weeping, begging. Saw something dash into the darkness. The figure of a man, followed by another. Moncho.

Bobby.

Thompson pocketed his phone and reached for the keys in the ignition. If he started driving, what would he do? Go after Bobby, run him over? Save his female cargo? He knew he had a quarter tank of gas left. Would that take them far enough to get away?

He heard a gunshot. His blood went cold. His fingers impotently grazed the keys as Bobby reappeared. Moonlight glinted off his .38.

Bobby trotted past Thompson to the other vehicle. Some conversation ensued. Silence. Bobby climbed back inside, shut the door, and studied Thompson for a moment.

Then he said, "Let's go."

Thompson turned on the ignition and put his foot on the gas. They drove for a couple of minutes and then Bobby said, "I got him. Shot him in the head." Thompson nodded, deadening himself so he wouldn't react. Bobby sighed. "Fucker had to try to be a hero." Thompson nodded again.

Bobby slid a glance at him. "Just so's you know, Fug had his Uzi trained on you while I was out of the truck. You did okay, Carrot Top."

"Thanks," Thompson said. His carrot-top hair stood on end.

They reached a sad little border crossing—a guard gate and a lot of barbed wire fence. There were also guards on the other side, Checkpoint Mexico. Two gringos on the American side, two Mexicans on the *vampiro* side. They looked surprised to see two trucks pull up, engines idling.

Moncho was—had been?—an American citizen. He could spill the beans.

The teenage boy was nearly dead. By their detached expressions, Thompson figured the guards were going to wait him out. The girl was throwing herself at them, telling them the horrible story. Saying there had been one more, her cousin, *Norteamericano*, who was forced from the truck and made to run, and the one with the beard had shot him.

Bobby shook hands with all four guards. He was slipping them something—money, drugs. Bribes, at any rate. They took all the illegals off their hands including the girl, who was shrieking, shrieking for help. Thompson kept his hands easy on the wheel, and the two trucks trundled back across the desert.

– 5 –

They went to the Shaft that night. Thompson threw them back. The TV was on, and in some kind of sick karmic joke, Yuki Nitobe was interviewing Luther Swann.

"This is happening to these people against their will," Swann was saying. "We need to be tolerant while we search for a cure."

"Yeah, tolerate this," Bobby said, giving the flatscreen the finger. He put his elbows on the bar and picked up his shot. Cocked his head and downed it. "Those assholes don't know what it's like out here in the trenches. Swarming across the border. *Damn*, did you see them? They're like jackrabbits."

"Rats," Fug said.

"What if someone comes looking for Moncho?" Walker asked quietly. His face was drawn, tense. He didn't like what his brother had done. Thompson wondered if he could be flipped.

"Who? Who is going to look for him?" Bobby said. He signaled to Bodie to bring another shot. "Two," he said to Bodie. "One for my little brother, who seriously needs to loosen up."

Bodie set down two shots. A nod from Thompson, and he was off to get him one, too.

"We still feel that we can avert a crisis." It was some Pentagon general pontificating away, in the way that all bureaucrats did.

"You asshole," Bobby yelled at the screen. "We're at *war!*"

"Fuckin' A, Bobby!" a patron called from across the room. He was a toothless, grizzled desert rat. Thompson recognized him from his apartment complex.

"We're at *war!*" Bobby shouted again. Four of the O.M.s cheered. Thompson smiled grimly and Walker stared down at his empty shot glass. Then he glanced past his brother at Thompson, and caught his eye. Held it.

Thompson excused himself, walked into the corridor that led to the greasy kitchen and the filthy bathroom, and pulled out his cell phone. Dialed.

His handler did not pick up. He erased the call and went back into the bar.

– 6 –

No one in town said a word when, at Bobby's suggestion, Thompson moved into 12 Vega.

No one asked where Moncho was. No one came from out of town to investigate his disappearance. The O.M.s started referring to 12 Vega as "Carrot Top's house," and by virtue of occupying a house, Bobby said he had moved up to recruit and the other soldiers began to treat Thompson with more respect than a recruit was due. It was unconscious on their part; it made him nervous, because it conferred increased full-patch worthiness on him as well. No one became a full patch without passing a test—committing a felony, usually a murder. Next time they ferried illegals back across the border, he might be the one running through the darkness with a glinting .38.

His handler answered three weeks later. Thompson said, "I need to get the hell out of here."

His handler said, "Sit tight," and hung up.

Thompson methodically went through all Moncho's mail. There were coded letters—*coyote* assignments, he assumed. He didn't show any of them to Bobby. He burned them over the flame of a vanilla-scented candle he'd found underneath Moncho's bathroom sink. He'd been living in Moncho's house for over a month when Moncho got a letter from the IRS, telling him he'd overpaid his taxes. A refund check was enclosed. $219.21.

Thompson went into the bathroom, lifted the toilet seat lid, and stared downward, as if he could see himself, treading water so as not to drown.

Then, as he stood and headed for the door, Moncho lunged for him, fangs extended.

Moncho's eyes glowed red and his canines were an inch long. Moncho was a vampire, and he hurled himself, hissing, at Thompson. The bathroom was tiny but Thompson's extensive martial arts training included knees and elbows, and his body supplied the adrenaline to add deadly force to his moves as he beat Moncho back. Moncho had a reflection, and he was bleeding. Beneath Thompson's fists, his flesh felt warm and he was panting, breathing.

Thompson pummeled him into the hallway and Moncho slammed backward against the wall. He left blood on the wall as he pushed off, hissing at Thompson. Thompson kept hitting. One of Moncho's fangs broke off. His face was hamburger.

Thompson hit him so hard that Moncho whirled in a half-circle. Thompson saw the gunshot wound. Bobby had only grazed the side of Moncho's head.

Thompson hit him again. Then Moncho collapsed on the floor with a weird, high-pitched keening that Thompson translated as crying. Through shredded lips, Moncho said in English, "This. This is my house."

Then the bright red glow in his eyes went out.

✹

"JUNK" PT.2

Jonathan Maberry

– 6 –
Christopher Street, West Village, NY
September 30, 8:36 a.m.
Thirteen Days before the V-Event

When Detective second grade Jerry Schmidt and his partner, detective third grade Mike Yanoff, arrived at the crime scene, they already had a pretty good idea that this was going to be a pisser of a case.

The chatter on the radio had been exceedingly formal, and that was never a good sign. It usually meant that this was either something internal—and Schmidt didn't think so because he usually got a cell call with a heads-up—or it was something that had headline potential. Cops who had political aspirations loved the political cases, but cops who wanted to do their jobs didn't. Nothing could make a case go colder than press coverage. Bad guys read newspapers, too. With the speed of Internet news, a perpetrator in a hot case was often inspired to get on a train or bus, or take a long drive in the country and be somewhere else before forensics finished collecting hair and fibers. That kind of early warning system hurt a lot of good investigations.

And, Schmidt knew from personal experience, headline cases often dialed up the pain for the families of the vics. Schmidt had seen the crushing effect on people who were already having the worst day of their life.

Now the press would be everywhere. Those pricks were often talented investigators, which meant that way too often they were interviewing witnesses and suspects long before the detectives could get there. Pissing in the pool, polluting lines of investigation, spoiling leads.

All of this ran through his head as he and Yanoff got out of their unmarked Crown Victoria on a side street adjacent to the crime scene. Uniformed officers had already blocked off the street and were doing active crowd control. So far, however, there were no news vans and no reporters doing stand-ups.

"Gonna start soon," said Yanoff, reading Schmidt's mind.

"Yeah."

They badged the uniforms and were passed through to the lobby of the small townhouse and climbed the steps to the third floor.

They saw the bloody handprints as they entered the apartment.

Schmidt and Yanoff had seen everything. Mob hits, homicidal hack jobs, gang war slaughter parties. They'd seen carnage ten times worse than this.

Even so, as soon as they entered the apartment, they both stopped and stood there in silence. The blood was terrible. Of course it was terrible. Everything about their jobs was terrible. In terms of the actual damage done, this wasn't even on their personal top ten.

And yet...

They stood there.

It wasn't the blood.

It wasn't the degree of harm inflicted on this young woman.

It wasn't that.

"Jesus," murmured Yanoff.

"Christ Almighty," murmured Schmidt.

They had seen everything, and yet...

Both of them knew that they hadn't seen this before.

–7–

NYPD 6th Precinct

October 12, 5:51 p.m.

One Day before the V-Event

"Do you think they'd let me have some cigarettes?" asked the prisoner.

"Sorry, but I don't think so. Smoking isn't permitted in public buildings."

The prisoner grunted. "Yeah," he said darkly, "those things'll kill you, right?"

They both laughed. It was brief and so brittle that the pieces of it fell around them.

"You called the police?" asked the interviewer.

"Yeah. From a pay phone. And, Christ, it's hard to find a frigging pay phone anymore."

"Everyone has cells."

"I couldn't call from my cell."

"I suppose not," agreed the interviewer. "Was that the first time you blacked out? Like that, I mean?"

There was a long pause.

"I…don't know."

"What do you mean?"

"I mean, I don't know. I can't account for every night."

"Wouldn't you remember a night like—"

"No, that's not what I mean," said the prisoner. "There were other nights, other chicks. But…I never woke up in someone's place. Not like that."

"What happened on those other nights?"

"I don't know. I'd see some broad, I'd make a move, or I'd let her make a move. You know, at Starbucks or at a party. Maybe at a club. I know how to work that scene. It's all acting. Everyone's acting."

"How many times did this happen?"

"I said I don't know. How can you remember a blackout?"

"You remember those times when you woke up in an…um…situation. Like the first one?"

"I guess."

"Tell me about those times. Tell me what happened."

"I *am* telling you. I'd hook up with some chick and we'd go back to her place."

"Not your place?"

"No."

"Never?"

"No," said the prisoner. "No way. You bring a piece of ass back to your place and then they know where you live. They know shit about you. Last thing I need is some chick going stalker and waiting on my doorstep. Screw that."

"Okay. Let's discuss what actually happened when you went to their places."

"Well…mostly it's what you think happened. We'd go there, we'd have some more drinks, do a line or split a blunt, and then I'd tap that and head home."

"You didn't sleep over?"

"I don't like to sleep over."

"Why's that?"

"Like I said, man, it sets up a connection. I'm there for the pussy. I'm not looking to establish a meaningful relationship. Been there, done that, have the tattoo."

"Okay. What about those nights? Did you black out on any of them?"

"I told you, I don't know. You live that life and you're always pretty much hit in the ass. By the time I'm getting my dick wet, I'm so sauced I could be screwing the hottest chick in the world or Rodan the Flying fucking Monster. Sober's not a destination, you dig?"

"Sure," said the interviewer, careful to keep his feelings out of his voice. "It's all about the sex."

"It's about having a good time. Making a bad day end good."

"But no sleep-overs?"

"No."

"If you were that, um, under the influence…how did you get home every night?"

"Cabs, mostly. Sometimes I'd drive."

"No accidents?"

"No."

"No tickets for DUI?"

"No."

"Then what?"

"Then I'd wake up in the morning."

"Were there ever any signs of—"

"Signs of what?" the prisoner cut in, his tone heavy with accusation and sarcasm. "Signs of violence? Blood, scratches? Yeah, the cops asked me that, and the answer is no."

"Never?"

"No. Not once."

"Did you ever contact any of those women again?"

"Christ no."

"Did they ever contact you?"

A pause.

"Did they?"

"Sure. If I picked them up at the coffee shop, sometimes they'd come in again, looking to see if we had any chemistry, maybe hoping for another hook-up."

"And—?"

"Once is fun, twice is a pattern. I'm not looking for anything more permanent than what I was doing."

"It…doesn't sound *fun*."

The prisoner looked away for a moment. He sighed and then slowly turned back to face the one-way mirror. "What can I tell you, man? Life sucks and then you die." He shrugged. "But I got a lot of pussy. More than you ever got, I'll bet."

"It's not a competition."

"Yeah. That's the kind of thing a shrink would say."

"I'm not a shrink."

The prisoner looked genuinely surprised. "What?"

"Not in the way you think. Yes, I have a degree in psychology, but it's only a bachelor's. I'm not a therapist of any kind."

"Then what the hell are you?"

"I'm a folklore professor from UCLA," said the interviewer.

"Folklore…?"

"Yes," said the interviewer, "I suppose it's fair to say that I'm one of the world's top experts in vampires."

– 8 –

Mark Hotel, 25 E. 77th Street, NY

September 30, 9:01 a.m.

Thirteen Days before the V-Event

Yuki Nitobe thought it was all junk.

Her career, her supposed upward mobility. Fame, fortune, the works. Junk.

She wasn't sick and she wasn't ice skating. It was her career that was circling the drain. The Pulitzer she'd won eleven years ago was a career high and she'd surfed along on that from one job to another, climbing higher each time. That story had been a godsend, and she'd stolen it right out from under another reporter. Yuki did not so much flinch at the moment of commission or in the weeks following when that reporter bleated and cried about it to their editor. The editor was old school: the story belonged to the reporter who filed it, and everyone else simply should have hustled better. Yuki was a hustler, and for a while that really worked for her.

44

Eleven years is a long time to wait for a second home run, though. Yuki sometimes wondered if the reporter she screwed had cursed her. It felt like a curse. Yuki went to Afghanistan three times and each time there was a freakish lack of anything interesting blowing up. She'd been in Libya covering the fall of Gadhafi but when the story went cold she came home; the following day the rebels found and killed the dictator.

That kind of luck.

Day late, dollar short, wrong time zone.

Her looks kept her on TV. She had a great face, with all of the exotic appeal of her Japanese parents and her American nutrition. Four thousand dollars' worth of fake tits and the best smile money could buy; Yuki knew that she was a knockout. But she was a thirty-four-year-old knockout, and soon she'd be thirty-five. Pretty soon she'd cross that dreadful line when she would be referred to as either "still pretty" or, worse, "a handsome woman." If she couldn't gold plate her credentials she'd never sit behind the anchor desk. As it was, she was filing field reports that lacked actual news, pouring grease on the career slope.

Each morning she woke up to the realization that she was becoming a stereotype. The failed reporter with no real friends and no real future. Her own life would make bad TV. It would make a weak punch line for a dull joke.

She'd kill for a story that she could make her own. A really good hurricane with her first on the scene, or an earthquake with a triple digit body count.

Then she got a phone call from a friend of hers, police dispatcher Serita Sanchez. Well—not a friend, really. Serita was one of the people who fed tips to Yuki. And, well, not "fed," exactly. Yuki paid for those tips and she paid very well.

Mostly it was money pissed down the toilet.

Until today.

Yuki was the first reporter who learned about the murder in the West Village. She was the first one on the scene. Serita gave her the address, the phone number, and the name of the victim. Serita wanted the money; the economy blew.

Yuki was ecstatic.

She broke speed laws and endangered both pedestrians and fellow motorists getting to the crime scene. Her cameraman, Moose, was already on the way, plowing through the morning mess to meet her there. Yuki had a good quality portable recorder with a crystal clear satellite uplink. If Moose was late, Yuki could still file a verbal report, which the station would play with her headshot as a placeholder for the live feed. That might even work. It would be like she was deep in Indian country, filing from the edge.

As she hurried up the street to the police line, her smile grew a little brighter. The cop working that crowd was Charlie Sims. Charlie was one of Yuki's "people."

Charlie was smiling, too. Charlie had two kids, and in this economy kids were expensive.

"Talk to me," said Yuki Nitobe.

Patrolman Charlie Sims, the officer at the barricade cut a quick look around. Most of the crowd was around front, but the side streets were still pretty clear. The only spectators were yards away, peering at the parked police cars as if the empty machines held some answers to the big commotion.

"It's a mess up there," said Sims. "I wasn't up there for long, but it was long enough to see how bad it is."

"Tell me," she urged. "Remember the Boddinger thing a couple of years ago?" She chewed her lip for a moment, accessing the vast heaps of data stored in her head. Every major crime, every disaster, every drop of blood that came onto her personal radar was filed away. She nodded. "Husband and wife killed, right? Russian mob was suspected. Is that what we have here?"

"No, not the Russians, or at least I don't think so; it's the *way* it was done. Blood everywhere, and I do mean everywhere. And even though I was only a few feet inside the door, I could see through into the bedroom. The bathroom door was wide open, and it was all right there."

"What was right there?"

"The girl. In the bathroom and in the bedroom."

"Which one?" asked Yuki, confused.

"What?"

"Was she in the bathroom or the bedroom?"

"Both," he said with a crooked jack o'lantern smile. "Whoever did this cut her to frigging pieces, Yuke."

She hated being called "Yuke," but right now she didn't care. This was good stuff. This was really, really good stuff.

"I need to get in there," she said.

Sims laughed. "Not a chance. The Goody-Goody Twins pulled this one."

Yuki cursed. With most of the detectives, Yuki could manage to bribe, bully or flirt her way right up to the edge of the crime scene. Close enough to get a quick photo or some footage with a lipstick cam. But not with Schmidt and Yanoff. They gave nothing to the press. Not a word, not an inch. The miserable pricks.

"Tell me what you saw," she said. "Everything."

"We good with the rates?" he asked.

"Come on, Charlie, don't be that way. You know I'm always good. But let me say this," she added, "If you can get me a copy of a crime scene photo, there's an extra hundred."

"They'd fry me."

"Only if they figured out who leaked the photo, and you're too smart for that."

Sims gave her a sly look, well aware that he was being played. But the money was sweet, and he had a friend in forensics who could get him pretty much anything.

"A hundred for a picture," he said. "But if there's more, then we talk."

"If it's *good*, we'll talk."

He thought about that, then nodded.

"Okay," he said. He told her everything he knew.

—9—

75 Bedford Street, NY
October 4, 8:36 a.m.
Nine Days before the V-Event

It was junk.

Broken. Tangled. Smeared.

Junk.

Three hours ago it had been beautiful.

Two hours ago it had sweated and groaned and clawed and cried out a name that wasn't his. Not really his. Not deep down.

One hour ago it had screamed.

Now…

Now it was junk.

He watched it change colors as the night changed. As clouds moved in front of the moon. As the slashed and stained curtains moved in the sluggish breeze, painting the debris with translucent shadows. There were colors he had never seen before. Nothing was black. Nothing was white. But there were ten thousand shades of blue and gray and red.

Before, he had never suspected such colors existed. Now, he could not bear the thought of never seeing them again. Nothing could be as beautiful as this. Not in daylight. He wasn't sure—*he* had never seen daylight—but he was positive that its glow would wash colors to a uniform opaque nothingness. For him, at least. The way night did to them.

To the other him.

The old him.

To Michael Fayne.

Fayne. The one whose perceptions were blunted. Christ, how could he have managed to walk down a street with perceptions as fractured and useless as that? How could anyone?

He was not yet Michael Fayne, though. Not entirely.

He wrapped his arms around his shins. It wasn't to protect himself from the sting of the October breeze. No, he liked that. He liked that just fine. Wrapping his arms around his legs was comfortable. It felt somehow more natural as he crouched there on top of the refrigerator. Barefoot, naked. Painted in a thousand shades of red.

Staring at the junk on the floor. And on the table.

He counted the pieces. He frowned and counted again, coming up short again.

Where was the rest?

He cut a glance at the window, wondering if he'd thrown some pieces out. It's possible. For a while there he wasn't tracking everything that he was doing. For a while he just *was*.

Now he was aware of everything. The colors, the smells. Some of them were smells he used to hate. That was all changed. Every smell had a thousand layers. Peel one back and there was another. And another. It frustrated him that he couldn't identify them, but then he thought about it. He would have time to catalog each and every one. If he was right about things, he would have time.

If he was wrong…

The thought of losing all those smells, all those colors, all those tastes—God, the million subtleties of taste—was the only thing that frightened him.

And suddenly he realized that it truly was the only thing that frightened him. Everything else just didn't. Not anymore.

Not since the change.

How long had it been?

Time meant almost nothing to him, and he realized that with barely a flicker of concern.

No, that was wrong. That was a lie.

Time did matter.

Time meant change. Time meant night and day.

He looked out of the window at the cloudy sky. It was deep into the night now. Maybe two o'clock. Or was it three?

Suddenly fear was there, blossoming like a tumor inside his chest.

What if it was four or five o'clock?

What if the end of night meant the end of this? The end of all these beautiful smells and tastes and sounds and textures? What if it meant the end of him?

He closed his eyes, trying to hear the pulse of the night. New York was so loud and loud in so many ways. A minute ago he loved that symphony, now it was a cacophony. On one side of a fractured moment, it spoke to him in its ten thousand voices, revealing truths to him, and on the other side it yelled so loud that he could not understand any single thing. The change was that fast, that complete; and he was aware that it was not an actual change. It was perceptual, but that made it no less terrifying.

What was the night hiding from him?

What did time mean to him?

As he struggled to understand this sudden mystery, he realized that the color of the night was different. Someone had splashed blood on the clouds.

He stared at it for a long minute, eyes unblinking.

"Oh, God," he said in a voice that was thick and wrong. There were too many teeth in his mouth, and too much mucus in his throat. Too much bile in the blood that burned in his mouth.

The bloody clouds whispered an awful secret to him.

It was not five o'clock.

It was *dawn*.

And dawn was going to tear him apart. As he had torn her apart.

It would reach into him and rip out whatever it was that allowed him to smell ten thousand smells and see ten thousand colors. It would smash down his perceptions, cracking them, blunting them.

Turning them all to junk.

Turning him to junk.

Turning him back.

He jumped down from his perch, landing in the lake of blood that covered the kitchen floor. He stared down into it, seeing his naked body, seeing the belly swollen with quarts of blood. Seeing the face that was new and not at all like the face he had worn for thirty-four years.

Seeing the teeth.

Seeing the eyes. And only in this muted reflection did black and white exist.

White, white teeth.

Bottomless black eyes.

Yet, even as he watched, the teeth changed. The eyes dimmed from a totality of blackness.

"No," he begged. Still in his voice, not in Fayne's.

He looked wildly around the apartment. His clothes were smeared with blood. His shirt was torn.

It didn't matter. He dressed as fast as he could. If he hurried, if he was fast, maybe he could make it home before true daylight stripped the magic off the sky. Maybe he could wash away the blood, hide the clothes.

Would *he* forget this? Would *he* think this was all a dream?

"Please, God, please…" he begged, though he was not at all sure to which God he prayed. *He*—the imposter who would soon reclaim this body—believed in nothing. Maybe he believed in money, maybe in his dick, but nothing else. Nothing grander. There were no mysteries in *his* mind.

But since the change, the new him—the true him—knew that there were many mysteries. Vast mysteries. Beautiful secrets waiting to be whispered in his ear. Secrets waiting to be torn from the flesh and read in the movement of blood through capillaries and veins.

Would the god of that world listen to prayers?

"Please," he whispered as he hurried out of the apartment. "Please."

If he was what he knew that he was, if this change was what he believed it had to be, then there must be a god of this dark world. Nothing else made sense.

He closed the apartment door behind him and fled down the back stairs. His car was parked behind the building.

Suddenly he was behind the wheel and did not remember opening the door or getting in.

He blinked.

He was ten blocks from the apartment.

How—?

He was reaching for a doorknob. His. No, *his*.

How had he gotten here, though, so fast?

No…how had it gotten so light. Pale red along the edges of the cloud cover. It shouldn't be this light for half an hour yet.

Inside his house.

No…inside *Fayne's* house.

The wall clock.

Six minutes past six.

Impossible. He was at her apartment not a minute ago.

He stood naked and dripping in the hall. Was it raining outside? No, the trail of wet footsteps led from the bathroom. The clock said six-nineteen.

"No," he said.

The dawn whispered, "Yes."

He turned to run but his cheek moved against the cool pillow and his legs tangled in the sheets.

"Please, no."

He stared at the brightening shadows in the room. They were so pale, so empty and featureless. There were no colors in them. No secrets.

He tried to smell them.

Nothing.

"This is not who I am," he said to the empty shadows. "This is not *what* I am."

But it was.

Michael Fayne stared through the open window and was surprised that he did not see the flickering fires of hell.

"Oh, God," he whimpered. "What *am* I?"

"LOVE LESS" PT.1

John Everson

–1–

"And that is why you should never let a plumber look at anything but your pipes," Danika Dubov concluded, flashing a row of perfectly white teeth and strikingly ice-blue eyes at the camera. The audience followed the cue of the stage manager hovering just behind Camera 2 and exploded into instant applause. Danika held the knowing grin for exactly ten seconds while the camera pulled back, and then she rose from her seat on the set and shook hands with her guests, a swarthy guy with a blonde crew-cut and a petite girl with hair almost as dark and long as Danika's.

The credits rolled as the talk show host smiled and chatted and led her guests off-stage. But as soon as they stepped off the stage and her producer, Lon Lawrence stepped up to meet them, Danika's smile evaporated. "I need five," she said simply, and Lon nodded. They had worked together at the Chicago ABC television affiliate for a long time, and had a code between them. Lon knew that when 'Nika needed five, he needed to shepherd the guests away ASAP. Or something bad would happen. Something for media columnist Robert Feder to feed on in tomorrow's newspaper. The show didn't need that kind of publicity. For "talent," Danika wasn't too difficult to work with. But everyone had their moments.

Danika flashed a half-smile at the plumber and his mistress. "Thanks again," she said, and then walked away, moving fast to her small office at the other end of the hall.

It wasn't much of an office for a popular morning talk show host, but it was private and held a desk and a small couch she could escape to. She shut the door behind her and leaned her back against it, staring out at the grey day outside. "Shit," she whispered, holding a hand to her belly. Something gurgled inside. She could feel the skin tremble beneath her palm.

Danika lay down on her couch. It was too small for her to totally stretch out on, so she kicked her heels off and rested her calves on one couch arm as she propped her head on the other. Then she swore again to the empty room.

"I'm tired of feeling like this," she complained. Deep inside her, something shifted and the nausea came again. She'd managed to keep it under wraps on camera, but now…now she wanted to go puke her guts out.

Someone knocked on her door three times. But didn't wait for her to answer. Instead, the door opened before the echo of the last knock had faded and Lon walked in. "What's wrong?" he demanded. "I thought the show went well today, though the next time you ask a plumber about the subtext of Shakespeare, I promise I will walk onstage and slap you."

"C'mon," Danika grinned. "It was fun to watch him sweat. I mean, how often can you get someone to compare *A Midsummer Night's Dream* to a Jenna Jameson movie?"

Lon grinned, in spite of himself. "Good TV, *baaad* talk show host." He walked across the room and knelt in front of her at the couch. "Now what's the matter? Same thing as yesterday?"

Danika nodded. "Every morning. It feels like my intestines are trying to slither right out of me."

"Ah yes, the dreaded snake gut disease. Sounds like the flu. Maybe you should go to the doctor and get some antibiotics."

She shook her head. "Not to be gross, but…nothing's coming out. At least, nothing unusual. And by mid-afternoon today, I bet you I'll be perfectly fine again."

"Hmmm…maybe you've finally developed a healthy dose of stage fright. It's about time; have you watched your reels?"

Danika slapped his shoulder and stuck out a tongue at him.

"Keep that in your mouth unless you're going to use it on me," Lon grinned.

"Oh, I'll give you a tongue-lashing alright," she said. "But it's not going to be the kind you want. Wait 'til Legal hears about this sexual harassment case: Producer bursts into a sick girl's office without permission, and then takes advantage of her loose tongue…"

"I think Legal has other problems with your loose tongue to worry about. You know the Catholic Church is not letting go of the transcript from the 'Downtown on their Knees: Nun Prostitutes' episode."

Danika shrugged and flashed her trademark wicked smile. "Sisters are doing it for themselves!"

"You're incorrigible," he laughed and got back to his feet. "Remember, we have pre-production at 2:00 p.m. Call me if you need anything before then?"

"I'll be fine," she said, and smiled as she watched him leave. He really cared about her, and it was sweet how he worried. She knew that his sexual innuendoes and jokes were meant to sound funny, but in reality, they were all serious. He wanted more with her. But she just didn't feel the same. It wasn't that he wasn't attractive. Lon reminded her a little of the character Stephen Keaton from the old *Family Ties* TV show. He was probably five-foot-ten and looked in decent shape behind the business shirts and green ties. (He always seemed to have a green tie, even when the shirt didn't call for it. She thought it was his way of being obnoxious. A statement against the corporate uniform, when he'd rather be in sandals, old jeans and a tie-dye T-shirt.) His hair was thinning a bit and going a little grey, but he had a good, warm face, and behind those black-rimmed glasses, he had sea-grey eyes that seemed to see right into your soul when he listened. Maybe it was the beard—a thick but close-trimmed brown halo around his mouth—that made her feel more sisterly than sexual towards him. He reminded her of her older brother.

She shifted on the couch as her insides moved again. The past couple days she'd run to the bathroom every time that happened. But nothing ever came up. Or out. So she wasn't budging now. Eventually the feeling would pass. Maybe then she could eat something. She was constantly hungry, but whenever a plate was in front of her, her insides turned to snakes.

Danika closed her eyes and thought of her favorite, the Southwest

Chicken Salad from the corner bistro. But somehow, just before she drifted to sleep, the image of the grilled chicken somehow transformed in her mind into a rare, bloody steak…

–2–

54

The lights on set felt hotter than usual. Danika was sure her makeup was running. They didn't need to put too much on—she had naturally high, Slavic cheekbones and her skin was flawless. The makeup girl always accentuated her bone structure with a touch of rouge and shadowed the electricity of her eyes with a dark liner. But right now, Danika felt beads of sweat popping up all around her hairline.

"Remember, we promised that we wouldn't ask any questions about him being gay or coming out," Lon was saying. He pointed to a sheaf of papers in his hand. "Stick to the Chicago Northside boy-makes-good-in-Hollywood angle. Ask him about how he's gotten along with Rob Lowe and Mel Gibson and Jennifer Aniston on set. Ask him what it's like to live in Los Angeles after growing up in the Midwest. But no gay stuff. This is his hometown, and he just doesn't want to accentuate that here."

"It's not like his family and friends don't see *People* and the *National Enquirer*," Danika pouted.

"Play nice, huh?" Lon walked off the set as the assistant director called out "One minute!" to the crew. Danika stepped up onto the stage and settled into the host seat at center stage. Lynnie, her makeup girl, rushed out and cottoned her forehead quickly before disappearing again as the count began: "in 5, 4, 3, 2…"

"Well good morning, Chicago!" Danika smiled. She held up a mug of coffee and said, "I hope you've had your caffeine fix for the day. If not, no worries: we've got a great show for you, so we'll wake you up no matter what! First, we have Brian James, that amazing North Side sensation who's been taking Hollywood by storm. It's summertime, so you know what that means—another Brian blockbuster. Later we'll talk with Heather West, the former adult dancer from Wrigleyville who has launched a line of energy snack bars. She recommends keeping them in your night stand, because sometimes after a long late night, you need a little boost to go one more round."

Danika raised an eyebrow at the camera in mock surprise. "I have *no* idea what she means, do you? But we'll find out later in the show. Right now, let's catch up with Brian James!"

The band kicked into the "intro guest" music and the thin, dark-haired actor walked on-sct, grinning at the audience with those heavy lips that had been making women swoon for the past three years. Danika rose to shake his hand, and barely stifled a look of horror as her guts twisted again. She prayed the mic didn't pick up the sound. It was worse than ever this morning. Her whole body ached. Even her gums felt tender. They'd bled when she brushed her teeth this morning.

"It's great to see you," she said, beginning the usual pleasantries. Inside, she began to panic. What if she couldn't get through the show?

"It's great to be back home," Brian answered, smiling as someone in the audience yelled, "We love you, Brian!"

"You've made, what, six movies now in the past couple years?" she asked.

"That's right."

"When do you sleep? It's got to be hard to keep up any kind of social life with that kind of schedule. Are you dating anyone?"

"It's been hectic," he agreed. "But I love it. I've just been focusing on the work for now."

"What was it like to work with Rob Lowe?" she asked with a dreamy look in her eyes played for the camera. "I think he's sooo hot, don't you?"

Brian didn't rise to the bait. "Rob's a great guy, and a great actor," he said, before going into an anecdote about how the two of them climbed a tree in the tropical rainforest during the shoot.

"I bet that was hot, shooting in Brazil for so long. Did Rob Lowe walk around a lot with his shirt off? Because that would have me melting. Does he have great abs or what?"

Brian laughed. "We wore as little as possible during that shoot! But you had to be careful with all the leeches…"

"Tell me about Mel Gibson," Danika said. "Don't you think he's hot? I mean, he's an older guy now, but still…"

–3–

Fifty minutes later, Danika forced herself to stand and grin at the camera while holding one of Heather's "Boost" bars. But as soon as the "live" light went off on Camera 2, she bolted from the stage. Her nausea had grown throughout the show, and as she talked with Heather about sex and fast food, her body had flashed hot and cold. The idea of eating one of the chewy granola bars (imbued with ginseng for sexual sharpness and some rare herb that supposedly acted like caffeine with a jolt to the libido) made her almost physically sick, despite the fact that her stomach was now growling constantly for food.

"Nice job," Lon said as she hurried through the door. "We'll never get Brian James on the show again after that stunt."

"What?" Danika said with false innocence. "I never asked him once about his gay lovers."

"No," Lon admitted. "You just asked him five times about what male actors he thought were hot. And the question about whether he liked to eat bananas fast or slow was *really* nice."

"I wish I'd thought to have a prop for that," she mused.

"Jeez, Danika, why did you have it in for him?"

"Not now," she said. Her eyes went wide as the sickness inside her shifted and growled. She felt heavy pressure in her stomach and saw a blaze of red across her vision. And then something hot passed her chest and slid up her throat in a sour belch. "I gotta lay down."

"Do you want another one of my Boost Bars?" Heather called from behind her.

Danika shook her head and felt her stomach heave. Her walk turned to a run and as she pushed open the door of the ladies room, the nausea finally won. Something dark and watery spewed from her mouth to the floor, and Danika didn't mince words. "Motherfucker," she coughed, and staggered to the sink, leaving a trail on the floor.

–4–

"You've lost weight," Mila Dubov observed, holding the door open to her third floor apartment. "It's very flattering that you only come to visit me when you're sick. I'm here all the time, you know, not just when you need some good old Russian soup."

"You could give me a hug before you crucify, you know," Danika answered her sister. The two were in some ways like night and day. While they shared their family's perfect cheekbones, Mila's hair was blonde, and her whole complexion just a bit lighter. On Danika, their mother's crystal blue eyes looked seductive; on Mila, they looked wholesome.

Mila shut the door and opened her arms. Danika accepted the hug, and leaned her head on her sister's shoulder. Mila was like a favorite pillow; warm, soft, familiar. She smelled like home, even after all these years of living apart.

"I have missed you," Danika said, pulling away as her stomach shifted and growled. Her throat felt like it was swelling.

"Funny way of showing it," Mila said.

"It's not nice to kick someone when they're down, you know."

"Well, when it's your only opportunity…"

"Got it, got it!" Danika shushed her with a hand. "Feed me now, beat me later. I've gotta get over this bug fast. It's been killing me all week."

"You could go to a doctor, you know?"

"Nothing works on a bad cold like Grandma's soup, and you're the only one who knows how to make it."

"It'll be ready in a little while," Mila promised, and walked into the kitchen to stir the pot. The room was thick with the smell of garlic and chicken. Danika's stomach churned, as she watched Mila work, tasting a spoon of the broth and adding a dose of spice from the cabinet. Her body seemed to grow hot, and her gums ached again. She'd had hot and cold flashes before, but what kind of flu made your teeth hurt?

"Have you talked with Dmitri lately?" Mila called from the other room.

"Not in months," Danika answered. She had to admit that as much as she loved her family, she wasn't really good at keeping in touch with them. Since her brother had moved to the east coast last year, she'd probably only talked to him on the phone twice.

"Well, at least I'm not the only one that you ignore."

"No, I'm an equal opportunity self-centered bitch," Danika laughed. But that laugh was cut short as a sudden pain shot up her gullet and into the back of her mouth. She choked and doubled over on the couch. It felt like barbed wire wrapped and tightened around her belly. Red fireworks swam across her vision, and Danika moaned.

"Oh God, what's wrong?" Mila said, rushing into the front room. As she did, Danika's whole body spasmed, and she fell forward from the couch, landing in a ball on the floor.

A guttural moan emanated from her throat. Her whole body felt on fire. Mila bent and put her hands on Danika's shoulders. Inside Danika's chest, the fire seemed to burn hotter.

"Pain," Danika gasped, struggling to look up at Mila. "All through my stomach and throat."

"Your eyes are bloodshot," Mila said, staring into her sister's face. "Danika, you don't need grandma's soup, you need a doctor."

Tears welled in Danika's eyes. "I don't know," she whispered. "I didn't feel this bad a little while ago. Since I got here though…"

"You need to take better care of yourself, honey," Mila said, and pulled her sister up from the floor to cradle her in her arms, hugging her close. As Danika rested her head on Mila's shoulder and returned the embrace, she felt the ache in her mouth and the back of her throat flare again. In her head, everything suddenly got fuzzy as the warm scent from Mila's neck and hair tickled her nose and the heat of her sister's chest warmed her own. She opened her mouth to let out a yawn, but the exhalation didn't come, something else did.

Something sharp.

Something hungry.

Something that bit down on Mila's neck like a wolftrap.

Mila screamed but the sound only made Danika bite harder. Danika felt an excitement she had never felt before. It surged through her body, hot, electric-deadly. Her consciousness seemed to have been shoved into a narrow hole and buried deep by the animal that owned her now. A monster used her bones, and the monster's teeth had somehow supplanted her own. All Danika really knew in that moment was that for the first time in days, the aching hunger and nausea in her belly went away. As the hot burst of blood slid down her throat, she felt instantly drunk. The pain turned to exquisite pleasure. Her groin throbbed as if she were in the throes of orgasm; her legs burned with power and an itch to run; her arms felt strong, and wrapped like a vise around the back of her sister, who shrieked and struggled to pull free.

"Danika STOP!" Mila cried. But almost instantly her voice lost its strength. "What's wrong with you? What are you doing…That hurts… Danika, please…"

Her sister's questions quieted. Danika saw Mila's eyes watching her, but she no longer struggled. Danika bit down again and again into the soft white flesh beneath Mila's ear. She latched on finally to one spot and truly drank, guzzling the rich iron life of her sister. Her eyes swam with red. Each swallow seemed to bring with it a small orgasm of ecstasy in both her belly and her sex. She let herself go to the feelings, no longer trying to figure out what was happening. She just let go. So much so that she didn't even see Mila in front of her. She only saw blood, and instinctively, she drank and drank until the flow had ceased and her stomach finally felt full and sated again.

And then Danika sat back on her haunches and like a feral cat licked the blood from her hands and lips until slowly the haze in her mind began to fade and she realized what she was doing.

She pulled a bloody finger from her mouth and stared at the spots of crimson still remaining on the back of her hand and wrist.

Comprehension dawned, and Danika felt her chest tighten. In front of her, Mila lay on her back on the front room floor, one leg crooked and bent at an awkward angle. Her face was slack and her eyes lolled open. Below the puncture wounds in her neck, the floral pattern pink shirt was drenched in gore. The holes glistened and still wept blood.

"Oh my God," Danika whispered, and leaned forward to put her hands on either side of Mila's cheeks. "I'm sorry, baby. I'm so, so sorry."

For the first time in years, Danika Dubov cried. Mila remained in the same spot, unmoving. Danika knew she had killed her sister.

When her tears were done, she took a deep breath, and composed herself. Then she stripped off her blood-drenched blouse, washed herself in the bathroom sink and found a fresh shirt in her sister's closet.

A coldness slipped over her, giving her strength to do what she had to do. It was the same feeling she had always had when hardship threatened her life. The ice of determination had always seen Danika through. It had gotten her through school and helped her step over all the other television hopefuls to take and hold her own starring seat in front of the camera. She hated what she had done to Mila. But she would not let herself wallow in it. The act was done, and it told her something that she needed to know.

She wasn't sick at all.

Danika turned off the gas on the kitchen stove, and considered pouring herself a bowl to take home. But the very thought of eating it made her stomach tremor again. Poor Mila had made this soup for nothing, because Danika didn't need it. All of the news reports from the past few weeks that talked about people spontaneously changing, becoming…something else…becoming monsters…flashed through her mind.

No, Danika wasn't sick.

She also wasn't really human anymore.

Danika Dubov was a vampire.

"I can get through this," she said to herself, as she took a paper towel and a bottle of Windex, and wiped down anything in the kitchen, bath and front room that she'd touched. She'd seen plenty of CSI shows and knew better than to leave obvious evidence that she'd been there. She took the Windex and her bloody shirt with her, using the paper towel to open the door to the apartment building hallway. She paused for a moment, and took one last look at the bloodied body of her sister.

"Now I just have to figure out how," she said, finishing her thought as she closed the door.

– 5 –

The next day at the station, Danika's trademark smile was fully back in place. She felt really good for the first time in a couple weeks, and while she'd been good at faking smiles the past few days, people could still tell that she was in better spirits. After the morning production meeting, Lon came up to her and put a hand on her arm.

"You seem a lot better today," he said. "But are you really sure you can do the show? We can put on a rerun and give you the weekend to rest. I don't want you to collapse in the middle of this one."

Danika smiled and shook her head. "Sleep is the drug I needed, I think. Last night I slept like a log for like, ten hours. Today, I feel great."

"Okay," Lon said, still looking a bit skeptical. "I hope so, because you've got a circus today. Cheating husbands and love triangles always make for a crazy show."

"Crazy, but fun," Danika laughed. "Maybe that LaShondra woman will use those two-inch fingernails of hers on that ass of a husband when the lie detector test results are announced."

"Just so nobody turns on you. Watch yourself."

"People are predictably stupid," she said. "I can steer them where I want the show to go."

"That's exactly what I'm afraid of."

– 6 –

The show went off without a hitch. And for the first time in days, Danika didn't feel like hurling on the set, so she could truly enjoy her "ringmaster" role. She honestly loved pitting people against each other on camera. She was a natural at it—somehow she had always been able to gently corral two people over the course of a conversation and manage to generate a passionate fight without ever looking like the bad guy.

Today though, as she deftly directed two trailer park couples and the cleavage-rich mistresses who had driven a spike through the middle of marital "bliss," Danika found herself looking at them all as cattle. She stared at their necks, and wondered if she could lead them into a dark corner and bite them, would she get the same kind of rush that she had gotten from killing Mila? Because that moment, despite how horrible it was that she had murdered her sister for it, was truly the best, most pleasurable moment of her entire life. Not that she could really feed on the guests on her show. She may have had a steady parade of candidates to choose from, but it wouldn't take people very long to notice that there seemed to be a high mortality rate for her guests, and she certainly didn't need *that*.

Danika knew and accepted that she was a vampire. It was a shock, but not unbelievable—vampirism was like the new AIDS. People were turning at an alarming rate; the news had been full of reports. Danika was pragmatic about it. She didn't fret over how unfair it was, she just pondered whether she could do what she needed to do in order to survive as one. And she had questions. Like…how often did she need to kill? Did it have to be every day? Every week?

She wanted to know what to do in order to survive this silent, invisible transformation…but her new self didn't come with an owner's manual. And there was nobody she could really go to ask for help in sorting it out. "Help me, I'm a vampire and I need to know how often I need to kill," wasn't going to earn her anything except a lock-up.

"Earth to 'Nika!" Lon's voice jolted her back to awareness. She'd been walking down the hall from the post-show recap and planning meeting, lost in her thoughts. "Still thinking about who did what with whose sex toy?"

Danika grinned. She'd come up with an impromptu question during the lie detector test, asking about whether the mistress had used the wife's dildo when the husband snuck her home to his own bed. And she'd had to laugh at the answer. The audience had. The wife had shrieked and jumped out of her chair.

Animals. All…just…animals, with fancy clothes and expensive cars. They reached the double doors to the parking lot, and Lon pushed one open for her. "And on that note," he said, "TGIF."

Danika agreed. "Have a great weekend. See you on Monday for another amazing look into the dirty linen of the American Dream."

– 7 –

Saturday slipped by like a dream; Danika ran errands, paid bills and did all the other mundane things that she never seemed to have time for during the week. She tried to fix herself a couple meals, but just the thought of forking a bite into her mouth made her stomach tremble. Ultimately, she scraped two plates of food straight into the trash. Other than that, she felt great, with no trace of the sickness she'd fought with for the past couple weeks.

When Sunday dawned, however, Danika got the answer to at least one of her questions. How long could she go without eating in her new condition? Just over two days apparently. Because she woke up with a dull ache in the back of her jaw, and a heat in her belly.

She showered and stalked into the kitchen, angry that she had seemingly lost control of her most basic function. She made a piece of toast, buttered it, and shoved it into her mouth, despite the rising swell of panic from her gut. As she chewed it, her saliva ran heavy, filling her mouth to the point where she almost needed to spit.

Danika didn't spit. She swallowed. And smiled as her stomach rumbled in protest. She'd be damned if she'd let some freakin' disease tell her what to eat.

But the toast didn't help. The hunger remained, and grew as the day wore on. Sometimes she felt flushed and broke out in spontaneous sweat. Sometimes she shivered as if she'd just entered a freezer.

"This is ridiculous," she complained. But she knew the answer was inevitable. The only question was how was she going to *deal* with the answer. It didn't take too long to formulate a plan, but once she had it, she had to wait, until night began to fall. Then she drove to the south side of the city, and parked.

Clad in her oldest, grungiest jeans and T-shirt, Danika left the car on a side street, and walked down the alley behind Flynn's Tavern. If there was one place she was going to find what she needed, it was here. Where the lonely and busted hung out and panhandled. Who would miss a lowlife?

She'd barely been in the alley for more than five minutes when she spied her first mark. He looked to be about fifty-five. He was tall, thin, had graying hair. She didn't know how to choose a "juicy" one yet, but she figured this guy would do for starters. She could always trade up and find another if he didn't give her the rush she needed.

"Hey," she yelled, and the guy looked up at her with bleary eyes. "Can I ask you something?"

The man shrugged. "Whaddayou wan'?" he gasped. The cloud of alcohol from his breath washed over her like a wave.

"I just need a hug," she lied. "It's been a really shitty day."

Danika held her arms out, and the drunk wandered right into them. This was too easy, she thought to herself. Then she put her lips to his neck, and rubbed them against the rough stubble at the edge of his jaw. He stank of sweat and booze, but he was warm. She could feel his pulse with her lips. He groped at her ass as she waited for the feeling she'd had when she'd hugged Mila—a building need, desire, the sharp ache in her jaw…but her stomach only gurgled angrily, as it had been doing all day.

She opened her mouth to bite him, but still felt no response. No heat, no rush, no hazy blur across the eyes. Nevertheless, she tried to go through with it anyway. Opening her mouth as wide as she could, she bit down hard on his neck.

The taste was sour, and the drunk's yell of complaint loud.

He dove away from her, losing his balance in the process. "Wha da fuc'?" he yelled. "Fuc'n' freak show."

The man staggered to his feet and moved faster than Danika would have thought he could have in his state. In seconds, he'd disappeared around the corner of an apartment building. Danika fingered her incisors and frowned. Why hadn't her vampire fangs descended? She'd done nothing to make them extend when she was with Mila; just the nearness of her sister's flesh had brought them down.

Maybe her inner vampire was a lesbian? Danika snorted at the thought. She may have undergone a change, but she didn't believe she could have changed *that* much. Maybe she just needed someone a little more her type. Someone who didn't smell. Were vampires "turned on" by their food based on scent and looks? Another question.

She got back in her car and considered what to do next. She did not want to do the show tomorrow feeling like she had last Monday, so she had to address this somehow. Cars passed by on the side street, and Danika realized that her drunken mark may have gone for help, in which case, she should leave. But she didn't want to go home. Not yet.

If there was a chance she could put this disease to rest for another couple days...She started the engine, and drove a mile or two away before finding another dark street to park on. There was a bar on the corner, and a restaurant down the next block. She turned the key and killed the engine. "One more for the road?" she said to herself, before getting out to look around. Nobody was currently out, so she walked slowly towards the restaurant. There was a bus stop shelter near the corner. A perfect place to sit and wait!

So she did.

It wasn't long before her wait was rewarded. From nearby, she heard voices and faint laughter. A screen door slammed. Moments later, a well-built guy in shorts and a blue Nike T-shirt walked up to the bus stop enclosure. He nodded, and leaned against the steel pole that held up the roof. Danika sized him up. He appeared young, attractive, healthy. She assumed he probably smelled okay, unless he'd just been jogging...and even then—she didn't mind the cologne of a workout. She grinned in the dark at the word that came to mind: manly! So yeah, maybe he was a better candidate than the bum. She could hear her stomach growl, and hoped he didn't notice.

She considered how to lure him over, but before she had a plan, he took care of the problem for her. He joined her on the bench. "Do you know when the next bus is due?" he asked.

Danika shook her head. "I'm actually just here waiting for a friend. You headed home?"

"Yeah," he said. "Just was at my girlfriend's, but I've got to get home. Early start tomorrow."

"Cool," Danika said, and let the silence rest for a moment. Then she composed her face, and considered the inflection of her next words carefully. "This is going to sound weird, because you don't know me from Adam, but...I've had a really bad weekend. My sister died a couple days ago, and..." she coaxed two tears on silent command as she paused. "I could just really use a hug right now, you know?"

"Geez, I'm really sorry," the man said, and slid closer to her on the bench. "Don't worry about it being weird. I know what you're going through," he said. "I lost my mom last year. At one point, I think I hugged the funeral director."

He opened his arms to her and she slid in close, stifling the urge to smile with victory. People were so easy to push.

"Thank you," Danika said, as she laid her head on his shoulder. She closed her eyes and breathed him in. She could make out the clean spike of his deodorant and the faintly floral scent of perfume, but also the sharp spice of recent sweat. And the musky smell of...sex? Again Danika stifled a grin. Was she really smelling the aftermath of this guy's sex with his girlfriend? She'd never had a good sense of smell, but this seemed strong to her. Another gift from her new disease?

Maybe the rich scents of life would awaken her inner vampire, she thought. She hugged him tighter, and he returned the gesture, patting her back gently. "You'll get through it," he promised. "It's hard, but you do."

"I know," Danika said, taking the opportunity of speech to flex her jaw. She held her teeth open, centimeters from the pulse of his neck and felt...nothing. Well, she felt nausea mixed with hunger pains, and her entire body ached with a dull heat. But her jaw didn't swell. No demanding pain shot from her groin to her teeth and changed her in that instant to make her ready to feed. Danika waited for a minute, and then gently kissed his neck, thinking that perhaps that gesture would trigger her body. But nothing came, and so, before the moment became embarrassingly long, she pulled back with a sad smile.

"Thanks, I needed that," she said.

"Happy to help," he answered. "I've been there."

She got up and began to walk away.

"Hey, I thought you were waiting for a friend?"

Danika looked back and shook her head. "I don't think he's going to come. Goodnight."

– 8 –

They discovered Mila was missing on Monday. When she hadn't shown up to work again, and didn't answer her phone or email, one of her coworkers had driven over to her apartment at lunchtime, and saw that her car was there. When Mila didn't answer the door, she called the landlord, who unlocked the door to look inside.

He walked the apartment; then picked up the phone and called the police. There was a dried pool of blood on the front room carpet, and smears of it on the couch and end table. But Mila's body was not there.

Danika got the call from the police that afternoon. But she didn't understand it.

"There's blood all over…but my sister isn't there?" she repeated to the officer on the phone.

"Exactly," the cop said. "We'd like you to come down and give us a statement, tell us anything about your sister that might help us find her." She agreed to be there in an hour, and then dropped the cellphone back in her purse, looking perplexed.

Lon noticed. "What's up?"

Danika shook her head. "They found blood in my sister's apartment…but not Mila."

Inside, she relived the scene from last week again and again. Mila's wide-open eyes, and the gashes on her neck. She had killed her, she knew she had. She had sucked all of the blood from the poor girl's veins. *Mila is dead!* Her inner voice repeated. *So where is she?*

–9–

Danika gave her statement at the police station and went home and thought about all she knew of vampire lore. The recent outbreaks of vampirism that had been reported all across the world seemed to point to some kind of disease or mutation, nobody was sure which yet. But people had been suddenly turning feral and strange without warning. No bites involved. Yet…the legends said that you *could* be turned into one by the bite of a vampire. Usually, they suggested that the person had to still have a trace of life left in their veins to allow the change. Danika thought she had drained Mila, but could she have left enough life in her that she'd changed?

Was her sister now stalking the night too?

–10–

On Tuesday, Danika thought that she might die. There was a throbbing pain that ran from her skull to her toes, and her belly churned and turned and spasmed. Pains shot through her joints every time she moved a finger.

She tried to keep smiling on set, but a haze was growing over her vision, and she found it difficult to focus on the questions she was asking her guests. Her normal sassy patter was missing. Errant pains shot through her guts and head without warning. It was tough to mask that when you weren't expecting it, and there was a camera trained on your face.

It all came to a head when she stood up to thank her guests at the end of the show. Danika opened her mouth to speak but instead, her legs turned to water. She toppled to the ground.

Lon rushed out to help her as the cameras quickly shifted to focus on a wide shot of the crowd as the credits rolled. One of the other stage managers hurriedly escorted the guests off-stage.

"Danika," Lon said, cradling her head in the crook of his arm. As he did, her eyes shot open. "What happened?" she said.

"You tell me!" he answered, eyes fraught with concern.

"Shit," she said, taking his arm to get to her feet. "I fainted, I guess." Then she groaned. "Crap. I fainted on camera!"

"We'll take care of it," Lon said. "We'll just put out the word that you've been sick and your sister was reported missing yesterday...Everyone will understand—probably get us lots of positive PR, actually."

"Shit," she whispered again, and then turned to wave at the audience. "I'm okay," she called out.

With that, Lonn rushed her offstage and back to her office. As they walked, Danika felt the heat in her body grow. It burned so hot, she could barely move. Lon wrapped his arm around her waist and she leaned into him as he opened the door.

"I want you to sit down here for a couple minutes," he said. "And then I want you to go to the doctor. You have not gotten over whatever you had last week."

She felt the red haze before she saw it in her vision; it rushed up the back of her spine like a wave, and the molten pain in her jaw returned as it crested. She knew what was going to happen next.

"Lon," she said, looking him in the eye, as he settled next to her on the couch. "I need something from you," she whispered.

Hope flickered in his eyes, as he mistook her tone for something else. Something that would answer his own long-held dreams.

"Anything," he answered, and Danika laid her head on his shoulder. She could feel her teeth descend, and the pains of the past three days changed to a symphony of sensations that all pushed towards one thing. Her mouth ached to open, and her arms throbbed with the desire to embrace. She didn't have to force this encounter, her body had chosen.

Danika opened her mouth and sank inch-long fangs into Lon's bared neck. He jumped as the pain hit, but this time she didn't waste time or blood. She locked her mouth to him, suckling, and slapped her hand over his mouth, stopping his initial attempt to scream. His legs kicked out and his arms pushed against her, but Danika found some secret well of strength in the moment—she easily pinned him and continued to drink, the warmth of his blood setting off explosions of ecstasy down her throat. In seconds, his body relaxed and stopped struggling. His eyes stared at her, just as Mila had. If Danika didn't know better, she would have sworn that his mouth was smiling.

The heat spread to her belly and then her groin, and Danika moved to straddle his thigh, rubbing herself against him in a gentle rhythm. She could feel that Lon had an erection. Danika laughed inside—she was killing him, and he got hard! The blood inside her somehow turned her on as no man had ever been able to—it only took seconds from the initial brush of her crotch against his thigh to feel the first explosion of orgasm. The sexual heat joined with the vampiric, and Danika longed to rip off her clothes and revel in the sensations. She lifted her face from his neck, and threw her head back to moan as her moment crested, and as she did so, she saw a vacant stare in Lon's eyes. He looked to be in a euphoric trance. She could feel his blood drooling down her chin, and saw it staining Lon's shirt as it ran quickly down his neck.

With much of her hunger sated, some moment of sanity returned, and through the haze of bliss, Danika told herself to stop. "I don't want to kill him," she told the beast inside her.

She bent and licked the blood from his neck, and then pressed her fingers to his throat, staunching the flow. She held them there for several minutes, and still Lon didn't move. But he was breathing, his chest continued to move. She could feel the hard-on beneath his pants, as she hugged him. He was still turned on!

The thought made her snicker and Danika slipped away from him to her desk and found a first aid kit in the bottom drawer. She bandaged the wounds, and then held her hand against them, hoping that the pressure would help seal the holes she'd bitten.

But what would she say to him, when he woke up?

A few minutes later, he finally did. And he took her off the hook when he looked at her in total confusion.

"What the hell happened?" he whispered. "I feel horrible."

"You don't remember?" Danika said, hope rising in her chest.

"I was sitting here, and you were here and then…" She could see him struggling for the memory. "No, I don't," he admitted.

"The fainting seems to be contagious," she said. "You fell forward, and caught your neck on the coffee table corner there.. I bandaged it up for you, but your shirt's ruined, I think."

"Wow," he said, still looking foggy. "How long was I out?"

"Just a few minutes," she said. "I think you need to rest for a little. Let me take you home?"

"Oh sure, and have you faint again at the wheel? What a pair we'd make on the road."

"I'm fine now," she promised, and soon had hustled him out the back of the studio and into her car.

She made sure that Lon got into his house okay, and set him up with a tall glass of orange juice. "You need Vitamin C and fluids right now," she explained. They always gave you juice when you gave blood to help the body's sugar levels. Well, Lon had just given a lot of blood.

She had promised to pick him up in the morning too, since they'd left his car at the station. Danika wanted to make sure that he made it through the night. She wondered if he would now become like her. She hadn't brought him to the brink of death or beyond, as she had her sister. So would he change? Another question.

But the real question on her mind right now was, where the hell was Mila?

– 11 –

The bedroom was small and dark. And hot. Mila threw the covers off, and hitched up her nightgown to expose her legs, but it wasn't enough. She rolled and turned in the bed, whimpering in frustration, and finally, pulled the nightgown over her head and lay back in the bed, naked, staring at the ceiling fan. She watched the blades go round and round and heard the *tick tick tick* of the motor as it moved them. She'd been keen to every tiny noise and overcome by every faint smell since she'd awoken on her living room floor, throat ripped up, blood everywhere.

Mila wasn't sure exactly what had happened; the visit with her sister had taken on a fuzzy, blurred perspective in her memory. But she knew two things: Danika had done this to her, and Danika hadn't even bothered to eat the soup she'd made. Mila resolved to eat it all herself, once she managed to clean herself up.

Only...later she found, she couldn't.

She bandaged her neck, and thought about calling an ambulance, but she hated doctors. She knew she'd lost a lot of blood; the carpet told that story well. But Mila knew that if she just lay down on the couch and ate and drank healthy things, she'd build her own blood back. She didn't need anyone else's pumped into her, and she couldn't afford the hospital anyway.

The only problem with her home-cure solution was that every time she tried to eat a spoonful of grandma's cure-everything soup, Mila felt like throwing up. She found she could drink water, but anything with any flavor threatened to evacuate upon ingestion.

Plus, her neck and throat hurt like hell.

For the first night, she'd stayed on the couch and slipped in and out of consciousness. Friday came and went in a haze, as the world seemed to grow warmer and every motion sent heat tingles down her limbs. She had managed to choke down some soup and milk, but it made her stomach churn and cramp.

When her boyfriend Adrian had dropped by on Sunday and found out how sick she was, he'd taken her back to his apartment. And that's where Mila had struggled with sleep ever since. As well as other things.

Mila was no fool. She'd known what the bite-marks on her neck meant. And so when the heat and the wanting and the need came—especially, dizzyingly strong when Adrian had sat close to her—she knew only one thing. She had to find a way not to give in to this temptation.

She would not be as weak as her sister and feed on her best friend.

Adrian opened her bedroom door and came in to sit on the side of her bed, asking if she was okay, and stroking the sweaty hair on her forehead. The heat inside Mila spiked with his touch, and she felt the teeth in her mouth move, fangs shoving forward.

She would not.

– 12 –

"I think we should get Luther Swann to come onto the show," Danika said. Lon had been staring out the window of her passenger's seat since she'd picked him up at his house. Now he looked at Danika with a frown. "Luther Swann?" he said. "You mean the vampire guy?"

"He's a folklorist," Danika corrected. "I saw him on cable last night, and he was fascinating."

"He's the vampire guy," Lon said again. "He's been doing the circuit for the last couple months thanks to the stuff he's written on vampire myths."

"Well, they don't really seem to be myths," Danika noted, "since people appear to be turning into blood-sucking freaks every day now."

"True," Lon admitted. "But why would we want to bring him on the show? That's like, serious shit, given the stuff going on out there. We're a topical show, but not that kind of topical. We're check-the-brain-at-the-door entertainment, nothing more. We don't focus on current events."

"But that's the beauty of it," Danika pressed. "Everyone has heard of the whole vampires are real—and more of us are them every day— thing. But it's not just a news thing. It's freaky and weird—just like the stuff we usually focus on. "

"Luther Swann has been turning up everywhere lately," Lon said. "So I don't know if we can get him. But even if he can, why would we want to?"

"Ratings," Danika smiled. "Vampires are hot right now. Let's get some of that."

Lon nodded. "Okay, I can see that, sure." He blinked a few times, as if trying to clear his head. "I'll make some calls."

"Cool," Danika said, pulling her sporty little Honda into the station parking lot with an abrupt squeal of a turn. "By the way," she added, almost as an aside. "How do you feel today?"

Lon squinted at her and shrugged. "I've had better mornings," he said.

Danika nodded, as if she understood. "Coffee's on me," she said. "I need to wake you up to find us Luther Swann. And hell, get that Michael Fayne guy too if you can."

As they exited the car, Danika Dubov wound her fingers together and flexed her hands. "I think this is going to be the start of a great week," she said with a toothy grin.

Lon moaned, and staggered towards the employee entrance behind her.

— 13 —

The search for Mila ended on Wednesday, when she returned to her apartment, shocking the hell out of her landlord. Danika found out, not from her sister, but from the police, who called to tell her that her missing person/possible foul play case had been closed, since her sister was now back in her apartment, unharmed.

Danika hung up with the police and reached out to dial and call Mila herself, but then hesitated. What would she say? *Gee, I tore your throat out last week, I thought you were dead?*

She pulled her hand back, and set the phone down. If Mila wanted to talk, she'd call. Until then…Danika had some things she wanted to find out. She needed to know more about what she'd become. About what she assumed *both* of them had become…

On Thursday, Danika woke in a hot sweat, with her stomach turning cartwheels. The need to feed was back. She told herself that she would control it. She would live through the pain until tomorrow. Because on Friday, Lon had managed to book Luther Swann. Maybe at last, she could get some answers about her condition. As the heat built inside her through the day, she prayed that she would last, especially since every time that Lon came near, she felt a throbbing in her jaw…it was almost as if she could feel her teeth grow.

– 14 –

On Friday, Danika prayed that her makeup wouldn't run on camera. She was burning up. When Lon came up to suggest a possible question to ask, she snapped. "Just let me handle my own interview, okay?"

He backed off, and Danika breathed a sigh of relief. As soon as he walked into the same room with her, she felt her jaw shift and the change begin. She did not want to feed on him again. So far, he seemed to have recovered from her first attack, and seemed oblivious to what had happened. But she didn't know if she could stop herself from killing him if she bit him a second time. And she was hungry.

Deadly hungry.

And for some reason, he was the one she wanted to eat. What the fuck? She said it over and over again in her head all week during production meetings, as she tried to muffle the groans from her belly, and smile without showing fangs, because Lon sat nearby.

WTF? WTF?

WTF?

– 15 –

"Luther Swann, you've been an expert on vampires for a long time, and a year ago my first question to you probably would have been 'Do you believe vampires are real?'"

Swann grinned in his leatherback chair, but let her continue uninterrupted.

"But now it's no longer a question of *are* they real, but *why* are they real? Why now?"

"That is the question, certainly," Swann said. "And I don't have an answer there. I've studied the vampire legends throughout history, and I believe they have always been among us, but over the past few centuries, as a truly dying breed—a mutant strain of humanity that has teetered on the brink of extinction. And not just one breed, honestly—there are at least a dozen variants on the vampire mutation alone. And then there are the werewolf strains."

"So, are these vampires and werewolves still human, just with a disease?"

Swann pointed a finger at Danika in the shape of a revolver, and let his thumb down to simulate pulling the trigger. "Bingo," he said. "That is exactly the question. There are those who theorize that these mutations are actually caused by a disease that is transferred through the saliva and blood, much like the AIDS virus. But my personal theory falls in line with what some scientists at Stanford University are looking at. They believe that there is an actual genetic mutation that is triggered by something. Maybe it's a built-in racial control sort of thing—when an area becomes overpopulated, the gene is triggered in someone and pretty soon you have some quiet crowd control happening."

Danika nodded. "That makes some sense—kind of like how rats live in a community until there are too many of them and then they all turn on each other."

"Right," Swann said. "The question of the day is, why have so *many* been triggered now, at this moment in time. There has never in recorded history been an outbreak of this magnitude."

"I'm guessing you don't have an answer for that one."

He shook his head. "Afraid not. But believe me, there are plenty of scientists looking at it. Studying the genes of the infected. Trying to determine why a seemingly normal person yesterday is suddenly possessed of long fangs and a burning desire to eat his neighbors. What I have found interesting is that the changes do seem to relate to the genetic history of the infected individual. The *jiangshi*, or Chinese hopping vampire, lives in dark places and hunts by night, but moves by hopping, with its arms outstretched. The *wampir*, from Russia, do not have fangs, but rather a stinger beneath their tongues. Vampires from India appear as crones with two heels on each foot. And the *strigoi* from Romania have two hearts and the ability to adapt the shapes of animals. We've seen all of these types of vampires emerge over the past few months, and what's interesting is, that in each of the vampires that we have been able to study, the mutations these people have undergone correspond to the folklore of their racial types. In other words, Norwegians don't become *jiangshis*, and Indians don't become *wampir*."

"How often do vampires need to feed?"

Swann shook his head. "There's no real agreement on that. Some evidence seems to suggest every day or two. But there are also stories of vampires only rising to feed during the light of the full moon. And there are stories of vampires surviving for months and even years without feeding."

The heat in the back of her belly flared, and Danika gasped. She couldn't imagine going a *week* without eating.

"How could anything survive without eating for so long?" she asked.

Swann shrugged. "There are those who say vampires are not alive. That's what most of the mythology suggests. From what we've seen recently, however, they do seem to be alive, just in a mutated state."

"Is it true that they have to eat blood? And does it have to be human?"

"The mutation does seem to revolve around the thirst and need for blood. There are stories of vampires surviving on animal blood, and even managing to sit at public dinners and eat normal human food. But the digestive track of a vampire undergoes a change…and the things that would have given the body sustenance before no longer serve. Vampires need blood to stay vibrant and active."

"Do vampires have to find their victims attractive? Or can they really eat just anyone?"

Swann laughed. "The majority of the stories about vampires seem to indicate that any live body will do. As I said, some manage even to feed on animals. And there are plenty of stories of vampires feeding on derelicts—who certainly would not fit into the good-looking category."

The historian paused and held out his hands, palms up. "That said, there are some vampires that do not feed on blood at all. And there are some, like the Russian *wurdulac*, who can only feed on loved ones. *That* can really limit the potential food supply for vampires without a lot of family and friends!"

"Yikes," Danika said. "So Russian vampires are basically incestuous!"

"That's not the way I would put it, since it's not about sex, but…you have the right idea."

Danika suddenly found herself searching for the next question. Because Swann had just given her the key. She was of Russian descent…and the only people she'd been attracted to feed on had been her sister and her best friend at the station. Perhaps, when the mutation hit her, it had drawn on some latent *wurdulac* gene from her ancestral past.

But now that she knew *what* she was…how to control it?

"How close would a *wurdulac* need to be to someone before it could eat them?" she asked.

"Hard to say," Swann said. "Presumably some emotional bond needs to be established, so whether one would have to live with the victim for a time, or just go on a really good first date…it's hard to say."

"If a *wurdulac* chomps down on its parents and siblings, won't they all become *wurdulacs* too?" Danika asked. "Or don't those old myths of the bite changing the victim into a vampire hold up?"

"No, you're right," Swann said. "If a *wurdulac* sucked the blood of its brother, the brother might also wake up a *wurdulac*. Unless all of the blood was drained. If the *wurdulac* truly bleeds out the victim, it's all over. Despite all those movies and myths, dead is dead. Over the past few weeks we've come to realize that real vampires are about mutation, not coming back from the grave. But all of the stories of the *wurdulac* type of vampire tend to show the vampirism curse being passed on like wildfire—whole families and everyone associated with them being wiped out in a matter of weeks."

"Wiped out?" Danika said. "What happens to them?"

"Well, the *wurdulac* tends to exhaust its food supply fairly quickly, especially when you have a mother and brother and sister all competing for the same group of friends and relatives to eat…pretty soon, the original *wurdulac* goes to the grave because the food supply is depleted."

Danica felt a horrible pain stab at her heart. She had virtually no relatives and hardly anyone she'd call a friend. And at the moment, she was weak to the point of fainting. The only thing keeping her going was the adrenaline of getting some real answers from this interview.

She looked up and saw Lon signaling to her from the side of the stage. His facial gestures looked frantic. And she knew why. The red countdown clock which told her when to wrap-up had gone into negative numbers. She was overtime on this segment.

"So where do we go from here?" Danika asked. "Do we need to

search out and destroy all of these new vampires? We can't really live with them, can we?"

Swann looked at her in horror. "Surely you're not suggesting that we set up death squads to go hunting down people? That's genocide! Remember, vampires are human…they are just…different. We need to find a way to co-exist with them. They evolved for a purpose, and there are many theories as to why. All I can say is, there is strength in cooperation, and death in isolation."

"So there you have it," Danica smiled, raising one eyebrow for the camera. "Love your vampire. Especially if he sneaks in your window after dark. One cautionary note—make sure he wears a condom, and you wear a neck guard. That's all for this morning, just remember… vampires are people too!"

She turned to Swann and grinned, giving him a hand as she stood up while the audience applauded and the credits rolled.

"That's not exactly what I meant," he said.

Danica shrugged. "You don't think we should kill them, but they will definitely kill us. I think I captured it pretty well."

"They may be the next step on the evolutionary track," he suggested.

Danica waved and smiled at the camera as she moved Swann towards the exit.

"That step appears to be somewhat self-defeating," she noted.

– 16 –

The door to Danika's office slammed. Lon strode in with a look of complete incredulity. "Well, that was great," he said. "If our viewers haven't gotten it from every other TV show over the past six months, we successfully gave them a complete primer on vampire legends today. I'm glad that we've broken new ground here."

Danika looked up from the pillow on her office couch. Her eyelids barely raised. "Yeah, like we broke a lot of new ground with the love triangle polygraph too," she said, and then let her head fall back to the pillow.

"You know what I mean. Interviews about science and history aren't what our viewers tune in for."

The cramps in her belly grew and Danika's skin burned. In her mouth, something changed that made it difficult to talk.

"I get it," she mumbled. "But I really am too sick to talk about it right now. And frankly, I don't want you to catch it….sooo…" Her voice slurred, but Danika's intention was clear. "I'd like you to leave now."

Lon opened his mouth to protest, but couldn't come up with a great comeback, so he did just as she requested.

As the door shut, Danika picked up the phone. She had an idea.

– 17 –

"I was surprised to hear from you," Craig said. He held his wine glass towards her in a silent toast, and Danika smiled as their glasses clinked. They were having dinner at one of his favorite Italian places on the North Side, and Danika could almost smell his excitement. Actually, as she thought about it, she realized she *could* smell his excitement. Not in a bad way; there was just a hint of heavier musk in the air around him that was separate from the perfume of his deodorant. She caught him staring at the amount of cleavage her black dress was allowing, and she shifted slightly in her seat to pronounce it even more. The lace at the top of her bra cup tantalized him.

"I've missed you," she lied. "But it just seemed like…well…things were over between us really, and I was busy and, you know how it is."

"And you're between boyfriends," he said, politely getting a dig in.

"And I'm between boyfriends," she admitted. Danika bent her face to the table but raised her eyes to stare hard into his. "Are you implying that this is just a booty call?"

Craig laughed and delayed his answer with a sip of wine. Danika's eyes didn't leave him. "I said nothing of the kind," he said at last. "Where do you want to go after dinner? Your place or mine?"

"Yours," Danika said. "Mine's a mess. I haven't made my bed in a week."

"So," he grinned. "Easy entry."

Dinner dragged for both of them after that, as they caught up on each other's social circles. When the waiter brought the dessert menu, Danika passed.

"You barely touched your pasta," Craig said. "Wasn't it any good?"

"It was great," she smiled. "I'm just hungry in a different way."

He hurried to pay the bill, and then escorted her to his car, hand possessively placed on the small of her back. Spirals of sensual heat moved down her spine with every slip of his fingers.

They didn't *run* to his apartment, but the walk from his garage was not slow either. Danika was in his arms before the door had fully closed behind them.

"I love what you've done with the place," she whispered, breathing in the heat from his neck.

"You haven't even looked at it," he laughed.

"I love it anyway."

His hand worked at the clasps on the back of her dress, and she followed suit, punctuating the unbuttoning of his shirt with hard fast kisses. She shivered out of the dress and kicked it to the side of the foyer as he dropped his shirt to the floor, and then Danika hugged him tight again. The hair on his chest prickled against her; Danika could feel the blood rising in her nipples.

"Did you…want to…*see* the apartment," he said, in between the touch of her lips.

"Soon," she said, and pressed her hips against him. Suddenly she shivered. An icy heat shot from her groin to her neck. The feeling blossomed into a warmth of pins and needles and then morphed again, into a desperately pleasurable sensation that made Danika moan.

"Don't start without me," he laughed.

"No worries about that," Danika said. Her words sounded slurry. "You're my dinner and dessert."

Her jaw shifted in a heartbeat, and Danika didn't wait an instant. She opened her mouth to suck on his neck. And bit him.

Craig's yelp of surprise only lasted a moment, as Danika's fangs found their home and released their poison before accepting his life. Between what she'd learned from Swan and the various theories she'd read, she knew that part of her change involved the development of a tiny gland in the back of the jaw. Now, with that knowledge, and her experience, she paid attention and could feel it pulse as her teeth slipped beneath Craig's skin. What she gave through her bite, she didn't know, but it quieted her food quickly. His blood flowed hot and fast down her throat and she sucked and sucked. It was both a hunger and an erotic sensation to feed, and unconsciously, she ground her hips against him as she drank from his veins. As her belly felt close to bursting, she climaxed, pulling her mouth back from his neck to gasp.

He lay there, on the floor, head just a foot from the door. Eyes rolled back. Quiet. Blood continued to leak from the holes in his neck, but Danika wasn't hungry anymore. She stood up, wobbling slightly from the sense of fullness, and the aftermath of orgasm.

"Wow," she said, staring at his body for a moment, before walking into his living room. There was a new couch and recliner there since the last time she'd slept with Craig. And a much bigger widescreen TV. Danika picked up the remote and flicked the set on, settling back on the couch. She wiped her hand across the sweat on her chest, smearing some blood across the edge of her bra in the process. Danika took a deep breath and looked around the room as she relaxed. She didn't plan to stay long, but at the moment, she didn't feel much like moving. She flipped to Channel 7, and laid her head back.

"I *do* like what you've done with the place," she said.

— 18 —

The only problem with being constrained to feed on people you had a strong emotional relationship with was, at least for Danika, the very limited supply. In the weeks after inviting Craig out to (be) dinner, she rekindled relationships with five other past flames. But her "Little Black Book" was quickly running dry. Danika was an exceptionally social person, but also a driven one. She "knew" a million people, but she was close to very few. She had not taken time to cultivate friends and lovers over the past few years, as she focused instead on her climb at the station. Driving ratings had been her passion. Which was why Lon stood in her office with his arms crossed, looking…cross.

"A scientist?" he said. "You want to have a scientist on the show? Have you completely lost it?"

"Not just any scientist," Danika said. "Maggie Ruiz! Nobody knows more about the whole vampire wave than Maggie."

"I'm sure that's true," he said. "But let me remind you, that's not what we do!" We explore the world of trailer trash. Husbands sleeping with babysitters. Love triangles with the postman. We don't talk about the hard science of an epidemic."

Danika crossed her arms. "Well, maybe we should."

Lon shook his head. He knew when he wasn't going to win. "I'll look her up."

— 19 —

"You've been studying Michael Fayne for a while now," Danika asked. "What have you learned about vampires, and what do we still need to find out?"

The cameraman focused in on Maggie Ruiz. The epidemiologist had gotten a crash course in how to handle TV interviews over the past few weeks, and she looked comfortable as she formed her answer.

"Well first of all, we've learned that there's no magic about this," Maggie smiled. "All of those stories about garlic and crosses keeping vampires at bay, and not being able to see their reflections in a mirror…well, I'm afraid none of that's true. Vampires are human and alive…or, at least, they're a type of human. But they've undergone a genetic change. We've identified the change in Michael Fayne's genetic structure that has altered his digestive track and created his need to consume blood over any other sustenance."

"But why him? Why now?"

Maggie nodded. "That's the question, isn't it? We don't have the answer yet. But we do know that it's not happening because of some mystical bite, and I can assure you, Michael Fayne's heart is still beating."

"So wait a minute," Danika said. "You're saying that people can't become vampires from being bitten?"

Maggie hesitated. "Well, I guess I wouldn't say 'can't'…but we have not found any evidence of it in our studies. Victims seem to be either drained and die of blood loss, or they recover and continue to live normally. We've not found any evidence of a gene-altering agent being transferred. So something else is activating the change in those whose genes have altered."

"So a vampire can't give away eternal life with his bite," Danika said. "You've dashed all of my dreams of meeting a tall, dark and handsome vampire and living with him in his mansion forever."

Maggie laughed. "Sorry. Vampires die, just like you and I. You might be able to find one to live with for a while, but he'd likely end up killing you and that would be the end of the story. They do not appear to have any ability to transfer their condition. Of course, we also have noted that the gene produces different changes in different racial types, so anything is possible, I suppose."

"That's an interesting point," Danika said. "We talked with Luther Swann last month, and he mentioned that there were all sorts of vampire types. He even talked about a vampire that can only feed on people that it is close to."

Maggie nodded. "I've studied all the legends, given what we've been dealing with. The Russian mythology talks of a *wurdulac*, which can only feed on its family and friends. The interesting part about that legend is that the creature is somewhat self-defeating. I mean, if your food source is constrained that way, your race would quickly become extinct, or, at least, have a pretty self-limiting aspect. The *wurdulac* strain might live on as it carried from family to family, but the individuals would run out of prey fairly quickly and die. I honestly can't see a biological benefit to the limitation, so I suspect that this is part of the cultural embellishment of the vampire reality, rather than a true limitation of the strain."

Danika nodded and smiled…but she knew better. After she finished her interview and escorted Maggie from the set, she told Lon that she'd have to miss the afternoon pre-production meeting for tomorrow. She had a couple of appointments she had to keep.

Appointments with ex-boyfriends that she'd killed.

She had a theory.

Her first stop was Craig's apartment. And when she knocked, Craig answered the door. He looked a little pale. But mostly he looked angry.

"What the fuck did you do to me?" he asked. Then he grabbed her by the shoulder and yanked her through the door.

"I woke up here on the floor," he pointed at the carpet of the foyer. "And then I spent the next two days throwing up. And then I went to my mom's house…and I ate her! I fucking ate her!"

Danika nodded. "My sister was my first. I know you're probably pretty pissed."

"Pissed? I'm gonna fuckin' kill you, you damn bitch. I should have known better when I got your voicemail that day. Of course you didn't miss me. You've never cared for anyone but yourself."

Craig raised a fist in the air as if to slug her, but Danika smiled and only moved into the circle of his arms.

"I missed you Craig-y, I did. And yeah, I was hungry too."

"I took a vacation this week," he announced. "Because I couldn't freakin' work anymore. All I could do was think of biting my mom. And Ginny."

"Did you?" Danika asked. "I always liked her."

"Yes," Craig admitted. "She came here a few days after I killed mom, wondering why I wasn't answering my phone. So…thanks. I killed my mom *and* my sister."

"Have you talked to them since?

"No," he admitted. "That would be a little difficult, wouldn't it? I killed them!"

"I killed you too, right?"

Craig looked at her with anger. "You tried, but clearly you didn't drink me dry."

"Sure looked that way," she said.

Understanding dawned, and a smile grew on his face. "So…maybe they're not…"

"Maybe," she said. "There's a lot of blood in the human body. I thought at the time that I'd drank enough to kill you and Mila. But then I realized, maybe I hadn't. Maybe that venom in my teeth just put you in a coma for a few hours. That's why I came back to check on you. Maybe you should…"

He shoved her out of the way. "You're still a bitch," he said. "And I fuckin' hate you."

"Yeah, that's not what your lips said a couple weeks ago." Danika said. "Just remember, if anyone else finds out, they're going to come after you. I think there's one cardinal rule here."

"Keep it in the family?"

"Right."

Danika smiled as Craig slipped out of the doorway.

– 20 –

She visited three more of her ex-boyfriends that afternoon. Each of the doors were answered by a man who looked very much alive, despite her memories of their faces as she'd left them. Tongues lolling, eyes rolled back. None of them were happy with her.

She could stomach that.

The real key was…Danika was making vampires. Despite what Maggie said. Maybe it was all scientific, but there was something about her particular *wurdulac* change that *was* transferring a physique-altering gene to her victims…er…dinners!

Danika considered the ramifications of that. Not everyone was going to be happy to be a vampire. Certainly none of her boyfriends were. And while keeping their own condition secret was sort of a mandatory self-preservation strategy, sooner or later, someone was going to talk.

She needed to pull them into a fold. She needed them to wake up and have a guide.

Danika considered.

Then she pulled out her cellphone, and called Mack. He'd been her third victim, and even though she hadn't talked to him in a year prior to sucking his blood a week ago, he was one of her favorite people.

She wasn't surprised when he answered. Sounding angry, like Craig.

"Here's the thing, Mack," she said, and launched into her plan.

The idea of a pyramid scheme was not a new one. But usually, pyramids had to do with money, not food.

Danika's idea…was all about staying alive. Secretly. That and, having your cake, while eating it too.

The talk show was the perfect opportunity for making new friends. And what did Danika need more than friends?

"We all need to get along," she told Mack. "More than that really… we need to *like* them. We need to establish a bond before we can break it!"

"Can you maybe hold a segment on beautiful lifeguards?" he asked. "After all, it is summer. And I could get really attached to lifeguards… if they're girls. And tan."

"And what's in that for me?" Danika asked.

Mack had an easy answer. "Their boyfriends. You don't think lifeguards date trolls, do you?"

–21–

The trick to having a houseful of live food was to keep the food fed. And in the case of a *wurdulac*, not to kill it when *you* fed.

That's what Danika and Craig and Mack and Hannah and Sarah learned very quickly. Craig made the first mistake after befriending and sucking on a girl named Julia just a little too long. He left her comatose in the room where they had locked in their human "cattle." But that night, instead of waking up groggy but normal, she turned. When Danika and Craig and the others woke the next morning, they found all of their food lying dead on the floor. Because, of course, the caged "human cows" all forged some pretty strong bonds thanks to their mutual situation.

Danika instituted the time clock method after that. Nobody fed unless the timer was set. They set up individual pens for the nighttime at Hannah's house, who had a full basement that they turned into a series of holding pens. Nobody could access the basement until the timer was set. And once the timer was set, a major alarm went off five minutes later that could only be turned off once someone returned to the top of the stairs to hit a button. It meant that feeding was successfully interrupted enough to allow the cognitive aspects of each vampire to surface, at least enough to restrain its fatal instincts.

Danika's "family" grew...a little at a time. Each day after the show, she held dinners with her guests, and anyone she "clicked" with, she invited on a date the next night and the next...until she felt that familiar surge in the back of her throat. She added someone to her own personal food "pen" almost every week. But she didn't always need to feed in the pen.

—22—

It was a Friday night, and Danika was happy to be done with work for a couple days...but still, her belly growled. She knew she needed to feed soon. Her new hunger had certainly made her change a lot of aspects of her previously "normal" life. But now...she went to Hannah's house after work just to see how things were going, and Mack met her at the door.

His normally dark hair looked darker. His normally pale skin looked paler. Danika felt strange, looking at him. "I want to kill you," she said, without thinking.

"Yeah," he said.

She could still feed on the ones she was close to, even if they were vampires. They kissed, and then, almost as one, their mouths moved. In a heartbeat, their mouths shifted, and their teeth slipped into each other's necks. They drank from each other. The taste was rich. And deep. In seconds the sexual charge became overpowering, and they ground their hips hard against each other while sucking.

"I want to kill you too," he whispered, between sips.

"Yes," Danika said, and bit harder.

"JUNK" PT.3

Jonathan Maberry

—10—
Department of Anthropology
New York University
October 9, 11:03 a.m.
Four Days before the V-Event

"Are you the vampire guy?"

Luther Swann looked up from his laptop and smiled. It was the kind of question he got a lot, and not the worst phrasing he'd heard.

The two men standing in the doorway to his office were neither students nor fellow faculty. They were both big, dressed in off-the-rack suits that were of the timeless style that would look equally uninteresting no matter how fashion shifted. They had similar mustaches and haircuts that might have been the result of a two-for-one sale at Super Cuts.

They might have come from central casting.

Cops.

The taller of the two—a sad-faced man with dark hair that was turning a dull shade of gray—reached into an inner pocket of his jacket and produced a leather identification which he flipped open. Swann peered over his glasses at the gold badge and name card.

"Detective Schmidt," said the man. He closed his case. "This is Detective Yanoff."

"Okay," said Swann, "and I guess that makes me the vampire guy. How can I help you?"

"Mind if we close the door?" asked Schmidt.

"Not at all."

They did and accepted seats in the two worn-out swivel seats across the desk. Swann smiled encouragingly at them, but neither detective smiled back.

"Dr. Swann," began Schmidt, "have you ever done consulting work for a police department or the district attorney's office?"

"Like expert witness work? No. Not much call for that in my field," admitted Swann. "Been on TV a few times. Discovery, History Channel. Shows about vampires and the supernatural. They rerun them every Halloween."

"Yeah," said Schmidt. "That's how we heard of you. Detective Yanoff DVR'd a couple of them. Very interesting."

He said it in a way that suggested that they were, in fact, not at all interesting.

"You write books, too?"

Swann nodded toward the bookshelf to his left. The top three shelves were crammed with multiple copies of the same eleven titles. The word vampire appeared in every title.

Schmidt nodded. "Yes, we have those."

Swann leaned back in his chair. "Really?" he said. "Should I be flattered?"

Instead of answering, Schmidt asked, "Would you be willing and available for a consulting job?"

"Sure—as long as it doesn't interfere with my class load. I can give you a copy of my schedule and—"

"We have it," said Yanoff. It was the first time he'd spoken.

Swann smiled. "Then sure. Is this a paid gig?"

"Yes." Schmidt named an amount and Swann tried not to let the excitement show on his face. His books pulled in enough to keep his salary from putting him in the poverty category, but he wrote scholarly books about folklore. He had never been within long rifle shot of the bestseller list.

"That will be fine," he said, keeping it out of his voice, too. "What will I be consulting on?"

Schmidt and Yanoff sat there and didn't say anything.

"Let me back up and ask another question first," said Swann. "What kind of detectives are you? Is this a theft of some kind? Holy relics, or antique books? Something like that?"

They said nothing.

"Is it a cult thing? I did a book on vampire cults in modern times."

Nothing.

"Come on, guys. You have to tell me something here. What kind of case is it?"

Yanoff glanced over his shoulder to make sure the door was still shut. There was no one visible through the frosted panes of glass on either side of the door. The hallway was quiet.

Schmidt said, "It's a homicide case, Dr. Swann."

Swann couldn't keep the smile from creeping onto his face. "A… homicide case? And you need a vampire expert? Really?"

The two detectives said nothing. Their eyes bored into him and there was not one trace of humor anywhere on their faces.

–11–
75 Bedford Street, NY
October 8, 9:46 a.m.
Five Days before the V-Event

Michael Fayne sat on the floor of his apartment, tucked in the corner between the dresser and the wall. It was the smallest space into which he could flee.

On the wall of his bedroom, the plasma TV kept telling him awful things.

Terrible things.

The reporter, that Asian chick, kept saying things that Fayne could not bear to hear. But the remote was on the bed and he dared not move.

He dared not.

"…sources within the department describe the murder as one of the most brutal they have ever seen," said Yuki Nitobe. "Authorities have blocked reporters from the crime scene, but in a Regional Satellite News exclusive, we have video footage taken at the scene. We warn viewers that the following image is explicit and disturbing. Viewer discretion is heavily advised."

Christ, thought Fayne, *she's milking this whole thing for ratings.*

He knew that with a disclaimer like that, no one would turn off their sets.

The image popped onto the scene, clearly taken with a lapel or lipstick camera. It was shaky and fuzzy and poor quality, but that gave every gruesome detail a documentary reality.

What it showed was unclear. More of a suggestion of the horror than anything explicit. And Fayne knew that this was even worse. Blood on the walls, a shapeless bulk on the floor, and one outstretched hand laced with a pattern of blood. That would have every viewer conjuring the worst possible images, filling in the blanks, feeding off it as surely as that succubus reporter did.

Fayne jammed his fists against his temples and squeezed his eyes and mouth shut. He tried not to scream.

He tried.

There was no one else at home in his five-apartment condo.

No one to hear the screams that he simply could not stop.

– 12 –

NYPD 6th Precinct

October 12, 6:07 p.m.

One Day before the V-Event

The prisoner stared at the glass, his mouth open, but so far he had not made a single sound since Swann told him what he did for a living.

Usually when he told people that he was an anthropologist, they looked bored. When he said that he was a vampire expert, they looked amused. The kind of amused people looked when they met a grown man who was doing something silly. Hotel staffs look at conferees at Star Trek conventions in the exact same way.

Finally the prisoner closed his mouth, but his eyes were wet with hot tears. His eyes slid away and for a moment he studied the empty air in the far corner of the room, then he covered his face with his hands and bent forward as if he'd been punched in the gut.

Which, Swann mused, was probably a fair assessment.

Swann cleared his throat.

"I'm sorry," he said.

The prisoner just shook his head.

"Really," said Swann, "I am sorry."

"For what?" asked the man without looking up.

"For springing that on you. It was clumsy and hurtful, and I apologize."

Slowly, as if the act caused him physical pain, the prisoner straightened. His face was wet with tears and snot, and flushed with anguish. He sniffed but didn't wipe his nose.

"Well, I guess we had to put a name on it, didn't we?"

"We're not putting any names on anything yet."

"Sure you are. The cops wouldn't have brought *you* in here if they didn't already know what's going on."

"No," said Swann, "that's not really true. The police don't know what's going on. No one does. They're trying to understand it."

The prisoner snorted.

"Come on," said Swann, "surely you have to agree that this isn't a common set of circumstances. Not for you and not for the police."

"Maybe not, but they went out and got fricking Van Helsing fast enough. They must have some idea."

Swann leaned closer to the glass. "Okay, fair enough. But tell me, Michael—I'm sorry, would you prefer Michael or Mr. Fayne?"

"Whatever. Michael, I guess."

"Michael, not Mike?"

"Michael."

"Michael, then. Tell me, Michael, if you were in their shoes, if you were investigating a case like this, what would you do?"

"I'm probably not supposed to answer that kind of question."

"Why not?"

"It's entrapment, right?"

"No, it's not. At least, it's not any kind of trap on my part, and remember I'm not a cop. I'm here to assess and advise. I want to understand what's happening."

"Why?"

"Because it needs to be understood. By the police and by you, I suspect. If you're having blackouts then you must be very afraid of them. I would be."

Fayne chewed his lip for a moment, then nodded.

89

"Michael," said Swann, "tell me about the last one. The last black-out. The one where they arrested you."

– 13 –

Tribeca, NY
October 8, 7:16 a.m.
Five Days before the V-Event

The next time it was worse.

Much worse.

He woke up in an alley.

Naked, filthy.

Covered in blood.

Michael Fayne lay there, his body filled with strange sensations. He expected pain. He expected damage. But what he felt was…wonderful.

At first.

Even before he opened his eyes, he was aware that he was not in bed. Not his, and not…anyone else's. He tried to piece things together. He remembered the last few days, remembered the horror and the shame. The crushing guilt and bottomless self-loathing. He remembered going into churches. Four, five of them. He had no idea what denomination they were. Whoever was open. Whoever had candles he could light.

He remembered sitting in pews. The ones furthest away from the statues of Jesus and the saints. Head bowed, hands clutched together so hard that he could feel his hand-bones grind together. Praying.

Praying.

Begging.

In the silence of those holy, empty places.

Last night he remembered leaving one of those churches. Maybe it was a Catholic church. It was big. One of those cavernous places in which you can feel the breath of ghosts on you. He'd shoved money into the poor box and lit a dozen candles. He'd prayed for hours. Fayne could not remember any of the prayers he'd learned as a kid. They hadn't mattered enough to him to be committed to memory. He found books in racks on the backs of the pews and read anything he found, opening them randomly. Looking for key words. Mercy. Forgiveness. Absolution.

Redemption.

Fayne remembered leaving one of those books open on the cold, wooden bench. Or…had he dropped it on the floor?

He couldn't recall exactly, because by then something was happening.

The light was going.

Not ambient light. In fact, Fayne's eyesight seemed to sharpen. He could see everything, *hear* everything. Smell every single thing. Even the air tasted different, and the surface of the polished pew was filled with new sensations under his fingertips.

No, it was not his eyesight that was failing.

It was the light inside his mind.

It was changing. Growing weaker. Fading.

Leaving in its place a featureless darkness into which no sight or sound or smell or taste or touch could intrude.

There was a moment of panic when Fayne thought that he was dying.

Don't let me die with this on my soul, he thought. Or had he said that aloud?

Then there was a moment when he felt like he was leaving his own body. It was like the feeling he sometimes got when he was sitting in a chair and starting to fall asleep. It was a toppling sensation, like his soul was sliding sideways out of his body. Normally he'd awaken with a start, slamming body and soul back into one conscious, unified place.

Not this time.

As the darkness in his mind expanded, he felt *himself* slip away. He felt his mind slide down into the darkness.

There was a strange transitional moment when he could feel his body begin to rise from the pew. But at the same time it was not *his* body. It moved without his will, without his control.

No! he tried to say.

But then the darkness took him.

Now he was somewhere else and it was some-*when* else. The darkness was sliding away, falling from him like a tarp being pulled off of an old car that had been put into storage. His mind awoke, dusty and disused.

In an alley.

He opened his eyes and saw the tall gray-green slab of a dumpster above him. Beyond that were the dirty bricks of a building that rose a dozen stories above him. The black zigzag of a fire escape gleamed with dew in the humid morning.

Everything stank.

Of rotting garbage, of human and animal waste. Of sweat and piss and…

…and…

Fayne's mind snapped back into its slots with a click, and immediately all of his senses were his own again.

His eyes bugged wide.

The side of the dumpster was not merely gray-green, the bricks not merely a dirty red. Both were smeared with blood.

Not his own, Fayne knew that right away.

He scrambled to his feet. He was naked.

The alley was long, but it opened onto a big street. He could see cars. People. Even this early in the morning.

The sight of them filled him with panic.

How was he going to get home? Naked, covered in…

Then he saw it. Hanging like a piece of trash from under the lid of the dumpster. Bent, but not at the elbow; twisted and broken in ways that were impossible.

He could barely even tell that it was a woman's arm.

He was sure that it wasn't attached to anything. It was held in place by the weight of the metal lid.

Fayne did not want to touch it. He wanted to run screaming from it. Even now he could feel the scream bubbling in the back of his throat.

And yet he had to touch it.

Not the arm. The lid.

He gripped it with one trembling hand and raised it. The lid was huge, heavy, but it moved under his touch as if it weighed nothing.

As soon as he shifted it the arm fell forward and down, landing with an empty sound at his feet. Fayne yelped and almost dropped the lid. Almost.

He stared at the arm for a long moment, and then raised his eyes as he leaned forward to look into the dumpster. There, amid the torn trash bags and soiled diapers and empty pizza boxes, was the rest of the woman.

She was not…

Whole.

And she was not alone.

Three white faces stared up at him from inside the dumpster. He did not recognize any of them, and in a mad moment, he felt as if that was the greatest tragedy of all. That they were dead, ripped apart, drained of their life and their blood…but they were strangers to him. Somehow he knew that he'd never known their names. Not before. Not now.

They were meat.

They were blood.

They were nothing. Garbage to be thrown away.

Fayne realized that on some level he believed that. Or, some part of him did.

It made it worse.

It was a sin. An unbearable one.

The last one, the one that broke him.

The bubbling scream rose to a full boil and he whirled away, vomiting a shriek into the fetid air of the alley.

After that, it all became so fractured.

He remembered running. Naked and wild.

He remembered other screams as people fled from him.

The blare of car horns, the screech of brakes. The bang and crunch of cars rear-ending each other to keep from running him down.

The shouts.

The yells from police.

He ran from them. He ran at them.

For some of the time he simply stood in the middle of the street and screamed at God, cursing His name, begging Him to explain how and why.

And what.

Then he remembered the hands on him.

And his own hands. Moving. Hitting. Shoving.

More screams, again not his own. Screams of anger and pain.

And then pain as the police came at him from all sides with their clubs and their pepper spray and their Tasers.

As he fell, Michael Fayne knew that it was not their violence that subdued him. He allowed them to beat him.

He needed them to do that.

He hoped they would beat him to death.

"EPIPHANY" PT.1

Yvonne Navarro

—1—

The desert is a beautiful and dangerous place.

When people say this, they refer to the heat and talk about the rattlesnakes and the scorpions and the vicious spines of the cacti that spread unchecked across its surface. Ultimately they know nothing about what can *really* happen out in the great emptiness, while the morning air is still frigid from the previous night and there are other creatures that seek to steal warmth and whatever form of sustenance from anything, or *anyone*, they can.

Mooney Lopez knows that the true danger of the desert walks on two legs and hunts not for food, but for the joy of causing pain and misery.

—2—

"I had hoped that the visit to the big city would clear your spirit and help you come back to yourself." Mother Gaso says. "That is why I agreed to give you money from your college fund to send you."

Mooney sits on the threadbare couch in the trailer's dim living room and says nothing. It is July in Sells, Arizona and the heavy old woman has the window air conditioner on high and the curtains drawn together. Mooney feels chilled and wishes she could go outside and lie in the sun. She's been back from New York for a week and hasn't felt well since. Aloud she says, "Come back to myself?"

Mother Gaso nods. "Forget." Her deeply wrinkled face is round and impassive below her long, iron-colored hair. "The past is gone. You must move forward."

Mooney does not raise her voice, but her hands ball into fists on her lap. Nothing has changed, either in herself or here on the reservation. The Tohono O'odham are still poor, she is still an orphan with a crappy future and who no one in her extended family wants to be responsible for, her guardian still waits for her to magically fall into the traditional ways of her so-called people…

And she was still raped in the desert by Mexican illegals a month and a half before Mother Gaso let her go on the New York trip.

"Come back to myself," she repeats. She makes her hands relax, then realizes she is gritting her teeth. "Why would I want to? That means I have accomplished nothing, have gone nowhere." Her eyes burn but she will not cry. Maybe later, but not now, not here. "I just wanted a distraction, something else to think about for a while." She sucks in air. "It didn't work."

"You must go back to before the men violated you," Mother Gaso tells her firmly. "Then move forward."

Mooney stands. "Seriously, old woman? Just forget about it…" She snaps her fingers in the air. "Like *that*." Her mouth twists. "Pretend it never happened, pretend everyone in town doesn't know and treat me like I'm something dirty." Three steps is enough to take her across the tiny space and she yanks open the door, enjoying for one blissful moment the swell of heated air that blasts inside. "I'm getting out of here. It's as cold as a damned refrigerator." Before Mother Gaso can protest, she marches outside and lets the door slam behind her.

It's a hundred and ten degrees in the shade and the sun is cooking the already scorched earth. The landscape is nothing but dust and weeds in varying shades of tan and dying green. For all its brutal appearance, the desert's hot breeze warms her skin and loosens the joints that had stiffened in the trailer's over-processed air. Mooney stretches then picks up a good-sized flat rock, using it to warm her fingers more quickly. It is hot enough to bake something on but it just feels good against her skin, and she rubs it over her knees and elbows with a sigh of pleasure. She wants to close her eyes, but if she does, she knows what she'll see.

There are three of them. They are sweaty and filthy from days of walking in the heat and nights of sleeping on the cold ground. Her guardian has ordered her to gather mesquite pods for flour, so Mooney has taken a heavy canvas sack and gone into the desert just before the sun heaves itself above the mountains, hoping to finish before the day's temperature rises. She is listening to her MP3 player and not paying attention to anything but where she is stepping when her head jerks up and she realizes she is surrounded. There is no one but her attackers to hear her scream, and the rest, as Mother Gaso insists, is the part that should be left behind.

Hours later two Border Patrol officers find her and load her into their car. Mooney wishes she could forget, that she could just get past it and "move forward," but the gossipy townspeople who see them help her into the doctor's office won't let her.

—3—

Two weeks later, Mooney knows she is a vampire.

"*Slut.*"

She is on her way to the Circle K Store off Main Street. It's two in the afternoon and there are plenty of people around, and even if they won't socialize with her, just their presence is enough to make her feel as safe as is possible given what happened. That complacency is shattered by the sudden, venomous tone of someone who walks past her on the sidewalk.

Mooney blinks and the forward step she is taking almost turns into a stumble. "What?"

"I'm pretty sure you heard me." The speaker is a teenager a couple of years younger than herself, a girl Mooney has seen around town but never talked to. Mooney doesn't know her name or anything about her, but the other girl apparently thinks she knows plenty about Mooney. Despite the triple-digit temperatures, the teen is dressed like so many people on the reservation, in jeans and a long-sleeved plaid shirt on which is pinned a tag from the local burger joint that says her name is *Ponka*. Mooney refuses to follow the ridiculous convention and has opted for cool, knee-length khaki shorts and a T-shirt with a dinosaur on it.

"Slut," the other young woman repeats, as though the first time wasn't enough to burn it into Mooney's brain. Her tormentor is with another girl who is the same age and two older boys; the boys leer at Mooney and look her up and down. The ugly speculation in their gazes makes her face flush with humiliation.

"I could get me some of that," the shorter of the two boys jeers. His skin is dark from being in the sun and his shoulder-length black hair is greasy. Mooney tries to remind herself that there are plenty of good people in this town; this guy, however, is not one of them, nor are his friends. "I hear you give it away to the Mexicans. It must be free for us, too. Right?"

Mooney stands, frozen, unable to speak and not knowing what to say if she could. They all laugh nastily and the other boy, who is the biggest of the group, grins and steps toward her. "C'mere, baby."

Before Mooney can react, he seizes her by the wrist and pulls her to his chest, then his other hand grabs her at the thickest part of her braid so that he can jerk her neck forward and control her head. Her face crashes against his neck and she gasps; he smells of sweat and dirt and the desert, just like—

Mooney opens her mouth and sinks her teeth into his flesh.

He screams like a scalded cat and flings her away, slams his hand over the wound.

"You're bleeding," shrieks Ponka. She and the other girl gape at each other and then at Mooney. Their faces look like real-time renditions of Munch's famous painting, *The Scream*. "Oh my God, she *bit* you!"

The first boy looks like he wants to say something but changes his mind. Instead he and the girls gather around their injured friend, then fixate again on Mooney with undisguised loathing. Mooney steps forward but she doesn't hear herself hissing until they all back away from her. A moment later they're running like terrified jackrabbits and she's standing there, watching them go, and wondering what the hell just happened.

–4–

It's not something Mooney ever considered might happen to her until now, although she's heard all the news—it seems like they talk about nothing else anymore. There are statistics, predictions, reports of attacks that occasionally come with lurid photographs of the horrific results. She's been paying attention only in that offhand way folks do when something big, a hurricane or enormous forest fire, takes over most of what's being broadcast on the television or talked about on the radio. You listen because that's just what you do, period. Thinking back, it isn't even difficult to figure out how she was exposed—

Michael Frayne, "Patient Zero," is one of the employees making coffee at some Starbucks she stops at during her endless wanderings around New York. Mooney remembers him now because although back then he'd still been handsome in a kind of GQ chiseled way, he'd also looked kind of… odd, distracted in that distant manner that people act when they're functional but not particularly feeling well; there hadn't been anything she could specifically point to, although while she stood in line and watched him—after all, he was *eye-candy—she'd seen him surreptitiously wipe the back of his hand across his jaw line at least twice. That movement, so small, had apparently been enough for him to spread the virus in the way that disease often did, airborne and invisible. She has seen his picture a thousand times on television since he became that famous first vampire. The trip is something that the old woman insists is going to somehow "make it all better," but that simply isn't happening. Mooney stands in a line that has more people in it than the number of employees in her town's grocery store and wonders how and when this "making it all better" is going to happen. Is this enormous city supposed to make her forget the rape, or the sad reality that now she fits in even less than she did before it happened?*

Surely it can't be because New York is known for shopping and shows and culture. She doesn't belong here, that's for sure. Mooney can enjoy none of the clothes or museums or tchotchkes—*New Yorkers use that word a lot—because all but the cheapest, tackiest things are priced out of her reach. Even the frozen vanilla latte she buys is an extravagance—back home she can buy an entire can of coffee for just under the cost of this pretentious* grande *concoction of trademarked coffee and flavoring,*

*Everyone has always claimed that Mooney's old guardian is clever, like the fox—*gaso—*that is her namesake. Mother Gaso approves of nothing Mooney does, from the way she dresses, to her "Get over it" attitude about the white man, to the way she refuses to use her given name, Wegi Mashath. Its translation of* Red Moon *is cute but too archaic for Mooney's taste. Maybe Mother Gaso thinks she will do something stereotypical of the rebellious young—meet a boy, move in with him, try drugs and booze, then refuse to return home. Be that as it may, Mooney is pretty damned confident she never planned on her foster kid returning to the Tohono O'odham reservation with some weird strain of DNA in her body reactivated thanks to a virus that seems to have the whole world in a panic.*

Fooled her.

Mooney is too buried in her own thoughts to remember the walk home from the Circle K. Although she knows she moved quickly, she is not tired or winded when she pulls open the front door and steps inside the overcooled trailer. As reluctant as she is to leave the spectacular warmth of the sun, common sense tells her she needs to get cleaned up. The nameless boy's blood rims her mouth and is smeared down her chin from where he pulled away; a few drops have dribbled onto her T-shirt, looking like black dots against the dark blue fabric. Mother Gaso is sitting at the tiny kitchen table sorting through beans; she glances in her direction but Mooney turns her face away as she passes and the old woman goes back to her chore without noticing anything. Mooney takes a clean T-shirt from her shelf in the closet and slips into the cramped bathroom to change, wash her face, and brush her teeth. The toothbrush and the water she spits out are stained with red but she doesn't mind the taste in her mouth. Instead, she kind of likes it and wishes she had more of the same.

She rinses until the water runs clear, then looks at her teeth in the mirror and smiles. The incisors are long and thin, much thinner than anything she's seen in the ludicrous horror movies or the panic-stricken pictures that are being splashed across the television nowadays. They are like the teeth of a…rattlesnake, a *wamad,* and on impulse she undulates just like one in front of the narrow, full-length mirror on the back of the bathroom door. She has never been a good dancer—no sense of rhythm or coordination—but now she finds herself admiring the way her muscles move effortlessly to and fro. Her arms and legs feel longer and stronger, as though they are ringed with muscles in the same way as the body of a rattlesnake.

Mooney's heard enough on the endless TV specials so she understands the concept of how the virus sometimes triggers a person's junk DNA—stuff left over from who knows how many eons ago—and makes them into something else. The key word, of course, is *sometimes,* which in scientific terms generally means rarely. People being what they are, the world's populace was jumping to conclusions first and not asking questions until later, if at all. Of course, *something* is also an interesting unknown, because according to the news, those whose DNA is reactivating are manifesting in all kinds of fascinating ways. Most, unfortunately, don't seem to be friendly, but all the ones she's heard about are definitely higher on the evolutionary scale of physical strength and abilities. She wonders for a moment what hers will be, then undulates again in front of the mirror. It takes only a few minutes of practice to make her movements markedly smoother and more graceful, more menacing. Watching herself, she's already pretty sure of the characteristics carried by her ancient ancestors.

The sound of a vehicle makes it through the wall and Mooney tilts her head. Not a car, heavier—a truck, coming up the property's long, dirt driveway.

Yeah, she is expecting him.

–5–

"Need to talk to Red Moon, Mother Gaso."

The trailer is small, a living room, tiny kitchen, and a bathroom just off the bedroom where her guardian sleeps. Mooney is not afraid, just curious about what he intends to do, so she watches from just beyond the door as Chief of Police Delgado takes off his hat in a false display of respect. The big man steps into the trailer even though the old woman doesn't invite him. He has to squeeze his oversized shoulders through the doorway and Mother Gaso has no choice but to back up until she is in the kitchen area. He sits on the couch—Mooney's bed—again without being asked, then looks at the elderly woman expectantly. Mother Gaso's gaze is emotionless and as unfazed as the surface of the sandstone cliffs that start the mountains miles to the north; she has no use for the Reservation Police, the Border Patrol, Highway Patrol, or any of the other entities of modern law enforcement. To her, they are just various ways the white man has dreamed up to subjugate her people. She believes in the old ways, where the elder tribesmen would discuss a problem and devise ways of handling it themselves.

"She's in the bathroom," is all Mother Gaso finally says.

"I'll wait."

Chief Delgado looks around the living room and Mooney sees his gaze linger on the things that speak to the fact that he is sitting, literally, on the limited space in which she is allowed to live. After a couple of minutes, he becomes uncomfortable under Mother Gaso's unwavering scrutiny.

"She coming out?"

"She might be awhile."

He shifts on the couch and looks as though he wants to force the issue but doesn't know how. When the old woman still refuses to make conversation, he can't stop himself from filling the void. "I'm not leaving until I talk to her. There was an incident in town this afternoon."

The sun-worn creases in Mother Gaso's face deepen as she frowns. "What?"

"She bit someone."

At last there is a change in the old woman's expression. Even so, it is fleeting, there and gone. It is hidden so quickly that the Chief doesn't notice. Mooney sees it because she knows Mother Gaso, sees her face every day. "Then that person must have done something to her first."

Delgado sighs. "That not the point. People don't just go around biting other people—you know that." He pauses, then adds. "Especially not with what's going on nowadays. It doesn't matter what the boy did, she—"

"Seriously?" Mooney asks. She has moved so silently from the back to the front of the trailer that her sudden appearance makes both Mother Gaso and Chief Delgado jerk in surprise. "Because I don't like to be touched. And after what I've been through, I *really* don't like it when someone grabs me on the sidewalk and pulls my hair as a start to something a whole lot more unpleasant. Did that really *not* matter, Chief? Was that really an all right thing to do?"

For a long moment all Delgado can manage is to stand there and shift uncomfortably. "No," he admits at last. "It wasn't. And if you want to file charges, I'll take care of that. But you need to be aware that the boy's got quite a few people up in arms." He hesitates, then just blurts it out. "He says you're a vampire."

Mooney laughs. "I guess I probably am."

"What did you say?" Mother Gaso demands. Delgado just looks at her unhappily.

"I said I am," Mooney repeats. "At least, I think so."

"When did this happen?" the old woman asks. "How?"

Mooney shrugs. "The trip to New York, I guess. I was at the coffee shop where that guy worked, the one they say started the whole thing. I must've been exposed to what he had."

"Michael Frayne," Delgado says.

"Yeah."

"So the boy you bit, he's going to become a vampire, too."

Mooney rolls her eyes at the older man. "No, he's not. Please don't tell me you're going to go out there and start a town-wide panic by spreading a bunch of wrong information. This isn't *Lost Boys*, Chief Delgado, or *Dracula*. Haven't you paid attention to anything they've said on the news?"

The lawman is turning his hat around and around in his hands. His fingers look like they want to wad it into a ball. "Not so much. I never thought it was something we'd have to worry about it."

Mooney laughs again. "Surprise!" When neither of them says anything, Mooney shakes her head in disgust. "Then I guess I'll have to fill you in. Being a vampire is not contagious, okay? It's—"

"But it's a virus, right? So…"

"That's different," Mooney explains with exaggerated patience. "The virus they're talking about doesn't give anyone a disease. Sometimes it activates really old DNA in a person's body. For most people nothing happens. For a very, very few—like me, I suppose—something inside them changes and makes them into what their ancestors were thousands of years ago."

Delgado snorts. "You expect me to believe that? Where's the proof?"

Mooney just looks at him. "I can show you more proof that it's true than you can show me that it's not."

Before he can retort, she steps even closer to him and opens her mouth wide. The motion feels absurdly good. The way her jaw pulls downward and her lips stretch is almost erotic, and the sensation of her new and improved teeth moving, actually *sliding* forward toward the man standing in front of her, is unlike anything she's ever experienced. It fills her with anticipation and a faraway…*tingling* in her stomach that it takes a second to identify as hunger. With a start, Mooney realizes she can't recall the last time she ate.

Suddenly she can smell Chief Delgado. His scent is not unpleasant—faded Old Spice and light perspiration, a hint of vanilla fabric softener on his well-worn uniform. He has a dog and when he kissed his wife goodbye this morning, she rested her head on his shoulder and hugged him—her hair left the odor of shampoo and her hands imprinted the back of his uniform with the smell of what they had for breakfast…chorizo, beans, and fry bread. The whole package is an intriguing combination and the memory of what the boy's blood tasted like rises strong in her mind. Without warning her mouth fills with saliva and she barely stops herself from drooling. Her tongue flicks over the sharp, tapered tips of her teeth—her *fangs*.

"Jesus!" He stumbles backward but it's only a couple of steps before he bumps into the wall and has nowhere else to go.

Those few feet are enough to let her clear her head and Mooney closes her mouth and smiles. "Don't worry," she tells him. "I'm not going to bite you, too. I promise." Mother Gaso stands frozen in the kitchen area, her face as impassive as it always is except for her eyes. Those are brighter than Mooney has ever seen them. Fear will do that to a person.

Delgado pulls himself up in a valiant attempt to regain his composure, to put himself back in control. Mooney realizes that it is useless. As sure as the sun rises above the mountains to the east, he will never again be in control of her. No one will. "So what now?"

Mooney raises one eyebrow. "Excuse me?"

Her hearing has improved and she can actually *hear* him when he swallows. "What are you going to do now? I mean, you can't stay here. So…" He trails off.

Mooney frowns. She knows what is coming but she is oddly unafraid. "Why not?"

"If you're a—you know. If you've got that disease, it's not a good idea, right? You should go somewhere and get treatment." He's floundering and he knows it. Mother Gaso still hasn't moved but Mooney can feel the tension building. More than likely it's because she agrees with Delgado, not because she intends to defend her foster child. Never that.

"I don't have a disease," Mooney says. She speaks very slowly, as though she is trying to make a confused child understand something. "I've changed, that's all. And there's nowhere for me to go. Even if there were, it's not going to happen. Yeah, I graduated high school last May, but I'm only seventeen, remember?" She glances at Mother Gaso but not for support, just to make sure the old woman is clear on what she's saying. "I have three classes at Tohono O'odham Community College that start next month. I'm very much looking forward to them." She had stopped smiling at his question, but now Mooney lets her smile return, full and bright…and toothy. She makes sure that Mother Gaso also sees it.

"I have a great future ahead of me, Chief Delgado. And this town is where I belong."

–6–

The first time she vomits is right before geology class.

It is a day of firsts—her first day of college, her first class, the first time in her life she has ever thrown up. That she has become a victim of the changes brought about by the vampire virus is ironic because she has never been ill, not ever. People say that all the time, but the truth is that it's usually bullshit and their childhoods were filled with the same number of annoying head colds and infected scrapes as other kid down the street. Not so with Mooney—no colds, no infections… not so much as a single fever or headache. Which is, of course, why she is so completely shocked by the roiling that starts in her belly and slides up her throat so quickly that she nearly doesn't make it to the women's room right around the corner from the classroom.

She crouches over the toilet and spits, trying to cleanse her mouth. "What the fuck?" she asks aloud, then she vomits again. It becomes a vicious circle—she vomits and the smell and sight of the inside of the toilet and her own mess makes her gag and vomit again. She does it over and over, until there is nothing left in her stomach but the feel of her abdominal muscles spasming and a thin line of bile-laced saliva going from her mouth to the less-than-white porcelain. "Gross," she tries to say but the only thing she can manage now is a whisper. She has expelled more than she would have thought possible, and judging by the chunks of chicken and white beans mixed in with smashed donut bits, she has lost all of her meager breakfast and most of what little she ate for dinner last night.

The college is tiny and the buildings aren't much more than trailers; she has locked herself into one of two stalls in the women's room. When she first bolts into it, someone else is in the other one. Now Mooney can hear the woman washing her hands and messing around at the sink. She's making a big show of pretending to put on her makeup, but in this runt-sized town, Mooney knows that the other is simply stalling because she desperately wants to know the identity of the Vomiting Woman—Mooney actually sees these two words as capitalized in her mind—who's in the closed stall. The minutes tick away and finally, *finally*, the unseen student leaves rather than be late for whatever class is on her schedule. Only then does Mooney manage to stand upright, unlock the door, then stumble to the sink.

What she sees in the mirror stuns her.

She expects her face to be pale and tired-looking, the stereotypical image of illness learned from countless hours of having the television in Mother Gaso's trailer on as background music to a life of stagnancy.

Instead, her face is an image of vibrancy—her black eyes are clear and shining and her dusky skin glows above lips that are glossy and burgundy-colored, as though they are covered in sleek lipstick. She squares her shoulders and lets go of the basin's edge, then realizes that she feels as good as she looks, both of which are damned good now that she's rid her system of everything she's eaten over the last eighteen hours. And she is absolutely ravenous.

Ignoring her hunger, she goes to class. She's late but it's the first day and everything is disorganized, even in a class of only eight students, so the teacher doesn't notice; if the woman in the bathroom is in here, it's doubtful she'll connect the violently ill person in the bathroom with the robust-looking Mooney. She has only two classes in the morning but it feels like forever until she has a long enough break to head for the Papago Café and grab four beef tacos. A year ago these had been her favorite, now she can barely tolerate the spices and the cheese; she forces herself to eat them anyway and hopes they won't come back up in the middle of her small business management class this afternoon. If she can make it through that, she is done with classes for the day.

And thus begins the pattern of her life for the next three weeks, until she realizes she is pregnant.

–7–

When Mother Gaso is not home, Mooney strips off her clothes and examines her naked form in the bathroom mirror.

Ten weeks.

It isn't an estimation. She remembers all too well the day in the desert, the *exact* day, that the three Mexican men left her, beaten and bleeding, in the desert. They probably thought she would die of exposure and thirst—they had taken her water, of course—and she would have, had the Border Patrol not found her. She had listened to the doctor and to the psychologist he had insisted she subsequently see, and had decided on her own that she wanted exactly the opposite of everything they directed her to do. Her only experience with sex had been violence, pain, and force. All Mooney wanted to do was forget.

Apparently that will not be possible.

Ten weeks.

She is three weeks into the first sixteen-week semester of her associate's degree program, and the rape is two and a half months behind her.

Mooney looks like she is four months along.

It's odd, to say the least. From a straight-on view she still has a very attractive waistline. With her hip-length hair and unlined face, she looks like any other teenager. But from the side, there it is—the baby bump, starting about three inches below her sternum and rounding nicely into the V of her legs. At this stage, most women barely show, and others have to push their stomach out intentionally if they want it to be noticed.

She tilts her head and leans closer to the mirror, then pulls her hair over one shoulder and inspects it. Her belly isn't the only thing that's off. Her hair has changed color or…something. Now it has a peculiar sort of *design* to it, as though it's been lightened by the sun but in a pattern that, if you look carefully enough, is quite symmetrical, with recurring patches of brown that are both light and dark. She frowns and looks closer, but that only muddles things, makes it seem as though she is looking at a bunch of weirdly stretched rectangles. She rubs at her eyes and steps back from the mirror as far as she can—not much in the closet-sized bathroom—then sees a hand mirror in the basket on the back of the toilet. When she holds it up, turns, and positions it so that she can see the back of her head, she discovers yet another of the unique surprises that just keep coming her way.

"What are you doing?" Mooney jumps at the sound of Mother Gaso's raspy voice. "Why are you undressed like that?"

The old woman smells like sweat and the desert and Mooney turns to face her, unashamed at her nakedness and not trying to hide anything. "I'm looking at myself."

"You already know what you are," the old woman retorts. Before Mooney can comment on the double entendre, her guardian tries to step pass her in the narrow hall, then freezes. "My God, girl. You're carrying a child!"

This is not a surprise to Mooney, so all she says is, "Obviously."

"Who's the—"

"Don't insult me," Mooney interrupts in an icy voice. "Have you ever seen me with a boy? No one in this town will even talk to me, much less hook up."

Mother Gaso ducks her head, then slides past Mooney and goes into her bedroom. Mooney can hear the woman putting away her purse and changing into a fresh blouse. She puts down the mirror and slips on her own jeans and T-shirt, then combs back her hair and twists it into a bun at the nape of her neck. Mooney is not afraid, but one step at a time. Right now might not be the best time to reveal that there is a wide swath of her hair from hairline to end that resembles the skin of a rattlesnake.

"You need to see a doctor." Mother Gaso's voice has dropped a notch; now she just sounds tired and old.

Mooney blinks. "No, I don't," she says. "I feel fine."

"You're pregnant. One way or the other, you need to take care of… it."

Heat explodes into Mooney's cheeks, so fast and full that it makes her stagger back into the bathroom. It takes her a few seconds to realize that what's she's feeling is anger, no, *rage*. She is back into the hall in an instant, filling the doorway of Mother's Gaso's bedroom and leaving the old woman no hope of escape. "What do you mean, *one way or the other*?" she grinds out. "And *it*?" Her heart is pounding so hard that she can feel it push blood through the artery in her neck; her vision pulses with each beat. She has never been so furious in her life, not even after the rape when the psychologist tried to encourage her to express her anger at what those men had done to her, what they had stolen from her. As it turns out, one of them gave her something in return; she doesn't know why, but she wants to keep *it*, as the old bitch standing in front of her called it. Yes, it is a child of violence, but the *it* is her child. And she will die to defend it.

Mother Gaso looks up, but the defiance on her wrinkled face disintegrates when she sees Mooney's expression. But she has spent too many decades speaking her mind to use caution now. Even so, she cannot disguise the shakiness of her voice. "An abortion," she ventures. When Mooney just glares at her, she adds, "Surely you understand that would be best, don't you? It's horrible enough that this pregnancy is the result of a rape, but now you're a…a…" Apparently Mother Gaso can't bring herself to finish, so she simply lets the sentence trail away to nothing.

"The word is *vampire*," Mooney says. "Try it out. It's pronounced *vam-pie-er*."

"Being sarcastic isn't helping anything. And you didn't answer my question."

"I'm keeping the baby," Mooney says with as much acidity as she can.

Mother Gaso looks at her for a moment, then shrugs. "It's your life. If you insist on screwing it up while you're so young, at least make sure the baby's healthy." She pauses just long enough to let that sink in, then added, "With all the changes that virus has caused in you, who knows what it will do to an unborn child."

Mother Gaso steps forward expectantly and Mooney lets her pass. As her guardian trudges into the living room, turns on the television, then pulls a pot of leftover tepary beans and beef from the refrigerator to heat up for dinner, Mooney watches her but doesn't really see anything. The rage is gone and now her brain feels swollen with all the thoughts suddenly banging around in her head, ricocheting from one side to the other and leaving little bloody dents in their wake. Saying she felt fine was a half-truth—she does, until she eats. Then her existence becomes a parody of the famous old lather-rinse-repeat shampoo commercial: she eats, she vomits, she feels great; she eats, she vomits, she feels great. Somewhere in there she is taking in enough nutrients to keep her going, but just barely. Her belly is big enough to be noticed in non-baggy clothes so she has switched to extra-large T-shirts, but she has lost weight everywhere else. Her cheeks are hollow and her jeans are loose everywhere but the waist, yet she is absurdly muscular, cut in the way that runners or kickboxers are and—when she's not puking up everything in her gut—she is faster, stronger, and has more stamina than she has ever had. She's almost in the best shape of her life.

Except for the vomiting.

And the minor fact that she's knocked up.

She opens her mouth and stares at her teeth...no, not teeth. *Fangs.* They're bright white, like a puppy's, and just about an inch long. Wide at the top, narrowing to a sliver at each tip, and curving under when she closes her mouth; barely noticeable when she talks, if she opens her mouth and pulls her upper lip back, like now, they drop forward... just like a rattlesnake's. She has lived in Arizona all her life and knows a lot about rattlesnakes—their habitat, their behavior, their feeding methods. Venomous reptiles have teeth like hypodermic needles to inject their prey. Were hers channeled as well, but for a very opposite purpose?

God, she thinks. *What am I turning into?*

An hour ago she had been proud. Ostracized from everyone, yes, but that hadn't mattered. Her mother and father had been like that— loners, different not in any kind of physical sense but shut out from society on the reservation because they had married in defiance of their families' wishes, then refused to bow to outdated traditions and oppressive rules. The had shaped Mooney to be just like them, irrevocably instilled in her the belief that time had marched not on, but *over* the Native Americans, and there was no turning back. Why scratch in the dirt and live in poverty when there was an entire world out there, beckoning at every turn? But her parents had died five years ago, killed after dropping her off at school when her father's old truck had blown a front tire on the way home and rolled. The attitudes of her parents had carried over to her, and although she was related by blood to probably more than a hundred people on the Tohono O'odham reservation, ultimately not a single relative had stepped forward to take her in. So at twelve years old, Mooney had been introduced to the spectacular environment of state foster care.

Native American.

The white man's world.

Now she fits in neither.

Without warning, pain ripples through her lower abdomen. Mooney gasps and clutches at the edge of the sink, fighting to keep upright only because the room is too small for her to double over. After a moment she manages to pull the door closed, then she sits on the closed lid of the toilet and rocks quietly, imagining she can feel something shifting below the surface of her belly. Is she losing the baby, miscarrying? She doesn't know why but the idea fills her with an excruciating sense of loss and she realizes she is crying. She manages to keep silent only by jamming the back of her fist into her mouth—she doesn't want the old bat out there to hear her weeping, although it would be a miracle if she could be heard above the clamor of the idiot box. It takes about five minutes but the pain fades away and that strange sense of movement disappears. By the time she's ready to go out and face the rest of her day, it is like nothing has ever happened.

Physically.

—8—

A week later Mooney is in Dr. Guarin's office. He is an older man with the typical swarthy skin of the Tohono O'odham but with fewer wrinkles because he works inside rather than in the sun. He folds his hands on his desk and looks at her steadily. She has no friends in this place, or anywhere else, but of all the people in town, he is, perhaps, the only person she does not dislike. She doesn't know if the feeling is mutual but he is one of the few old-timers who calls her by the name she prefers rather than Red Moon.

"According to my calculations and the lab work, you are just under sixteen weeks along," he tells her. He knows when she was raped, but there is no judgment in his eyes. His expression is professionally placid and infers that she can tell him anything, he will keep it confidential, right to privacy, and all the rest of the modern, politically correct bullshit.

"I was attacked less than three months ago," Mooney reminds him. He says nothing.

"I was a virgin," she says, even though she told him all this on the day the Border Patrol brought her in. "I never had sex with anyone before then."

He stays silent, she stays silent. It is an odd battle of wills, a standoff between the two of them. Mooney will not give in; she knows the truth of what she is saying. Whether or not he believes her, the facts will not change.

"There were some abnormalities in the blood work we did this morning," he finally says.

Ah, she thinks. *Now we'll get to what he really wants to talk about.* She has a feeling that he has known all along that she is telling the truth about her sex life—or lack of it—and that whatever is about to come out of his mouth is what he has been driving at since he finished his examination. "I expected that," is all she says.

"I don't have the equipment here to fully analyze the results," he continues. "I need to send it up to Tucson Medical, see what they come up with."

"You know full well what they're going to say. The whole town knows it already."

They stare at each other and after a bit she sees his shoulders slump. He sits back and sighs. "Mooney," he says, "this is an enormous thing. Sells just isn't ready for something—some*one* like you. The people here won't know how to handle it, how to act, what to expect. The reaction may not be positive—"

"I already know that," she interrupts.

"All right then," he says calmly. "Then let's look at it another way. I don't know what to expect."

"I'm not exactly an expert either."

"Not only with you," he continues stubbornly, "but with the pregnancy. You've told me you experience terrible nausea, but I'm reluctant
to give you anything to stop it because I don't know how you'll react. I
don't know your physiology, and with a child inside you, assuming you
intend to keep it, there are tremendous risks involved in giving you any
kind of prescription medication."

He stops, waiting for her to say something, but Mooney is silent.
She doesn't know what to say. She thought he would be as excited as
she is—not only does he now have a vampire patient, but a pregnant
one, at that. She feels embarrassed when she realizes that her assump-
tion about that was immature, something that would come from a
teenager rather than a young woman who's undergoing massive bodily
changes. If she changes her perspective, she sees that Dr. Guarin is not
a young man; he is in his mid-fifties, unimaginative and complacent. He
is used to nice, predictable clientele who bring him head colds, diabetes, an occasional broken arm or perhaps alcohol abuse, and he no
doubt likes it that way. Her rape last summer was probably the worst
thing he's seen in years.

The minutes tick past and at last he tells her, "You need to go somewhere where they have the resources to help you, like Tucson or
Phoenix. I don't know if they've had any cases as a result of the virus
or not, but either way—"

"I'm not leaving Sells," she cuts in. "There's nowhere else for me to
go. No one will take me in, you know that. As it is, I'll be eighteen in
January. The state will stop paying foster support and Mother Gaso will
put me out of her house. I won't have any medical insurance." This is
just a fraction of the things that have been going through her mind, the
same deliberations that she realizes adults dealt with constantly, a
life-load of responsibilities, worries, and if-thens, then-thats. It stings
to spell it out to this man who is only slightly more than a stranger, but
he has to know why. She doesn't know him that well, but in the months
to come he may be the only person who will stand by her side, even if he
isn't *on* her side.

"I can't say for certain, but my guess is the government can be convinced to treat you for free."

Mooney feels her face flush and her pulse rate triples. She wills herself to stay in control before the feeling can escalate to the fury that

she experienced last week with Mother Gaso when the woman called her unborn child *it*. He is only laying out options but he has not thought things through. The dual surprise of discovering the changes Mooney has undergone has not given him the time needed to do that. At least this is what she tells herself, and it is enough to cool her down and make her heartbeat drop back to something vaguely normal…whatever that is for her now.

113

"No," she says with utter finality. "If I do that, it's just like donating my body to science. They'll lock me away in some medical facility and God only knows what they'll do to me in the name of finding a 'cure.' You've seen the panic and heard the whacked-out stories. The news reports air them for sensationalism, and the fact that they retract them the next day or say they were just rumors doesn't do any good. It's like uploading a picture of yourself naked on the Facebook, then taking it down. Once it's up there, it's there forever." She sit there quietly for a few seconds, then adds in a soft voice, "And what do you think they'll do to my baby in the name of science, Dr. Guarin?"

It is only a slight change of expression, but Mooney picks up on it. Oddly, she can also *smell* something different, a spike in pheromones that her senses register as fear. For her? If so, it is the first time anyone in Sells has ever exhibited anything resembling sympathy for her.

He looks down at the papers on his desk again, flips one up and scans it, then another, and another. "I don't know what to give you for the nausea," he says again. His next words are enough to make her raise her eyebrows, but the fact that he won't look up indicates he's completely serious. "Have you tried rare meat? *Really* rare? I can't recommend raw—everything I've been taught just won't let me do that. But your physiology, what I've read in the science journals, it all seems to indicate…" His voice trails off but he doesn't need to finish for Mooney to understand.

"No," she answers. "I haven't. Mother Gaso buys the groceries. She gets the money from the state for me. It's not a lot so we don't eat fancy. I don't get much spending money."

Dr. Guarin nods. "I understand that, but she needs to rethink your diet. You're bordering on malnutrition, Mooney. Instinct tells me a normal diet isn't supplying you with what your body needs. If this continues, your baby may not get enough nutrients. You could miscarry or worse."

"Worse?"

"The child could be born prematurely, underdeveloped, or even deformed. I just don't know. But it's not worth taking the chance." He finally looks up at her. "It doesn't have to be steak. Hamburgers, whatever's on sale. As rare as you can make it and still get a little cooking heat on it." He puts the papers in a file with her name on it, then closes the folder and runs a finger across the calendar pad on his desk. He picks up a pencil and writes her name on the pad. "I want to see you in two weeks, sooner if you don't get any better. Just stop by after your last class. And remember—

"Rare, red meat. *Lots* of it."

–9–

The thing with the rabbit happens so fast that Mooney doesn't even know what she's doing until it's done.

Mother Gaso tries, more than Mooney expects. She expects the old woman to disregard Dr. Guarin's instructions, especially since red meat is so expensive—money is always the driving force in their existence. Mooney thinks her guardian probably doesn't give a bat's ass whether Mooney is healthy or not, and she certainly doesn't care about some vampire baby (or whatever she and the other old cronies in town are calling it these days). But no matter what Mother's Gaso's personal opinions are, the day after Mooney relays the doctor's instructions a cheap, family-sized package of ground beef appears in the refrigerator and suddenly there is meat on her plate at every meal. As Dr. Guarin had suggested, it isn't the expensive stuff—just a quarter-pound patty, cooked on the outside, bloody on the inside.

At first it's good, better than it has been…but not as good as it should be. The meat is okay, but the blood—and this is a hard thing for Mooney to admit—is better. She works it in her mouth, savoring the flavor and the juice, before finally swallowing; the urge to vomit every time she eats subsides, but never truly disappears. She feels better after each meal, ultimately eating the meat and leaving the rest, the beans, the rice, the fry bread, until the old woman no longer puts them on her plate at all. It's not a miracle cure but almost immediately Mooney fills out a little. She no longer feels like she's starving, going through each day like some sort of high-functioning shadow of herself that watches while her body consumes itself but her belly gets bigger.

And then, the rabbit.

She is three days away from her appointment with Dr. Guarin when it darts across the road in front of her on her way home from class. One moment it's a gray-coated blur four feet away—

The next her teeth are buried in its neck.

Her backpack lies in the dust where she dropped it. She's standing at the side of the road and sucking on the bunny like it's a popsicle and she's a thirsty kid on a hundred and ten degree afternoon. The taste that fills her mouth is salty, thick and heavily metallic, with a texture like hot gravy. It is unlike anything she's ever had and it slides down her throat, coating the hollowness that has been deep in her core for months and wiping it out of existence.

It is the best thing she's ever had.

The gamey smell of the rabbit fills her nostrils and she presses the animal's fur tighter against her face and revels in it, pulling harder at the bite she's made in its flesh. It kicks in her grip and the movement does something—pumps adrenaline into the animal's bloodstream, perhaps—to the flavorful liquid sliding down her throat, making it even better. Mooney doesn't know how long it takes for her to drain the creature, but it seems like only seconds. When she lifts her mouth from its throat, her lips, tongue and hands are tingling, and her fingertips have become so screamingly sensitive that she can literally feel the small carcass already cooling beneath its fur. She stares at it for a moment, then flings it into the desert for the scavengers to take care of, watching impassively as the effortless flip of her wrist sends it sailing at least forty feet before it disappears into the waist-high scrub.

For the first time since before she learned she was pregnant, Mooney isn't sick to her stomach. She feels halfway decent for a change, not entirely satisfied but not precisely hungry, either—it's as though she's been given half a sandwich when what she really needed was the whole thing. She's not a fool and she knows what this means, even if she hasn't been willing to acknowledge it.

Until now.

There is a part of herself, the human part that has controlled her existence until very recently, that views the idea of drinking human blood as disgusting and vaguely filthy. The new part of her, the DNA-activated mystery creature who just had its first decent meal, finds it so appealing that her mouth instantly waters. A thousand horror movie images flip through her mind like a slide show on warp speed, and they all end in splatter and gore and death. Does she really want to go there, to *kill* other human beings in order to sustain herself? Although small by comparison, the rabbit has made her realize that she can likely do just that to anyone without much effort. She has the speed, the strength, the *bite*, and instinct tells her that the more she feeds on what she really needs—blood—the stronger she will get. But as much as she despises almost everyone in town, there is no one in Sells she hates so much that they warrant dying.

But what are her options? A scene from another movie, an old comedy called *Love at First Bite* starring George Hamilton, blots out the bloodier scenes in her mind and Mooney laughs out loud at the idea of breaking into a blood bank in the middle of the night. She cannot remember the last time she laughed at anything, a joke, a television show, something she read in a book, and it feels good. She raises her face to the sun and luxuriates in its warmth and in the almost-complete sensation of fullness in her belly. For the first time, she dares to think of herself as not human and to accept that without it feeling wrong. She is what she is; not human, but better. There are things on which she can feed, rabbits, coyotes, other creatures of the desert. She might crave human blood, but she's just not ready to take that huge, permanent step.

Not yet.

– 10 –

"What's up with my hair?" She is sitting on the side of the examination bed in Dr. Guarin's office, swinging her legs like an energetic kid. The glossy black mane of her ancestry—at least the human part—is gone. What now falls from her head to her hips is hard to describe, like thin, shimmering strips of rattlesnake hide lying side by side. It's still hair, but the pattern and its perfection are something neither she nor the physician have ever seen before.

"I can't answer that, Mooney." He lifts an inch-wide piece of it and peers closely at it, then lets the lock of hair drop. "If you haven't colored it, obviously it has to do with whatever chemical changes are going on in your system. I warned you on your last visit that I'm in a no-information zone here." He listens to her heart, then takes her blood pressure and temperature before having her lie back so he can examine her stomach and press a stethoscope against it. "You seem to

be doing much better," he finally says. "You've gained a few pounds,
your blood pressure is good. Did you try changing your diet as I rec-
ommended?"

"Yes."

"And?"

"It helped some," she answers. Although she's not lying, the truth is
that she hasn't eaten anything at home since killing the rabbit three
days ago. Until then she had thought she knew the desert, its climate,
its creatures, its good and bad, light and dark. After all, she had been
born in the Sonoran desert, grown up with the blistering heat and frigid
nights, played with the four-inch grasshoppers and horned lizards, and
avoided rattlesnakes and tarantula wasps. The desert *had* taken her
parents and she had been raped in it, but she had never realized what
a rich source of food it could be until she'd slipped out of the trailer
just after dawn two days ago and gone hunting for the first time.

When she doesn't elaborate, Dr. Guarin gives her a sharp look.
"You're not telling me everything," he finally says. "I admit that I don't
have very much knowledge about how to help you, but to give me the
best chance at it, you need to be honest, Mooney. You can't know how
to fix an engine if the driver doesn't tell you what it does wrong out on
the road."

Mooney looks at her hands, then just blurts it out. "I've been catching animals in the desert."

She expects him to looked shocked but he doesn't. "And you feel
better."

"Yes."

"Then keep it up," he tells her. "Just be careful." When she sends
him a puzzled look, Dr. Guarin adds, "Rabies is not unknown around
here, Mooney. Do you know what would happen if you consumed the
blood of a rabid animal?"

"No."

"Neither do I. Let's not find out." He writes something on her chart.
"How much blood are you ingesting per day?"

Mooney hesitates. She had started with the rabbit, then quickly
graduated to animals that could provide a heartier meal, discovering
immediately that it was easier to snap the neck of something larger than
have it struggle within her grasp. As much as the old man insists he
wants honesty, she doesn't think it will sit well if he learns that last

night she killed a twenty-five-pound bobcat with her bare hands and drained it dry. "Whatever I can get," she finally says. "A couple of coyotes yesterday."

"Well, at least it will help keep them away from the livestock," he comments. He catches her with his gaze. "The baby's heartbeat is strong," he tells her, "but there's something odd about it, almost like an echo. I don't know what's causing that so I'd like you to take it easy if you can."

"Okay," she says, but the *if you can* part is not lost on Mooney. How many creatures that have to hunt their own food can *take it easy*? She slides off the table and stands, but Dr. Guarin makes no move to step out of the room so she can get rid of her gown and back into her own clothes.

"Mooney," he says, "the baby is growing at an astounding rate, much faster than it would in a normal pregnancy. I really recommend you go to the clinic for an ultrasound."

She shakes her head. "I can't do that. Even if the state covers it—and I'm not sure they will—there's a chance it could raise a whole bunch of flags. We just talked about what that could mean." She shrugs and wishes she could somehow convey to him the sense of well-being that has been tickling at her senses over her the last couple of days. "I feel great, really. It grows as fast as it grows. I can hide it for bit longer, but I can't stop that." She raises her eyes to his and doesn't flinch. "I can't change whatever this baby turns out to be, and I won't stop it."

He walks to the door but stops and glances back at her unhappily before leaving. "Are you sure, Mooney? *Absolutely* sure? Because I have no idea how this is going to turn out."

She nods. "Yeah, I am. Mother Gaso was watching this old movie last night and the blonde woman who starred in it kept singing this French line, over and over. Stupid thing is stuck in my head. *Que sera, sera.*"

"Doris Day," he says. "Whatever will be, will be."

Mooney nods again. "What she said."

"JUNK" PT.4

Jonathan Maberry

-14-
NYPD 6th Precinct
October 12, 5:51 p.m.
One Day before the V-Event

"Did they hurt you?" asked Swann.

Fayne shrugged. "Who cares?"

"I do."

"No you don't. Nobody cares."

"You must care, Michael," said Swann frankly. "You obviously don't want to be executed. You don't want to die. Okay, not in the heat of the moment, not when you were freaking out and the police were all over you, but later—now—you clearly don't want to die."

"Maybe."

"What does that mean?"

Fayne shrugged again. "Maybe *I* want to die but *he* doesn't."

" 'He'?"

"He, it, whatever the fuck this is. The thing inside me. The *thing* that killed nine goddamn women. Jesus."

Swann leaned forward; at that angle he could see his own reflection superimposed over Fayne's. In that light his face looked as pale and ghostly as the prisoner's. It was a disturbing insight that Swann did not need to see, so he sat back and crossed his legs.

"You refer to this 'thing,' Michael," he said. "What is it? Are you hearing voices?"

"No. It's not like that."

"Then what is it? Help me understand."

Fayne stood up abruptly and walked right up to the glass, stopping so close to it that his breath smoked the surface. "Listen, motherfucker, why don't *you* tell *me*? Tell me what you think? What have you assessed?" He slapped his palms against the glass so hard that the big pane trembled in its frame. "What am I?"

"Michael—"

Fayne slapped the glass again. Harder. The door to the observation room banged open and Detectives Schmidt and Yanoff came hurrying in.

"The hell's going on in here?" demanded Schmidt, but Swann waved them to silence.

"C'mon!" yelled Fayne, and again he slapped his palms against the glass. The whole wall seemed to shudder under the impact. "Tell me! In your *professional* opinion, you self-righteous prick, you tell me what's living inside me. Is it a monster? Well? Am I a goddamned vampire?

Another slap.

Swann covered the microphone and whispered to Schmidt. "Can he break that?"

"No way," answered Yanoff. "It's half-inch tempered glass. He could swing a chair at it and not—"

"*Am I?*" screamed Fayne as he struck again and again.

Spider-web cracks suddenly jagged out from both points of impact. Fayne froze.

So did Swann and the detectives.

Fayne stepped back and looked at his hands. They were unmarked.

He looked at the cracks, and then once more seemed to stare through the glass to the observation room.

He half-turned away, then paused. His body trembled with inner turmoil.

With a howl of rage and pain, Fayne swung back and slammed his palms once more against the glass.

It exploded inward, driving Swann, Yanoff and Schmidt backward with arms flung across their faces to protect their eyes. Chunks of rcinforccd glass slashed at them, cutting their arms and shoulders and thighs. None of the cuts were deep, but Swann felt like he was cut everywhere. He staggered backward and lost his balance, falling against a row of chairs, slipping, collapsing to the ground as the glass disintegrated into a million fragments.

Yanoff fell, too, his right thigh cut to the bone by a sliver of glass as thin and sharp as a sword blade. He screamed and dropped, blood pumping from the gaping flesh.

Only Schmidt remained on his feet. Swann and Yanoff had both been closer to the window and their bodies kept him from the greatest harm. He was bleeding, but with a growl he whipped open his jacket and tore the Glock from the nylon holster.

"Freeze!" he bellowed. "Freeze right there, you son of a bitch or I will kill you."

Fayne had already frozen in place, shocked by the enormity of what he had just done, and by everything that impossible act conveyed. He stood wide-legged, his hands still palm out from where they had struck the glass. His eyes were as wide as his gaping mouth.

"Oh God…," he said in a voice that was hollow, empty of all emotion and certainly of all hope.

Swann stared up at the young man and he said it as well.

"Oh, God."

– 15 –

October 12, 3:18 a.m.
New York Presbyterian Hospital
Zero Days until the V-Event

Swann sat on the edge of the gurney in a hospital johnnie and his socks. Everything hurt. His body, his mind, and his heart. He glanced at the wall clock. It was nine hours and change since the doors banged open and both rooms—interrogation room and observation room—had been flooded with cops. Everybody had been yelling; everybody had a gun.

Fayne did not protest, did not resist, but the cops still clubbed him down and piled on him. They put plastic cuffs on his wrists and ankles. One of the officers stood over him with a Taser and dared him to move. Fayne face was covered with blood that leaked from his scalp and from his nostrils. He screamed and screamed, but not to be let go. Fayne simply screamed.

After that, things got a little hazy for Swann. There were so many people crowding around him. First police officers of every kind, then EMTs, then hospital staff. He remembered injections and tweezers and stitches, but now as he sat there, it all seemed like it was something that had happened to someone else. After all, he was a college professor. He could not have been injured by flying glass in a police interrogation room after interviewing a man who was suspected of the brutal murder of at least two people, and who might actually be a…

122

A what?

Even now, even with everything that he'd seen and heard, Swann did not want to put the name to it. To do so would be to cross a line. He preferred to stay on the sane side of that line. On that side of the line, vampires were a cultural phenomenon. Vampires were the creations of superstitious people who could not otherwise explain things like plagues and Sudden Infant Death Syndrome and catalepsy and porphyria. Vampirism was the stuff of folktales and movies and pop culture and his own heavily footnoted scholarly books.

Vampires were not young men in holding cells in New York police stations.

No. They were not that. That was all on the *other* side of the line.

Swann was an academic. For people like him, there was no other side of the line. There could not be.

He sat there, swathed in bandages which hid proof that he was wrong.

Swann closed his eyes and tried not to see anything.

He heard the soft scuff of a shoe and opened his eyes to see Schmidt standing there. The detective had a line of butterfly stitches across the left side of his forehead but no other signs of injury. Schmidt's face was on the dour side of blank, with a hint of a frown and eyes that held no light.

"Professor," he said.

"Detective," said Swann, and they studied each other for a long, silent moment. From a detached angle, Swann understood the implications of this moment. They had both been there, they'd both seen what happened, and they both knew the rest of it. The crime scene reports, the lab work. All of it. Until now, however, it was nothing more than a collection of bizarre and anomalous information that had no common thread.

But now…?

Now they were going to have to talk about it. Now they were going to have to put a name to it. Both of their lives and all of the world around them hinged on that conversation.

Swann wanted no part of it, though, and he tried to stall. "How's Detective Yanoff?"

"Resting," said Schmidt.

"His leg?"

"He'll keep it. Might have a limp, though."

"That going to affect him on the job? I mean, will they let him—?"

"He'll be fine, professor," said Schmidt, his tone curt, his eyes dead. They studied each other and the moment stretched.

"Say it," Swann said softly.

"No," said Schmidt. "I want you to say it. You were in that room, you spoke with him. I want you to tell me what happened."

"I don't know what happened."

"Bullshit. You saw the medical reports and you spoke with him—"

"I saw blood work, detective. I need to see the DNA."

"That's going to take days."

"I know. While we're waiting for that we should be getting a team of specialists in on this. Hematologists, physiologists, a pathologist, maybe an epidemiologist and the best diagnostician in the city. We need to do a full work-up. Everything."

"And we'll do that, professor, but that isn't what I need right now."

"I know what you want me to say, detective but—"

Schmidt suddenly pulled the curtains around their tracks and sealed off the examination room. When he spoke, his voice was low and urgent. "Listen to me, professor," he said with heat, "Fayne broke that glass with his bare hands and I want to know how. Understand me here…I've seen methed-out freaks and three hundred pound Hell's Angels throw chairs at that glass and not so much as scratch it. I know for a fact that a gun was fired in that room three years ago and the bullet—a nine millimeter round—*bounced* off of it. So why don't you tell me how a one-hundred-seventy-pound barista smashed shatter-proof glass with his bare hands?"

Swann said nothing. His mouth was as dry as a desert.

"How did he do that, professor?" demanded Schmidt, his voice still low and fiery. "How does anyone do that? What are we dealing with? What *is* he?"

Luther Swann closed his eyes for a moment and sighed. Schmidt's anger and fear were like fists punching him in the chest.

"Detective," Swann began slowly, "I don't believe in any of this."

He opened his eyes and Schmidt was right there, right in his face.

"This isn't real," said Swann. "It can't be."

"Then what is it? What is *he*?"

"I…"

"Say it, for Christ's sake." There was a mad light in Schmidt's eyes and he looked like he was going to cry. Or scream.

But Swann shook his head. "Listen to me, detective, hear me out for a moment. We have to tread very carefully here. If we put a label on this and we're wrong, then both of us are done. Our careers are done. You'd be laughed out of the police department, and I'd be lucky to get a job teaching English as a second language at a community college. If this is…what it seems to be…then any label we put on it is going to change the world. Not just this case, and not just our lives. Do you understand that, detective? This is so much bigger than a murder case, even a multiple murder case. If we are *right*, then we stand at an open doorway into a future that no longer conforms to any version of reality that either of us has ever understood. We are stepping out of our world and into something else. Do you understand that?"

Schmidt nodded, but he said nothing.

Swann licked his lips. "We need that DNA and we need those specialists. You get me that, you get every test done, and then I'll say whatever you need me to say."

The detective nodded again. "I need you to tell me that we're wrong about this."

"I know," said Swann. "I know.

– 16 –
October 12, 5:22 a.m.
Offices of Global Satellite News, NY
Zero Days until the V-Event

"Hey," said Officer Sims, "it's me."

Yuki already knew that from the caller I.D. on her phone. "What do you have?"

"I got enough for a bonus," he said bluntly.

"If it's good stuff, then count on it." Yuki was able to make that statement without a blink. The footage she'd gotten from her lipstick camera had all but made her news director come in his pants. It had so thoroughly scooped the other networks that a few of them had offered cash and other incentives to replay the footage. However, Regional Satellite News was only leasing it to the wire services, and even then the fees they were charging was a half-step short of actual armed robbery. Yuki was suddenly operating with a budget for sources.

"Okay," said Sims, "I got a name, a social security number, a home address, and the information on where he's being transferred to."

"Transferred? He's not in the precinct lock-up?"

"Not anymore," said Sims with a chuckle in his voice, "and that's the other thing. That's the thing that's going to double the bonus."

"Hey, I don't like to be fleeced here, Charlie."

"Believe me, Yuke, you'll think you're getting bargain prices on solid gold when I tell you what just happened."

"Don't screw with me, Charlie. I mean it."

"I'm not. Really, this is pure frigging gold. I mean…this is some very, very weird shit here. Creepy weird."

"Okay," she said, her chest tingling with excitement despite the reluctance she was faking into her voice, "hit me."

He did.

By the time he was finished telling her everything about Michael Fayne, Dr. Luther Swann and the incident in the interrogation room, Yuki Nitobe felt dizzy. She had to drag a chair over and sit down. Her heart was hammering in her chest.

"They just took him out of here," concluded Sims. "They're taking him to the psych ward at Bellevue."

"Why?"

"At a guess I'd say it was a combination of four point restraints, padded rooms, and a lot of tranquilizers."

"Wait, wait, wait," said Yuki, fanning back through her notes, "This professor? Swann?"

"Yeah."

"You said he was an authority in *what*?"

"You heard me," Sims laughed. "Vampires, baby. Count Dracula. Team Sparkly. Vam-frigging-pires."

"God, Charlie, if you're scamming me here I'll cut your nuts off."

Officer Sims was laughing when he disconnected the call.

Yuki grabbed her purse and ran out of her office, screaming for a camera crew.

–17–
October 12, 6:55 p.m.
Bellevue Hospital
Zero Days until the V-Event

"This had better not be a prank," said the fierce little woman behind the desk.

Luther Swann stood shoulder-to-shoulder with Detective Schmidt in the spacious office of Alice Feldman, Bellevue's chief of psychiatric medicine. Feldman had a wall full of certificates and a shelf lined with awards. Her books were required reading in the very best medical schools, and she was a frequent talking head on the Discovery Channel and MDTV.

"This is no joke," said Schmidt in a flat voice that left no doubt.

Feldman studied him. She had eyes that were almost a perfect teal green and a mouth so tight with disapproval that Swann wanted to check his fingernails to make sure they were clean.

She studied the men for another few seconds, then gave a single curt nod.

"Sit."

Like obedient schoolboys, they sat, perching straight and stiff on the edges of the two guest chairs in her office. She continued to study them from across an acre of polished desktop. Between them were the statements, photographs, X-rays, charts and lab reports that comprised Michael Fayne's file. Swann knew that one of those papers was a copy of his résumé. Dr. Feldman picked it up, studied it for a moment and dropped it on the desk without comment. As they waited, she went through each piece of evidence with an expression that rarely changed except for an occasional lift of one eyebrow and a mild grunt. When she was finished she sat back and sipped the last of a cup of coffee that had gone cold.

"DNA?" she asked.

"We're waiting on that," said Schmidt. "Might have it tomorrow. I put a rush on it."

Another grunt.

"I'll want my own people to redo all of these tests."

"Yes," said Swann, "that's pretty much what we want."

She narrowed her eyes at him. "Why? Don't you trust your own results? No…of course you don't. Who would?"

They waited.

"What injuries did he sustain when he broke the glass? I don't see that report here."

Schmidt cleared his throat. "The suspect sustained no enduring injuries."

Feldman frowned. "That's interesting phrasing, detective. What is it supposed to mean?"

"It means that although the suspect appeared to receive several lacerations from the glass, there was no evidence of recent wounds when he was examined by an emergency room doctor."

"Then the doctor missed it."

"No, ma'am," said Schmidt. He bent and retrieved his briefcase, opened it, and produced a file folder. He cut a quick look at Swann, took a breath and handed it to Dr. Feldman. "The wounds were noted and photographed before the suspect was transported to the hospital."

Dr. Feldman looked at the photographs. She pushed her glasses down to the end of her nose and peered at the prints as she slowly fanned through them. She paused at the last photo, which Swann knew was a high-res shot of Fayne's palms taken just prior to transporting him to this facility. The photo showed several thread-thin white lines crisscrossed over the heels of his palms.

Swann tensed, expected the harsh and certain denial that such evidence should evoke.

Instead, Dr. Feldman closed the file and placed it neatly in the center of her desk.

"I'll want affidavits from everyone. Every officer who entered the interrogation room, the ambulance staff, the E.R. staff. Everyone. And we may even need to do polygraphs on some of them."

Swann and Schmidt nodded.

"And…," she said, pausing for a moment before completing her next comment, "we may want to attempt to reproduce those results under clinical conditions. Multiple video cameras, witnesses, the works."

They nodded again.

In the ensuing silence, she once more picked up Swann's résumé.

"Professor Swann," she said softly, "a cynical person might think that this was all somehow staged in order for you to get on the best-seller list."

"I—" he began, but she cut him off.

"You look too scared to be playing a game."

"Scared doesn't begin to touch it." He leaned forward with his elbows on his knees. "If I'm wrong about this, then I'm going to forget it ever happened. I'd be an idiot to put it in my books. I'd be an idiot to even talk about it. My career would be in serious trouble."

"And if you're right?"

"Then the whole world might be in serious trouble."

"LOVE LESS" PT.2

John Everson

−23−

Sometimes the hours felt like days. The need burned in him stronger than anything he'd ever known. And he'd needed a fix of something or other for half his life. But this latest drug…he craved it more than any snort of cocaine or rock of crack that he'd ever had.

Pete was a junkie, and he wasn't ashamed of it. That's why he'd agreed to go on that talk show a few weeks ago. He had known then that his addictions would kill him. This latest jones was different in some ways, but not in that. But if he had to die, there was no better way to go than this. His latest addiction kept him safe and warm, put a roof over his head and fed him. After a day or so without, the need became so powerful that he could feel it inside his veins. His jones was like a thousand tiny roaches running up and down his arms and legs. He itched himself until he bled, but it never touched the need. Sometimes watching TV with the others helped; sometimes he could get his mind off the need. They understood; a couple of the others had also been junkies before they'd come here. Sometimes he played video games with the little Spanish girl Chelsea. That chick had it really bad…she'd been on meth before she came here…and now whenever the waiting for her next fix grew too intense, her wrists and elbows and eyelids began to twitch. So bad she couldn't walk. Sometimes Pete held her on the couch, trying to hold back the shaking.

"It will be nighttime soon," he'd promise, as he struggled himself to keep from tearing new trails in his flesh with his fingernails. "You know they'll be here soon," he whispered, stroking the limp hair away from her eyes.

Tonight though, Pete lay waiting in his own bed. He didn't have the energy to console Chelsea. His own need was too great. He could taste it. Funny how the symptoms of the old addiction had transferred so easily to this one.

The lock on his door clicked.

Pete's eyes snapped open in the dark, and he stared at the faint silhouette of his cell door. The light blinded him as the door opened. But it closed again quickly, and he heard the faint sounds of clothing falling. Then the heat of her body was next to him in the bed, the silk of her thigh slipping easily over his.

"Did you miss me?" Danika whispered.

Pete slipped his arms around her, enjoying the soft curves of her body.

"Yes," he gasped, as her fingers slipped between his legs, measuring. "Hurry," he said.

Danika opened her mouth and kissed him on the lips…He could feel the points of her teeth as she broke the kiss and trailed them across his cheek to his neck.

And that was it for the foreplay.

Danika bit, sliding her fangs inside him slowly, easily.

Pete moaned as the warmth of her venom began to flow from her teeth into his flesh. She pumped her fangs in and out, releasing precious drops of poison inside him. A neck fuck. This was the best drug ever. The waves of heat shot down his back and up his cock like an electric jolt. His world turned from a grey thirst to kaleidoscope of orgasmic color. He barely even noticed when Danika shifted and straddled him in the bed, guiding him inside her. She used him for more than just blood.

All he cared about was the hit to his head, an amazing tunnel of color and light and sound. He was lost in the drug of her.

Danika's hips slowly moved as she moaned…and drank.

−24−

Mila Dubov turned away from the TV in disgust. She could see the change in her sister. She could almost feel the blood lust inside her pulsing. How could Danika go on pretending? She was a vampire. Feeding on the very people she sought to entertain.

They were both damned.

Mila looked at her boyfriend, who lolled without cognizance on the couch. Part of her laughed at her self-righteous indignation aimed at her sister. Who was Mila to talk? She had maimed Adrian, and still, without any real conscious thought, he served her. But she knew it wouldn't last long.

She had stopped short of killing him the first time she'd drank, and she'd continued to feed on him in smaller bits ever since. So far, he seemed to still be human, though he walked about in a daze much of the time. But she'd done her best to avoid killing or turning him. She did not want to make Adrian like her.

But Mila was constantly hungry. How long she could hold off from taking too much…she didn't know. All she knew was that she could not suffer to eat grandma's chicken soup anymore. And that was a penance as frustrating as the need to hurt in order to eat. She had always loved that soup.

Mila turned away from Adrian's still body in disgust with herself, and her sister alike. Frowning, she picked up the phone and dialed her sister's cellphone. She hadn't talked to Danika since the day she had cooked her chicken soup to cure Danika's "cold." She hadn't asked her sister's help when she confronted the change. She wasn't going to ask for it now.

But there were some things she needed to know. She looked at the man on her couch, and shook her head in bitter sadness. "I have a responsibility," she whispered.

–25–

"It's about time you turned up," Danika said.

"That's about what I said to you the last time I saw you," Mila retorted. They sat at a streetside café, two unsipped iced teas on the table before them. Mila would try to drink some of hers, because blood or not, she believed the body needed to be hydrated.

Still, the body didn't want it. She choked, struggling to contain it.

"I could ask you why you did this to me, but I already know the answer," Mila said, after she got herself under control. "Because you're selfish. You always have been. Why would you care about my life if you were hungry?"

"I didn't know," Danika began, but then stopped, throwing up her hands. "I'm not going to argue with you. You didn't come here for that."

"No, I didn't," Mila agreed. "I came here to find out how you're surviving so well. I've seen your shows. Anyone paying attention would know something was up. It seems like some of your guests have turned up missing lately. I've noticed that. And you've been interviewing vampire experts. I've noticed that too. Plus, every now and then, you get a little twitchy on camera…I guess most people aren't going to put two and two together, but I can see what's going on."

Danika laughed. "You have no idea."

"Why don't you tell me, then?"

Danika smirked. "And ruin all your fun? You should have to figure things out for yourself, just like I did. The whole *wurdulac* thing was a bit of a surprise to me, and frankly, it has some built-in barriers that just don't bode well for the continuation of the race!" Danika rolled her eyes at what was apparently a private joke.

"*Wurdulac*? " Mila asked.

"A vampire that can only feed on its loved ones," Danika said. "You didn't think I *wanted* to eat you, did you? I had no choice."

Danika stared her sister in the eye, measuring Mila's response, before she continued. "Speaking of which, how are you keeping yourself fed, by the way? You look hungry to me. I can see it in your eyes. Bloodshot and a little yellow."

Danika held out her arm. "Do you need a hit, baby sister?"

"You are a bitch, you know that?" Mila hissed. She struggled to hold herself at bay, because Danika had her pegged. Her fingers longed to reach out and grab that arm. She could almost feel the heat pulsing in that blue vein that ran across the inside of Danika's wrist.

"I can help you, if you want," Danika whispered. "You don't have to be hungry all the time. All you have to do is make a few new friends… and then keep them safe and tucked away."

"How many have you done this too?" Mila asked, shocked.

Danika smiled. "It was hard at first, because I didn't understand."

"How many?"

Danika shrugged. "Fifteen or twenty? The first few got away before I knew what was happening. Since then I've kept them a little closer at hand."

"Murderer."

"I haven't killed anyone," Danika said. "They all walked again after I kissed them. That's one thing you have to learn—if you drink too much, they die. And stay dead. If you only drink a little, they get a little groggy...but after a couple days, they're back to normal. If you drink a little too much though...some of them sleep for a day or so and then grow fangs of their own."

"How many have *you* done?" Danika asked, genuinely curious.

Mila said it under her breath. "One."

Danika frowned. "Did you say one?"

Mila nodded.

"How is that possible...it's been weeks."

"He's been enough," Mila said. "But I feel horrible for what I've done to him."

"Yeah, yeah," Danika said. "I feel like a shit too. But, you do what you need to if you want to survive."

"You have to stop," Mila said. "You can't do this to people."

"You do what you have to do," Danika said. She rose from the table. "I have to get back to work," she said. "But my offer stands. If you need a drink..." She smiled, and then held out her arms. Mila couldn't help but to focus on the swell of the veins in her wrists. Danika reached for her sister, teasing, "Can I get a hug?"

Mila's heart flared and she longed to get close to Danika. But she refused. "You'd like it if I bit you right here in public, wouldn't you?" Mila said. "Great publicity for you, and you'd walk away the wounded hero."

Danika winked. "We all need good PR," she said.

"Some of us just need someone to love," Mila said.

Danika snorted. "Love less. Eat more."

–26–

The reports had been there, but Mila hadn't noticed. And then it all came home when the 10 o'clock news anchor showed a special report on *Vampires: Stake or be Steak?*

The camera swept through an empty house, pausing periodically to focus in on a patch of reddened floor or wall. Places where someone had died.

"The strange thing is...nobody is here." The reporter was Baird Lang, an attractive thirty-something guy with a luster in his black hair that most women would kill for. He played up the confused look perfectly, as the camera flipped from him, to the blood-stained walls, to the obviously empty hallway from kitchen to bedrooms, and then back to Baird's face.

"Authorities have confirmed that more than three dozen homes have been discovered in this state over the past month…and the numbers are now snowballing at an alarming rate. There have been reports of screams and commotion at some of the locations, but each time, by the time police have been called and dispatched to the scene, the victims…and their assailants…are already gone. We talked with South Precinct Captain Josh Brant, who offered this theory."

"Look, it's no secret that there have been outbreaks of vampires and even werewolves around the globe for the past several months now. Given the evidence we have been able to find on the scene, and this situation, we believe these are vampire-related abductions. Or killings. Perhaps both."

"But Captain, don't vampires usually drain their prey and leave?"

The policeman nodded, blue eyes flashing perfectly for the cameras. "Absolutely…from what we've seen up to now, they always have before. But how much experience do we really have with this? Our legends of vampires go back a thousand years, but our actual experience—that only goes back a few months. Let's face it, we are dealing with a creature that is intelligent…if there is a group of vampires who have decided to take the evidence with them for some reason, well, it does limit our choices in terms of pursuing and prosecuting, doesn't it? There is no body, so we're not even sure who has been injured. One thing we have noticed, however, is that there appears to be a connection between many of these empty houses. The home we're standing in front of right now belongs to Lucas Branson. He and his wife disappeared three days ago. They were considered a very happy couple. Last night, Lucas' parents disappeared from their house just a few miles away from here leaving behind bloodstains on the sheets of their bed. And at the same time, the brother and sister-in-law of Lucas' wife Naomie, also appear to have disappeared. Their apartment is currently empty, and has been for more than twelve hours, though a bloodstain is clearly evident on the floor near their rec room couch."

–27–

Mila thumbed off the television remote in disgust. It was no mystery to her what was going on. She'd looked up the clue that Danika had thrown her during her lunch. She'd learned more about what the word *wurdulac* really meant, and she understood now. It was all crystal clear. Her sister's genetic transition had not simply been to change into a creature that fed on humans. Her physical alteration had turned her into a transmitter. When she bit friends and lovers, so long as she didn't drink them dry, she basically paralyzed them for a time, and somehow transferred a retrovirus that impacted and inserted itself into their genes, initiating the deadly mutation in others. While by nature, the *wurdulac* was self-limiting, given its boundary of relationships, Danika had, as usual, found a way to play outside of the rules, and in doing so, had set loose a horde of *wurdulacs*, thanks to her insatiable appetite. Mila had no doubt that you could follow a thread of relationships from every Chicago *wurdulac* back to Danica. The question now was…what should she do about it?

— 28 —

Lon brought her the FedEx package. There was something in his face that made Danika open it immediately. The Network office in New York didn't often send FedExes to Chicago talk show hosts.

"It looks important," he noted. Danika set down her list of potential guests for next week, and took the package. It was thin, and she ripped open the top with a quick pull.

There was only one thing inside. A one-page letter.

The letter was from the president of the network and the content said essentially this: "We'd like you to come and jack your show off next week in New York instead of Chicago. We think we can make you a star."

"National syndication!" Lon gasped.

"Leaving Chicago," Danika answered, with a trace of panic in her voice.

"And the problem with that is…" he asked.

Danika didn't answer. Mentioning that she had a blood farm going that would be hard to instantly replace in another city was not really something that sat on the tip of her tongue.

"Do you think you can take me with you?" Lon asked. "I'd like to keep helping with the show."

"I'm sure they'll ask me about that, and I'd like to keep you involved. So I'd say…pack your bags, we're going to the Rotten Apple, baby!"

"The Big Apple," he corrected.

"Yeah, whatever," she said. "It will be rotten when I'm done with it!"

– 29 –

Mila grinned in the dark. Her teeth shone white as the moon, but nobody saw. She slipped around the corner of the small bungalow, and walked up to the front door. She twisted the knob, and it opened easily. She'd figured it would. Lucas Branson was in a hurry, and he wouldn't be worried about locking the door behind him.

She stepped into the dark foyer and carefully closed the door quietly behind her. Then she slipped quickly down the hall towards the kitchen. A faint yellow light emanated from there, and she already knew that Lucas was there. She'd seen him through the back window, chewing on his sister's neck.

Mila reached into her back pocket and pulled out a gun. It didn't have silver bullets and it wasn't a stake to the heart, but she was pretty sure it would do the trick on the modern version of the vampire. No head meant dead.

"The family that eats together shouldn't eat each other," she said, as she stepped into the room. Lucas leaned over a mousey-haired woman who lay stretched out on the kitchen table. He looked up in surprise at her voice, blood dripping down his chin. As he did, a thin squirt of blood sprayed the side of his face, as the wound continued to pump out his sister's life.

"Call for an ambulance," Mila demanded. She pointed the gun first at him, and then at the phone.

"She's going to die no matter what," he complained.

"Maybe," she said. "But that's not going to be on my hands. Call."

He watched her for a minute without moving. Mila notched the hammer of the gun back, and Lucas put up a hand. "Okay, okay," he grumbled, and picked up the phone to dial 911.

"It's my sister," he said. "She's been hurt."

When he hung up the phone, he looked at Mila and asked, "How did you find me? How did you know?"

"I looked your family up online after the police found your house empty but full of bloodstains," she said. "I looked up who you all were related to, and I've been driving back and forth for the past two days watching a half dozen houses."

He looked puzzled. "Are you a cop? Why would you do that?"

"Because I'm like you," she said. "And I don't think there should be any more of us."

"Try it," he grinned, letter her see the blood coating the whites of his teeth. "You might like it."

"I like the ones I love to stay alive," she said.

"They will," he said. "Everyone I've bitten has gotten up and walked away."

"Yeah," she agreed. "To go find others to kill. It's a bloody pyramid scheme, but I've got news for you…you'll all run out of family and friends that you can feed on, and then what?"

"Then I'll be hungry, I suppose," he shrugged.

"You will starve and you will die," she said. "You'll all eventually die. Dying of hunger when there's food all around you. That's what a *wurdulac* does. It sentences everyone it loves to a slow, painful death. Is that what you want for your family? Really?"

"Fuck you," he said. "My family is my business."

"Who turned you?" Mila asked.

He laughed. "You'll never believe it."

"Try me."

"Okay," he said. "Get this. My brother-in-law was on Danika Dubov's talk show last week, cuz of he banged his niece. Danika did a big exposé program about incest. She liked him, I guess, and asked him out to dinner. Next he's waking up in his apartment with blood on his shirt. And not so much later, he's got a craving for my sister. And not too long after that…she's got a craving for me."

"So you already figured out that you can't suck on just anyone?"

"Yeah," he said. "That don't work at all."

Mila shook her head. "Well, you got that right. But I can't believe you don't have a problem with killing your own family."

He looked at her with complete disgust. "Look, I don't know who the hell you are, but get the fuck out of my sister's house. My family is my business. This has nothing to do with you."

"Not true," she said. "It has more to do with me than you'll ever know. But I'm not going to argue with you. Hell, your brother-in-law fucks his niece. What do you people know about family? Here's the thing. The ambulance will be here soon. Maybe they'll be able to help your sister. Maybe they'll even manage to help you. But I'm not sticking around to find out."

The gunshot rang out with a sharp, immediate snap. Lucas crumbled to the floor, blood beginning to stream from a hole just above his right eye.

"Sorry man, but this has to end. And I'm here to end it."

Mila slipped out of the apartment, already thinking about how she could trace down every other family member of Lucas Branson.

She wondered if she had enough bullets.

– 30 –

"Our guests are dying," Lon said.

Danika looked at her producer and smiled. "As long as it's not on the show, we're good."

"You have a heart of…"

"It doesn't matter," she said. "We're moving to New York. As of August 1, we're officially on the biggest network in the world…and Chicago is just a dream."

"And a bad one, at that," Lon said.

Danika smiled. "Yeah."

– 31 –

The colors were indescribable. Danika said that he looked at her as she drank, but her face was never what he saw. He saw purples and greens and blues that swirled like some strange oscillating blender churn. But it was more than that. Every time the colors moved and swirled, the pleasure centers in his brain responded. Orange triggered the taste of pure sugar. Pink felt like the envelope of the softest velvet robe against his skin. Purple was that moment of release when you were deep inside a woman and could no longer control your moans. Black was that moment when the needle released its load beneath the skin.

Pete saw/felt all of those colors and sensations at once as Danika sucked and fucked him in his tiny cell. And the sensations continued for hours after she left him. It was the best high *ever*.

"Pete," Danika was saying. He realized she'd been shaking him for a while. "I need to talk to you"

"Uh-huh," he gulped, trying to look at her through the haze of a psychedelic orgasm that wouldn't stop. Her hair was wet and matted; perspiration shone on her breasts. She'd used him for a long time tonight.

"I have to leave," she said.

"Okay," he whispered. He was good for now.

"Not just for tonight," she said. "Forever."

The pain of fear that shot through his heart roused him from the stupor. "What…?"

"I'm going to New York," she said. "But Hannah will stay here with you. She'll be good to you."

"No, I need you…" he begged.

"She's sucked you before," Danika nodded. "Was it good for you?"

Pete had to admit, Hannah's drug was just as powerful. He nodded.

Danika kissed him on the lips. "Give her what she needs," she said, as she left his bed.

– 32 –

Mila crept along the old bungalow and paused every few steps to listen. Her hearing seemed to have improved with "the change" and she made use of it, angling her head towards the house to hear if there was any movement within. She didn't need any surprises.

And there were none. She saw what was happening inside the house through the kitchen window. The blood was obvious. Mila didn't need to see much before she moved. Toward the front door.

She opened it and stepped inside, taking in the dark carpet and shadowed walls as her eyes adjusted. Then she moved fast down the hardwood floor into the living room, where the woman was crouching on top of the man, her fangs extended and active…they plunged in and out of his neck like oil derricks.

Mila didn't wait too long to issue justice.

She trained her sites on the earlobe of the woman and didn't say a word. Instead, she simply pulled the trigger.

And like jellied spam, the woman's brains plastered the paneled room wall in a weeping pink behind the man that she had been trying to eat.

"Sorry," Mila said, under her breath. "We don't really need any more *wurdulacs*."

She quickly, and quietly slipped her way back out of the house. Under her breath she whispered, "I never wanted to be this."

In her mind, she saw herself as an angel…and avenger…and felon. She moved with the air of someone already defeated. She kept going, carefully tracking down and picking off the spawn of her sister's hunger. But with every confrontation, she had to ask herself over and over again…"can I do this anymore?"

And she answered that question every time with the image of Danika emblazoned in her mind.

"Yes," she thought. "Yes, I have to. Until it's finished."

– 33 –

Danika Dubov packed the last T-shirt into her suitcase and then stood back to look around. She felt empty. And a little afraid. It had been hard to "will" the "blood farm" over. But she couldn't exactly take it with her. Her friends Sarah and Hannah Kerstin would take care of her barn of humans. Hannah loved to "milk" the cows. She had fangs that never wanted to quit. And Sarah had a mothering instinct that kicked in every time they fed. She was the one who kept the food alive.

But for Danika? There would be more opportunities in New York than she could ever have had in Chicago. It might be tricky at first, but she needed to do this.

A knock tapped quietly but firmly on her front door, interrupting Danika's thoughts. Even as she stood up, the idea of sitting in a New York studio, with real New York cameras pointing at her filled her mind.

She was finally there. She was *arriving*.

Absently, Danika stood up and walked through the mess of boxes and suitcases to open the door.

Her sister barreled through the opening as soon as she turned the knob.

"Going somewhere?" Mila said, observing the stacks of boxes.

"You say you watch the show, so you know where I'm going," Danika said. "Is there a problem?"

"No problem," Mila said. "Except that you seem to have developed a bad habit of turning people into vampires."

"*Wurdulacs*," Danika said, stepping backwards. "And habits are not necessarily a bad thing." Mila seemed agitated.

"No," Mila agreed. "Except when those habits include murder."

"I've not murdered anyone!" Danika said.

"How fast the vampire's memory fades," Mila laughed. "You murdered me, you rotten selfish bitch of a sister…or did that slip your mind?"

Danika had to laugh. "Murdered? Then what are you doing standing here in my apartment when I'm trying to pack for a trip?"

"You're not packing for a trip, you're packing to go on a slaughter."

"You always were the dramatic one," Danika laughed.

"No," Mila said. "That was *you*. I'm just here to stop you from hurting anyone else."

Danika smiled and raised an eyebrow.

"Well," Mila said, pulling a pistol from beneath the back of her shirt to hold it at Danika's left temple, "I'm pretty sure you can't bite anyone if you don't have a working brain."

"What do you want?" Danika whispered, cringing at the touch of metal on the cool skin of her temple.

"Take me to the place where you have your food stashed away," Mila said. "That's what I want to see."

"You can't eat off the smorgasbord if you're not a friend already," Danika warned.

"I'm well aware," Mila answered. "And I'm not concerned."

She held a gun out and leveled it at her sister's face. "My goals go beyond food," she said.

$$-34-$$

Danika was at a crossroads. She had never meant to hurt Mila, and didn't want to, even now. But at the same time, she didn't want to expose Hannah or her roommate, Sarah. They had enough problems keeping the "farm" secret. She didn't want them having to fight Mila after she left for New York.

Of course...there was always the possibility that she would never make it to New York because Mila was just plumb fuckin' crazy.

But Danika didn't believe that, not really. Her sister had a bleeding heart that ran redder than the red sea after the locusts came. Mila felt guilty after swatting flies.

"Fine," Danika said. "You want to see food, I'll show you a smorgasbord."

$$-35-$$

Mila kept the gun trained on her sister's head during the entire ride across town. When they finally pulled into the garage of a large house on an otherwise empty, wooded street, she finally spoke for the first time. "Nice," she said. "In the woods, nobody can hear you scream."

Danika held her palm out to block Mila's gun.

"Please," she said. "We eat from them, we don't torture them…or kill them. That would be somewhat counterproductive. Our food is happy here. And until feeding day, they're all pretty happy going about their lives."

"Lives in a cage," Mila reminded.

"Well, yes, a very cozy padded one," Danika agreed. "It's a good life. They're taken care of, and we're fed. We do care for them, or this arrangement wouldn't work, you know."

"You are a twisted bitch, aren't you?" Mila whispered. "Care for them my ass."

"I never knew you had such a foul mouth," Danika said. The faint trace of a smile colored the edge of her lips.

"That's because you were always so busy looking at yourself in the mirror."

"And a jealous little sister too!"

"Just show me what you've done here," Mila insisted, and Danika shrugged.

"As you like. But I have a plane to catch soon, you know."

Danika led her through the garage and into the basement of the large house. She had to key in a password in an electronic door lock system before it opened for her, and as she did, she found herself staring very self-consciously at all of the large-breasted women. A half dozen girls lounged inside wearing nothing but bras and panties, or, in some cases, ripped and stained T-shirts.

"Girls taste better," Danika said, smiling at Mila's obvious discomfiture. "At least that's what Mack says."

Danika walked slowly through the room, and the women barely acknowledged their presence. Most kept their eyes trained on the large screen TV playing an old episode of *Baywatch*.

"The trick is to keep them low on blood sugar," Danika explained. "Then they really are happy to just lie around here in their underwear."

"A frat boy's dream," Mila said under her breath. "Too bad there aren't any fratboys here."

"Oh, there are," Danika promised. "I keep them upstairs."

Danika pressed a key into a locked door, and waited until Mila passed before closing it and making sure the knob remained locked.

"Perhaps you'll enjoy this exhibit more," she laughed. "The male species. Every now and then, I have to admit, I enjoy playing with my food as much as eating it."

She stepped into a room painted in deep blue. Much like the downstairs "women's cage," this room held a couple couches and a large screen TV. Three men lounged around the room, all of them watching a car race on the television. Two of them didn't move or seem to notice that Mila and Danika had entered the room. A sandy-haired guy with a sleeveless T-shirt pushed himself off the couch slowly, and grinned at Danika as he stood.

"Hey sugar-momma!" he said.

"How's it hanging, Pete," Danika answered with a faint smile.

"Why don't you come see?" Pete staggered as he moved towards her. His brow knitted in some internal confusion, and then he lost his balance again just before reaching Danika. She held her arms out to catch him, and then slapped his ass as he righted himself.

"Was *he* on the menu last night?" Mila asked. The disgust dripped off her words.

Danika nodded. "Little going away party."

"What's going to happen to your favorites when you leave?"

"Sarah and Hannah and Mack have all really gotten to be friends with all of them now," Danika said. "We're all family here. If you like, I can introduce you…"

"How sweet," Mila said. "I've been looking for a nice family to have Christmas dinner with ever since Mom died. I just never suspected that my new family would *be* the dinner."

"You sound so bitter," Danika said. "You need to come to terms with what you are now."

"You mean, what you made me!"

Danika shrugged. "I didn't mean to do it. I didn't know what would happen."

"How many of these people will turn?" Mila asked.

Danika shrugged again. "Eventually? Maybe all of them. Maybe none. I don't know. We try not to take too much blood…and we keep them locked up separately at night, in case they do turn. But I'm not really sure what turns them in the first place. I know that I've drank from my producer at the station several times, a little at a time, and he's never turned."

"How many *have* you turned?"

"A few."

"I can't let you do it anymore," Mila said.

"I'm not sure you can stop me."

"This gun says otherwise," Mila said, aiming the pistol at her sister's face.

"What are you doing?" Pete cried, struggling to get back up off the couch where he'd just dropped himself.

"Taking care of a problem," Mila answered, not taking her eyes off her sister. Danika simply smiled. "I don't think so," she said.

Hands suddenly closed on Mila's wrists, yanking her arms up to point at the ceiling.

"Meet Hannah and Sarah," Danika said, stepping forward to embrace Mila. Above her head, Mila struggled to gain control of her hands, but the two women held her tight. Danika rested her face on Mila's shoulder, inhaling slowly as she hugged her sister closer.

"There's something about you that tastes even better than the others," she whispered in Mila's ear.

A heat shot through Mila's groin. Her mouth ached with hunger at Danika's words. At her closeness. She could feel her lips begin to peel back as something in her jaw moved. Her belly roiled and she could no longer keep up the struggle for the gun.

"You're anorexic," Danika said. "I can feel your hunger. You need me even more than I want you. Take some," she offered.

Danika tilted her head, offering her neck to Mila.

Mila opened her mouth to say, "I can't…"

But she did.

Her canines extended. Before she could finish her sentence, her mouth was on her sister. Part of her screamed inside, *no, no, no,* this was not what she came here to do. But the bigger part of her, the part that Danika had made, was in ecstasy. The gun was lifted from her hands and she brought her hands down to hold Danika by the waist as she drank deep from her sister. The blood was amazing; as it coursed hot and fast down her throat she felt sexual sparks of lust shoot through her thighs and crotch, while at the same time her mouth and belly warmed with sensations that surpassed the feelings of the most amazing meal she had ever tasted. Her nerves sang with every note of pleasure they knew, and Danika smiled as Mila drank greedily. Maybe now Mila would finally understand.

All of the pain and weakness Mila had suffered for the past few weeks dissolved as her sister's strength coursed through her body. She sucked hard and fire seemed to cover her vision. She didn't try to hold back, as she did with Adrian. The world swam in a haze of pleasure. From somewhere far away, she heard people calling her, begging her to stop.

And then hands were on her shoulders, dragging her back, and Danika's body fell to the floor, blood flowing from the wounds in her neck to stain the carpet.

The fireworks of pleasure faded and Mila's blindness lifted.

"You took too much," one of the women complained. The other, a honey-haired girl with a pleasant face, knelt next to Danika and offered her neck.

"Danika, it's Hannah," the girl said, slapping Danika gently on the cheeks, trying to rouse her. "Drink from me," Hannah demanded, but Danika didn't answer. Her eyes had rolled back in her head. The other woman, Sarah, bent down to help Hannah, and as her awareness returned, Mila massaged her arms a minute…and then spotted the gun. They'd left it on a coffee table near one of the couches. She picked it up and trained it on Sarah.

"Sorry," she said to herself. "I know you didn't ask for this."

Then she pulled the trigger. At the sound of the shot, Hannah pulled back from pressing her neck to Danika's mouth, but Mila didn't pause. She fired the gun again and Hannah's forehead exploded with a spray of blood that rained over Danika's still form. Hannah's body collapsed to the ground next to her.

"What are you doing?" Pete asked, staggering towards her. "Stop it! Leave them a…"

The bullet caught him in the neck and the word "alone" turned into a gurgle of death. The two other men in the room barely stirred and Mila put bullets through their brains without protest. She wasn't going to risk them turning.

She walked quickly through the house until she found them all. Shot after shot rang out, and she had to reload the gun before the execution was over.

Mila stood in the kitchen of the house. Tears slipped down her cheeks. Her lips and chin felt sticky with blood. It had warmed her a few minutes ago; she felt sick to her stomach now.

She looked at the spots of blood that streaked her arm and the grey metal of the gun. Mila hadn't asked to be made a vigilante. She looked at the stove and thought of her grandma's soup. There should be a kettle of it cooking here. That's what she wanted to offer. All she'd ever wanted to do was take care of people. Like her nana had taught her.

But soup wouldn't cure this cold. The only cure was in her hand. Mila knew that she was doing the right thing. The world did not need any more *wurdulacs*.

She walked once more through the quiet house, clicking the TV and lights off as she left the rooms where bodies now lay still. She knew that she would need to stay here for the night, to wait for the rest of the *wurdulacs* to come home. From what Danika had said, she thought that Mack lived here, and Craig apparently spent a lot of time here, if he didn't sleep here full-time. Mila didn't want to hurt them. She really didn't. But she would be ready.

Finally, she returned to where she had left Danika. Her sister remained on the floor, surrounded by her friends. The blood had clotted at her neck, and Danika's eyelids fluttered. She was conscious, just barely.

Mila bent down and kissed her sister on the forehead. "I know you didn't mean for any of this to happen," she whispered. "But I can't let you do it to anyone else."

She aimed the gun and her Danika's eyes widened in fear. One of her arms trembled as she tried to move away.

"I'm sorry, Sis," Mila said pulling back the trigger. "But you're not going to New York."

"THE BALLAD OF BIG CHARLIE" PT.1

Keith R.A. DeCandido

–1–

Walking into Bronx District Attorney Hugues Charles's office, it was easy for New York *Daily News* reporter Mia Fitzsimons to understand how he got the nickname "Big Charlie."

The office, located in the rectangular edifice of the Bronx County Courthouse on E. 161st Street, was surprisingly cramped for the biggest prosecutor in the borough—and "biggest" took on a whole new meaning as his six-foot-eight frame unfolded itself into an upright position. The window behind him had a view of Joyce Kilmer Park alongside the Grand Concourse. On this sunny spring day, people sat out in the park, and cars zoomed past giant apartment buildings on the Concourse.

Big Charlie's shoulders were wide enough to land a plane on, and he loomed over the five-foot-three Mia. She approached his metal desk, which was covered in papers, a small Droid tablet, an iPhone, and two computers—a laptop and a desktop. His head was long and widened as you went down, with no obvious neck—it was as if his cheeks went straight into those gigantic shoulders. He held out a huge hand to shake that Mia almost didn't return for fear that her own tiny hand would be lost.

No wonder he's such a good prosecutor. If I had to face that in the courtroom, I'd plea for fear of being eaten alive.

Then he smiled, showing wide teeth, and suddenly Mia felt at ease. He spoke with a light Haitian accent. "A pleasure to meet you, Ms. Fitzsimmons."

She put out her own hand. "Thank you, Mr. District Attorney." His hands were warm and all-encompassing, but the handshake was gentle.

His face turned quizzical. "Or have we met before?"

Mia nodded, impressed at his memory. "At the opening for the Homeless Voices exhibit at the Bronx Museum of the Arts." It was one of Mia's first pieces for the *News* years ago before she got moved to local politics.

"Of course, I should have recalled," he said, though there was no reason why he should have remembered her. Indicating the guest chair with one enormous hand, he said, "Please, take a seat."

She sat in the guest chair opposite him, and fished her digital recorder out of her purse. "May I record this?"

"By all means."

After hitting record, Mia said, "Yesterday, you announced that you're running for a fourth term for Bronx D.A. First off, why'd you do it on Mother's Day with your mom by your side?"

That prompted another smile from Big Charlie. Mia had missed the press conference, as she was having dinner with her own mother in Woodlawn. She was hardly the only one to miss the Sunday holiday presser, but she did see the footage on both New York 1 and Channel 12.

"*Maman*, she was seven months pregnant with me when she came here from Haiti," he said. "My father, he was killed by Papa Doc's *Tontons Macoutes*, and that was when *maman* decided to depart. She wanted what was best for her unborn child, so she boarded a boat and travelled to New York. She worked very hard to make sure that I had nothing but the best education, nothing but the best opportunities. It is due to her that I am here, and it is due to her that I am running again."

Mia nodded. "Is she also why you announced so late?" The primary was in September, after all, and while there was technically a general election, all local elections in at least four of the five boroughs were decided on Primary Day. Aside from Staten Island, this was pretty much a Democrat town.

Big Charlie got up and walked to the window, looking down at the park and the double-parked cars on 161st. "I was a boy in 1977. I recall watching the Yankees in the World Series on the television. The South Bronx—the neighborhood outside this window—was on fire. Howard Cosell was the announcer, and he said, 'Ladies and gentlemen, the Bronx is burning.' "

Mia couldn't help but chuckle at hearing the late sports announcer's trademark staccato monotone with Big Charlie's Haitian accent.

He continued: "I thought then that it was wrong that the place where law was made should be on fire like that. I wanted to protect this neighborhood so the law would still be made." Turning around, he hit Mia with the smile again. "I was a child, thinking childish thoughts, but they remained with me all my days. But once I had completed three terms, I was not sure of my ability to continue to fulfill that promise. It was *maman* who took me aside and said, 'Hugues, you're just being a fool, and I did not travel 3000 miles to raise a fool.' "

Frowning, Mia said, "Uhm, Haiti's less than 2000 miles from New York."

Big Charlie's laugh was deep and hearty. "Yes, I know. *Maman*, she has always been poor at judging distances."

"So she got you here and made it clear you wouldn't be a fool."

"Yes." Big Charlie squeezed himself back into the leather chair behind his desk, the view of Kilmer Park framing his long face. "I grew up in the public schools, but then I received academic scholarships to the Bronx High School of Science, to Columbia, and to Fordham's law school."

"You spent all of three years in corporate law before becoming a Brooklyn A.D.A. Why'd you make the switch?"

"I recall my first case when I began working for the District Attorney's office in Brooklyn. I inherited a case that was going to trial—a drug case. It had been almost two years since the arrest. All the police officers on my witness list had been promoted—and this arrest was not a significant contributor to those promotions, as it was a standard buy-and-bust. It is the sort of crime that often leads to a plea-bargain so that a greater crime can be prosecuted.

"But that did not happen here. Instead, this minor purchase of heroin was allowed to tie up the court system for two years. It was a colossal waste of resources, and one I swore would never happen were I to ascend to the position of District Attorney."

"Uhm, okay." Mia smiled wryly. "That doesn't actually answer my question."

He chuckled. "I suppose that I simply did not feel that my childhood dream of keeping the place of law safe could be accomplished behind a mahogany desk in an office with a view of downtown. I prefer the metal desk in front of me and the double-parked cars out my window. I feel more as if I am part of something rather than attempting to remain above it."

That came closer to answering the question, and Mia figured that was the best she was going to get. "We first met at an art exhibit opening, and that's hardly the only one you've been to. Every time there's an event at the Bronx Zoo or at a park or museum, there you are. That's a lot more dedication to the community than you see from your average D.A."

"I did not wish my legacy to be that of someone who was 'tough on crime,' because crime-fighting is the job description. Being a District Attorney who is hard on crime is merely someone who has shown up for work each morning. I wish to be remembered as one who went above and beyond such."

"You've hired Barel Grindberg as your campaign manag—"

Mia was interrupted by Big Charlie's iPhone, which made a three-tone beep and lit up. He glanced down at the status, and then winced. "I am sorry, Ms. Fitzsimmons, but that is one of my A.D.A.s and I'm afraid I must contact her immediately. Let me just say that Barel has managed all my campaigns to date, and she has done a superb job. I am quite fortunate to have her again."

With that, Mia hit stop on the recorder, dropped it in her purse, once again lost her hand in Big Charlie's oversized paw, and beat a hasty re-treat out of his office. She'd been hoping to ask more about Grindberg, who'd been a player in New York politics for years, but the quote would be enough for the op-ed piece she was doing. It wasn't as if she was going to be digging any kind of dirt in this interview. Maybe later, but for now, she was doing a puff piece that would make the candidate happy enough to give her more access.

Then, if dirt materialized, she'd be in a better position to find it. And if it didn't, then she would have the inside track of a beloved community figure's candidacy. She won either way.

– 2 –

News article in the Bronx section of the New York Daily News.

Several residents of the Edenwald neighborhood have reported a large dog or wolf roaming Needham and De Reimer Avenues near Baychester Avenue and Boston Road. Many garbage cans were turned over with the bags ripped open, and one resident—who asked to remain anonymous—said that the wolf or dog injured her cat.

NYPD's Animal Control has been notified, and a source at the 47th Precinct has stated that uniformed officers are keeping an eye out. No animals have been reported missing from the Bronx Zoo.

–3–

"The field's completely clear at this point. Ayala was the only holdout, and he's on board now, especially if you give him that promotion you've been promising him for a year."

Barel Grindberg looked up from the notes on her legal pad to see that Big Charlie was staring at the display on his iPhone, which sat on the conference room table. "Uhm, hello? Coulda sworn we were having a meeting here."

"Hm?" Big Charlie looked up. "My apologies, Barel, I am simply concerned about *maman*. I have not heard from her all day, and it is rather unlike her to be out of touch for this long a period. What were we discussing?"

"Bernie Ayala. He agreed to drop out and endorse you if you give him that promotion to homicide."

Shaking his head, Big Charlie blew out a breath. "I only have refrained from promoting him due to the budget. If he's willing to accept the job title without the salary bump—"

Barel grinned. "He'll pretend to be pissed, but he'll take it. He wants murders so he can run when you finally get around to retiring."

"That should be four years from now."

"Yeah, right. That's what you said four years ago."

"*Maman* changed my—"

Holding up a hand, Barel said, "Please. Save it for the reporters. By the way, I loved that op-ed piece Fitzsimmons did for the *News*."

That got the trademark Big Charlie smile. "As did *maman*. And she generally has very little use for reporters."

Barel filed that away. While she did tease her boss about it, Marie Charles' likes and dislikes often had a profound impact on her son's decisions. If Fitzsimmons was someone Marie liked, it meant that Big Charlie was likely to give her access. She jotted down a note to have her guys vet the reporter.

Running a hand through the mess of steel wool she laughingly referred to as her hair, Barel opened her mouth when she saw something out of the corner of her eye.

The conference room of their Boston Road campaign headquarters had windows on the east wall that looked out on the rest of the main campaign office. On the far end was the glass door to Boston Road, which flew open to reveal Judy Alejo, the D.A.'s press secretary. A tiny Latina woman, Judy had a lovely round face that looked disarming and charming most of the time—all of the time if she was in public or anywhere near a journalist or camera.

The only way she betrayed her mood was if she was biting her lip. The right side meant she was nervous or concerned about something. Having the left side between her teeth meant she was pissed.

"This isn't good," Barel said as Judy made a beeline for the conference room. She was holding a round disc in her hand.

"You're *not* gonna believe this," the press secretary said without preamble as she threw the door open.

"What is it, Judy?" Big Charlie asked.

But Judy didn't say anything, instead walking over to the DVD player on the table against the north wall and pushing the open button. After dropping the disc in, she grabbed the remote and turned on the flatscreen that was mounted to the west wall.

It was a Channel 12 news report. Based on the stamp in the lower-left-hand corner of the screen, it was just aired a couple of hours earlier that day.

"If you thought the Bronx D.A. race was over when three-termer Hugues Charles announced that he'd be running again, you'll have to think twice. Big Charlie has a challenger, and it's long-time activist Mickey Solano. Nishan—"

"You have *got* to be fucking *kidding* me." Barel was livid.

Judy hit pause. "I thought you said you took care of him."

Trying not to grind her teeth, Barel said, "I thought I did, too."

In a much calmer tone than either of the two women in the room with him, Big Charlie said, "I do not believe that it is entirely bad. Play the rest of the story, please, Judy?"

Nodding, Judy hit play. For her part, Barel thought she was, if anything, underreacting, but said nothing, wanting to see the rest.

"—da Henry has the story."

The image cut from the anchor desk to Nishanda Henry, a tall, striking African-American woman. Barel had always thought she was wasting her talents on the local level, as she had good instincts and camera presence. But she actually said she liked staying in her own borough.

"Mickey Solano hasn't been a practicing trial lawyer in many years, although he is a full partner in a local law firm, but now he's running for Bronx District Attorney."

Barel rolled her eyes. "That *momzer* was never a trial lawyer. Only time he saw the inside of a courtroom was when he got called for jury duty."

Now the image was that of the square jaw, slicked hair, and wide eyes of Mickey Solano. "It's time for a change. Hugues Charles is a good man, and he's done fine things for this city, but most of them have very little to do with being the man who prosecutes crimes in this borough. Mr. Charles has done a great deal to streamline the process, to unclog the courts, as his press releases would have you believe, but it's come at the expense of truly punishing those who deserve to be punished."

Rising to her feet, Barel gestured at the television. "That fucking *pisher* better not be pulling the death penalty *mishegoss* out of his *tuchas.*"

Judy stared at her a moment, then looked at Big Charlie. "Okay, that's four Yiddish words in a minute. *Now* will you agree that this is bad?"

"When did I use Yiddish?" Barel asked, confused.

Having paused the DVD again, Judy smiled. "*Pisher, mishegoss, tuchas,* and *momzer.* I don't even know what a *momzer* is. I mean, I can guess from the context, but—"

Waving her arms back and forth, Barel rolled up the sleeves of her cardigan and said, "Play the damn tape, would you please?" She hated when she started sounding like Uncle Eli.

Nishanda was back on: "Solano was an advocate of New York's death penalty statute that was passed in 1995, and w—"

"Did I call it?" Barel asked.

"—as a vocal opponent of the state supreme court ruling of that statute being unconstitutional in 2004. He has dedicated a large amount of time and money to advocating for the reactivation of the statute and allowing the death penalty in New York once again."

"*This* is what the *momz*—" She caught herself. "*This* is what the asshole's going with? Elect me D.A. so I can enact a death penalty that never got used during the ten years it was legal?"

Solano was talking again. "It's all well and good for Mr. Charles to point to the reduced crime rate, but that's simply him taking credit for a citywide and nationwide drop in crime since he took office. Advanced technology, better crime-fighting procedures, COMSTAT—these are what reduced the crime rate, not a man who happened to be in the right place at the ri—"

154

Judy talked over Nishanda. "Can you believe that shit? He lobbied *against* COMSTAT for three years, and now he's talking about how it did your job for you?"

Solano was talking again. "—ave nothing but respect for Big Charlie. I like him a lot. But this isn't personal. This is business, and I'm putting myself in the business of giving the Bronx a better District Attorney."

Barel turned to Big Charlie, who was staring at his iPhone. "So do you agree that it's bad? He's a legit threat to you. That was why I thought he was dealt with—the whole thing was that you'd run this year and he'd make a run in four years. So what the fuck changed?"

Big Charlie looked up, with a sad expression. "Nothing changed, Barel. He simply was upset when I announced, after the conversation we'd had in April."

Glowering at him, Barel simply said, "What conversation in April?"

"I told him that I was not going to be running. He was going to announce on Memorial Day."

"And you were going to share this with me, when, exactly?" Barel asked tightly.

"Or me?" Judy was chewing pretty hard on her left lower lip. "Jesus, Charlie, you can't just leave shit out. We need to *know* things like that. We can't afford to be blindsided."

"If it makes you feel any better, Mickey is not particularly pleased with me, either." He held up the iPhone, and Barel snatched it out of his hand.

Staring at the display, she saw an e-mail from Mickey Solano. "I guess you seen the news. I'm sorry, Hugues, but you TOLD me you wasn't running again. I ain't gonna air your dirty laundry in public, coz I don't play that, but damn, man, you said you wasn't running! You KNEW I had an exploratory committee, you KNEW I was scouting out campaign locations, so why do you wanna do me like that? Well, I'm sorry, but I been planning this for way too long to give up now. It's my TURN, and you ain't taking this away from me, no way, no how."

"Dirty laundry?" Barel handed the iPhone back to Charlie. "Is he kidding? Did you actually promise him anything?"

Big Charlie shrugged his immense shoulders. "I said only that I was not planning to seek re-election—which, at the time, I was not—and that the field was open to him if he wished."

Judy shook her head, and Barel feared she would draw blood from the left-hand side of her lip. "Why would you even do that? Especially to Mickey? He's a snake."

"He's not a snake." Barel was shaking her head. "He's the guy the snake sends to the bodega to buy his cigarettes. And now he's gonna be crawling up our *tuch*—our asses. Hope you're happy." She tossed her legal pad aside. "Well, that's useless now. It doesn't matter who dropped out, because it's a race again."

"It was always a race, Barel."

"No, it was a cakewalk. Your only opposition were the down-ballot nutjobs. We weren't even going to have to debate those—those guys." She managed to swallow another Yiddishism. "Now, though, we have to actually have a debate."

Big Charlie stood up, looming over both women. "Then we shall have a debate." And then he strode out of the conference room and headed to the front door.

"I guess he's going home. Great." Barel looked at Judy, who was now chewing on her right lip.

"I'll do up a press release, saying we welcome the competition, the airing of issues, and so on. Y'know, the usual bullshit."

"Yeah." Barel shook her head. "You know Mia Fitzsimmons at the *News*?"

Judy nodded. "Yeah, we went to the same high school."

"Friends?"

She grinned. "Not then. I was the cool Latina chick, she was the brainiac Irish girl."

"Well, she did a nice job on the announcement, and I think we should give her more access. If Mickey's throwing his fedora in, we're gonna need all the favorable press coverage we can get."

—4—

Mia Fitzsimmons stood on the steps of the Bronx County Courthouse, the midday June sun blasting down on her, and wondered what this press conference was about.

Big Charlie and Mickey Solano hadn't even had their first debate yet, though it was scheduled (finally) for two weeks' hence.

Jack Napolitano approached, his jaw arriving half a second before the rest of him. He went from being an anchor on Channel 12 to a political beat reporter for Channel 5, the local Fox affiliate, and with his chiseled good looks, he was bound for an anchor there, too, if not something national.

In case Mia ever forgot all that, Jack was likely to remind her of it.

"So I heard it through the grapevine that you got the other question."

Mia frowned. "Excuse me?"

"Judy told me only two people are asking questions after he makes whatever big statement he's making, and a little bird told me that you're number two."

In fact, the impression Mia had gotten from Judy's e-mail was that she was the only one asking questions, but thinking back over the text of it, realized that she'd never been that specific. It burned her britches a bit that she had to share with *this* jackass, but Channel 5 was the most-watched local news channel, so she could understand the logic.

"So you have any idea what this is about? I've been keeping my ear to the ground, but everyone's lips are sealed."

"No idea."

"He's gotta be dropping out." Jack shook his head, and Mia felt the need to duck, as his jaw had quite the turn radius. "Why else would mum be the word?"

Mia shook her head. "He's not dropping out."

"How're you so sure?" Jack asked, sounding offended that she would disagree with him.

Had she been she speaking to someone she liked—or respected—or didn't want to sock in his oversize, cliché-spouting jaw—Mia would have said something like, "His mother wants him to run, and he's the world's biggest *maman*'s boy," but instead she just shrugged. "Call it instinct."

"If you insist." He let out a sigh. "I hope this doesn't take long. I've got an interview with RSN. I think I'm a shoo-in for that one."

Mia suddenly experienced a massive coughing fit, which covered her look of disgust. Yuki Nitobe had broken the "vampire" story for the Regional Satellite Network, and that got her a promotion—once she was released from the hospital, anyhow. Mia herself had been dubious about the whole thing, but then Mick McCarthy told her, and the rest of the reporters in the city room, about what he saw at Bellevue that night. Just Mick's descriptions of it had given Mia nightmares. She couldn't imagine what it must have been like for Yuki.

But she'd broken the story and now was the go-to girl for I1V1, the virus that was turning people into vampires. "The V-Event," some marketing dork at RSN had called it. Her promotion meant a job opening, and Mia was completely not surprised that Jack had dusted off his résumé to take his shot at it.

"It's showtime."

At Jack's words, Mia looked up to see Judy Alejo approaching the podium that was set up on the courthouse steps. Big Charlie was just a few feet behind her, looking far more solemn than Mia could ever recall the jovial prosecutor appearing.

Once everyone quieted down, Judy spoke. "Thank you, ladies and gentlemen, for coming. Without further ado, here's Bronx District Attorney Hugues Charles."

Mia blinked with surprise at Judy's clipped tone and terse introduction. She usually provided a bit more buildup than that. It was odd on several levels, not the least being that she never had anything but a happy face on for the fourth estate. The last time Mia saw such a sour expression on Judy's face, it was in high school when she lost the election for Latin American Club president to Paolo Sandoval.

Something bad's going on here. She jotted some quick notes on a small paper notepad. Jack, who was cradling a tablet, made a *tch* noise. "Paper? That's *so* twentieth century."

"Thank you, Judy," Big Charlie said. "I have spent my entire career—indeed, my entire *life*—being truthful with the people of this community, and I do not wish to cease this tendency now."

The plot thickens. Mia noted that the reporters were unusually quiet. If not for the traffic noise of cars and buses on 161st and on the Concourse, it would've been eerily silent.

"Many of you are, I assume, aware of the I1V1 virus that has been spreading across the entire world. Several people standing in front of me right now reported on poor Michael Fayne, shot down while in custody at Bellevue Hospital only a few months ago. I1V1 has been especially strong here in our great city, and it would seem that I am among those who are affected by it."

That broke the quiet. Everyone around her started bellowing questions at once, voices overlapping each other into a wall of meaningless noise.

But Mia was just staring at Big Charlie as he said, "Please, calm down, my friends. I will take questions once I have completed my statement. Thank you."

A million questions went through Mia's mind, the most prominent of which was: *How did I miss this?* She'd been around Big Charlie for almost a month now, and hadn't seen a single sign of this.

That, however, was not the question she could ask him when the time came.

Once the noise died down again, Big Charlie went on. "It seems that I have *loup garou* in my ancestry. My mother told me stories of men who could turn themselves into wolves—I had no idea that I would become such a creature myself."

Mia noticed Jack frantically tapping on his tablet, cadging a wireless signal from the courthouse to look up *loup garou*. Mia would do likewise when she got back to the office, but she could afford patience. Jack was going to be on camera in a minute, where Mia had until late evening to file her story.

"Let me assure you of several things. First of all, I retain complete control over the transformation. It is not triggered by the full moon or by stress or by any outside factors that are out of my control."

One of the reporters standing behind Mia muttered, "So not Lon Chaney and not the Incredible Hulk." Mia snorted a quick chuckle.

"I can become the wolf purely by force of will. Indeed, I could demonstrate for you now—but the transformation changes my shape in such a way that it would destroy this rather expensive suit I am wearing…"

That got some more chuckles. Mia could see the trademark Hugues Charles disarming technique at work. The soft voice, the smile, the yes-I'm-massive-but-I'm-a-big-teddy-bear-really mien. But this time, she wasn't buying it.

"Secondly, I have gone to see a physician, and while there is much about I1V1 that remains unknown, I have received a clean bill of health. The results of that examination will be made public, rest assured."

That got a derisive snort from Jack. Mia looked over and saw that the Channel 5 reporter was salivating. This story would make a nice addition to the reel he sent RSN.

"Finally, I have not changed. I'm still the same man that ever I was. I am still the District Attorney of Bronx County, a position I intend to retain for at least another four years after this one. Now, then, I can take a couple of questions." Several reporters raised their hands, even though Mia and Jack were, as far as she knew, the only ones who would get called on. "Yes, Jack?"

At first, Mia was annoyed that he chose Jack first, but then she realized she had no idea what to ask. All the questions she had prepared in her head were based on what she thought this presser might be about. Big Charlie being the latest victim of I1V1 never made that particular list.

"So just to verify—you *are* continuing to seek re-election?"

A dumb but necessary question, to which Big Charlie replied, "Of course. Nothing of consequence has changed. One more question. Mia?"

And just like that, she knew what she had to ask. "If you have full control over the transformation as you say, Mr. District Attorney—then why reveal the condition at all?"

Jack stared down at her with a look approaching respect.

"Thank you for asking that, Mia," Big Charlie said, and he sounded sincere. Mia couldn't help but put on a self-satisfied smile. "I have been a part of this community for my entire life. Except for my brief sojourn in Brooklyn, I have always been a child of the Bronx. I have never lied to the people of this borough, Mia, and I see no reason to start now. Some might say I have everything to lose by sharing this information, but what, pray tell, is the alternative? Yes, I could hide it—and then what? What if Mr. Solano or an enterprising defense attorney learns the truth and reveals it? I would no longer be able to do my job—more to the point, I would no longer be *worthy* to do my job. The truth is, the only way I lose is if I do *not* disclose this condition."

Mia jotted down a few more notes. She was witnessing political history here.

"There are men and women all across the globe who are being persecuted for what is truly only a medical condition. I am continuing with my life to show others that they can continue with theirs. Thank you all, my friends."

More voices blurted out with questions, but Big Charlie had left the podium, and a slightly-less-sour-looking Judy had returned. "Thanks, everyone, I'm sorry, but no more questions. No more questions!"

"Oh, there'll be more questions, you can bet the house on *that*," Jack said.

–5–

Judy Alejo had deliberately timed the call to her older sister for five minutes before *Top of the News with Helen Lashmar* started so she would only have to talk to her for five minutes. It meant Perla had to concentrate her questions about when Judy would get a boyfriend, start going to church again, and stop doing that awful job and do something *useful*.

"Look, I have to go," Judy said in Spanish when the closing credits for the morning talk show that was just finishing on RSN rolled.

"You always have to go so fast," Perla replied in the same language.

"I'm the press secretary for a district attorney running for reelection. It's busy now. It'll get better after the primary."

Barel walked into the office just then. The older woman was wearing yet another cardigan, despite summer coming around. She seemed to have an endless supply of them.

"You always say that, Judy, but—"

"I really do have to go."

"But—"

Judy pulled the phone from her ear and hit end. She turned to Barel and said, "That woman will drive me up a—"

"How's that again?"

Shaking her head, Judy realized she was talking to Barel in Spanish. Switching to English, she said, "Nothing. Let's see how this goes."

She'd been dreading this broadcast. The first story Lashmar would be tackling was Big Charlie, and her producers had assembled an impressive cross-section of pundits to pick the whole thing apart.

"Some good news," Barel said. "Judy Gomez cancelled, so they got Mia Fitzsimmons on."

Judy's eyes widened. Mia had been a godsend, giving them excellent coverage. More to the point, hers was the only coverage that had been about Big Charlie as a *person* rather than a cause or a thing. Of course, she'd been the only one paying attention to him prior to that, as a local

D.A. election wasn't any great shakes. Now, though, everyone was on the story and everyone had an opinion—but very little of it had to do with Hugues Charles himself.

The opening music finished, and the camera cut to Lashmar—an attractive brunette in her thirties who looked great on camera and had done a superb job of never once having any kind of opinion. That combined with her strong interviewing skills enabled her to get really good guests on her show.

"Good morning," she said in her pleasant alto. "We start with our roundtable segment, where a panel will tackle the news of the day. Joining me today are John Generico of the Generico Politico blog, Mia Fitzsimmons of the New York *Daily News*, former Manhattan District Attorney and current columnist for *Newsweek* Allen Reimold, and the Rev. Michael Sookdeo, chair of the Religious Studies Department at St. Paul's College."

Judy frowned. "Religious Studies? What the hell?"

Barel shrugged. "The religious types've been coming out of the damn woodwork. Vampires, crosses…"

"Our first story," Lashmar said, "is from New York City. Patient Zero of I1V1 came from New York, and now the first politician to publicly admit to suffering from the virus has come out of the city as well. Bronx District Attorney Hugues Charles, known locally as 'Big Charlie,' has admitted to being a werewolf. We'll start with John—what do you think this means for Big Charlie's re-election chances?"

Judy noticed that Mia looked relieved that she didn't get the first question.

Not that she herself was all that thrilled with Generico getting it. He was either a textbook example of the triumph of Internet journalism, or proof that the Internet had destroyed journalism, depending on who you asked. Judy generally fell into the former camp, but Generico's bloviating blog was the exception in her mind.

He also had the proverbial face made for radio, as his wide mouth, twitchy gestures, and beady eyes meant he was better suited to carrying on where you didn't have to look at him. That didn't stop every cable news station from having him on since his blog passed a billion hits a week.

In response to the question, Generico said, "In the toilet. Seriously, did he think this would have any result other than total disaster? These people are being hunted down and shot—the ones who aren't hunting themselves. Plus, how do we know he isn't going around mangling people on the night of the full moon?"

Judy shook her head. "Here we go." The past few weeks had forced her to take a crash course in separating the wheat from the chaff of werewolf legends, but most people didn't go to that much effort, and just fell back on the obvious pop-culture stereotypes just as Generico was doing.

Mia spoke up. "Well, for starters, he has control over the transformation, and—"

Generico interrupted her. "We only have his word for that."

"We only have his word that he *has* the virus! And he didn't have any reason to tell anyone."

Dismissing her with one of his twitchy gestures, Generico looked at Lashmar. "He wasn't even sure he was going to enter the race. Now he's got cold feet, so he's admitting to the problem that probably led to his delay in entering the race in the first place. He probably just figured he'd have no opposition, then when Solano decided to run, he needed a reason to back out."

Judy's first job was in the mayor's office, and she'd met Allen Reimold when he was the Manhattan D.A. She'd always liked him—certainly more than the jackass who had the job these days—and so she was cheered to hear him run to Big Charlie's defense. "Except he isn't backing out. If he was, he would have by now. In fact, he's increased his public appearances in the three days since the announcement."

Generico shook his head. "I still think it's butt-covering. He's been pretty popular, so he doesn't want to let the community down."

"He's not just 'popular,' " Reimold said, "he's *good*. He's streamlined the D.A.'s office, reducing the average time between arrest and trial by months. Now part of it's the lower crime rate. I tried to do what he did when I was in the Manhattan office, but I couldn't get it done because there was just too much backlog. But he's taken advantage of that to really do some good."

Barel was nodding. "Nice." The campaign manager had been bitching for days about this show, that it was going to be a hatchet job, especially with Generico on there, and Judy hadn't been able to assuage her concerns.

Mia then joined in. "I think it's also important to recognize that he's doing something politicians almost never do: he's telling the truth."

Generico made a noise. "You think maybe there's a reason why they never do that? When they do, they fail."

"Actually, John, no, it's when they lie and get caught that they fail. We live in an age of a twenty-four-hour news cycle. Politicians—even local D.A.s—have reporters who follow their every move. Hell, I've been covering Big Charlie since he announced. With that kind of coverage, it gets impossible to have a secret life. End result, the bad stuff comes out. That's what killed Eliot Spitzer's career, just to give a recent local example."

Judy winced. Her mentor in the business worked for Spitzer's gubernatorial campaign and had really believed in him. The day the New York governor's career was torpedoed by a sex scandal, Judy had had to listen to a two-hour harangue over the phone over how you think you know somebody…

"I don't know about that, Mia," Reimold said. "I mean, you're right about Spitzer, but history is filled with examples of politicians who kept important health secrets from the public."

Barel snorted. "Generico's gonna mention either Woodrow Wilson or FDR."

Judy nodded. Woodrow Wilson had a stroke while in office, and his First Lady wound up doing much of the governing during the latter days of his presidency. Franklin Delano Roosevelt hid the fact that he had polio and was wheelchair bound from the world as he led the country through the second World War.

Sure enough, Generico said, "Woodrow Wilson."

"See?" Barel said with a smile.

"I was gonna say Roosevelt, but—" Reimold started.

Then, for the first time, Reverend Sookdeo said something. "FDR could still do his job, however."

Mia said, "Yes, but neither of them had to deal with television or the Internet. Wilson didn't even have to deal with radio, really."

Looking to the ceiling with glee, Barel said, "Oh, I could kiss her."

"Isn't anyone worried about what he'll do if he loses?" That was Generico. Judy figured he was suffering withdrawal from not having spoken in thirty seconds. "I mean, what if he goes all werewolf in the courtroom?"

Reimold laughed. "You've obviously never been a D.A. in New York, John. You don't have time to prosecute cases anymore once you reach the top office."

With a chuckle, Lashmar said, "Of course, he also might 'go all were-wolf,' as John said, on his opponent."

"If that is the case," Sookdeo said softly, "then this is a truly grave matter."

Lashmar's smile fell. "I was kidding, Reverend."

"I know that, Helen," he replied, though Judy didn't think he did, "however, your joke does raise a reasonable question, and it is one that John raised earlier. We do not know the true nature of Mr. Charles's metamorphosis. Mickey Solano is one of Mr. Charles's oldest friends. Were Mr. Charles to attack Mr. Solano while in his wolfen form—"

Mia put in, "We don't even know what his wolfen form is *like*!"

"Isn't that the point?" Generico asked snidely. "We don't know anything about what he's turned into, but if he's anything like the werewolves I grew up reading about—"

"You didn't grow up with them, John, you saw them in movies."

"Nice one, Mia," Barel said proudly.

"That's not the point," Generico muttered.

Before Mia could reply, the reverend said, "Actually, it very much is, Mr. Generico, because Mr. Charles has not been transformed into a werewolf. He is a *loup garou*."

"Forgive me, Reverend," Reimold said, "but isn't that just French for *werewolf*?"

Judy ground her teeth. If she had a nickel for every time someone had thrown that in her face, she'd be able to retire to the Bahamas.

"Not exactly." Sookdeo folded his arms on the desk, and suddenly Judy understood why a religious studies professor was on the panel. "There are many legends of the *loup garou*, but in many, the transformation is voluntary, and does not always come with the violent associations that the movies of Universal Studios would have us believe."

"What about—"

Lashmar, bless her, interrupted Generico's stupid question. "John, I'm sorry, I have to cut you off, as it's time for a break, and we still have three more news stories to get to. When we come back, what the origins of I1V1 mean for those who are against climate change? We'll be right back."

The screen cut to a commercial. Judy looked at Barel. "Whaddya think?"

"I think we should get Mia a fruit basket. If this is the tenor the debate will take, we may pull this off."

– 6 –

Sermon given by Rev. Josiah Mann
The Blessed Church of Enlightenment, Des Moines, Iowa
Broadcast live over the Good News Network.

The Bible states, "Thou shalt not suffer a witch to live." Except it doesn't actually say that, now does it? Y'see, the original Hebrew of Exodus 22.18 uses the word mekhashefah, which simply means someone who practices magic against people. Y'see, the Lord wasn't concerned about women in big pointy hats with green skin ridin' brooms. No, y'see the Lord was concerned about people who practiced unnatural arts. The Lord was concerned about people goin' against His will by usin' forces that were not meant for the people He created in His own image.

The Lord was concerned about people *usin'* magic.

Now, we have people all over the world who are usin' magic. The same scientists who try to convince us that we're descended from apes, the same scientists who lie about "global warming," as if God's Earth could possibly change because of man, are now tryin' to tell us that this is a virus. They give it a fancy name, I1V1, and they try to convince us that it's the flu. Just a little bed-rest and a couple aspirin, and you'll stop turnin' into a fanged killin' machine!

But y'see, this is *not* an illness! This is *not* a condition that people will get better from if they take antibiotics or if they pray or if they go to a hospital! This is people who are livin' in defiance of God!

And we have to be vigilant! Y'see, we have people—we have sorcerers, magic-users, and yes, *witches*—who are feedin' off of God's own creations. They're maimin' us, they're feedin' off us, they're *killin'* us!

And we cannot suffer them to live.

I am telling you now, ladies and gentlemen, that these are monsters. Y'see, they pretend to be the sick and the lame. They claim they have a virus, and they hope that they'll be healed the way that Jesus healed the sick people of Gennesaret. But these are *not* the ten lepers! These are *not* Lazarus needin' to be raised from the dead! These are *mekhashefah*, and they cannot be allowed to continue to contaminate God's Earth.

Now y'see, some may say, "Reverend Mann, I don't understand. I've read the 22nd book of Exodus, and it talks about fathers givin' away their daughters in marriage, and it talks about makin' sacrifices to other gods, and it talks about a whole lotta other things that don't matter in the world today." And ladies and gentlemen, people who say that are absolutely right. The Bible was written at a time when such things mattered. But y'see, Exodus 22 also speaks of not lyin' with animals, an act we *still* consider a sin. Exodus 22 also speaks of not stealin' your neighbors' belongin's, an act we not only consider a sin, but a crime. Exodus 22 speaks of startin' fires and of stealin' and of breakin' oaths—these are things that matter to us still.

Y'see, the 18th verse mattered to the people of the time as much as all that stuff about oxen and dowries and such. And for a time, people did not practice magic, at least not in the manner meant by the proscription in Exodus 22.18.

But y'see, ladies and gentlemen, times have changed. Foul magic is among us once again, and once again we must turn to the Bible, as the Israelites did so long ago, as we continue to do today to guide us in our daily lives, and we must follow the Lord's word.

Now y'see, there is a man who is currently in New York City. I know, I know—it is a den of iniquity in so many ways, but it is also considered by many to be the hub and heart of our great nation. It is where the Statue of Liberty resides, after all.

There is a man there who has been the District Attorney of the County of the Bronx, prosecuting the many criminals there, for the past twelve years.

Now y'see, I have no doubt that once Hugues Charles was a good man—*once*. But he has *admitted* to becoming one of these creatures. He has *admitted* to being able to unnaturally transform himself from a man made in God's image into something else—something wicked, something *horrible*. And he intends to keep his job. Y'see, even as I stand here talkin' to you all, Mr. Hugues Charles of New York City is runnin' for re-election. He intends to continue prosecutin' man's law even as his very existence remains an affront to God's law.

We cannot suffer this man to live.

−7−

"Have you seen this?"

Barel Grindberg blinked as she walked into Big Charlie's office in the courthouse and was hit with that question from its occupant. "Uh, well, if you're talking about the Reverend Mann thing, I e-mailed you about it half an hour ago. If you're not talking about the Reverend Mann thing, then I have no idea what you're talking about."

"I apologize, Barel, I have not as yet checked my e-mail. I have been too busy being livid about this. The man is calling for my death."

Unable to stop herself from grinning, she said, "I know, isn't it great?"

"I fail to see what there is to smile about, Barel."

"You kidding? This is *gold*. There's, like, a hundred different YouTube clips of it. They're all ripped from RSN. A bunch got taken down, but I think they finally gave up with the cease-and-desists after a day of fresh uploa—"

Barel cut herself at the expression on Big Charlie's face. She sighed. She supposed she shouldn't have been surprised that he didn't see the upside. "Barel—"

She held up a hand. "Look, I know it seems bad on the face of it."

Big Charlie was glowering now. "He is calling for my death."

"Well, technically, yeah, but it's not like he has an armed militia on his side. What he *does* have is a flock in the millions all throughout the Midwest, which means that people all over the country are talking about you, and that means more press coverage that we don't have to pay for. Now the whole country's talking about our little D.A. race, and it's *you* they're talking about. If they even mention Solano, it'll be an afterthought."

"I suppose—"

She held up both hands. "Look, I get that you're concerned, but the people who hang on this asshole's every word are all out in the fly-over states. None of them are registered Democrats in the Bronx, and those are your people, and they're the ones who're gonna get their backs up at some *schmuck* preacher calling for your head. The outrage votes alone'll knock us up five points."

Big Charlie stared at her for several seconds, and Barel honestly had no idea how he was going to respond to this.

Finally, he let out a long breath, and put a meaty hand to his forehead. "This is madness."

"Hey, you're the one who wanted to run with I1V1. We knew things might get crazy. May as well take advantage. I'm telling Judy to clear your schedule—I've already started getting calls asking for more appearances."

"And how am I to respond to people asking how I feel about this lunatic?"

"Well, for starters, don't call him a lunatic."

"Barel—"

"We take the high ground. Call Reverend Mann a decent, honorable man of God who was simply speaking his mind."

"Who wishes me dead."

"Trust me, I've dealt with the 'Blessed Church of Enlightenment' garbanzos before. They'll be spin-doctoring this puppy from here till doomsday. As soon as anyone actually *calls* them on their bullshit, they backpedal. We gain absolutely *nothing* by getting down in the dirt. Just stay above it all, and make use of all the new interview opportunities to point out how awesome you are."

That finally got Big Charlie to smile, his endless shoulders rumbling with a chuckle. "Very well." He tapped some keys on his computer. "Ah, I see your e-mail. Oh, and one from Mickey with the subject line of 'Rev. Mann.'"

That surprised, and concerned Barel. Solano at least claimed to be a devout Catholic, and she wasn't sure he'd come out against a man of God. Besides, Catholics were always going around forgiving people. "What'd he say?"

Big Charlie read off the screen. "'That's some serious bullshit right there. I won't be sayin' nothin to support that asshole Reverend Mann nohow. Sorry you had to hear that shit.'"

Barel gave a quick fist-pump. "Perfect. Not only do we get free airtime, we get Mickey going around agreeing with you at a time when he needs to be ripping you to pieces. This is *great*."

"I hope you are correct, Barel." Big Charlie sounded as serious as he ever did. "The reverend's words did not come out of a vacuum, and I do not believe that he is the only one who has this particular opinion regarding those of us with I1V1."

"What did I always tell you?" Barel said with a glare. "In a campaign, there is no long term. Worry about that when it happens. For now, let's deal with the hand we've got, and Mann just gave us three aces."

☾

"JUNK" PT.5

Jonathan Maberry

October 12, 7:28 p.m.
Bellevue Hospital
Zero Days until the V-Event

Yuki tried not to think about the money she was spending to grease the wheels. The bonus she'd promised Charlie Sims was nothing compared to what she'd had to pay to get this far inside the hospital where Michael Fayne was being kept. There was a point during the negotiations with a friend of a friend of a friend of Sims—a thick slab of a white boy named Jenkins who ran security for the psych ward—where Yuki thought she was going to have to open more than her wallet. Jenkins was the kind of creep who ought to be on watch-lists. The kind you wouldn't let your kids be alone with, not unless you wanted to pay some very expensive therapy bills for the next forty years.

But in the end, the thug's greed was hungrier than his libido.

Now she was inside. Complete with a white lab coat and an I.D. badge that identified her as a visiting specialist from UCLA Medical. With a Chinese name on her nametag, her red lipstick rubbed off, her hair in a bun and a pair of horn-rim glasses she kept in a bag of simple disguises she always kept in her trunk, no one gave her a second glance. A couple of the men checked out her legs, but no one connected her with the glitzy and glossy Yuki Nitobe from Global Satellite News.

Jenkins had provided her with a swipe card from a doctor who was on vacation in St. Thomas.

"Charlie said that there were bonuses," said Jenkins, shifting to block her from leaving his office.

Yuki stared up at him, hands in pockets. She'd managed to slip her little stun gun into her right lab pocket while Jenkins was fishing in his file cabinet for the I.D. card. Her thumb rested on the trigger slide.

"What kind of bonus are we talking about?" she asked cautiously.

He gave a nasty little laugh. "When Charlie called and gave me a heads up, I checked the nurses' logs and found out what room they're putting that guy in."

"That was part of the original price."

"The room number was, sure…but I got in there before the ambulance arrived and left one of my little toys behind."

"What…*toy*?"

His grin was wide and wet as he opened a drawer in his desk to show her a dozen small black cylinders. Lipstick cameras.

"The feed is sent to a portable hard-drive with a little built-in router." He produced one from his pocket and showed it to her. "There's a cable to plug it into any viewer. It'll even work for your iPhone. This one gets the direct feed from Fayne's room."

"These cameras are in every patient's room?"

He snorted. "Nah. We…um…use these to keep an eye on patients when we don't want them to know."

" 'We'? You mean the doctors, or you and your jerkoff buddies?"

"What's it matter to you?" he asked coldly, actually contriving to look offended; however, they both knew that those cameras were never approved by administration. Yuki wondered how many of them were covertly positioned in rooms occupied by young women. She felt mildly ill and wished she could spend a few minutes introducing Jenkins's nutsack to her stun gun. Instead, she nodded.

"Two hundred," she said.

"Screw that," he countered. "A grand or we're not even having this conversation."

"A grand? Not in this lifetime, Jenkins. Five hundred and I

take the hard drive with me. And that *is* the end of this conversation."

Jenkins tried to budge her, but Yuki could see from his expression that he knew he was wasting his breath. She gave him cash and he gave her the hard drive.

Once she left his office, Yuki began threading her way through the maze of halls and security checkpoints, going ever deeper into the most secure sections of the hospital's ward for violent patients. Her disguise worked so well that she felt invisible. The place was a beehive of doctors, nurses, orderlies and visiting families.

The one close call was when three people stepped out of an office right in front of her. Two were strangers—a short woman with an imperious air, a tall jock-looking guy with wire-frame glasses and Detective Schmidt.

Yuki did a fast right turn and walked into a patient's room while the trio passed, but after a moment it was clear that the detective had not recognized her. He probably hadn't seen her, and with all that was going on, Yuki could understand that.

She noted that the detective and the jock wore fresh bandages. That tallied with what Sims had told her. She looked at her watch. It was almost seven-thirty. Christ, the day was burning away. She'd missed the window for the six o'clock news and if she didn't come up with something solid, she'd blow the slot for the eleven o'clock broadcast. Without a homerun she was going to very quickly lose all of the ground she'd gained today.

"Are you here to ask me about the space dolphins?" asked the old man in the bed.

Yuki turned to him. He was about a thousand years old and apparently composed entirely of wrinkles. He looked hopefully at her.

"Space dolphins?" she asked.

"Yes. Don't you see them?" he said, nodding to the empty air beside his bed.

Yuki smiled. "Of course I do. They're quite lovely."

The old man blinked twice at her and then smiled. "They really are. Especially the green ones."

"The green ones are always the prettiest," she agreed.

She left him smiling and continued her search for a creature that was equally fantastic. One that should have been equally unreal. But wasn't.

– 19 –
October 12, 8:11 p.m.
Bellevue Hospital
Zero Days until the V-Event

172
🦅

Dr. Alice Feldman stood by the open door with an orderly right beside her. The orderly, Max, was one of the biggest men Luther Swann had ever seen. Max was easily six-eight, all of it his chest and shoulders. He looked like he could bench-press New Jersey.

Three other orderlies were clustered around Michael Fayne. Each of those men was also huge, and Swann wondered if sheer bulk was the principle requirement here. It probably was, he decided.

Max did the talking. "Mr. Fayne," he said, "these men are going to place restraints on your ankles and wrists. Do you understand me?"

Fayne nodded.

"Mr. Fayne, I'm going to need you to give me a vocal response. Do you understand?"

"Yes," mumbled Fayne in a broken voice. "I don't care what you want to do."

"You're not going to give us any trouble, are you?" asked Max.

"No."

"Nobody wants to hurt you, Mr. Fayne," said Max.

Fayne snorted at that and shook his head. "Just fucking do it."

Max nodded to the other orderlies and they applied the padded restraints with practiced speed and dexterity.

Swann leaned close to Dr. Feldman. "How strong are those things?"

Max smiled faintly, "Nobody ever gets loose."

"He's stronger than he looks."

The giant shook his head. "Leather, chain and airline cable, mister. They'll hold anyone."

Swann nodded, but he wished he actually felt reassured. He looked at Schmidt, who stood with his weight shifted to his left foot. Per protocol he had surrendered his sidearm, but Swann wondered if the detective had a back-up pistol in an ankle holster. Almost certainly. Schmidt caught him looking and when Swann pointedly looked down at his ankle and back up again, the detective gave him a cold millimeter of a smile.

Swann felt that was far more reassuring than the restraints.

But not as much as it should have been.

Dr. Feldman gave a tiny jerk of her head and the orderlies stepped back. The four of them stood like the pillars of Stonehenge around the bed. Swann and Schmidt lingered by the rear wall. Only Dr. Feldman approached the bed on which Fayne lay, his face turned away toward a blank wall. There were no windows in this dreary, cheerless little room. The walls were not padded; instead they were a featureless off-white that Swann thought was the least tranquil and comforting color choice he could imagine.

"Mr. Fayne?" said Dr. Feldman. "Can you hear me?"

Fayne said nothing and continued looking at the blank wall.

"Are you comfortable, Mr. Fayne?"

Fayne snorted.

"Do you understand why you're here?" asked Feldman.

Fayne turned his head very slowly to face her. Swann saw Alice Feldman start ever so slightly and a deep frown etched its way onto her face. She shot a quick look at her orderlies and then over at Swann.

Swann and Schmidt took a half step forward and then stopped. Even from that distance they could see that there was something different about Michael Fayne. Schmidt stiffened, and Swann could feel his blood turn to ice water.

Fayne knew that everyone could see the change. He wore a strange expression. Almost a smile, but not quite. His lips were curled upward but he looked like he was in pain.

"I know why I'm here," he said.

And his voice was different, too. Deeper. Thicker.

Feldman quietly cleared her throat. "And why are you here, Mr. Fayne?"

The prisoner closed his eyes for a moment but his half-smile lingered. "It's not because they think I killed those girls."

"No? Then why?"

He tried to raise one hand but there wasn't much slack on the restraint. The action made the whole bed tremble. The sound was unusually loud, as if there was a lot more power in the motion than there appeared to be. Than there *could* have been.

"I'm here because you got beds like this and a goon squad and lots of drugs," said Fayne. "That's why they brought me here."

He opened his eyes and Swann shifted again to get a better look, his heart suddenly hammering in his chest. The irises had somehow changed their color from a medium brown to a dark red, as dark as smoke-stained bricks. Almost black. The sclera had also changed, darkening from blue-white to a bloody red.

"Jesus," gasped Max. "Doc—?"

"He's hemorrhaging," Swann snapped. The orderlies surged forward.

"*No!*" growled Feldman. "Don't touch him."

Everyone froze, staring at the young man on the bed.

Schmidt gripped Swann's arm, maybe to stop him from moving, maybe because he was reaching for an anchor in a moment that was drifting into strange waters.

Michael Fayne looked at the doctor and the detective and the orderly and the man who studied monsters.

And laughed.

It was one of the strangest sounds Luther Swann had ever heard. It was a deep, rumbling laugh that was all bass. So low it seemed to ripple along the floor and vibrate in Swann's chest. Everyone in the room froze.

That laugh held so many emotions.

Insanity.

An unhinged mirth.

Absolute terror.

And a dark and endless promise.

"This is all a joke," said Fayne, and now his whole voice was filled with the weird bass rumble. "You already *know* I killed them."

Schmidt's hand tightened on Swann's arm.

"That I tore them apart. That I *drank* them." There was laughter in Fayne's voice but tears burned silver lines down his cheeks.

Three of the orderlies took small steps backward from the bed; only Max held his ground, but his look of calm control had slipped several notches. He kept flicking uncertain glances between Fayne and Dr. Feldman.

"That's what you want me to say, isn't it?" demanded Fayne, his voice low but filled with strange passions. "You want me to say it, don't you?"

"No," someone said, and Swann realized that it was own voice. In very real point of fact, he did not want this young man to say anything more. Not a word.

Dr. Feldman held her composure. "We want to know the truth, Mr. Fayne. We want to know what happened."

"Don't lie to me," snarled Fayne, and his voice was huge, like a physical blow made of sound and rage. Everyone staggered back, two of the orderlies clapped hands to their ears. Dr. Feldman cried out and turned sharply, digging for a tissue with one hand and pressing the trembling fingers of her other hand to her nose. Blood bubbled from both nostrils and flowed in red lines over her lips and chin. Bright scarlet drops splattered on the spotless white of her coat.

Fayne's eyes snapped in that direction and Swann heard him make a low, desperate sound. A moan. Of pain?

Or hunger?

"God…oh, God…," said Feldman in a small voice as she struggled to stem the flow of blood. "Mr. Fayne…"

Fayne's eyes burned as he stared at the blood. He struggled to sit up, to lean closer to the blood. "I–I…"

Max stepped close to the bed and placed a huge hand on Fayne's chest, pressing him flat down on the bed. The way Max moved, it was clear that he expected to slam the smaller man down, but there was a moment's delay between his push and any reaction. Muscles stood out in sharp definition on Max's arm and his face tightened with effort and anger. Swann saw surprise register on the giant's face.

"You settle your ass down, right now," growled Max.

Fayne reluctantly shifted his eyes away from Feldman's bloody nose; he looked up into Max's eyes, and in a voice that was once more totally human and totally vulnerable.

"Kill me," he whispered.

The moment froze.

Max said, "What?"

"Kill me," begged Fayne. "Do it now. Please, for the love of God."

Max looked momentarily confused. "Look…sir…I need you to settle down. I need you stop…whatever you're doing and act right, okay? No one wants to hurt you, so—"

"God, you're all so fucking stupid," whispered Fayne. He turned to

Swann. "You! You understand what's going on. Tell them. For God's sake, tell them to *kill me.*"

The orderlies glanced at Swann. So did Alice Feldman, who was finally slowing the flow of blood.

"Tell them what I am!" screamed Fayne. "Tell them that I'm a god-damned vampire!"

– 20 –

October 12, 8:24 p.m.
Bellevue Hospital
Zero Days until the V-Event

Yuki Nitobe cried out and nearly dropped her cell.

The digital image fed to her iPhone from the hidden camera carried a crystal clear picture and great sound quality.

She saw and heard everything.

Everything.

"Oh my…*GOD!*"

Part of her wanted to laugh. This was insane. It was bad comedy. It was some kind of trick the cops were playing on a mentally disturbed patient.

Part of her wanted to run. Those bottomless dark eyes. That voice.

Part of her need to stay right there. Watching. Recording.

Getting ready to become the most famous reporter in the history of journalism.

That part of her forced her to sit there in the empty office and keep watching. But a bead of cold sweat crept crookedly down from her throat to between her breasts, right over her wildly beating heart.

– 21 –

October 12, 8:28 p.m.
Zero Days until the V-Event

"Vampire?" one of the orderlies, a big redhead, barked out the word and then laughed. "What the hairy fuck are you—?"

"Shut up," snapped Swann, Schmidt and Feldman all at the same time.

The room crashed into a hard silence.

"Tell them," said Fayne, but his voice was weaker now, paler. Broken.

Max fished some clean tissues out of his pocket and handed them to Feldman. "Doc, you need to get out of here. We need to get that looked at."

Alice Feldman shook her head in irritation.

"Professor Swann?" she said.

Swann wanted so badly to just bolt out of the door and get the hell away from here. Far away from here.

"Luther," murmured Schmidt, and it was the first time the detective had used his first name.

Swann took a deep breath and tried to clear the terror off his face.

"Mr. Fayne...Michael...," he began, "do you know what's happening? Do you really understand it?"

Fayne's dark eyes were inhuman, but his tears were not. He slowly shook his head.

"We can't rush to slap a label on this, Michael," continued Swann. "You understand that, right?"

Fayne nodded. A sob broke in his chest.

Swann took a step forward, paused for another steadying breath, and then went all the way around to the side of the bed. He gently pushed past Max and stood close to the restrained man.

"I know how all this looks," Swann said, "but you need to understand that we're not looking to simply solve some crimes and—"

"Murders," interrupted Fayne bitterly. "Don't pussy around with it. Call it what it is. You got to have the balls to at least do that much."

Swann glanced at Schmidt, who gave a tight little nod.

"Murders," said Swann reluctantly; and yet saying it seemed to steady him. Murders were still part of this world. "We're not just trying to solve murders. You understand that, right? If it were just about that, they would never have brought me in and they would never have brought you here."

Fayne considered that, and nodded.

"This is bigger than that," continued Swann. "This goes deeper than that. We need to know what *caused* this."

"'Caused it'?"

Swann nodded. "When we were speaking earlier, you told me that this happens during blackouts, and that the blackouts—this kind of blackout—something that only recently started happening to you. Do you remember telling me that?"

Fayne nodded again.

"Was that the truth?"

"Yes." Fayne's voice was totally normal now, though it was small, almost childlike in a lost and broken way. He closed his eyes.

"We have to discover how this happened. When it happened," said Swann, "and why."

With his eyes still shut, Fayne shook his head in disgust. "Well, gee, man, you think I haven't thought about that? You think if I knew how this shit started that I wouldn't have told you? And told everyone? Christ! You think I was bitten by Count frigging Dracula?"

"No. Dracula is fiction, and what's happening to you is real."

Behind him he heard Max quietly whisper to Feldman, "The hell is he talking about?"

Feldman shushed him.

"If it's real," Swann went on, "then it must have an explanation. There will be physical evidence. I mean…you know that there are changes in your body."

"Yes." A single word, hissed out like a curse.

"Then those are symptoms of something real, something measurable. Dr. Feldman has a top team here. She wants to re-do the blood work they did when you were first arrested. She'll do that a lot more. She'll do everything, Michael. CT scans, DNA tests. Everything. She'll be looking for something that could tell us what's going on."

"Like what? Little bats fluttering around in my bloodstream?" sneered Fayne.

"No," said Swann. "Something much more practical. A bacterium, maybe. Or a virus. Some infectious agent, some genetic anomaly."

Fayne finally opened his eyes. The sclera was nearly white again and spots of ordinary brown showed among the brick red. Swann's hammering heart slowed by a single degree.

A frown of doubt twisted Fayne's features. "What are you saying? Are you telling me that this is something I *caught*?"

Swann forced a smile onto his mouth. "Why not?" he asked.

"That's stupid. You *know* what I am."

"No, Michael…that's just it. We don't."

"I'm a vampire!" Fayne said, but instead of shouting it, he whispered it, like a secret they all shared. Like a curse that was only real and powerful if spoken aloud. Like a sinner confessing his greatest transgression. "A vampire."

The orderlies and Detective Schmidt shuffled uneasily. Dr. Feldman, whose nose had stopped bleeding, stood with a handful of crumpled, blood soaked tissues. Swann glanced at them and then back at Fayne.

"Okay," he said, "but what does that mean? I mean…really. What is a vampire?"

"I…" Fayne began, but he had nowhere to go, so he shook his head.

Swann looked around the room. "Do any of you know? If vampires are real, do any of you believe that they're supernatural?"

No one responded. Not even a shake of the head.

"That's just it," said Swann emphatically, "*no one* knows. If vampires are real, and if that's what you are, Michael, then we have to be smart and practical about how we look at this, and we can't start with the supernatural. We can't. We have to start with common sense, with what we know to be true. With what we can touch and weigh and measure and photograph. That's science. That's practical."

He drew in a breath as his audience, the man tied to the bed and the others shackled to Swann's every word, listened. "I've been studying vampires my whole life. I've written more books on the subject than anyone. The police called me in because what they were seeing, both in the, um, murder victims and the suspect tilted them toward the concept of vampires. Okay, sure, we can all freak out about that. But we can't stay freaked out. Not even you, Michael. If you were some kind of supernatural monster then how could we hold you here?"

Doubt flickered across Fayne's face, and for him, doubt was a lifeline.

"In stories, vampires can turn into mist, or change in animals. You can't do that, right?"

"I—don't know," said Fayne.

"Sure you do. If you could, then you'd be out of here already. You'd have turned into something else that couldn't be held down by restraints."

Fayne said nothing, waiting.

"No one's using a magic charm to hold you here. No holy relics, no charms made from rosewood or garlic. None of that is happening."

"No," said Fayne softly.

"Jesus," whispered Max and Swann shot him a quick look and gave a small warning shake of his head.

Swann sat down on the edge of the bed. It was a calculated move on his part, a show of confidence to the orderlies, but more importantly a message to Fayne that he wasn't afraid.

However, he was afraid. Terribly afraid, and like everyone else in the room he was grasping at the words he spoke to pull him back into a world that made sense.

"Listen to me, Michael," Swann said gently, "one of the things we academics are good at is finding very rational and occasionally deeply boring explanations for everything. We balance folklore and science as a way of understanding why people believe what they believe. A lot of what's in vampire legends is distortion because these beliefs were created by people trying to understand things that were beyond them, beyond their understanding of the world as they knew it."

He fished for an example. "Take SIDS—Sudden Infant Death Syndrome. Imagine trying to make sense of that in the twelfth or sixteenth century. Parents put a healthy baby down for the night, and in the morning the baby is dead. There are no marks, no signs of disease, no bites from night predators or insects. There's nothing, but the baby is dead. It died in the dark of night.

"Now, put yourselves into the heads of those people. Villagers living in pre-industrial times. Deeply religious people who expected God and His angels to look after innocent babies. They cannot—simply can *not*—accept that God would take this child's life, or allow it to die of anything approaching 'natural' causes. Their entire belief system would shatter if they believed that, or if they believed that it was completely random, that 'these things just happen.'

"So, in order for the world to make any kind of sense, there had to be something deliberate which caused the child's death. Some malevolent force, some creature of evil who stole in during the night and stole the child's life. The priest of their church would agree with this, perhaps even suggest it. The people would pray for protection against such a monster, and since SIDS rarely strikes the same family twice, the next child would be born and would grow up, safe and healthy. What's the result? They believe that their prayers protected the new baby from harm, which both reinforced their belief in God *and* their belief in evil monsters."

"But how does that explain this?" asked Schmidt.

Swann shot him a *shut the fuck up* look. Schmidt said nothing else.

"Most of the monsters we believed in can be explained away by science. Even the word *'nosferatu,'* which Bram Stoker incorrectly translated as 'undead' in *Dracula,* doesn't mean that. It means 'plague carrier.' Most of the great plagues have been associated with increases in beliefs of vampires and other monsters."

Fayne's eyes were almost completely normal now. "He's right," he said, ticking his head toward Schmidt. "That doesn't explain me."

"No," said Swann, "but it clears the board of almost all of the supernatural elements of vampirism. It removes ninety-nine percent of the vampire myths."

"What's left?" asked Fayne, clinging to Swann's words.

Swann said, "Well, let's look at a parallel first. For years there were beliefs of a tribe of tiny, savage predators. They stood about three feet tall—smaller than pygmies—and they attacked under cover of darkness and stole babies to eat. Monsters. Science dismissed all of this as myth, just as science dismissed most 'monsters.' It was bad reportage from people who didn't understand what they were seeing. Or whisper-down-the-lane tales that had been blown out of all proportion. But in 2003, Australian and Indonesian scientists found a cave on an island east of Bali with the bones of creatures that matched the descriptions of these monsters exactly. Not closely—*exactly.* The Ebu gogo. National Geographic did a whole story on them. These little people are now known as the *Homo floresiensis* scientists nicknamed them 'Hobbits' after the little people in Tolkien."

"Yeah," said Fayne, nodding, "I saw that special. Little people. They found bones."

"Bones, tools, all sorts of things."

"But—how does that…?"

"The scientists determined that the Ebu gogo were not myths but rather an offshoot of *homo sapiens.* Just as *Homo heidelbergensis, Orrorin tugenensis and Homo ergaster* were different genetic lines from what became *homo sapiens.* Different evolutionary paths."

The silence almost screamed as everyone digested this.

Swann continued, "Science had been trying to figure out what happened to the Neanderthals. Why'd they suddenly vanish? What happened to them? Well, thanks to programs like the Human Genome Project, we now know that our cousins didn't just die out, and Cro-Magnon didn't slaughter them all. We intermarried, interbred. They became part of us. Everyone whose family line never left Africa has some Neanderthal DNA in them. Everyone."

"But—"

"So," said Swann, "what if vampires are the same"

"They're…Neanderthals?" asked Max.

"No," said Swann, "what if vampires were a different branch of human evolution? What if they really existed? Not as supernatural creatures, but as different kinds of humans? What if they existed, and over the years they died out as a separate line?" He touched his chest and then touched Fayne's. "We could both have the DNA for vampirism. For whatever it is that makes a vampire."

"But…how?"

Alice Feldman cleared her throat. "DNA. We've mapped the human genome, but we're a long way from indexing and annotating it. We don't know what most of the genes in human DNA code for. There are so many blanks to be filled in."

"And," said Swann, "there's all that junk."

"Junk?" asked Fayne, surprised.

"Junk DNA. Genes that are part of us that we simply don't know what they do. Maybe, like the DNA for Neanderthals and who knows what else, maybe somewhere in there is the answer to what's happening to you."

Fayne closed his eyes for a long time.

The room was utterly silent.

Without opening his eyes, Fayne said, "Please."

"What?" asked Swann. "What do you want?"

"Do what you have to do. Take blood, take tissue, do whatever tests you have to do. Find out what the fuck is happening to me."

"We will," promised Feldman. "I've already ordered a full workup and—"

"You'd better hurry," warned Fayne.

"Hey," soothed Swann, "it's okay. You're safe here. No one's going to hurt you and you don't have to worry about hurting anyone else. You're safe here."

"No," said Fayne in a whisper. "It's not safe."

He opened his eyes, and the irises were the color of blood.

"Hurry."

− 22 −

October 12, 8:41 p.m.

Bellevue Hospital

Zero Days until the V-Event

"Don't screw around with me, Yuki," said Murray Gold, senior editor for Regional Satellite News. "You made a lot of big promises and so far I've got bupkiss."

"Bullshit, Murray," Yuki fired back, "I got footage inside the murder scene."

"That was this morning. Now it's evening. What have you done for me lately?"

"Sometimes you're a real asshole."

"Yeah, and I know how to spell asshole, too. It begins with E and ends with R and rhymes with 'editor.'"

"Hilarious. Every bit as funny as the first hundred times I heard that joke."

"I'm not joking here, Yuki, tell me you got something or tell me why I'm not transferring you to writing obits."

"Murray, stop trying to be clever long enough to listen to me," she said. "I have a story that you won't believe."

"Don't try to jazz me with another 'story of the century.' I get ten of those a week."

"Not like this. And when I say that you won't believe it, I mean exactly that. You *won't* believe it. But…you will."

"That doesn't make sense," said Murray.

Yuki laughed. Short and nervous and full of excitement.

"You know Jerry Schmidt, right?"

"Sure. One of the Goody-Goody Twins."

"And Dr. Alice Feldman over at Bellevue?"

"Yes. Is that where they took the guy who chopped up that girl? Feldman's a stone, she'll never talk to you. She hates reporters."

"I don't need her to talk to me, Murray. I have her and Schmidt on video. With the suspect and with some guy named Luther Swann who's an anthropology professor at New York University."

"Already bored. So what?"

Yuki told him.

Murray Gold did not interrupt her or say a word until she was finished. There was a silence that was so tense and protracted that Yuki winced, expecting a tirade.

184

Instead Murray said, "And you got this on video?"

"Yes."

"Everything? Everyone's faces? Enough so that we can go with indisputable identity on all the players?"

"Yes."

"And…the suspect. Fayne. You got his eyes? You got all that stuff?"

"I got everything, Murray. I can send it to you from my cell."

"Vampires?" murmured Murray.

"Vampires," agreed Yuki. She could almost feel Murray's heartbeat echoing from the speaker.

"Okay," he said, and he sounded as winded as if he'd run up forty flights of stairs, "here's what I need you to do."

-23-

October 12, 10:19 p.m.
Bellevue Hospital
Zero Days until the V-Event

Luther Swann leaned against the wall outside of Fayne's room. He blew out his cheeks and rubbed his eyes. Schmidt stood beside him, arms folded, muscles bunching and flexing at the corners of his jaws. The hall was busy, but not with anyone associated with this case. Dr. Feldman was having her nose looked at, which she agreed to do only after dictating a list of medical tests to a nurse that included only five or six things that Swann recognized. The rest had been arcane, rattled off in medical code in a voice that quavered with fear.

None of the people in the hall so much as looked at the two haggard men. Orderlies pushed gurneys, nurses went from room to room with charts, doctors in white lab coats read reports and talked on cell phones and consulted with each other in low voices. None of it was related to what had happened in the small room behind where Swann and Schmidt stood.

"This is insane," said Schmidt quietly, cutting a look at Swann. "How are you doing, Luther? You look a little freaked."

Swann gave a hollow laugh. "Oh, I'm way more than a little freaked."

Schmidt nodded. "Tell me something…that stuff you said in there about this being something from nature, something scientific? Were you just blowing smoke?"

"No," said Swann. "I mean…it *has* to be that, right?"

Instead of answering, Schmidt said, "I'm going to call my captain and bring him up to speed. He's a good guy and he's very political. He'll understand what needs to be done to keep this way off the radar. And he's good at handling the press. He'll spin some bullshit story to keep them off our backs while the doc does her tests."

Swann ticked his head toward the room they'd just left. "I think we need more than just orderlies here, don't you?"

"Oh yeah. I'm going to hand-pick some officers I trust and get the captain to detail to me for security." He paused. "What are you going to do?"

Swann shook his head. "I need to get to my office and get my laptop. I have a ton of bulk research data there, and the contact info for other experts I can call if we need to."

They discussed the details as they walked away.

Behind them, one of the doctors who had been poring over a sheaf of medical records on a clipboard straightened and turned to watch them go. She was slim, pretty, and smiling.

When the two men turned the far corner, Yuki Nitobe casually stepped to the door to Fayne's room, knocked, and was admitted by one of the orderlies.

–24–
October 12, 10:22 p.m.
Bellevue Hospital
Zero Days until the V-Event

"I can't leave you alone with him, doctor," said the orderly as he stood holding the door to Michael Fayne's room. He was a big man with black hair and a nametag that identified him as "S. Riddle."

"I know," said Yuki, who stood in the hall. She stood very close to Riddle. Close enough for him to smell her perfume and very likely to look down the V of her blouse. "Dr. Feldman said that we have to maintain the strictest security. I'll just be a few minutes, anyway. A few background questions."

Riddle stepped close and lowered his voice. "Be careful with this patient, doctor. He's still a bit twitchy. They had some real trouble with him."

Yuki contrived to look up at him with the biggest brown eyes in town. She placed a hand lightly on Riddle's chest. "Thank you. I'll be very careful…and you'll be there if I need you?"

"Yes, ma'am."

"All the time?" She put the slightest bit of a smile on her lips.

"Yes, ma'am," he said, but this time he put different inflection in it.

"Thank you," she said again.

Riddle smiled and stepped back to let her enter.

Yuki went straight over to Fayne's bed. He lay with his face turned away. Even from that angle, Yuki could see the corners of his eyes. There was no trace of white.

"Mr. Fayne?" she asked, her voice low and soft.

Fayne said, "You're not a doctor."

He pitched his voice so that only she could hear him.

"What?" she asked.

"You don't smell like a doctor," he said, still looking away.

"I—"

"Who are you? Did I kill someone you know?"

"No," said Yuki, surprised. Partly by the question, but more so by the degree of hurt in this man's voice. She flicked a look at Riddle, smiling to reinforce it. He smiled back. Yuki spoke even more quietly to Fayne. "I'm here to get the truth."

"What truth?"

"About you."

He made derisive noise. "You mean about what I am."

"Yes."

"What do you think I am?"

She pretended to make notes on her clipboard. "Mr. Fayne, I have a camera in this room. I saw and heard everything."

Fayne turned toward her, but he closed his eyes before he did so. "You're…what? Another cop trying to get my confession?"

"Hardly."

Fayne appeared to think about it. He pursed his lips. "Oh," he said at length. "I get it. You're a reporter."

Yuki flicked another quick look at Riddle, but clearly the orderly could not hear the content of this conversation.

"Yes."

"You taped everything?"

"Yes."

"And you're going to put it on TV?"

Yuki hesitated, then plunged in. "Yes."

"Good," he said bitterly. "I always wanted to be famous."

"My network...we'll hire you the best lawyers, the best doctors," said Yuki. "We can protect you."

He said nothing. His eyes were still closed and he might have been asleep except for the occasional twitch of his lips.

"Mr. Fayne?"

"I did it, you know," he said.

"Did...?"

"I killed those girls," said Fayne. "All of them."

She said nothing.

"I didn't remember it before, because it happened during my blackouts. Do...you know about the blackouts?"

"I heard you say something. Is that what happens?" she asked. "You...black out?"

"Yes. Michael Fayne goes away. He isn't there when it happens. He doesn't understand what happens. He's afraid of what happens."

"I—"

"But *I'm* not."

Yuki frowned. "I don't understand."

"No," said Fayne in a voice that was strangely calm and unusually deep. It had been like that for a few minutes earlier, when Yuki was watching through the spy cam. "They don't understand either. Not the cops, not the doctors, not that idiot Luther Swann. They don't understand because they can't understand."

"I want to understand," Yuki insisted. She touched his arm, making sure that her body hid the action from Riddle, who leaned against the wall pretending to be casual.

Fayne chuckled. It was an ugly sound. "You only think you do...but you don't. I can smell how much you don't. I can taste it in the air. I can hear your heart beating. You really don't want to understand."

"Yes," she insisted, though her trembling voice betrayed her.

"Not even Michael Fayne understands it."

"But…you're Michael Fayne," she said, suddenly wondering if the police had arrested the wrong man.

The man on the bed laughed again. Louder this time.

"Is everything all right?" asked Riddle, starting to come off the wall.

"Yes," said Yuki quickly, waving him back, "it's okay. Everything's fine."

Riddle scowled, but he stayed where he was. "You behave yourself, Mr. Fayne. Nobody wants any more trouble today."

The patient said, "Mr. Fayne isn't here."

"Whatever," Riddle said under his breath.

Yuki leaned forward another few inches. "What does that mean? Aren't you Michael Fayne?"

The man's mouth curled into a tight-lipped smile. "Not anymore."

Yuki felt her heart pounding harder. "Then…who is it I'm speaking with?"

The man on the bed opened his eyes. They were no longer white with brown irises. They were no longer brick-redbrick red. Now they were totally black. Bottomless, endless black.

Yuki gasped.

The tight lips relaxed as the smile grew and grew, revealing his teeth.

His…

…teeth.

"God!" cried Yuki.

Riddle started away from the wall.

"What…what *are* you?" she cried.

The man on the bed spoke in a voice that was entirely unlike Michael Fayne's. It was entirely unlike anything Yuki had ever heard.

It was entirely unlike anything human.

"I don't know," said the voice. "Shall we find out together?"

Riddle made it only halfway to the bed before the thing that had been Michael Fayne tore both hands loose from the restraints.

Yuki Nitobe screamed.

Riddle screamed.

So did the thing that swarmed off the bed and attacked them.

"HEARTSICK"

&

Scott Nicholson

Never trust a goddamned Injun.

Artus Matheson couldn't make that declaration to the church folk down at Barkersville Baptist, because they proclaimed God loved every color in the rainbow. Like Artus would believe a crock of mule squat such as that. Why, the Mathesons, like most of the Great Smoky Mountain families, had never held slaves. And it wasn't just because they were too poor, or didn't trust outsiders.

And, hell, blacks had even come to the mountains to hide out when they ran away from the plantations on the Coastal Plain. There was even a Mulatto Mountain in Pickett County, where they settled and more or less lived out their days in peace and freedom, as much as anybody could when jobs were scarce and land was the only thing a man could stand on.

But, goddamn, the Injuns.

Never mind that they'd been here first, squatting on those granite ridges and hunting beneath the hardwoods in the silent and golden autumns. The college professors claimed the Injuns didn't even live here year round, because the Cherokee had enough sense to head for the flatlands when the first frost hit.

But professors also claimed that buffalo had once roamed these hills, and that good white hunters like Daniel Boone had followed the herds up here and turned them into steaks and skins. Made it sound like Boone did a bad thing. They even called him "the original tourist." Goddamn professors were about as bad as the Injuns when it came to bitching.

Artus squinted out the window. It was dusk, and he could barely make out the barn on the next farm across the black stretch of pasture. He figured the cows were safe, because he hadn't heard any reports of dead cows, except the one that sorry old Sonny Absher had poached and foisted off as the work of a heart-stealer.

But the heart-stealers apparently had easier meat.

He shouldn't have paid a visit to the McFall barn. That was a nosy thing to do, even if he hadn't seen Delphus McFall in a solid week. But he chalked it off to being a good neighbor, checking up on things.

He'd found the victims in the barn, scattered around in the horse stalls and pig pens like a pack of drugged mules. They had been pale in the lantern light, and it had taken a few seconds for his mind to make sense of what his eyes had seen. They lay on their backs and sides, a couple of them snuffling and moaning, with bloody bandages on their throats.

But the worst horror was in the corn crib, where three men were strung up into a sitting position, their scarred and ragged arms tied above them with a coarse rope. But one of them wasn't tied. No, this one had long, raven-black hair that swayed in greasy tangles as its head worked at the neck of one of the men. It was clearly an Injun, right down to the rough brown skin of those hands that clutched like a butcher making bacon.

The Injun was bent low over one of them, so busy that he didn't notice Artus at first. And then Artus banged the lantern into a locust post, and the Injun lifted its face from its work. Blood trickled from that dark, twisted-up mouth and two long teeth flashed, and the man's neck showed a wide red grin that was in the wrong place.

Artus had run back to the house so fast his boots barely touched the ground. All he could think was that the Injun had been *tending* those blood-stained scarecrows. Like livestock.

And if that goddamn Injun had his way, Artus and his wife Betty Ann were next on the menu.

"You see anything?" Betty Ann asked, and he hated the tremble in her voice. She'd been crocheting a little cap for their granddaughter, but it was busy work and she was making a real mess of it.

"Nah," Artus said. "Maybe he won't come tonight."

"What if he ain't the only one?"

Artus had considered that, which was why he'd left a loaded dou-ble-barreled shotgun propped by the back door. Most of the Injuns had left the area, and the professors made a big deal out of the Trail of Tears, as if anybody was going to cry over a few thousand Cherokee falling down dead. Hell, they'd been dying by the wagonload anyway, and there wasn't enough room for everybody, plain and simple.

But what if it wasn't just Injuns that turned into heart-stealers?

The television was on in the corner, the sound low. They had a wire antenna on top of the house and only got two channels, three if the wind and clouds were right, but Artus figured the same stories were on every channel anyway, even for those rich Florida idiots in town who had one of them silver dishes with four hundred channels.

The talking heads with their New York accents droned on and on in their big words, and it had been going on for days. At first it was just one of those little stories, some guy with a weird infection that they liked to scare everybody with so they'd sell their stocks, or buy their stocks, or whatever the hell the point of scaring people was. Artus had never had any stock except livestock, and with the FDA regulations and the taxes and the high cost of gas to drive them to stockyard in Wilkesboro, he'd whittled his herd down to the few he needed to keep his own freezer packed.

"The news said there was more of them," Artus said. "But that's off in the big city. It's always worse in the city."

"It don't make no sense, what they're saying." She hooked and tucked a length of yellow yarn, and Artus hoped little JoJo never had to wear that cap, because it had holes big enough to let a hummingbird through. Betty Ann wasn't much with her hands.

"Goddamn professors is the problem," Artus said. "Coming on with all these theories when they don't know mule squat from blackberry cobbler."

"I heard one of them say it's an outbreak of some kind," she said. She'd been watching the news nearly nonstop, but Artus could only stomach so much. He'd stayed busy around the farm, mending fence posts and getting ready for fall harvest. Pumpkins and feed corn were getting ready, and the last of the beans and tomatoes needed to be canned, if Betty Ann could get off her easy chair long enough to boil

some water. And potatoes, they laid right there under the ground waiting to be buried, shooting off new roots and getting soft. If he didn't get
them in the root cellar soon, they'd be eating nothing but cabbage all
winter.

"Well, if it's an outbreak, the best place to be is right here," Artus said.

"Maybe we ought to check on the Greenes."

Horace Greene had borrowed Artus's chainsaw two weeks back and
had never returned it. The Greenes were a sorry bloodline, right up
there with the Abshers, and there wasn't any difference between bor-
rowing and stealing if you never brought back the thing you borrowed.
But maybe in a head as addled as Horace's, stealing was okay if you
asked permission first.

"We mind our own business in these parts," Artus said, though the
truth was, he was afraid to walk the fifty yards in the dark to his Ford
pickup in the gravel driveway, and afraid to see what Horace Greene
might have turned into if the heart-stealers got him.

"The president was on TV while you was out in the barn," Betty Ann
said, and Artus finally turned from the window.

"What does that jug-eared son of a bitch got to say about it?" He
trusted the president about as much as he trusted Horace Greene.

"Said we all needed to remain calm, and that he was ordering all
resources put into addressing the issue."

"Addressing the issue? That's what they say when they don't know
a danged thing about what's happening. If it's something they can
fix, they fix it. If it's something else that looks like it ain't got no end in
sight, they call it an 'issue' and jabber about it until the election, and
then they forget all about it."

"Don't think they'll be forgetting this one. Important people are
dying, they say. Saw a TV star had caught it, and died."

"TV star?"

"From one of them reality shows."

"Huh." Artus checked the window again. He could barely make out
the hulking form of the two-story barn, hay in the top, stalls in the bottom, the chickens long gone to roost, those torn-up bags of men laying
around to be harvested.

He shook the image of Billy Standingdeer from his head.

"Well," he said, "Looks like they're fixing to get one hell of a reality
show, if this keeps up."

He glanced at the television, and although the sound was turned down, he could tell it was a live report from somewhere in a city, probably New York. That Japanese woman, the one who seemed to take up most of the news these days, was flapping her pretty lips against a microphone, and some words came up on the bottom of the screen.

Artus had dropped out of school in the ninth grade because he always got the letters backwards, and the teacher would mark what he did wrong and made him fix it, then got mad when he turned it in exactly the same. Well, it had looked fixed to him. Eventually they'd started in with some tests and a special teacher, but by then so many kids were making fun of him—the Abshers were a fine hand at that—he couldn't stand it anymore.

Besides, he'd planned on being a cattleman and a tobacco farmer like his daddy, not knowing the goddamned government would sue the cigarette makers to hell and back and make tobacco almost as illegal as green dope, but growing green dope paid way, way better.

So he couldn't parse out the words on the screen, but Betty Ann read some of them aloud. "Centers for Disease Control," she said, sounding a little smart-alecky because she knew Artus couldn't read. "Atlanta, GA."

"Centers? They need more than one? This must be a hell of a goddamn issue, then."

"The president said this was his top priority and he's putting his best people on it."

The television switched to a picture of a ramrod man in a dark green military uniform and enough brass on his chest to beat into a decent moonshine still. The officer was walking fast, shoulders back, head down, talking to a woman in a dress suit and a white coat. A bunch of people with cameras and microphones swarmed around them, which must have meant the two people were important.

"Well, we're a long way from Washington, so I guess we better take care of this ourselves," Artus said. He was a little ashamed for including Betty Ann in his plan, but he didn't want to admit he was scared.

"Why do you think it's Billy Standingdeer?" she asked.

"He was always going on about that Raven Mocker shit. You remember, the Cherokee legend where the evil spirit shows up at a dying man's house and steals his remaining days. If'n he eats the heart, he gets those days added to his own life."

"Blue Hartley died of natural causes, they said."

"Well, what else would they say? These peckerheads with the county been taking training from the federal government. Lies are contagious, too."

"You know something I don't?"

He didn't want to tell her about seeing Billy Standingdeer feasting on some poor fool in the barn. "When I was in town the other day, I talked to Frankie Fowler at the funeral parlor. Said when they went in to dress Hartley for his viewing, his chest was split open."

"I thought they took all the innards out anyway."

"Yeah, if the innards are still there, that is."

"You think Billy took it? Like he's living out that legend?"

"You know how these Injuns are. They never got over us taking their land. But they weren't using it no way. All they did was hunt and eat roots and such."

"I don't see what they got to complain about. The government set them up with a reservation and they got that shiny casino and everything."

Artus didn't want to talk about that damned casino. They'd driven out to Qualla when it had first opened, and Artus had paid eight dollars for one little glass of whiskey, and then the flashy, noisy machines had swallowed about twenty more dollars before he grabbed Betty Ann's wrist and drove the two hours back to Pickett County.

"Shut up and turn up the TV," he said, glancing out the window to check the barn again. No sign of movement.

Betty Ann groaned as she rose from her chair. She was putting on weight in her old age, and with her arthritis getting worse, Artus wasn't looking forward to the rest of their lives. But he wasn't ready to die, either, and if whatever was eating hearts in Pickett County tried to get in here, Artus had a double helping of twelve-gauge buckshot waiting.

The Japanese television announcer's voice boomed out, and the words had a little fuzz of interference in them. Artus thought she talked pretty good for a Jap, but she looked way too young to be jabbering about something as important as heart-eaters and blood-drinkers running loose.

"—the president has appointed an advisory committee to investigate the apparent mutations, what some are calling a contagious outbreak," she said.

The video cut away to footage of people standing in line in a department store, their arms loaded with goods as they pushed and shoved. "The reports have created a panic in some municipal areas, with people stocking up on batteries, food, and even firearms, despite the president's assurances that the situation is under control," the reporter said over the footage.

"Under control, my ass," Artus muttered. "Frankie said a man over in Whispering Pines was found in the back of a pickup, every ounce of blood drained out of him. I don't know what that Injun was up to in the barn, but it wasn't natural. I don't know what kind of disease does that. Whatever it is, it's here now."

"You think maybe Billy caught it and that's what got him acting crazy? Maybe if he has the fever, he started believing in the old legends."

"And come to revenge his ancestors? I don't reckon."

"According to sources, some bodies have been found in groups, suggesting the killers are somehow herding or confining their victims. Genetic mutations could lead to such predatory behavior." The Jap reporter was still rattling off a bunch of big words, which Artus ignored, because something clattered on the roof.

"Did you hear that?" Betty Ann asked.

"Shhh," Artus hissed. Betty Ann had made it through high school but sometimes she was dumb as a hitching post.

The Jap reporter started yapping faster. "The infection has been referred to as the 'vampire virus' because of the potential mutations—"

Artus grabbed his shotgun with one hand, scrambled across the room on his creaky knees, and punched the television knob so that the house fell silent. He strained his ears against the night, and a soft wind pushed the tree branches around, but other than that, he couldn't hear anything except the pounding of his own pulse against his eardrums.

Then came a shriek that might have been a high howling wind. Or maybe a giant raven cutting through the air.

"Do you think it's him?" Betty Ann whispered.

"Well, the Raven Mocker is a raven, ain't it?" he sneered, but he knew it was fear that made him angry. "And a raven is a bird. And a bird can fly."

"But the TV called them vampires—"

"Vampires ain't real. Any fool knows that."

Vampires, maybe not, but Raven Mockers...who knows?

Tin crimped and crumpled high overhead.

He didn't want to think about Billy Standingdeer walking around on the roof. Artus was pretty sure that people with the disease couldn't grow wings and fly. But there was a big oak tree that grew right beside the house, and a crazed Injun could scramble right up, shinny out on a branch, and drop down onto the house. Artus shook away the image of the young Cherokee perched there on the branch, long black hair swaying in the breeze as he peered into the lighted windows.

While Artus crept to the foot of the stairs, Betty Ann went to the window, clutching the little scrap of knitting. Something *thunked* on the roof, a metallic ripple that reached deep into Artus's bones.

"They's something moving out there," Betty Ann said.

Artus paused with one boot on the stairs. "It's just Billy."

"I thought you said Billy's on the roof."

"Yeah, and Billy's the only one of them. If he's on the roof, there can't be nothing out there. So shut your mouth."

"You heard the TV. They said it was spreading."

"It's only spreading in the city, where people are all piled up on top of one another."

She hadn't turned around yet. "Well, something sure is moving out by McFall's barn."

Artus wondered if Billy would be able to hook down off the eaves and sling himself in through one of the upstairs windows. He strained his ears for footsteps, and there they were—just over the boys' bedroom, unoccupied since they'd grown and moved away, nothing in there but some cardboard boxes and a few clothes in the closet. The window would likely be open, circulating air to fight off the autumn dampness.

Artus was about to head on up to the hall, planning to wait just outside the bedroom door, when he heard the second set of feet on the tin.

"A couple more in the cornfield," Betty Ann said, with a strange calmness, like she was watching television. "Ravens like corn, don't they?"

Artus didn't tolerate an uppity wife, but at the moment he was too distracted by these goddamned Injuns trying to get in the house. It wasn't his fault Daniel Boone and his ilk had taken over the mountains and driven the Cherokee west. And he'd never held a personal grudge against any of them, as long as they kept to their hardscrabble corner of the county.

But the Standingdeers didn't.

Billy Standingdeer had dated an Aldridge woman, and although the Aldridge family had fallen from grace since Prohibition and the days of moonshine, they were still white and local, two traits that people didn't like to see mixed with Cherokee blood. And a couple of his brothers had even taken a notion to enroll at the community college.

But they still held to their native customs, at least during the annual Trade Days, when the county historical association set up a festival in Melvin Eggers' cow pasture and brought the past alive. Some Cherokee dressed in their buckskins and feathers, performing rain dances for ten bucks an hour, and Billy Standingdeer was among them.

The festival also included storytelling, which was where Artus and Betty Ann had heard the Raven Mocker legend. It had been told by Granny Standingdeer herself, who looked old enough to have been cutting teeth while the world was born. Not that she had any teeth left now.

Legend or no legend, Artus didn't take kindly to people traipsing around on his roof. And whatever the Injun had been up to out in the McFall barn, that didn't mean any of those others had turned.

"Are they coming any closer?" he said, reluctant now to make the journey up the stairs. Even with the shotgun, he didn't feel so confident.

"One of them's down by the fence," she said. "I can see the porch light reflected in his eyes."

Artus kept a pistol in the bedside table, but it was upstairs. He had a .22 in the hall closet for hunting squirrels, and he'd shown Betty Ann how to point and shoot it, even though she didn't have much knack for marksmanship. Still, until he figured out what they were dealing with, a little extra firepower probably wouldn't hurt.

"Get the rifle out of the closet," he said, moving a few steps up the stairs. "Bullets are on the top shelf. You remember how to load it."

"I ain't shooting nobody," she said.

"It's just Injuns," he said.

"They're still coming."

"Would you shoot if they was vampires?" he said, taking another two slow steps up the stairs.

"Depends on if they was trying to drink my blood."

"And the Raven Mocker will eat your heart. Amounts to the same thing."

She was moving now. He couldn't see her, because he was near the top of the stairs, but he heard the closet door squeak open. The two pairs of feet above danced their metallic hoedown across the tin.

Artus reached the landing and tried the light switch. The government had cut the phone service but at least the power was still on. He wasn't sure whether the infection was the work of the government. He couldn't see the sense of it, unless they were just trying to scare honest taxpayers. But he had a feeling old Billy Standingdeer didn't give a hoot about taxes.

The door to the boys' room was ten feet straight ahead. The footsteps on the roof had stopped, but the wind had picked up, making it difficult to hear any unusual noises as the house creaked and groaned.

"You okay, honey?" he whispered down the stairs.

"Never been better," she said.

It was the same thing she'd said on their honeymoon, after he'd made an awful mess of things and she'd cried a little.

"Any more of them out there?"

"Sky's black as tar," she said. "If they's any ravens flying around up there, I can't see them."

Artus couldn't tell if she was joshing him or not. She didn't seem as scared as he was. But she hadn't seen Billy Standingdeer in the barn, grinning like a crazed fool and looking like he enjoyed the taste of the blood on his lips. And those eyes, with their red fire glinting in the lantern light...

Screw Billy and his whole heart-stealing tribe. I got a little twelve-gauge peace pipe for him right here.

Artus tiptoed down the hall, his heart hammering. He tried not to think of what that Jap on the TV had said about vampires.

If he's a vampire, don't you need silver bullets or sharpened wooden crosses or something?

But he didn't believe in vampires. Here in the Southern Appalachians, the Raven Mocker was the thing you had to worry about. That and the government.

The door was in front of him. Unlocked. All he had to do was reach out and turn the handle.

But he couldn't do it.

He heard more footsteps, but even over the noise of the wind in the trees, these didn't sound like they were walking across tin. No, they sounded like they were walking on *wood*.

The door rattled in its frame.

Gotta be the wind. The window must be open.

Then the doorknob turned, and it seemed like the house shivered a little against the autumn breeze.

He couldn't even turn, much less run, and his legs felt like knotty locust posts sunk in rocky soil. The shotgun grew heavy in his hands, and his lungs were dry and tight. His heart pushed frantically against his scrawny ribs.

The door swung inwards and the widening crack revealed only darkness.

He tried to recall Granny Standingdeer's stories from Trade Days, because there was a way to defeat the Raven Mocker. She said only medicine men could kill them, but what else did he expect her to say? A white man with a law degree?

But didn't a shotgun count as medicine? Artus would take the weapon over mumbo jumbo and owl feathers.

Granny said the Raven Mocker came to the house of the weak and stole their remaining days by stealing the heart. Artus, with his high blood pressure and diabetes, didn't think he had all that many years left, but he sure as hell wasn't going to give them up without a fight.

The door swung open another inch, and the house shook with a sudden surge of wind. Shutters flapped and a loose piece of tin spawned a rusty scream.

He wondered if the things outside—Raven Mockers, vampires, or just plain old Injuns—were moving closer, and if Betty Ann had the gumption to fend them off if they got too close. He didn't think so. Having a mousy wife had been fun in the beginning, when he laid down the law and she followed or got a quick rap to the kidneys if she needed a lesson. In a way, women were like Injuns, always wanting a little more than they were due, or else expecting equal treatment when they surely didn't deserve it.

But this one coming out of the bedroom was going to learn his place, or get blown back to hell.

The door opened another couple of inches, and Artus lifted the barrel of the shotgun. It seemed heavier, and his heart thudded and spasmed in his chest. He took a deep breath to steady his hand but it didn't work.

With the October night ripping itself to life, as if the mountains had opened and let loose the old gods, the floor shook beneath Artus's boots. The lights flickered, and his heart skipped a beat.

If the goddamned government decides to cut the power—

His finger tightened against the twin triggers. If the place went dark, he was letting loose with a bee's-nest worth of buckshot, and whatever was behind the door would be spattered across the room like a busted bag of soup.

The door opened six inches and a hand appeared, the reddish-brown fingers appearing ordinary aside from the black dirt under the scabby nails.

Do it, you old fool. Shoot.

But part of him was curious, wanted to see what the Injun had become. After the encounter in the barn, Artus now had a hard time believing what he'd really seen. Maybe it was just a bunch of migrant Mexicans from the Christmas tree farms, passed out from cheap wine and wacky weed. And maybe Billy Standingdeer was their drug dealer, dishing out powders from his medicine bag.

But that didn't explain the blood.

Artus felt the cold, firm nudge to his back just as the door swung open wide. The pain in his kidney rivaled the one in his chest, and the shotgun felt as if it were a soggy old piece of oak timber, heavy and useless.

And Billy stood there, pupils black as a bird's but the sclera shot through with scarlet, and his mouth was cracked into the crooked wedge of a smile. And there was them two long teeth again.

But Artus couldn't focus, because of the thing jabbing him in the back. As mesmerizing as Billy's appearance was, Artus turned his withered neck to glance behind him.

Betty Ann was pressing the .22 against him, her face set in a grim line. He'd never noticed before, but she had blue eyes, and they seemed cold as deep winter and hard as graveyard ice.

"Buh-Betty?" he murmured, confused. He shifted his gaze back to Billy Standingdeer, whose skin seemed to darken even as he stepped into the light of the hallway. But it was his eyes that were the creepiest, the sockets filled with purest black and red, not a sliver of white showing.

Raise the gun, you old fool—

But his arms were like damp ropes, and he couldn't even get it high enough to blow off Billy's kneecaps and stop him in his tracks.

"Shoot him," he grunted, hoping Betty Ann had more strength and willpower than he did, even though he'd always been the protector. The man of the house. The one who laid down the law.

Instead, she gave him another jab in the kidney. "Drop it," she said, and her voice was steady and clear even though the walls still shook around them.

"What?" Artus whispered, and the sap seemed to run out of his legs and he eased himself against the wall. The tip of the shotgun *thunked* against the floor, and he tried to make sense of the fire that had sparked itself to life behind his rib cage.

He sagged and slid down the wall until he was in a sitting position, fighting to catch his breath. Billy eased down the hall, his feet making no sound now, almost like he was gliding on a carpet of air.

Like a raven...

Artus looked up at Betty Ann, and she was pointing the .22 at his face, and she held the rifle as if she knew her way around it. Like maybe she'd been practicing behind his back.

Behind my back... that would be funny if I didn't hurt so damned much...

A noise on the stairs drew him out of his suffering long enough to see the others. One of the Standingdeer brothers, and a couple of other Injuns he didn't recognize. They had that same solid blackness to their eyeballs, like marbles that had been rolled from the deepest corner of the ancient night.

"He's all yours," Betty Ann yelled, and she wasn't talking to Artus.

Artus let the shotgun fall across his lap. The thoughts swirled as Billy and the others closed in:

The red-hot spike that had been yanked fresh from the forge and driven deep in his chest...

The pursed lips of Billy Standingdeer's grin, which made his mouth resemble a dark beak...

Betty Ann's face as calm as he'd ever seen it, and he wondered if he'd ever actually *looked* at her in their forty years of marriage...

But most of all, he remembered that Jap reporter talking about vampires, and he decided he was glad these things were Raven Mockers instead, because he sure as hell didn't want to die and come back as a goddamned blood-sucking Injun. Or worse, be kept around in a pen for the filthy redskin to feed on whenever he took a craving.

And then Billy was reaching for Artus's chest, for his wasted, flaming heart, and he wondered how they all would divide up his years they had stolen, and whether they'd get Betty Ann's years next.

The other Injuns huddled around, waiting their turn, with Betty Ann stepping aside to make room for them.

But just before the first heart-stealer reached inside, he decided Betty Ann had a lot of years left, and they might be the best years of her life.

While the rest of *his* life...

...didn't last long.

$$\text{\reflectbox{M}M}$$

"JUNK" PT.6

Jonathan Maberry

– 25 –
October 12, 10:33 p.m.
Bellevue Hospital
Zero Days until the V-Event

Luther Swann sank into one of the leather guest chairs in Dr. Feldman's office. Schmidt remained standing, hands in pockets, shoulder resting against a crammed bookshelf.

Alice Feldman had a thick folder open on her desk.

"We may have something," said Feldman. Her face was clean of all traces of blood, but she was very pale. Swann wondered how much of that was the result of blood loss and how much was because of everything that had happened. She tapped the file with her fingernail. "These are Michael Fayne's medical records. I had them faxed over from Presbyterian Hospital. Fayne was admitted there last March and spent two days being treated for acute dehydration and fever that were the result of a virus."

"Which virus?" asked Swann.

"I1V1."

"The ice virus?" blurted Schmidt? "I thought that was all a big nothing."

Feldman pursed her lips. "What do you know about it?"

"What everyone else knows," said Swann. "The news said that it was something released from melting ice caps. An ancient virus. It spread fast and a lot of people got sick—"

"But no one died," added Schmidt.

"—and then it kind of went away," Swann concluded.

"That's the oversimplified version," agreed Feldman. "I1V1 is one of many new—or, to be more precise, 'old'—viruses and bacteria that have been introduced to our modern biosphere by the melting of the ice caps. When it presented, there was a great deal of concern in the medical community, especially in the early days before we identified the source of the virus. Naturally, there was a fear that it was a bioengineered virus."

"Why?"

"Probably because it came out of nowhere," suggested Swann, "and didn't resemble anything currently going around."

Feldman nodded approval. "Like H1N1 in 2009, there was a sudden fear of a global pandemic. Every day there is a tremendous movement of populations around the world."

"Planes, trains and automobiles," said Schmidt.

"Global transportation is what helped the Spanish Flu to spread beyond control in 1918. Most major plagues that became pandemics can be tied to migration or transportation." Feldman placed her hand on the file. "And I1V1 cases turned up everywhere, on every continent. I did a check after reading Fayne's file and the estimated number of infected worldwide is a much larger number than ever made the news." She paused. "A conservative estimate by the World Health Organization is that twenty-eight percent of the human population experienced some symptoms consistent with this virus."

"Holy God," said Swann.

"The Centers for Disease Control put the estimate closer to fifty percent."

"But nobody died," insisted Schmidt.

"Most people experienced only very minor symptoms. The sniffles, a headache, that sort of thing," said Feldman. "But people *did* die, detective. Granted, most of those cases were in third world areas and related to the symptom of dehydration. What matters most, however, is that there are secondary effects to most diseases, and the CDC and WHO have been tracking them."

"What kind of secondary effects?" asked Swann.

"Genetic disorders," she said. "Specifically, the emergence of genetic disorders that had previously been dormant in the patients prior to the onset of I1V1. Many people carry the genetic potential for a variety of diseases, but these are inactive. Not everyone with the potential for Parkinson's or Sickle Cell or other disorders becomes victims of those diseases. You can see that in every family. We talk about traits 'skipping a generation,' which is a nonmedical way of saying that although the genetic potential is present, the gene has not actively coded for the symptoms. Am I making sense?"

"Yes," said Swann.

"Kind of," said Schmidt. "Pretend for a minute that I'm a cop, not a scientist."

She gave him a tolerant, almost pitying smile. "We have to look at the possibility that Professor Swann is correct in that vampirism may be a phenomenon that belongs to our complex evolutionary family tree. If we can strip away the more sensational and irrational elements of the vampire story, we can probably make a list of symptoms that are possible, even within our current understanding of human genetics. It may be that the potential for vampirism is in all human DNA."

"Junk," said Swann.

"Exactly," said Feldman.

"What?" asked Schmidt.

"In genetics," explained Feldman, "there are significant portions of the human genome sequence for which no discernible function has been identified. Junk DNA. That's a term coined in 1972 by Susumu Ohno, a noted geneticist and evolutionary biologist, and one of the seminal researchers in the field of molecular evolution. These noncoding DNA are components of DNA that do not encode for protein sequences. Recent genetic studies have determined that much of this 'junk' actually does serve biological functions, including the transcriptional and translational regulation of protein-coding sequences. With time we'll understand all of this, but there is much we don't know. Research indicates that many junk DNA sequences probably have unidentified functional activity, and others may have had functions in the past. And some may be entirely nonfunctional."

"Maybe," said Swann.

Feldman nodded. "Even those apparently inert genes are never discounted in science. Genetics, for all of its advances, is still a young science."

"How's the ice virus play into this?" asked Schmidt.

"Viruses have been known to affect genes in a variety of ways," Feldman told him. "Sometimes even in positive ways."

"But Fayne's not the only person to get sick with the ice flu," said Schmidt.

Feldman again tapped the medical records. "No, but there is something very significant here. Mr. Fayne is an actor and one of the movies he made was filmed in Alaska. He was among the first fifty people to present at a hospital in North America with symptoms of I1V1, and he was one of six whose symptoms were severe enough to warrant admission and observation. For now he is the index patient, the person around whom the research and any resulting science will be based."

"Patient zero," said Swann, and Feldman gave a short, reluctant nod.

"Does that mean that Fayne's behavior, his actions, and his blackouts are all symptoms of a disease?" asked Schmidt.

"Possibly," said Feldman. "And, before you ask, we're shooting in the dark here, so until we have completed an exhaustive series of tests, 'possibly' is as far as I'll go."

"Can we treat him in some way?" Schmidt asked. "Give him something to dial down the, um…outbursts?"

"Too soon to know that," said Swann, and Feldman nodded agreement.

"We're at the very beginning of this, gentlemen," she said. "We have no idea how Fayne will react to even ordinary drugs like over-the-counter painkillers. If he becomes violent again in ways that are a danger to himself and others, we may attempt to narcotize him, but even then I would hesitate before committing to any kind of treatment. This is an entirely unknown disorder—if it's even a disorder. What alarms me the most is how well developed Fayne's symptoms are. Genetic traits don't suddenly appear. This has been happening to him for a while now. Weeks at least, probably months. That isn't good news because it opens the door to so much speculation."

They sat in silence with that floating in the air between them.

Swann knew that everyone was probably thinking the same thoughts, and they were bad thoughts. Dangerous thoughts.

It was Schmidt who put them out there.

"If Fayne is patient zero," he asked, "does that mean that there will be more like him?"

Feldman opened her mouth to answer, but the door to her office suddenly banged open. Riddle stood there, one hand on the doorknob, one hand clutched to his own throat.

To what was left of his throat.

Riddle's mouth worked as he tried to speak a word. A name.

But that throat was no longer constructed for speech.

Blood spurted from between his fingers.

Feldman screamed. Swann screamed, too.

Schmidt yelled with sudden fear and anger as he yanked up his cuff and tore the thirty-two caliber throwaway pistol from the nylon holster. He racked the slide and brought it up just as Riddle's legs buckled.

"Fayne!" yelled Swann.

And then they rushed into the hall, and into hell.

– 26 –

October 12, 10:45 p.m.
Bellevue Hospital
Zero Days until the V-Event

"Stay back," ordered Schmidt, but Swann was right at his heels. Swann didn't want to be there, he wanted to flee, to find some place to hide, but his body would not listen to the cringing pleas of his mind. He pelted down the hallway after the detective.

Alarms began blaring overhead. People ran, people screamed.

In the private rooms the patients howled like dogs.

There was a long, crooked trail of blood leading all the way back to Fayne's room. Doctors and nurses crouched against the walls, many of them spattered with red.

As they wheeled around the corner, Schmidt tripped and fell over a body that lay sprawled on the floor. A nurse. Her head was canted obscenely to one side and there was a red ruin where her trachea should have been. Her eyes stared at the ceiling and even as Swann dropped to his knees beside her, he knew that there was nothing he could do.

Schmidt was on his knees, his pistol in one hand and a cell phone in the other. He shouted into the phone, calling for backup. Calling for SWAT.

God almighty, thought Swann as he reached out to close the nurse's eyes. They always did that in the movies. His fingers brushed the lids, but even though they rolled down, the lids popped open again as soon as he let go. He withdrew his hand like he'd been stung.

Down the hall, all of the doors were open. Some of the patients peered out. Most looked absolutely terrified. A few were laughing.

One pointed to a set of double doors that led to another wing.

"It went in there," said the patient in a voice that was small and fractured.

It, thought Swann. Not "he."

The patient said, "It had a girl. It dragged her in there."

God.

Schmidt shoved his phone back into his pocket, clambered to his feet and hurried to the double doors. They were closed, but there was a small Plexiglas window. Schmidt did a quick-look through the window and ducked back as if expecting to be shot at.

"Can you see him?" whispered Swann.

"No." Schmidt was sweating and he held his little automatic with two powerful hands. Those hands trembled.

"How long until your backup arrives?"

There was a single piercing scream from beyond the doors. A woman's scream. High and shrill and filled with more terror than Swann had ever heard in a human voice.

"Too fucking long," growled Schmidt, and he wheeled around, kicked open the doors and ran into the hall. Swann bounded up and got to the door just as he heard the first shot.

The sound was followed almost instantly by another scream. A man's this time.

It was not Fayne's voice.

It was Schmidt's.

There was no second shot.

In the distance, even with the blaring alarms, Luther Swann could hear the sound of sirens approaching and, even louder, the thunder of his own beating heart.

–27–

October 12, 10:51 p.m.
Bellevue Hospital
Zero Days until the V-Event

It took all of Swann's courage to approach those double doors and peer through the window.

He saw three things. Three figures.

He saw a woman. Asian, pretty, terrified beyond the capacity to move. She cowered on the floor. Her clothes were covered with blood, but Swann could not tell if any of it was her own.

He saw Jerry Schmidt, lying sprawled, bent backward over a gurney, his automatic hooked uselessly on one twitching finger of his out-stretched right hand. His body trembled and his legs jerked with invol-untary spasms as his body tumbled through pain and into a terminal shock.

And he saw Michael Fayne. Or, the thing that had *been* Michael Fayne, bent over and tearing at the detective's throat with savage teeth.

There was blood everywhere.

It was the defining characteristic of the tableau.

Blood.

Blood and death.

Fayne suddenly raised his head and stared down the hallway, through the little window, right into Swann's eyes. He raised his drip-ping mouth from the dying detective.

And he smiled.

If there was anything human left in the man, Swann could not see it. Not in that smile.

All he saw was a monster.

All he saw was a vampire.

The vampire spoke a single word as his fingers caressed the ragged, pumping veins.

"Mine."

He stood, frozen to the spot, frozen into the moment, trapped by the power of those black-within-black eyes

Swann could not tear his own eyes away. He was helpless, lost in this new reality. He stared at the monster, at the thing he had spent his life studying. The thing he had sometimes secretly wished was real. The thing he had lauded and written about and aggrandized and devoted his life to. No longer a thing of myth and legend. No longer a creature of film or fiction.

Real.

Here.

Now.

"God…"

Schmidt's words from just a few minutes ago replayed in his head with dreadful clarity.

If Fayne is patient zero, does that mean that there will be more like him?

He was still standing there when big men in black body armor and automatic rifles came barging out of the stairwells. He made no protest as they pulled him aside and shouldered past him. He was dazed, numb, horrified beyond speech or action. One of the officers pushed him to the floor and he went down without resistance and did not argue or speak even a single word when the roar of gunfire filled the air, drowning out all other sounds.

— 28 —

Secaucus, NJ

Now

The V-Event plus Twenty-six Days

Luther Swann picked up the phone on the fifth ring. The phone had been ringing off and on for weeks. He knew that he should probably change his number. Or maybe throw the damn thing away.

But he recognized the screen display.

"Hello," he said quietly.

"Luther…?"

"Alice? How are you?"

"Oh, god, Luther," said Dr. Feldman in a tiny voice. "Where are you?"

"I'm in Los Angeles," he said. "Following up reports. So far…nothing."

"No," she said urgently. "Turn on the news. God, Luther…Detroit. Mexico City. Cairo…."

"What…what do you mean?"

Feldman was sobbing. "It's everywhere, Luther. Oh my God…it's *everywhere.*"

"ROADKILL" PT.2

Nancy Holder

— 8 —

Rampage. Thompson didn't get his full patch for killing Moncho, because he didn't tell anyone that Moncho had returned, seemingly from the dead, and that he'd been a vampire. No seemingly about that. He didn't tell Bobby because Bobby had started seeing vampires everywhere—behind the counter in the liquor store; driving the school bus; sitting in one of the seats on the school bus. Bobby saw them flying across the moon at night. Bobby heard them sucking out the blood of the town's few remaining cattle and chickens.

It didn't take special training in nonverbal communication to know that Bobby was losing his shit.

Luther Swann kept insisting that vampires didn't fly. Bobby said he'd seen a wedge of them flying over his house, like geese flying south for the winter. No one contradicted Bobby.

But they did trade looks.

In the middle of the night, Bobby would burst out of the house in a pair of jeans, brandishing a semi-automatic, and paint the night with starbursts of live ammunition. One night he killed a cat. Another night, he killed an old man.

He insisted the old man had been a vampire. He said the Mendozas came up to the windows at night and taunted him, promising to steal their own children so that they could turn them into vampires and be together again forever. And he went out there to cut them in half and instead, the old man died.

No one else saw the Mendozas. If Little Sister and Manuel overheard Bobby's raving in the middle of the night, they didn't show it. Or maybe they had forgotten that the vampires he was talking about had once been their parents. More crosses went up on the turquoise door and the walls of the Morrisey home. But Yuki Nitobe had explained that crosses didn't serve as deterrents against vampires. Bobby said they did.

As the months went by, Little Sister stuck to Walker, which upset "Manny" no end. Thompson understood why. No one had adopted him with any special affection. Manuel went through weeks where he clung to his sister day and night. Then he'd ignore her completely, making a show of hanging out with the O.M.s. Thompson could see a one-percenter in the making, but he stayed well away. Manuel was not the mission.

Little Sister had a birthday—sweet sixteen—and all her uncles gave her presents, mostly jewelry, and some makeup in the original packaging, which meant that it had probably been stolen because outlaws stole things. Thompson refrained from pointing out that in Latin cultures, fifteen was the big birthday for girls. Their *quinceñera*. She layered on her treasures and strutted around in a cropped T-shirt and low-slung cutoff jeans, practically in her own original packaging, but no one came near her. Maybe Walker had staked his claim. If that were the case, in the old days, she would have a tattoo somewhere prominent that read *"Property of my Old Man Walker"* by now. Now it was nearly three day's ride to get to a decent tattoo parlor.

Walker himself kept dozing off during the day and when he was awake, he was silent. He was haggard and gaunt. Thompson walked to the compound from 12 Vega a few times, keeping to the shadows, confirming his suspicion that Walker was staying up all night, every night, maybe in hopes of seeing the Mendozas or maybe trying to stop Bobby from shooting unsuspecting passers-by. Walker was very troubled. The vampire that was feeding off Walker Morrisey was the vampire of stress.

When they went into town, Bobby bought lots of coffee. For Walker, he said, but Walker said, "You drink more than I do."

"Only in the morning. You're a fucking addict," Bobby said.

Thompson got a reputation for hard drinking because he went to the Shaft as often as possible. He worked there to make money, washing glasses and cooking meth. For a while he also went to contact his handler. His handler kept promising an extraction. *Sit tight. Sit tight. Somebody will get in touch with you.*

Sit on this.

Thompson stopped placing the calls.

– 9 –

"He's a vampire. Anybody can see that," Bobby yelled at the TV in the O.M. bar.

Thompson, Bobby, Fug, and Walker were watching the primetime show, *Freedom Fighters*. It was set in World War II, because that that was the last war where people could express their patriotism without getting smacked down for it. Even with the world simmering in hellfire, if you said the wrong thing in public about the president or vampires or mutations, you might get a little visit from Homeland Security. Unless, of course, you lived in a place like Sonrisa. Sonrisa got little visits of another stripe—"relatives" of the locals, who were really people escaping over the Mexican border. People who had not gotten the memo that Bobby Morrisey was the mad emperor of Sonrisa. Bobby, who waited until they tried to sneak back out of town. Then Bobby and the O.M.s roared after them in the desert, killed them. They died easily.

They died more easily than Moncho, even if you counted Moncho's headshot wound as a simple graze. These desperate people died like ordinary people. So far, Thompson had gotten away with aiming wide. He hadn't killed anyone. Walker had gotten away with aiming wide, too, which Thompson knew by observing him. No one could keep score of the kills, although they tried. The others bragged, counted coup. Walker mostly looked down, then excused himself to check on Little Sister and Manuel. The kids were not allowed at O.M. club meetings, or murderous romps in the desert.

At the Shaft, the actor on the screen gave a speech about the dream that was America and the O.M.s immediately threw back their shots. Bobby and Fug hooted like apes. Walker looked drunk and tired, and Thompson maintained his cool detachment. It was a drinking game to go with the show—a belt every time someone said "America" or "these United States," and a shot for the death of every Nazi, French collaborator, or beautiful Japanese propaganda slinger. The rules of the game were updated on the Internet, and somehow, Bobby kept current on them.

They still went to the post office box, and Bobby still retrieved his mystery deliveries. Thompson still didn't know what was in them, but he was beginning to suspect it was LSD or some kind of other hallucinogenic. Because Bobby was going off the deep end in a big way.

"That actor, he's a vampire," Bobby said again, and the scattering of patrons in the bar nodded. "Those Hollywood liberals protect them. *Tolerate* them."

"Fuckin' A, Bobby," a grizzled old man said at the other end of the bar. "Bodie, give Bobby a drink on me."

"Tequila," Bobby said, grinning over at the man.

Thompson pondered the amount of alcohol being shipped to Sonrisa. He watched trucks come in with booze, food, and other supplies; the town's single trash truck chugging around on trash day; the school bus lighting out each school day. The wheels of civilization went round and round. Infrastructure had not yet uniformly shattered in the U.S. the way it had in Mexico.

The way it so had in Mexico.

The four O.M.s were waiting for Monster, Poison, and Johnny Rocket to come back from the hunt. The O.M.s were the real vampires of Sonrisa, flying over the sand in their trucks; running illegals to ground; swooping after the vans and SUVs of *coyotes* who still dared cross the vast, uninhabited wastelands to transport their human cargo. Maybe the *coyotes* and wetbacks had heard of the Ocotillo Militia, and maybe they figured, *Orale, chinga*, there were only seven of those biker guys in a huge desert.

Seven biker guys with trucks and guns, and plenty of food and water. Even Walker gave up saying prayers over all the people Bobby shot. Bodie put the tequila shot on the pitted wooden bar. Bobby tore his gaze from the flat screen to pluck it up, and in doing so, glanced at Bodie. Bobby froze with the shot glass halfway to his mouth. Bobby's eyes narrowed, studying the bartender, his crow's feet causing deep furrows that reminded Thompson of the Bog Man of Mexico. Thompson felt the sudden tension flare up around his president like a wall of flame.

Bodie didn't notice. He was watching the TV, cheering with the others when one of the Freedom Fighters garroted a Nazi. Then he moved away, whistling the *Freedom Fighters* theme song as he lined up shots for the drinking game.

"Oh, Christ, they got Bodie. They got to him," Bobby slurred under his breath. His hand went to his quick-draw pocket, where he kept his .38.

Walker jerked his attention away from the TV and looked at his brother. He traced Bobby's line of vision. Bodie was clearly in Bobby's sights. Walker ticked his glance toward Thompson. Thompson looked steadily back.

"They got Bodie." Bobby's lips were rubbery from all the alcohol.

Thompson had learned not to underestimate him when he was drunk. Thompson stayed quiet, focused. Walker was fighting to do the same.

"They turned him into a fuckin' vampire," he went on. His hand wrapped on the .38 and he began to pull it out of its holster.

"No, Bodie's okay," Walker said.

Thompson tried to warn him off with a headshake. After all this time, you'd think Walker would know better than to argue with his brother when he was wasted.

Bobby's head whipped toward Walker. He drew his lips back, showing his teeth in utter rage, like a pit bull. Thompson watched Walker's spine straighten. Fight or flight.

Stand down, Thompson thought, wishing there was such a thing as ESP. *Shut the hell up.*

"The hell?" Bobby said finally. "Look in the mirror behind the bar. Tell me what you see." He swung his head at Thompson. "You, too."

Thompson complied. First he saw the crack he had made when he'd thrown the empty tequila bottle over a year ago. Then he saw Bodie's face as he capped the tequila bottle—untroubled, older, not unusual.

"You can see it," Bobby insisted. "You can see his eyes glowing."

"No, Bobby," Walker said, glancing again at Thompson. "He's fine." He pursed his lips. "Tell him, Thompson."

Don't you dare try to throw me under this bus, Thompson thought. Where adrenaline should have rushed in, Thompson just felt tired. He probably deserved this.

Bobby's head bobbed in Thompson's direction. "You want your full patch?"

Walker and Fug both stared at Bobby. Fug remained inscrutable. Walker was freaking. Thompson kept loose, same as in the desert, same as when he had killed Moncho. In a motorcycle club, if your president told you to do something, you did it. Or else he wasn't your president.

"It's not the old days," Bobby said to Thompson. "Recruit like you, you can't just leave."

My bike says I can, Thompson thought, but thanks to his government education, he kept his features neutral. He had done all these equations in his head. He had a mental big wheel with everyone's name on it that he could possibly think of, and he gave it several spins a day: What if Bobby decided Father Patrick was a vampire? What if he went after Johnny Rocket? Or Manuel? Or Little Sister?

"He's probably bleeding into our drinks," Bobby said, "to turn us."

"Vampirism is not contagious," Luther Swann had assured the public, over and over and over. *"You can't catch it, and no one can give it to you."*

But vampires could kill people. They did kill people. In the past six months, there had been seven deaths in Sonrisa, not counting the people Bobby had killed out in the desert, not counting the old man he had shot by accident while he was trying to gun down the Mendozas. The community had fragmented into clusters of gossip. The little medical clinic was gone, so no one could pronounce cause of death. Dehydration, an accident with a chainsaw, a heart attack. Straight up blood loss. Others started looking funny at the Ocotillo Militia. Who the fuck needed to use a chain saw in Sonrisa?

"You have to kill him," Bobby said to Thompson in a low voice. "If you don't kill him, you're not an O.M., and there's nowhere for you to go."

My bike says there is, but it would be six against one in the deep damn desert and for all he knew, Bobby had jimmied his brakes or punched a hole in his gas tank. There was the Uzi.

"I'll do it if you tell me to," Thompson said steadily, "but maybe I should watch him. He may have turned other people. Or we can find out who turned him." He cocked his head as if the thought had just occurred to him, but he had practiced this contingency a dozen times in front of the mirror in Moncho's bathroom.

Bobby swayed on the barstool. "You can torture it out of him. Shove a cross down his throat. Make him eat garlic 'til his guts dissolve."

Neither of those things affected vampires. It was a mutation. It was just DNA. It wasn't Bram Stoker or *Vampire Diaries*. Bobby said Swann and that reporter bitch Nitobe and all the people in authority were lying to people to save themselves. That they had made a deal with the vampires—throw them the little people and live to lie another day.

"Make him tell you who they are," Bobby said, pushing off his bar stool with his .38 in his hand. He aimed it at Thompson. "*Now.*"

"Bobby, no," Walker said.

Behind the bar, Bodie stood stock-still and the other patrons fell silent. Fugly stood behind Bobby with his own hand inside his own vest. Thompson had a crazy hope that Fug meant to shoot Bobby in the back if things got out of hand.

But Thompson doubted that was Fug's intention.

"Guys, are things straight up?" Bodie asked with a quaver in his voice. He obviously hadn't heard a word, had no idea the confrontation was over him.

Three motorcycles blared outside. Bobby's eyes glazed over as he lowered the .38 to his side and looked expectantly at the door to the Shaft. Soon there was laughter, the heavy clopping of biker boots. Johnny Rocket burst in first, and he was grinning. Good hunting in the desert tonight.

"We got one!" Johnny shouted. A cheer rose up. "We shot him. And we brought him home!"

"What the hell?" Walker said.

"We've got him outside. Says he's Bodie's brother," Johnny Rocket declared. Everyone looked at Bodie. The man went white and put down the shot glass he had been drying with a towel.

"I have a brother," he said. "His name is Stan."

He moved around the bar and headed for the door. Bobby followed him out, the other O.M.s falling into line, and then everybody in the bar filed behind them. Beneath the moonlight, a bound man with light brown hair was kneeling with his head bowed in the trash-strewn parking lot of the Shaft. What was left of the blacktop looked like large-sized pieces of gravel. Monster and Poison stood on either side of the kneeling figure.

"Stan?" Bodie shouted.

Monster reached down and slid his fingers through his prisoner's hair. He yanked back the man's head, revealing a face that clearly resembled Bodie's. A groan of pain escaped the man's throat. He was wearing a denim jacket that was drenched in blood. There was so much blood that he should have died by then, if the blood was his.

"Oh, my God. What did you do to him?" Bodie cried.

The bar patrons gathered around in a circle as Bodie tried to run to the man—to Stan—but Johnny Rocket restrained him, grabbing his arms and holding him back. Bodie struggled in Johnny's grasp.

"Let me go! He's hurt," Bodie yelled.

Monster tugged harder and Stan grimaced, revealing the sharp canines of a vampire. The crowd gasped and drew back. Red light glowed beneath Stan's swollen, bruised eyelids. He was a vampire, all right. Thompson ticked his glance from Stan to Bodie, to Walker.

"Bodie," Stan said in a weary, agonized voice. "Bodie."

"How did this happen to you?" Bodie asked. "Who did this to you?"

"I didn't know where else to go," Stan said. "As soon as I knew, I left Jane and I started driving—"

"What did I tell you?" Bobby crowed. He pointed a hand at Bodie. "He's a sucker, too!"

"No, no I'm not," Bodie said, looking shocked...and uncertain.

"It's in the blood," said the grizzled old man who had bought Bobby a shot of tequila. "It runs in families."

"No. You have to be attacked," a woman said. "It's genetic," another man said.

Thompson looked at Walker. Thompson gave his mental wheel of fortune a spin, and it stopped at Little Sister's number. It certainly had not been lost on anyone that if the Mendoza parents had been vampires, their children might turn out to be suckers, too. No one had brought it up. Little Sister and Manny were under their protection.

Stan hissed. It was the worst thing he could have done. It sounded so creepy, so evil, that a woman wearing a tube top and the shortest skirt in Arizona let out an ear-piercing shriek.

"*Now* do you get it?" Bobby shouted at the crowd. "You get what we've been doing for you? To save you?"

He raised his .38 still in his hand. Aimed at Stan. Pulled the trigger.

Bodie roared in protest along with the bullet as it slammed into Stan's chest. The man—the vampire—was thrown backwards, slamming onto his back. But he wasn't dead. He writhed, hissing like a Gila monster, like someone sneezing. Blood was spurting out of the wound like a geyser.

"Don't let it get on you!" Monster cried, ducking the spray.

Then the grizzled man ran up with the baseball bat Bodie kept under the bar and slammed it into Stan's face. Someone else had a pipe. It came down. There was another gunshot.

Walker turned to the side and quietly threw up. Then he ran to the line of motorcycles and climbed on his, started it up, drove away. No one noticed.

Thompson did the same. He doubted anyone noticed, either.

Thompson followed Walker, who drove straight back to the house, looking over his shoulder as Thompson pulled up. He didn't shut the turquoise door with all the crosses and Thompson entered the house a few steps behind him.

Walker strode down the hallway toward the bedrooms, knocked softly on a door marked with a paper sign that read *Angela* in childish crayon letters—Manuel's creation—and said, "Angela? It's me."

There was a muffled reply, and Walker went into the room, pointedly glancing Thompson's way as, this time, he shut the door behind himself. Thompson remained in the hall, listening for the rest of the O.M.s. He figured that the club had batted the wisdom of adopting the Mendoza kids back and forth before he'd arrived. If their parents were vampires, then they could be vampires.

But what if no one had ever believed the Mendozas were vampires? Maybe their deaths had been the result of something else—turf war, drug deal gone bad. Maybe they'd been killed because of the post office box deliveries.

The deliveries he'd been sent to investigate in the first place. Thompson knew which room belonged to Bobby. Of course Bobby's door would be locked. But it wasn't.

Thompson kept listening hard. He heard crickets. It amazed him that in the midst of all the death, the desert still teemed with life. Owls, bats, jackrabbits.

As he turned the knob of Bobby's door all the way, he told himself it didn't matter what Bobby was receiving through the mail, except that it did. Just not enough to take a chance like this.

He cracked open the door. Except for a pie shape of light from the hallway light, it was dark inside. He couldn't turn on a light.

He re-shut the door just as another door opened. It was Manuel, who frowned at him. Thompson's ginger-colored hair stood on end as the boy smiled at him shrewdly.

"What were you doing in there?" Manuel asked.

"I didn't go in there," Thompson said.

Manuel smirked. "Uh-huh."

Thompson stayed loose. Remained calm. Suddenly, crazily, he realized how hungry he was. They had gone to the Shaft for burgers. Bodie hadn't cooked them yet. He wondered what they were doing to Bodie. Stan was a lost cause. Hard to kill, like Moncho had been. Maybe that was the upside of vampirism, except for tonight.

"What do you want?" he asked the boy.

"I want to go hunting next time," Manuel replied.

No, you don't. You really don't, Thompson thought, but he knew he was wrong.

Manuel knew it wasn't a game, and he wanted to play anyway. Thompson felt sick down to his soul.

The motorcycles blared above the scraping of crickets. They would be there in seconds.

"I'll put in a good word for you," Thompson said.

Manuel jutted out his lower lip. After all, he was only nine.

"*Make* him take me."

"I can't make Bobby do anything," he said. "He's Bobby."

Then, on a hunch, he asked, "What does he get when he goes to the mailbox?" The bikes were pulling up to the house.

Manuel was making a decision. "I'll tell you if I get to hunt," he said.

"I'll take you myself," Thompson promised. He went to Little Sister's door and knocked. "Walker," he called.

The front door burst open just as Walker came back out of Little Sister's room. Walker's hair was tousled and he smelled of very cheap perfume.

Bobby strode in, followed by the others. His eyes were bulging and when he looked at Thompson and Walker in the hallway, Thompson wasn't sure that Bobby recognized them. Fug and Johnny Rocket were blank-faced, practically catatonic. Monster hung back. Poison was missing.

"I'm starving," Bobby proclaimed.

They went into the kitchen and Fug started pulling out bread and salami from the fridge while Johnny Rocket produced two bottles of tequila from the pantry. Bobby flopped down in a metal dinette chair and grabbed up one of the place mats Little Sister had purchased on a run into town. There were little bears on them with hearts on their chests. Bobby wiped his forehead with the placemat and held it between his hands.

Thompson came close enough to show respect yet remain on the perimeter of whatever was happening. Walker hesitated, then edged around Thompson and stood beside Bobby's chair. Neither brother said anything.

Johnny Rocket opened one of the bottles and passed it to Bobby, who took a swig. He handed it to Walker, who simply held it against his chest.

"Is he dead?" Walker asked flatly.

"He was so fucking hard to kill," Bobby said. Then he got up, wove down the hall, and disappeared into his bedroom.

That reminded Thompson that Manuel had been standing in the hall. He turned to see the little boy taking in all the drama, flexing his hands like he wanted to make something happen. He looked imploringly at Thompson, all his blackmail bravado forgotten. Manuel was scared. Thompson remained silent.

"Where's Poison?" Manuel asked in his little child's voice.

"Ssh," Walker cautioned him.

Johnny Rocket grabbed the tequila from Walker. "Poison was an asshole." He took a long swig. His hand was shaking.

"But where is he?" Manuel insisted.

"Let's get you to bed," Walker said. He turned the boy away.

"Isn't that Little Sister's job?" Monster said to their retreating backs.

Walker halted. He pivoted on his heels and fixed Monster with an ice-cold stare. It was a look that said, *Don't forget who I'm related to.* So then it was Monster, Fug, Johnny Rocket, and Thompson in the kitchen. Johnny Rocket handed the tequila bottle to Thompson. As Thompson took a drink, he smelled thick, oily smoke. He didn't ask what was going on.

"Liquor store's going up," Monster said, staring at his placemat. "And a few other buildings, too."

"We don't have a whole lot of buildings," Fug put in.

"*They* don't," Johnny Rocket corrected him. "We've got the road, man."

"We've got the Shaft," Monster said. "And our lab."

"We can burn them down if we fucking feel like it," Johnny Rocket insisted.

Fug clenched his jaw as he studied his placemat. "That Stan guy. That vampire. He was practically indestructible." He tapped the heart on the bear. "Those other ones we killed, it was just one bullet."

"Two slugs at the most," Monster put in. The two glanced at each other, then dropped their gazes again.

"So what are you assholes saying?" Johnny Rocket demanded. "That we haven't been killing vampires? Bobby said…" He trailed off. Thompson could see the wheels turning as he put two and two together; Fug and Monster were doubting their president.

"Hey, that is not cool." Johnny Rocket said, raising his chin. "Bobby got attacked by suckers. You've seen his scars. He *knows* about vampires."

"Bodie went down with one bullet," Fug muttered.

"He didn't have fangs or any of that shit," Monster added.

"This is bullshit." Johnny Rocket paced back and forth in the kitchen. Thompson could see that he was just as rattled as they were. "You two are *traitors*. If I tell Bobby—"

"If you tell Bobby *what*?" Bobby asked from behind Thompson. Bobby's eyes were practically spinning as he swept into the kitchen, arms crossed over his chest as he loomed over Fug and Monster. His fingertips pressed against the scars on his bicep.

"Someone talk to me *now*," he said. "Hey, you, no-patch." He glared at Thompson. "What the hell is going on?"

Thompson mentally took a deep, long breath. He had worked so hard for so long to stay out of the spotlight.

"It's hard when it's people you know," Thompson said. "Or thought you knew."

Bobby locked gazes with him. Thompson remained calm. "Yeah," Bobby said. "You got that right. You *thought* you knew." He sneered at the two O.M.s seated at the table. "This is a war. You know what happens to deserters."

"The hell, Bobby." Monster sounded offended. "I've ridden with you the longest. But it's…this town is bad, man…maybe we should find a new one."

"Fuck that." Bobby spat on the kitchen floor. "This is my town."

— 10 —

Your town is burning, you fucking wackjob, Thompson thought, as he drove back to Moncho's house. The smoke was thicker, but he saw no flames.

He put his bike in Moncho's garage and was about to go inside when he realized someone was already inside. It could be any one of several hundred people—a mob, a commission on behalf of the townspeople; it could be a vampire. Thompson had a piece of his own now—a .38 like Bobby's, purchased illegally in the town with Bobby's post office box. He pulled it from its holster and kicked open his own front door.

Father Patrick rose from Moncho's couch with his hands in the air. Thompson didn't put away his weapon. He just waited.

"Please, shut the door," Father Patrick said, trying to sound calm. Not quite pulling it off.

"It's probably broken," Thompson replied.

"I'm sorry," Father Patrick said. He took a deep breath. "You seem like a reasonable man. The most reasonable O.M., anyway. So I–I came to you."

"You could have knocked. Or left a note."

"I really needed to talk to you," Father Patrick said. Thompson assessed the priest. Shoulders tight. Nervous, afraid. Circles under his eyes—not sleeping. Worried about things.

Thompson put away his weapon and Father Patrick sat back down on the couch. Thompson didn't so much lock the door as reposition it in the frame. Then he walked into the kitchen and poured himself and Father Patrick two glasses of water. He brought them back to the living room and held one out to Father Patrick.

The man took a sip. "I'd think you'd drink something stronger after the night you've had," he said.

"I didn't have that night," Thompson said, but he was an O.M., and what one O.M. did, they all did. That was the code, anyway.

Father Patrick leaned forward with his forearms on his knees, his expression very earnest. He really did look just like a Catholic priest.

"Bobby gets paid to keep illegals from crossing the border," the priest said. "But I think he's taking his job way too seriously."

Thompson thought of the post office runs. Where they government payouts, those deliveries?

"How do you know that?" Thompson asked him. "Not even I know that."

"Priests hear all kinds of things," Father Patrick said. He shrugged.

"I was in the bathroom at Bodie's one night. Bobby thought he was alone in there with Walker and they talked it over." Father Patrick sipped his water. "So apparently, Bobby's not splitting up the payments."

"On the other hand, we do okay with our bar and our side business," Thompson said, meaning their lab. It wasn't a big secret. Just no one talked about it.

"So…maybe your president is helping himself to too much of your product," Father Patrick said. "He's acting strung out."

Thompson couldn't argue with him there.

"I've been watching Bobby Morrisey for a long time," Father Patrick said, "and I have a theory. Angela and Manuel's mother, Emilia Mendoza, was a *curandera*. Well, that's how she started out. She got into the shamanic business, brewed up a lot of heavy-duty drug cocktails to send people on 'spirit walks.' She fed her clients a lot of peyote, mushrooms, things like that. She kept her supplies in a sandalwood box from the Holy Land. She told me all about it during confession."

He took another sip of water. "She told me where she kept it. After she died, I went to the Mendoza house. The box was there, but it was empty."

"So you think Bobby's tripping on mescaline?"

Father Patrick shrugged. "Maybe he doesn't know that he is."

Thompson spun his mental wheel. "Why would Angela Mendoza slip Bobby loco weed?"

Father Patrick made water rings on Moncho's wooden table. "Revenge?"

"He's her protector."

"*Walker* is her protector," Father Patrick corrected him.

"But that still doesn't jibe. Bobby sane is scary enough. Bobby off his nut is terrifying. As we are seeing. She's a Mendoza, and he's seeing vampires everywhere."

"Maybe she didn't realize this would happen," Father Patrick said. "She's just a kid."

Thompson thought a moment. "Or maybe Walker *did* realize this would happen."

Thompson had the man's attention. "He wants to get rid of Bobby?" Father Patrick asked.

"He might. He doesn't like what's happened to the O.M.s. Maybe he wants it to get so bad the other soldiers will have to get rid of Bobby for him."

"Walker could just leave," Father Patrick argued.

"Bobby's laid down the law and he owns a rocket launcher. Besides, Walker's an operator. I think he's been trying to lure me to his side of the force." He smiled wryly to himself for having the arrogance to assume that he, Thompson, had been on the verge of flipping Walker. "Do you know what happened to Poison tonight?"

Father Patrick nodded, his eyes clouding over. "I'm not sure anyone knows who shot him in the back. But he's dead."

"How many bullets?" Thompson asked; then, at the man's confusion, he drained his water and set down the glass. "Where's the body?"

"In the church. I'm going to bury him myself." Father Patrick drew a little cross in the air. "As in, with my own shovel."

"I'll help you," Thompson said.

– 11 –

Thompson hadn't realized that Catholic churches kept a few coffins on hand—at least, the Catholic church in Sonrisa did—and they packed Poison into a simple wooden box and laid him in the ground by the light of the moon. Father Patrick conducted a beautiful funeral without once glancing at the missal he asked Thompson to hold for him. Then the two parted ways, agreeing to compare notes in a couple days.

After he left the churchyard, Thompson drove up and down the streets of the town. There weren't that many buildings on fire. The Shaft was fine.

Someone took a shot at him, and he went home.

In the morning, he found a dead rat on his front porch. It could have died there, or maybe it was a calling card.

He showed up at Bobby's around ten a.m. He knocked on the turquoise door with all the crosses and Manuel opened it. The boy's eyes were enormous, and he was blinking rapidly, as if he were trying to speak to Thompson in code. Maybe he was saying, *Get me the fuck out of here.*

Manuel led him into the kitchen. Only Little Sister and Bobby were there. Little Sister was picking apart a six-pack of cinnamon rolls and putting them on paper plates. Then she carried two of the plates and plopped one in front of Bobby, who was seated, and one in front of an empty seat.

"Manuel, come eat," she said. She sounded nervous. The fragrant scent of coffee wafted through the room.

Bobby gestured for Thompson to take a seat. Bobby was covered in sweat and his hands were trembling. He looked like he was OD'ing.

Thompson sat. He didn't ask where the others were. He made no comment. A cinnamon roll appeared on the placemat before him.

"More coffee," Bobby said, raising a black coffee mug decorated with a white motorcycle.

Thompson focused on the cup as Little Sister crossed over to Bobby. Then, as she took the cup, her glance darted at Thompson. Her cheeks reddened. And he knew:

She's been lacing the coffee with her mother's drug cocktail. As first a recruit and then a hang-around, Thompson had never eaten breakfast at Bobby's house before. And that's when Bobby drank coffee. Only at breakfast. He'd said that.

But won't it taste off?

He watched her as she poured the cup for Bobby. They had a drip coffeemaker. She looked at Thompson and suddenly dumped the remaining contents of the coffee pot into the sink. Set it down. Brought Bobby's coffee to him. Practically ran out of the room.

The front door opened again and Walker, Fug, and Monster came into the house. Walker sat down. Fug got the half-empty six-pack of cinnamon rolls and brought them over to the table.

"We use plates," Bobby said pointedly. He looked around. "Where'd she go?"

Walker picked up the stack of paper plates and brought them to the table. He ticked his glance at his brother's coffee cup.

Thompson took note.

"Tell her to come out here and make another pot," Bobby ordered his brother. So maybe the O.M.s weren't that enlightened about women after all.

Walker disappeared down the hall, and returned a minute later with Little Sister. She dutifully made another pot of coffee. It was a drip coffee maker, into which she inserted a filter, then poured in pre-ground coffee from a dark green bag.

"Today is town patrol," Bobby announced. He wiped sweat off his forehead. Consternation went around the table. There had never been "town patrols" before. "There's going to be a lot of civilians scared out of their minds," Bobby went on. "They're going to think leaving's their best option. But we've been out there. We've *seen* what's going on."

Oh, shit, Thompson thought, and it looked to him like his brother O.M.s were thinking the same thing.

Little Sister ferried four cups of steaming coffee to the table. Then she edged the used filter packed with grounds out of its container and threw it into a white plastic trash can beneath the sink.

Thompson ate his cinnamon roll. Fug and Monster drank their coffee. Walker brought his mug to his lips, but he didn't drink.

"Man, that's hot," he said. Then, "Bobby, maybe we should let them find out what's in the desert."

Bobby reached across the table and thwacked his brother on the forehead. Like he probably did when they were little. Walker didn't even flinch. Like he'd gotten used to it through the years.

But Little Sister's lips parted as if she were going to say something about it. A furtive look from Walker silenced her.

"Why'd we start patrolling the border, huh?" Bobby asked Walker. "Why'd we take our lives into our own hands by riding through the goddamn desert day in, day out? To keep America free!"

"Fuckin' A, Bobby," Fug said, taking a big swallow of coffee.

"This is our country, and our town, and our people!" Spittle flew from Bobby's mouth. "And no fucking vampires are taking any of it away from us!"

– 12 –

"He's a patriot, in his own twisted way," Father Patrick said two weeks later, after Thompson had joined him in the parish hall. Father Patrick was sitting on the corner of a desk drinking a beer. It was almost midnight.

"One per-centers usually are," Thompson said, drinking the beer Father Patrick had given him.

It was Thompson's turn to be on patrol tonight. Last night, on his watch, Bobby had identified a Sonrisa citizen named Joaquin Mendez as a vampire and executed him with a single bullet in the back of his head. Fug and Monster, high as kites, had kicked the body and spat on it, then zoomed away to single out someone else. Walker had gotten his wish. The O.M.s were monsters, and Thompson figured it was only a matter of time before Walker felt safe enough to get the hell out of Sonrisa—with or without Little Sister, was Thompson's only question.

Meanwhile, Thompson was at the church to help Father Patrick bury Mendez.

"Okay, I ran some tests with my little chemistry set," Father Patrick said. The good father copped to being an occasional, small-time drug dealer himself, but Thompson knew by his body language that he was lying. Either Father Psychedelic was or had been a much bigger player, or he was making drugs himself on the side. Either way, the priest offered to check some coffee ground samples Thompson had snagged out of Bobby's trash.

"It's a definite that she's been putting the cocktail in the coffee," Father Patrick said, reaching around and setting a paper bag on the desktop. Thompson glanced inside. It was the coffee grounds minus a few handfuls.

"Walker knows I haven't been drinking it," Thompson said. "Neither has he."

"And that brings us to tonight's big event," Father Patrick announced.

Thompson assumed he meant tonight's burial. But Father Patrick threw off an aura of excitement as he rose from the desk and led the way from the parish hall to what looked like a potting shed. Mendez— brown skin, black hair—lay on a wooden table. He was wearing blue jeans and a blue T-shirt. His eyes were half-open, and glassy-dead.

And there were two large holes in his neck. Fresh. Thompson grunted. Then Father Patrick took the man's left hand in his own and gently turned it over.

Chunks of veins and flesh were missing. Fresh.

Thompson's stomach did a flip. He bent over to inspect the wounds more closely. He saw teeth marks.

"Do vampires eat human flesh? Isn't that ghouls?"

"Or zombies?" Father Patrick asked. "Luther Swann hasn't mentioned any flesh-eating vampires."

Thompson exhaled. "When did this happen?"

"Earlier tonight," Father Patrick said.

"Jesus. Do you think one of the O.M.s came in here? Did this under the influence?"

Father Patrick smiled grimly. "I don't think it. I know it."

Thompson blinked as Father Patrick reached around the corpse and picked up a laptop. He opened the clamshell and hit the power button. While it was booting, he said, "This isn't the church's. I brought it with me. When things started heating up, I mail-ordered a couple of cameras. They feed images to my laptop. I saved some pertinent footage for you."

While Thompson wondered precisely which of the many heated up things prompted the priest to buy some surveillance equipment, Father Patrick clicked on a large blue arrow in a circle, and a grainy video started running.

"I wish it was clearer," Father Patrick said. But it was clear enough.

— 13 —

Thompson had to work it just right. He spun his wheel and did his calculations and then he went to Bobby's house. The guys were out, probably killing innocent people, which was what Thompson wanted. Not that they were killing people, but that they weren't home.

He'd spent years sneaking up on criminals, so he was silent as death as he let himself into Little Sister's room. To his surprise, she had a nightlight—a cross that glowed in the dark. It cast a soft glow across her empty bed.

Damn.

He'd planned to have a heart-to-heart with her, but she was gone. He thought about searching for her mother's stolen herbs, but her absence threw him. As quietly as he'd entered the room, Thompson backed out. When he closed her door, Manuel opened his. *Déjà vu.*

The little boy's face was blotchy with tears, and when he saw Thompson, he began to cry.

"Hey," Thompson said, taking him by the shoulder and squatting down to his eye level. He had a bad feeling. "Hey, Manny, what's up?"

"They left me here," he said, with a hitch in his voice.

"They," Thompson said, leading the witness.

"Walker and Angela. *She* said they're going to get married and they'll come back for me but..." He pressed his fists into his eyes, whining.

"Married." Thompson fought to stay loose. To sound calm. "Were they going to see Father Patrick to get married?"

Manuel lowered his head. "No. He said Father Patrick didn't like him. They have to go someplace else to get married."

Father Patrick didn't like him. "Did she say where?"

"*He* said they had to ride for a while. That's why they didn't take me. That's what he said."

Suddenly, unexpectedly, he threw his arms around Thompson's neck. He wailed with grief. "But they're not coming back."

Shit, shit, shit, Thompson thought, as he let Manuel hang on him longer than he should have. Longer, because he had to catch up to them.

"If you help me find them, I'll bring them back," he told the boy. "Now, think hard, Manny. Did they say anything about where they were going?"

The boy was crying so hard he couldn't talk. Thompson eased him away and cupped his thin little chin with his fingertips.

"Manuel, *escúchame,*" he said in Spanish. Listen to me. Tell me.

"No," Manuel said, "*nada.*" They told me nothing. Then he said, "Walker said there should be another envelope in the post office box in the morning. He said they'd take it and he would buy her a Horchata and a wedding ring."

The dusty town two towns over. An envelope with government money in it. The grocery store.

"How long ago did they leave?"

"I don't know," Manuel said. What was time to a nine-year-old?

"You've been a big help," Thompson said. "I'm really proud of you. Now go back to bed and I'll take care of this."

"I don't want to. I want to go with you."

"I have to move fast."

"I'm fast," Manuel insisted.

"You need to stay here," Thompson said.

Manuel sat in the hall and wept. Thompson put a thumb drive and the CD he had burned off Father Patrick's laptop on the kitchen table, betting that via one technological delivery system or the other, Bobby would be able to view the footage. Then he wrote a note:

Bobby, I'll take care of this. Thompson. Then he hit the road.

—14—

Thompson didn't know how much of a head start Walker and Little Sister had, so he pulled it out and barreled down the highway at speeds he had never dared before. Was Walker really planning to marry her?

Or was he getting rid of the loose ends of the let's-screw-up-Bobby-plot?

Thompson had been right. Walker had been feeding Bobby's head as a form of misdirection—but for a different reason. See vampires everywhere, and you won't see the one sitting across from you at breakfast. Or if you say you do, no one will believe you.

Thompson rode hard. Maybe someone else would have let them go. What the hell, Bobby was right. Vampires were coming over the border. Vampires were everywhere. Why not let Walker...walk?

Because she was only sixteen.

He rode all night. Once, a trio of shadows blipped across the road—animals, refugees?—but he blazed past, on his mission, wondering if Little Sister would be alive when he got there.

The dusty town two towns over was still asleep. He pulled across from the post office and waited. Dawn washed the horizon with lavender and pink, and he remembered a world before the ice melted and released the trigger. The world he'd known then was gritty and diseased, but he'd taken cold comfort in the knowledge that it was an underworld, practically an alternate dimension, separate from where the majority of human beings lived. But this new world was a world war. The V-War, they were calling it. There was no barrier.

The sun rose, and still no sign of Walker and Little Sister. Thompson wondered if Walker had passed disinformation via Manuel. If, in fact, he had planned from the beginning to ride somewhere else entirely.

Thompson rode out of that town and on to the next one. And the next. Down the ribbon of highway with its ever-receding watery mirage. Past miles of nothing, and more nothing, and less than nothing. The heat pushed down hard, and he thought about the Bog Man.

In frustration, Thompson squinted up at the bright yellow desert sun.

And that was when he saw the buzzards. They were circling slowly, way up high, barely recognizable in the bright blue sky as they rode the thermals; then they angled downward, almost as if they were tiptoeing down a steep flight of stairs.

Thompson headed in their direction, trying to keep them in his sights, wondering how far away they really were. He found himself thinking of all the desert miles he had covered in service of his country, fighting the onslaught of controlled substances. Things were certainly out of control now.

The buzzards disappeared and he swore under his breath. Then more appeared in the cloudless blue, as if the word had gotten out that there was good eating to be had.

He put the pedal to the metal, stayed on the highway, and then he saw dark shadows to his right on the sand. One was moving, one was not.

The engine roared as he pushed against the road; and then he saw the whole tableau: not the *Pietà* this time, but *The Nightmare*, by Fuseli—the succubus crouched on top of the inert woman; the horse—this time a motorcycle—angled behind the couple.

Walker was crying. His lips were outlined in Little Sister's blood. The vultures hopped close by, impatient for him to finish up so that they could get some, too. Sloppy seconds were the best.

"Thompson," Walker cried. His eyes were coals in his sunburned face. His femur was protruding from his jeans leg. The white bone glistened. It had to hurt like hell. "We had an accident and we ran off the road. My fucking leg is broken. But she fell off the bike. I'm giving her mouth-to-mouth. God, call an ambulance!"

But Little Sister was in no pain at all. She was dead. Her eyes were unfocused, like Mendez's.

"Walker," Thompson said, "you know why I'm here."

"I took the money out of Bobby's room," Walker said, crying and stroking Little Sister's hair. Blood dribble down his chin.

"You know it's not the money. I went to the church," Thompson said.

Walker groaned. He cried a few more tears. Then he said, "I didn't see the camera until after."

"Yeah, it looked that way on the monitor," Thompson said. He was reading Walker's body language. Walker was try to figure out how to get out of it alive. And he was deeply remorseful about Little Sister.

That was nice.

"There's a couple thou. Take it and leave me alone. I–I won't do anything like this again. "

A couple thou? There had to be more.

"I thought you loved her," Thompson said.

Walker sobbed. "I did. I just, you know, we were out here and she was dying and it's not a good way to go. And-and I was thirsty."

"Hungry, too," Thompson said. "You take chunks out of her?"

Walker shook his head. "No. I couldn't, not to her."

"If it makes you feel any better," Thompson said, "it wasn't just the camera. I already knew about the coffee cocktail. I knew you and Angela were planning something."

Walker blubbered. "She wanted to do it for revenge. For her parents. It worked out with-with my…situation. I was afraid someone would figure it out. I thought it might you. You're so quiet. But they were already so crazy. Bobby is so crazy."

Walker stared down at Little Sister and whimpered like a whipped dog. "He's crazy. The others are just loyal." He wiped the tears off his face, then looked at his fingers. "God, there's blood all over me."

"Yeah, there is," Thompson said. Then he added, "But *you* never figured it out."

Then, stirred by the blood, by so much blood when he'd been fasting, because he stayed quiet and careful and under the radar, Thompson felt his own fangs extend. Knew his own eyes were two coals glowing.

Walker started screaming. He dug his hands into Little Sister's chest for purchase, struggling to drag himself away. "You're a fucking vampire!" Walker shrieked. "Like me!"

"Exactly like you," Thompson confirmed. Walker screamed some more. Thompson kept coming. "I drink, and I eat, too," he told Walker. "Eat their flesh. All those people Bobby killed in the desert? They've been my stashes. But *you* had to go fresh."

"I'll tell my brother! I'll fucking tell him!" Walker shouted. And then he seemed to think better of that plan. "I *won't*, Thompson. I swear I won't. I won't," he babbled.

"You won't," Thompson affirmed.

Walker stared at him in horror. He burst into fresh tears and Thompson let him have his cry. He sounded younger even than Manuel. Thompson remembered all those impromptu funerals Walker had held. His dismay over Bobby's savagery.

"We can team up," Walker said. "Leave together."

Thompson shook his head. He knew he had to sacrifice Walker. Let Bobby see the vampire across the breakfast table so he wouldn't see the one riding behind him in the desert.

Riding behind him so he could do what?

Walker cried forever. Then he looked from Thompson to Little Sister. "I really did love her," he said. "I didn't mean to kill her."

"I know," Thompson said, although he didn't know.

– 15 –

234 The roar of three motorcycles split the heavens like an atomic blast and the vultures shot back up into the sky. The president of the Ocotillo Militia, Bobby Morrisey, rode point; then his sergeant-at-arms, Fugly, and Johnny Rocket, his V.P. By then, Thompson knew that the flesh of vampires did have a special tang. It was extra spicy. By then, he had shot Walker in the chest to hide the evidence of his feast, and washed up with the bottles of water in the cooler strapped to Walker's bike.

He hadn't touched Little Sister. He showed respect.

The O.M.s were almost there.

I'm going to get my full patch, he thought, *or I'm going to die.*

He found, unexpectedly, that he was fine with either outcome. Except there was Manuel. Somebody had to look out for him, help him become something in the new world order besides a hardened biker chasing nightmares in a dead end desert.

And as the Ocotillo Militia arrived, he watched the buzzards, circling. Then he watched them give up, and fly away.

"VULPES" PT.1

Gregory Frost

–1–

Ruksana Vulpes pushed up her helmet and glanced across the glistening wall of ice to where Harry Gordon was descending on his separate line. Two ice axes hung off Harry's harness, and both had orange snow baskets on them because Harry was terrified of losing them and finding himself stranded a thousand feet down. A ridiculous fear, given that they could be hauled up on winches if they didn't choose to climb. Then again, three axes dangled, clinking, from her own belt; in case she lost her grip on one while climbing back up the side of the calved ice shelf. Everyone had their superstitions.

They went down in pairs. She was buddied with Vincent Dusault. He rappelled separately, too—above her at the moment. Harry was teamed with another American, John Bail. John and Vincent carried the core drills, like rifles slung on their backs. She and Harry had the rucksacks with the polymer tubes.

The ice shelf had calved only two hours ago, introducing more than a thousand feet of glacial face that hadn't been exposed in millennia. By rappelling down the side of it and taking their samples horizontally at various levels, they avoided the longer process of drilling down from above while eliminating all possibility of contaminating their samples with matter from the upper strata. Plus, the four of them liked to rappel down mountains and climb glaciers. It was part of the reason they were here.

The mountains were in Ruksana's blood, as integral as iron. Even though both her parents had died while climbing, caught in an avalanche when she was three, she had not been dissuaded from developing the same skills. If anything, it had impelled her. On some unacknowledged level, she had likely thought that she would find them one day, on some mountain top. Them or their ghosts.

In the end, a lifetime of climbing had won her a place on the USAP team.

Vincent called out to her, and she dug in her sabertooth crampons and waited for him to reach her on his lead. He stopped beside her. Though he was smiling coolly, his face was flushed. It wouldn't be from the exertion; more likely he had bulked up with too many layers of clothing. It was a balmy 40 degrees Fahrenheit here in Antarctica and he was overdressed for the occasion.

Vincent was tall, thin, and fashion-model handsome. The only thing he lacked was humility. He'd been raised to be a god, and it was his opinion that he had succeeded. During the first month here, he'd managed to convince her of the same. Their affair had lasted about as long as it had taken her to realize that she was convenient and discardable, and that she had made a terrible mistake giving into need, inveigled by Vincent's smooth self-assurance. From collaboration to sex to truculence in a month with another three to go. She'd spent a lot of her time climbing. And now her tour of duty was nearly at an end—just a few more days until they and the other fourteen members of their group rotated out.

"We should drill here now," Vincent called down to her. "According to the altimeter, this is the median." He tapped the dial on his wrist.

Lost in thought, she replied automatically, "Desigur." When he just blinked at her like a gecko, she sighed and called out, "D'accord."

Of course he had selected a spot that required her to climb back up to him. She unclipped two axes and in short order had pulled herself up the ice face to where he wanted to drill. She swung off to the side, away from him, and tied off the line to suspend her there.

Vincent leaned out from where his crampons were dug into the ice, and let the double figure-eight knots keep him in place on his super-dry Mammut line. He unslung the core drill. The cylindrical saw attachment was a good half-meter long. It didn't really matter if he went in straight or not, so long as he carved out a cylinder of ancient ice around which she could slide her tube, fill it up and cap it. It was a slightly perilous suspension, with both of his arms engaged in drilling. The fundamental rule of climbing was to maintain three points of contact.

She glanced far below, at the black sea water speckled with ice like oyster crackers. A zipper fall from here would either plunge you into the water where you would die from hypothermia before anyone could rescue you, or else you would strike one of those chunks of ice and die much quicker. No worse than a fall off a mountain.

The drill whined to life above her, sounding like a circular saw, and in a matter of two minutes Vincent had punched in the full depth of the cylindrical bit. He backed it out, looked at his handiwork then at Ruksana as if to say, "I made it perfect for you."

He shouldered the drill again, careful to keep the hot bit away from his body, took hold of the line and swung away from the sample, giving her access.

Ruksana swung over to it. She pulled the rucksack to where she could get a hand into it, pulled out the first tube, unscrewed the cap, then slid it into the drilled ice. His cut angled slightly up, and she wrestled the end of the tube up to snap off the plug of ice before she slowly withdrew the container, now filled with the sample. The ice in it was speckled with dirt and other organic matter that had probably been washed from the surface of the earth a thousand years ago. She capped the sample and slid it back into the rucksack.

While she worked, Vincent had taken off his jacket and tied it to the back of his harness. His face shone with sweat. He kicked loose and dropped below her on his way to the second sample as though she didn't exist.

A hundred feet away, Harry and John had descended to a different height, staggering the samples. They were just getting ready to drill their first sample.

Ruksana put away her axes, placed her left hand between the anchor and rappel device, her braking hand against her hip, and let herself continue to follow Vincent down.

–2–

At a height of a hundred feet above the ocean, they collected their final sample. The chunks below now resembled pancake ice, as if individual chunks were partially freezing into a wider temporary formation. The water remained dark and turbulent in the aftermath of the calving, even though the huge mass that had broken away had already drifted out of sight. The surface was playing tricks on Ruksana's peripheral vision. She kept almost seeing something moving under the ice, but when she looked directly, there was nothing. Thus distracted, she paid little attention to Vincent as he started the drill.

He went in at a steeper angle than before, and when he withdrew the bit, a dark viscous fluid began seeping out after it. Ruksana felt the ice shavings sprinkle onto her helmet. She looked up to find a syrupy greenish liquid oozing down the ice face. A few drops spattered off Vincent's boot onto her cheek. Furious, she swatted at the stuff, feeling it smear. It was on her gloves now, looking like some ancient health drink made from mushed kelp or algae. No doubt the drill had heated up the ice in the hole, liquefied some of it. *Vincent, you idiot.*

On crampons, she maneuvered to the side, got out her axes and climbed spiderlike up the face again.

Vincent, shouldering the drill, swung on his line beside her. The arm and back of his jacket glistened with the stuff, but clearly he didn't see it. He said, "Well?"

Ruksana drew out another tube and shoved it up into the slot he had carved. The fluid continued leaking out, onto her gloves and sleeves. When she withdrew it, the tube was slimy with the stuff, too. She screwed the cap back on and pushed it into the rucksack. She tried wiping her gloves against the blue wall of ice but to little effect.

"What's wrong? You all right?" Vincent asked.

"Cred ča da," she answered, angry and unthinking, and again had to translate for him. "I think so. Sure." She spat even though the goop wasn't in her mouth. "I need to wash off this stuff you dripped onto me." She gestured at him. His jacket, tied behind him, had goop all over it. "You have it, too."

He looked over his shoulder at the shiny smear. "Must be Pleistocene escargot. As big as this." He held his hands up as if to hold a human head. A string of slime hung between his gloves. He ignored it, grinning in that cocky way that had first persuaded her to make a mistake with him.

She unclipped her ice axes once more, took one in each hand. "Let's get out of here," she said. She started up the wall.

"You don't need to climb, you know!" he shouted up at her in French.

He drew the small walkie-talkie from his harness and ordered Martin McCabe above to start the winch.

A moment later, Ruksana found herself tugged along. This should have been her final climb and she had looked forward to scaling the vertical ice face. Now she was annoyed, sticky, and helpless as the winch pulled her up. The only benefit, she supposed, was that she remained above him the rest of the way up.

Where the stuff was on her skin it itched, although the sensation was likely psychosomatic. Finally, she admitted it was her inattentiveness and not his that was responsible. Usually she was very attentive, very focused; and the one time she wasn't, this happened.

She clipped the ice axes to her harness again and watched the shape of her reflection, like a dark doppelgänger, rippling along the deep blue ice.

–3–

"I don't want you to tell anyone what happened," Vincent said.

They were standing beside the Range Rover, waiting now for Harry and John, who were being winched up by Martin and Brian Childs. In her hand was a rag she'd taken from the vehicle to wipe her face and neck.

"What?" Surely, she hadn't heard him correctly. Her French wasn't all that reliable.

"I don't need a black mark on my record because you didn't get out of the way."

She had conceded already that it was her fault she'd been below him. But his insistence got her back up. "But you did start drilling without checking to see. You stopped following procedure." She gestured at her cheek with her bare hand. "For all you know, I've been poisoned."

"Really?" He leaned in close as if he saw something on her skin, then at the last moment kissed her. His hand was on the back of her head and kept her from pulling away. Then he tilted his head away. "You taste okay to me. I don't think there's anything wrong with you, and anyway, if you've been contaminated, so have I." He licked his lips, then wiped his fingers across his wadded up jacket, held them up. "Maybe the escargot came from outer space, eh? If it did, I can tell you they won't let you go home in two days or even two weeks. You'll be a lab rat at the NSF's pleasure for a long time. More to the point, so will

I." He snatched the cloth from her hand and wiped it over the jacket. "You will have to decide. If it reflects badly on me, it does on you, too. And Henderson is a former Marine. He will believe me if I tell him you and I had a relationship that went sour and you're just trying to get back at me with a parting shot. Gordon knows about us, as well, so if asked he will have to agree. You see, you gain nothing and lose almost everything. Anyway, all you did was get dirty."

She couldn't believe it. Her opinion of him could not have sunk any lower.

"Fuck you, Vincent," she told him. She turned on her heel and circled around the Range Rover.

"You did," he called after her.

— 4 —

Despite his behavior, when they returned to the base, she said nothing about the incident beyond turning in her Polartec jacket and gloves so that Kwasi Nkrumha, a biologist from Tanzania, could take samples. Vincent followed her lead and handed over his jacket. There was more of the stuff on the last tube and, it appeared, inside it as well. Kwasi wouldn't lack for samples. The true focus of concern was as to whether the stuff had contaminated the other core samples. But she had sealed the first two tightly. They were safe from the greenish sludge. It did seem to be a localized phenomenon—Harry and John had encountered nothing akin to it.

Three days later, on February 9th, their four month stint came to an end. The long-term staffers threw the eighteen of them a party on the last night. Harry got drunk and went around hugging everyone as if they were the dearest friends he had in the whole world, whom he never expected to see again. Their group included Deb Arliss and Brian. The chatter was about families and relationships, and about a series of stories on CNN about real-life vampires who had set themselves up in New York City. At least, that was the way Deb characterized it. She was going back to New York.

At one point Vincent caught Ruksana's eye. He was standing in a small group alongside Henderson, Harry, and John. He made a point of raising his glass to her. He said something to the others, and they faced her, gave her a nod. Vincent winked. Harry set down his glass and came over. "Rooksie, it has been so good working with you. If I ever come out of retirement to put together a team to explore volcanic geological formations, you are at the top of the list." He gave her a wet kiss on the cheek as he hugged her. "And I know I'm faced, but I mean it."

"You're retiring?"

It was obvious he hadn't meant to let that slip. He was sixty-one, and his wife had died of cancer the previous year. His children were long gone, and he wasn't looking forward to returning home.

"I, uh, I might be. But you, sweetie, you have your whole life ahead. Everything is yet to be done. I'm envious as hell, but you knew that already, same as you know that if you weren't my daughter's age, I would have been fighting that prick Vincent for your favors." He blushed and broke out with a nervous grin at the same time. "Sorry. That Johnny Walker pops the lid right off."

She held his hand. "It's okay, Harry. Really." She leaned in and kissed him. "I'd work with you any time."

The core samples they'd brought in had already been filed away in a freezer for later study. Leaving Harry safely parked at a table with Deb and John, Ruksana found Kwasi and dragged him off into a corner. She asked him what had been on the jackets.

"Something organic I imagine," he said, his eyes big. "It looks like algae. I see clear evidence of photosynthesis." He speculated that maybe when the ice shelf calved, the algae responded to the sunlight, activated. "Then again, perhaps it's prokaryotic given where it's survived, but it's too soon to know. Considering how much ice has calved this year, there's a good chance the majority of whatever it is has sailed off into the ocean anyway.

"We'll get to it, just not before we've cleared out our backlog. You guys accomplished a lot, but a few more lab biologists and a few less mountaineering climate scientists would be helpful in the next rotation." He winked at her. He couldn't have known how much that reminded her of Vincent.

Kwasi was staying on another three months. He promised he would contact her when they finally analyzed the samples and had some definitive profile.

The next morning she boarded an LC-130 and flew out of McMurdo. Vincent sat at the opposite end of the plane. He chatted with Deb and acted as if he barely knew Ruksana. Harry, with his Red Sox cap pulled down to shield his bloodshot eyes, gave her a little shake of the head as if to say "Forget about him." There had been a point where she'd worried about how she would explain her relationship with Vincent to her boyfriend, Costin. But Harry was right. Vincent was best forgotten. Unfortunately, the two of them continued sharing jets up until she boarded her flight back to Romania.

– 5 –

Decebal Vulpes stood up as she walked into the terminal at Henri Coandă airport outside Bucureşti. In his heavy old coat he strode forward, arms wide, intense dark eyes above a crooked nose, his thick mustache rimed in yellow from his cigars.

"Bunicul, bunicul," she said, making it an affectionate term.

"*Floare mea*," he replied and folded her into his great arms, into the smell of cigars and winter. He pushed her back, his large hands on her shoulders. "They starved you in Antarctica. Was there nothing to eat but penguin?"

"Nothing," she answered. "But it was very good penguin when we had it."

He *tsked* her. "I hope you didn't develop too much taste for it. Tonight it's tocana cu carnati and for dessert—"

"Cozonac." She smiled at him.

He shrugged. "Your mother's recipe."

"It's the only dessert you know how to make, bunicul."

"Foo. I only make it always because it's your favorite. I *could* make anything."

Walking with him, she had to go slowly. She didn't remember him being this stiff in his movements four months ago. His walk was almost a shuffle; and she wondered if she had simply not noticed a steady decline, whereas now his freshly encountered aging was shockingly apparent.

After they collected her bags, they took the 783 train into the city center. It was getting dark by then. He smoked a small cigar as they walked along. On the way to catch a trolley, they saw a pack of four dogs across the street at the mouth of an alley. The dogs were tearing open a large plastic trash bag. No doubt there was food in it. At first only one dog glanced their way while the others shredded the bag. Then, as though a signal had been given, all four stopped and turned to watch until they'd rounded a corner. It reminded her too much of Vincent and Henderson's group at the party.

They kept going, heads down against the wind coming off the lake to the north, bitterly cold. Antarctica seemed tropical to her by comparison. On the trolley, she said, "So the wild dogs are still a problem then."

"That's the first pack I've seen in awhile. The extermination program continues, but it never will wipe out all of them. They are clever. Did you see how that one watched as we approached? No different than a street gang, except probably much smarter."

The trolley took them almost to the door of their apartment on Strada Virgiliu. The computer store still occupied the ground floor. The Microsoft sign in the window was the same one as when she'd left, just more yellowed by exposure. Its presence was oddly comforting.

The apartment looked as if her grandfather hadn't moved anything since she'd left. It smelled of the rich sausage stew he'd promised. He lit the burner under the pot to reheat it, then opened a bottle of wine. "It's Bull's Blood," he announced as he poured her a glass. "You'll need a glass or two to shake the cold."

"Did you teach?" she asked.

He dipped his head. "I am teaching. It's only February, my flower. I have months to go. Ah, but they are distracted anymore with their iPads and their earphones. What I am telling them is from another planet. Folklore? It's an empty word to these runny noses. What could it possibly have to do with them?"

"I don't believe you," she said. "You could make shadows come to life."

He bowed his head, smiling. "Only for you, little one. But you wanted them to come to life. You made my task easy." He scraped a fingernail along a front tooth as if cleaning it. "Did you call Costin?"

"That's a leading question. You've been with me every moment since I got back. When would I have called him?"

He pointed his wine glass at her. "And that's a telling answer. I remember four months ago, the tearful goodbyes, and the granddaughter who didn't want me going to the airport with her because she didn't want to cry in front of me and Costin both."

"She's still here," she replied, but she knew how attuned he was to her behavior. Her whole life he had been able to suss when she was upset and when she was concealing something, no matter how she tried to hide it.

Now he abandoned pursuit and said, "Go wash your face and we'll eat. It's ready."

Once they had sat down to their meal, however, he picked right up as if no time had passed. "She is still here, yes, but something has happened to her. Something that has her holding Costin at a distance when she knows he will be watching his calendar, too, and worrying if he hears nothing."

She ate awhile, sniffling from the spice of the sausages—he preferred them very spicy. Finally she remarked, "There was a man."

Decebal nodded. "Of course. And as you say was, I will assume this has not proved superior to your nice musician so you're, what, ashamed?"

"He was a scientist. Very beautiful. Very full of himself. I was stupid." She then described everything including the last days in Vincent's company.

"Me, I should have killed him, cut his rope," Decebal said when she'd finished. "Then again, I have no reason to spare him. Did they run tests on you? You are all right?"

She shook her head. "No, no tests. No cause for it. They are analyzing it, eventually. At the depth we were drilling it had probably been fermenting for many thousand years. Frozen and dead slime that we heated up with a drill. Pretty stupid. Really, I'm fine."

He said, "I would still kill him though."

"Me, too."

He laughed. "Then you learned a valuable lesson from this Vincent. Not to be persuaded by your loneliness and pretty men with facile ways."

"Yes," she agreed. "I certainly did that."

"In that case—" he dipped two fingers into his water glass and flicked them at her "—I absolve you of your sins. You have grown from the experience, my child. Go forth and sin no more."

"Bunicul," she laughed.

"Fată drăguţă," he replied. It was a tease. He called her a "pretty girl" whenever he wanted to incense her by pretending to dismiss her intellect. "Go call Costin so I can serve you dessert."

– 6 –

She did not call Costin. To herself she rationalized that she lacked the energy. To her grandfather she lied and said that she'd left a message on his cell. After the dessert she went to bed. Cozonac was her favorite, but as she crawled into bed, she couldn't even recall how it had tasted, as if it had been taken away from her in her exhaustion.

A fitful night's rest awaited her, and this time she could not blame jets and airports. It was her own bed and she should have sunk into a deep sleep.

No dreams stayed with her, but she had a sense of floating just below the surface of consciousness like someone trapped and drowning under a dark red layer of ice, half-impressions of people in the room with her. In the middle of the night she was sure she came groggily awake and saw someone crouched next to the bed, which startled her, but there was nobody there after all. She must have gone right back to sleep. It was a weird hallucinatory dream.

She woke up in the gray of morning, feeling that other impossible things crawled just outside the periphery of her recall. She felt as tired as if she'd had no sleep at all.

From the kitchen came soft noises—her grandfather moving about—and finally the snap of the lock on the apartment door that signaled his departure. Silence reigned, and only then did she truly drift off and sleep deeply for a few more hours.

She awoke lying on top of her down-filled duvet, warm despite having, it seemed, cracked the window at some point during the night. She'd no memory of getting out of bed. Her flannel nightgown had risen up to the tops of her thighs, and she pushed it down as she lay there.

The air coming in was cold. She got up and cranked the window shut.

The kitchen had been cleaned up and it appeared her grandfather had stolen off to the university without making himself any coffee, probably worried that the smell would wake her. She sat awhile, worried about him, wincing at the way he shuffled now like an old man. He had been so hardy. How had he declined this much in four months?

She cut off a slice of the cozonac and then boiled water for tea while she tore off and chewed a hunk of it. It was definitely better the second day, just as everyone said.

Her grandfather had left a newspaper for her. A photo of a huge orange moon filled the middle of the front page, and above it the headline ran "Supermoon Tonight!" She skimmed the accompanying article. The moon was almost at perigee and if the skies were clear, it would look as enormous as in the photo. She wondered if they would be able to see it from their little balcony.

She was going to have to call Costin and tell him something. Maybe she could make up that she had come home ill and shouldn't see him right now. But all that would do was prolong the—

The door buzzer sounded.

With her mug in her hand, she walked barefoot in her nightgown across the apartment to the door. Leaning up on her toes, she peered through the peephole. An enormous eye stared at her. Then it drew back. Costin had eyelashes so thick that at times he seemed to be wearing mascara. His black hair was windblown. A cowlick stood up at the back.

She stared at him, and for a long moment she debated whether to pretend not to be home. Internally she argued how it wasn't fair, she wasn't ready, didn't know what she wanted to say, what she should say, and damn Vincent again for fucking up her life. But then Costin smiled that goofy, demented smile of his, as if he knew she was on this side of the door and watching, and desire surged through her like the heat from a shot of vodka.

She unlocked and flung the door wide.

Costin wore his long green and purple scarf over a jacket too light for the cold they'd come home in last night, but he didn't seem to notice. Like a magician, he drew his arm out from behind his back and produced a bouquet in green cellophane.

"Welcome home, stranger," he said. He stepped forward and kissed her in the doorway.

Ruksana tasted him, the flavor of the coffee he'd consumed on the way over, probably on the trolley. She smelled his body washed fresh with a hint of peppermint in the soap, citrus in the shampoo, and beneath it all the smell of him so familiar and yet newly discovered. She sensed her own body reacting to him with an urgency coming from somewhere undiscovered; a new sensation but she liked it. She tugged at the flowers just hard enough to lead him in, took them and placed them. Somewhere.

She drew him through the kitchen, past the table and the sweet bread. Her tea—she must have set it down. Into her room they went, she walking backwards all the way. Her eyes bored into his, her fingers working at his belt, his zipper. He was hard underneath it.

She turned him, pivoted on her heels. When he was aimed at the bed, she tugged down his pants and pushed him. He fell across her duvet. His feet frantically worked to kick off his shoes, to get at least one leg out of his jeans.

She lifted her flannel nightgown over her head and flung it away. Every bit of her wanted him right now. She dropped to her knees over him, took hold of his penis and fit him into her, surprised by her own wetness. She looked at it on her hand, then held the hand out to him. He licked her palm. *Like a dog,* she thought, and the image propelled her toward a surprisingly sudden orgasm. She sat on him and groaned, amazed. She never orgasmed without using her fingers or his tongue.

Half sated but still aroused, she rode up and down on him. She leaned forward to kiss him. His palms grazed her nipples and a current jolted through her. When had her breasts ever been so sensitive? She rocked and shivered, bore down on him and thrust her pelvis against him. He came with a gasp, his legs twitching, his head back, over and done in just minutes. She continued to ride a little longer in the sensation of the flood. Her fingers cupped over her pubis, the tip of her middle finger flicking rapidly until, with a shudder and a deep groan of release, she lowered herself to him, her nose in his scarf, her head processing scents of fresh air, coal, car exhaust, and him. When had sex ever been like this?

After a minute, his hands slid up and closed over her shoulder blades. "It's nice to see you, too," he muttered in her ear.

Finally, she leaned up on her elbows, felt him shrink out of her. She smiled into his eyes. "Four months is too long," she said. He barked a laugh. That was what he had said to her at the airport just before she boarded her flight to Antarctica.

"Yes," he answered. "By about four months. I didn't even get my clothes off. Of course you cheated by having only one item to remove. Maybe we should start over." His glance rose then above her eyes. "So, did someone do something to your hair for fun, or did some of it freeze in the cold?"

She tried to look up at her own hair. "What are you talking about?"

"That." He reached up and pinched a forelock of her hair.

Still thinking that he must be teasing, she got up from him and crossed to the bathroom sink. She barely noticed the cold trickle along her thigh.

In the mirror her short-cropped auburn hair had a solid patch of white in it the size and shape of a rabbit's foot. She brushed at it, pulled: White all the way to the roots. She tried to think if it had been like that last night. But, no, it couldn't have.

She met her own gray gaze, saw the concern in her eyes, and lowered her eyelids before turning away. She went and lay beside him on her belly as if she might crawl back into her covers.

"Hey. Did something happen, was the flight back a rough one?" he asked. "I've heard of people's hair turning white from fear."

She knew that wasn't the case. This had happened overnight. It was a moment before she turned her head and looked his way. "It's your fault. Sex with you, that's what did it. I didn't have any white hair last night when I went to bed."

"Sex with me." He said it as if vaguely impressed that he could cause such a transformation.

"Well, was it white when you came to the door?" she teased.

He pondered a moment. "No, I don't think it was. I didn't notice anyway."

"You see?"

His eyes went sly. "We need to repeat the experiment, to see if you're right."

She inhaled him. Her fingers went to the scarf. Her other hand started down the buttons of his shirt. "At least one more time," she said.

–7–

Where the energy came from she could not say, but rather than exhausting her, the sex seemed to charge her battery. Even though they went slowly the second round, her whole being seemed to be humming with life. She wanted to bite Costin all over, and did finally, her teeth closed on his shoulder until he twitched, and she let go, aware that she'd lost control. She still wanted to bite him, but restrained the urge.

By the time he rolled aside, fully naked now, Ruksana's fever and exhaustion had vanished, replaced with something like a pheromonal high.

"You know, I did come by for a reason," he said, "I mean, another reason than this. I wanted to remind you that we're performing in two nights."

"The orchestra?"

"Yes. Dukas' *Ucenicul Vrăjitor* first, then a wonderful Şostakovici concerto for violoncel, and a Sibelius sinfonia to finish. Mihai Marica's the soloist. It's going to be stunning. And you love the cello."

"Of course I'll come," she replied, "but I'm only going to hear your violin."

"That's right." He ran a hand along her side and rested it against her hip. "Now, tell me about Antarctica. I want to hear everything about your periglacial..."

"Zones?"

"Yes, right." He smiled sheepishly. "You see, without you here to quiz me all the time, I forget. I've missed you." He leaned over and they kissed. She lost herself in the taste, some of it her own, some of it his.

Lying back, she said, "You want to know about Antarctica. But, you know, if you quizzed me all day long, I still couldn't read music."

"Okay, so make it simple for me. Just hum the melody. But I want to be part of everything with you."

It took all her effort then to hold his sweet gaze and not tell him about the "everything" she was fairly certain he didn't want to be part of. She took his hand from her hip, kissed his fingers. They tasted of her. She denied the swirl of arousal that stirred. She seemed to be on the verge of arousal today. "I'll tell you all about it later," she said as if to the hand. "Right now I just want to enjoy how you feel and smell." She snuggled against him and closed her eyes. Behind her eyelids, she thought she could almost see his heartbeat.

– 8 –

By the time her grandfather returned, Costin had gone to a rehearsal, and Ruksana had the previous night's stew reheated. Before she could even tell him about Costin, he pointed at her and said, "What did you do?"

"Costin, he—"

"He painted your hair?" He flicked at the white tuft with his finger. "That's not...That really is your hair."

"I know. It happened this morning sometime. I'm not sure I know why—maybe a nightmare I had." She thought of the leaking glacial fluid, but that had fallen on her cheek. She'd been wearing a helmet.

Her grandfather brooded as if the hair meant something that he couldn't quite recall. He pressed a knuckle against his nose, but whatever he was thinking, he didn't voice it, and finally sighed, defeated, and went on as if it was nothing. "But he was here, your Costin."

She imagined that he could smell what they'd gotten up to even under the spicy aroma of the stew. "This morning. He came by to invite me to the symphony. You're invited, too."

"When?"

"Two nights."

"Ah. That's too bad. I cannot that evening."

She looked at him critically and he turned aside as if something in the other room had suddenly caught his interest. "Why, you have a date, don't you?"

He broke into a secret smile. "I have a life, you know. Like Costin, I didn't sit here and brood all the time you were away. Not that I think Costin is also dating a forty-seven year old widow."

"Forty-seven. You're robbing the cradle."

He looked at her, about to object, but then replied, "Yes, I am, and I'm enjoying the hell out of it." Then he waved the matter aside. "But let me tell you what I heard at university today. And it was on the radio. Talk of vampires. Not pretend ones. Real live vampires."

"Isn't that a contradiction, bunicul?"

He considered what he'd said and chuckled. "Once it might have been. This is something else. This is something exciting."

"One of the people on my team was talking about this. She lived in New York, and it worried her to go home. She made it sound like gang violence, not like something supernatural."

"But it is supernatural, you see? The supernatural merging into the natural."

She formulated a rebuttal about belief in the supernatural, but then stopped herself. He was holding onto his excitement with the pure zeal of a small boy. She didn't want to attack that.

Her mother had been the practical one who dismissed grandfather's flights of fantasy—his tales of Baba Yaga, of goblins, witches, and werewolves. It seemed to fall along sexual lines. The men in the family wallowed in the fantastic, the women were the practical, level-headed ones. Which wasn't to say that scientists didn't dream, too; only that it wasn't huts on chicken legs that populated their dreams.

Thus, while she suspected anything in the media to be at best a hyperbolic account, she let it go. As grandfather had so often said, folklore and fact could be mirror images, once you established how the distortions disguised the commentary or the cautionary warning about real dangers. She believed him, although for her, the two really did not mix any better than reality and religion.

-9-

Two nights later, she ate a small dinner alone and then left early to get to the Ateneul Roman on time. She wanted to drive there, and needed to retrieve her small, dark blue Dacia Logan from storage parking. Her grandfather did not drive, and while she could have ridden the trolleys, she hoped to stop at university and collect her departmental mail on the way home after the performance.

The concert was wonderful, which was hardly a surprise. The George Enescu Philharmonic always delivered a grand program. Their rendition of Dukas was both sinister and comic, the Sibelius rich and emotional as his work always was. But it was the Şostakovici that most affected her. Marica, the handsome cello soloist, drew a full range of passion from the instrument as it conversed with and cajoled the orchestra. In the fourth movement she sat with eyes closed as the music painted a world behind her eyelids, whisked her on a mad, unstoppable run through a forest. Where the imagery came from, she didn't know, but it was so precise, so certainly a forest around her; it was all she could do to make herself sit still as it swept her along. This was unusual from something that wasn't program music—that didn't claim to be telling a story from the beginning.

She wasn't the only one affected, as witnessed by the standing ovation for Marica, the director, Valentin Raymond, and the whole of the orchestra.

Afterwards she joined Costin and five others in a celebration. They might have been classically trained musicians, but they drank and partied like rock stars, and some had their groupies, too. With the exception of Toma, who was a new boyfriend of Aurelia, the second violinist, Ruksana knew them all, as they knew about her situation. So the first round were all "Welcome home" toasts. Aurelia asked if Antarctica was colder than Bucureşti. She explained that along the coast it could be almost temperate, because it was summer there in February. Bogdan, a percussionist, announced, "Then, I am going to winter in Antarctica next year!"

Costin commented, "And if you wear this tuxedo, you can mate with a penguin."

Irina, a clarinetist, said, "He had better hope it's blind."

That sent them into a flurry of teases and insults until, in a lull, one of the older members, Sebastian, who played oboe and had crazy, thick eyebrows, asked "Did any of you hear about the vampires in America?"

"Isn't that one of their political parties?" Aurelia offered.

"Or a church. Over there they invent a new one every fifteen minutes," said Toma. He was short with black hair.

"Hardly new," replied Bogdan. "We Orthodox have been drinking blood for centuries in our rituals."

"Always ahead of the curve, are you, Bogdan?" asked Costin.

Bogdan wrapped a massive arm around Irina. "And what is wrong with that? Who wants to be behind it?"

"Maybe you should join these vampires."

"If they exist." Irina stepped out from under his arm, then added, "Of course, if he's joining up, we can be almost sure they don't."

Aurelia turned to Ruksana. "Your grandfather's a folklorist, isn't he? I've read one of his books even. What does he think of this?"

"I don't know," she replied. "But he heard the same report as Sebastian. He mentioned it as I was leaving for the concert."

Toma, who sported a burnt orange scarf and had nervous eyes, tossed the end of it over his shoulder for perhaps the third time. "Then there really was a report—there are vampires?"

Everyone looked at Sebastian. He shrugged. "I didn't create them." He tossed back his drink, and indicated to a waiter that he would have another. "Take it up with Vlad the Impaler."

"That's right," said Bogdan. "We've had the vampire much longer than the Americans. We own the franchise."

Irina shook her head. Aurelia leaned over to her and said loudly, "You can come stay with me tonight."

Toma gaped. Ruksana, seeing it, said, "Better have protection, Irina."

"Ooh. A condom or a stake?" asked Costin.

Irina replied, "Both."

"You're all *terrible*," said Aurelia.

"How many of us have you tried?"

It was Sebastian who said it, so unexpected that Bogdan choked on his ale and the table erupted with howls of laughter.

– 10 –

Ruksana decided to go home. She would have stayed with Costin, but he was happily energized for a late night, and she could feel herself already flagging. She wanted to get to the university and home before the sun came up—which made her laugh, as it sounded exactly like a vampire's complaint…at least, the old world version of a vampire. And a vampire would have loved the supermoon.

Costin insisted on walking her to her car, which she'd parked on a small side street, and along the way, she caught glimpses of the orange moon between buildings. He didn't seem to notice, but by then he had downed various beers and was weaving slightly as he walked beside her; not so drunk that she had to hold him up, but on his way.

"I'm more worried about you getting lost on the way back to the club," she told him as he held the car door for her to get in.

He laughed and pounded his chest like King Kong. "I'm not in any danger from anything except love!" He was about to say more, but she put her finger on his lips, then replaced it with her own lips. When she pulled away, he said, "You go home and sleep now, young lady, because tomorrow I intend to ravish you again." Then he leaned in, kissed her and shut the door. He stood in the cold, his breath a ribbon, until she started the car and put it in gear. In her mirror he waved furiously until she'd turned the corner. She decided then and there that she loved him beyond words.

The university was at the other end of the city center. She drove down the Bulevardul Nicolae Balescu and finally got a good look at the huge moon. Its light felt warm in the chilly interior of her car.

The university was all but deserted. She parked nearly on the sidewalk in front of the Old Building. What was unique about the University of Bucureşti was that it had no single campus. Its buildings were spread all over the city. No one was about, and she entered and went straight up to the central office.

Her small mailbox was full, in fact stuffed. Journals, notices about events that had already occurred, like the Christmas party, and books that she had requested had been crammed into the pigeonhole with her name on it. An overflow basket bearing her name sat on the counter beneath it, and that was full, too.

She sorted through most of it, tossing aside the obviously irrelevant, dead mail. The rest she carried or stuffed into her shoulder bag. She could read it more carefully at home, tomorrow.

Outside, the moonlight seemed to track her like a searchlight along the sidewalk. She watched her breath steam and glisten in the glow. The nearness of the moon made her want to buy a telescope and put it on their little balcony, where she and grandfather could try to look at planets and stars. She realized that they couldn't see many. It was the skies of Antarctica she was remembering, and the great exploding smear of stars upon the sky there.

The ground had a rime of frost on it. She saw nobody about, but it was so cold, there would be no one out. No lovers. Thinking that as she climbed in and started the engine, she imagined herself and Costin naked in snow. Now, why was that so arousing?

The door of her car was flung back suddenly. Before she fully comprehended, fully turned, a fist slammed into her cheek. Hurtled across the front seat, she struck her bag and it flipped, spilling its contents onto the floor. The shift lever stabbed at her belly. Sparkles scattered everywhere. Her thoughts refused to coalesce—what had happened? Someone had a hold of her, was turning her onto her back, at least she wasn't on the shift knob now. Fingers dug at her hips, under her slacks, her panties, yanking all of it down. Abstractly she understood what was happening and kicked out. Heard her shoe hit the pavement, heard the breathing. Then came the pressure on top of her, his stinking mouth on hers. She heard his blood whooshing through his arteries.

Lightning crackled through the car. It lit his scruffy face: Dark eyes wide, slavering lips—but almost immediately the face twisted with terror. A claw hooked the corner of his mouth and sliced it open, all the way to the ear. His scream must have shattered windows for a mile. A flash and she stood outside the car, above him. He was trying to crawl away. Her blood raced, heart hammered. She rose up, saw the moon all red now, and then lunged into blackness.

–11–

Blue lights were flashing all around. Ruksana began to choke, turned her head and spat out the fluid in her mouth. It tasted foul. She felt a hand on her and instinctively fought, kicked out. Then she realized it was a young police officer, who was saying, "It's okay, it's okay, don't move." She stopped. What was this?

She sprawled in the driver's seat, half tilted into the car, and naked from the waist down. Her coat was gone, her blouse in tatters. She covered her sex, looked at the cop accusingly, but he was trying to hand her his own coat. She grabbed and spread it across her lap. The lights flashed from three different cars and a medical vehicle, and she realized now there were more police behind this one, in the darkness beyond the door of her car.

"You were attacked," said the policeman, pulling her attention back to him. "Do you remember anything?"

She blinked, and took a moment to reassemble the fragments of her memory. "He had to have been waiting, watching me."

"You teach here?"

"He hit me." She reached up, touched her cheek. It stung. She could feel that it was swollen. When she looked at her hand, it was smeared with blood. Staring at it, she added automatically, "I'm on sabbatical."

Another car pulled up, screeching to a halt. The officer turned and started for it.

"My shoes, where are my shoes?" she asked, but he was already out of earshot. Ruksana carefully slid down until her bare feet touched the cold pavement. She kept the coat wrapped around her and stood up. That was when she saw what the other police were focused on: A body, half-dismembered, so freshly dead that steam still rose from its exposed entrails. It so little resembled a human beneath the blood and gore that she hardly reacted. It was like seeing something in a movie, separate from her and easily compartmentalized, denied.

"Here," said one of the inspectors who'd just arrived, "you shouldn't move, miss. We don't know the extent of your injuries."

"I'm looking for my shoes."

The inspector appeared to have raced here without shaving or brushing his thinning hair. He told her his name, but she forgot it even as she heard him. All that stuck was his rank: Inspector Principal. He stared carefully at her, then came closer and said, "I'll find the shoes for you. You stay in your car." She nodded and sat down again. The inspector turned back to the young officer and said, "She's in shock. See if you can find her shoes. If they aren't attached to that bastard, give them to her."

They were, as it turned out, under her car, but spattered with blood.

She rode to the hospital on a gurney although she insisted she didn't need this. On the way, one of the medical nurses asked her questions, which she forgot as fast as she replied. At one point she said, "Oh, I need to give that policeman his coat back," then realized she was lying under a blanket and the coat was no longer covering her. She didn't think she had her shoes on, either, and couldn't see them around her.

At the hospital, she was carefully examined, smears and samples taken amidst apologies for the invasiveness of this necessary procedure. It seemed to amaze everyone who paraded into her room that she had no external wounds other than where he'd hit her and a few minor abrasions. Once they had established that she wasn't bleeding or otherwise injured beyond a mild concussion, they let her shower. As a river of pink water poured from her and circled her feet, she began to understand why they were all so surprised and upset.

When she finally saw herself in the mirror, she almost overlooked the discolored swelling of her cheek because of her hair. The spade-shaped white spot above her forehead had tripled in size. "What is happening to me?" she asked her image. She put on the paper gown they'd left her and then sat down to wait for whatever came next.

Shortly, the same inspector turned up. He too expressed amazement that she hadn't been torn apart by the dogs.

"Dogs?" she asked.

"It seems fairly certain. He was clawed and mauled to pieces, and while you had some of his skin under your fingernails, I think we can rule you out as the perpetrator in this. I am curious if you had a dog with you, or even if one rides with you often perhaps, because whatever pack did this responded to something, and another dog, you know, the barking, the smell—"

"Dogs," she said again. It was preposterous. "No, I've never owned a dog."

"Oh." He looked down, disappointed by the news. "Well, it's no matter. My suspicion is, his being wedged in the door of your car accidentally saved your life, kept the pack from getting at you. And it's poetic justice, too. We're fairly certain he's a local rapist who has eluded us for some time. The M.O. matches and he has a record. You would have been his sixth victim." His eyes met hers again. "You're very lucky, Miss Vulpes. He did not succeed, and you'll never be bothered by him again.

Nobody will." He dragged the plastic chair across the room and sat in front of her. "So, please, even though you may not remember very much, walk me through whatever you do remember."

Eventually, after she had related everything she could recall, the inspector released her to her grandfather. He had brought with him clothes for her, which were passed to her in the room so that she could change there. She still had no coat or shoes. It seemed the police had kept them.

Decebal stood up as she came out, and she experienced a moment of déjà vu as if she was in the airport again, arriving home anew. A policewoman sat next to him. He hugged her to him, more tightly than the last time, and he snuffled against her, in tears. The woman had her coat and shoes. The coat was spotted with dried blood. The rest of her clothes, shredded and torn, would be kept as evidence.

A squad car drove them both home. Her car was being held for the moment as well. On the drive home she realized that the inspector's version of events made no sense: If her clothing was ripped up, too, why were there no cuts on her skin to match the...she hesitated to call him the victim, but for a second she flashed on the ghastly corpse she'd seen from her car door.

At home Decebal embraced her again. He had regained control of himself. He kept his arms on her shoulders, looked at her critically. It seemed to her he wanted to ask something, but finally he just ruffled her hair. "If you keep going with traumas like this, you'll be a white haired old lady before you're thirty." He sat her down and made her eat the last of the stew he'd made and drink some wine.

In her bedroom, he started talking and couldn't seem to stop himself. "I had to go through your things for the hospital, so here, I laid out your nightgown for you. I want you to rest now, dearest. They gave me something to help you sleep if you need it. Tomorrow you're going to have a very bad bruise on your cheek, but no bones are broken they said. I suppose you'll have to go back for more rabies shots, and if you want, I'll change any dressings before you sleep—but, that is to say, they didn't tell me where you were bitten or how badly, and I—"

"I wasn't. I wasn't bitten."

"But it was a dog attack. They told me."

"I know. But if it was, the dogs didn't bite me. They attacked the man who was trying to..." The word *rape* burst in her head. She couldn't speak it. The shock caught up with her then, rolling across her like a thunderstorm. Her body shook and she suddenly began to cry, collapsing on the floor like a rag doll.

Decebal held her in his arms and rocked her; but under his breath he was saying, "Impossible," over and over, and she knew he was right.

"ESCALATION"

Jonathan Maberry

–1–

New York

Fifteen Days after the V-Event

"Professor Luther Swann?" asked the big man in the black suit. He wore sunglasses and had a wire coiled behind his ear. His partner looked like a clone, and a third almost identical man stood by the open door of a smoke gray Crown Victoria.

Swann paused, the key to his Toyota Prius almost into the keyhole. He knew who these men had to be. FBI or worse. It saddened him. And scared him.

"I'm Swann."

The first man opened a leather identification case. Swann read as far as the initials and his stomach seemed to fill with ice water.

NSA.

"We'd like you to come with us," said the man. His voice was unemotional as his face. He had the kind of face Swann believed would bleed if forced to wear a genuine smile.

"Am I in trouble?" he asked.

The second agent stepped closer and to one side.

"Now, professor," said the first agent. It was not a request.

–2–

"Ah, Professor Swann," said a man Swann had never seen or heard of before, "thank you for coming here at such short notice. Have a seat."

Swann felt a little numb as he lowered himself carefully into an expensive leather chair. He glanced around. At the blue rug with its American eagle embroidery. At the famous desk. At the curved walls. At the seal on the wall.

This was the Oval Office—a fact that made his head swim—but the man who sat down across from him was not the president.

"Is this about what happened at the hospital?" asked Swann.

The man waited until the NSA agents left the room and closed the door. He crossed his legs and took a thick blue folder from a side table, glanced at the contents for a moment, then closed it and placed it on his lap.

"Do you know who I am?" asked the man.

"No, sir. But those guys were National Security agents, so…does that make you their boss?"

"I'm Bill Gabriel, the White House Chief of Staff."

Swann cleared his throat. "I'm sorry, but I don't really know much about national politics."

Gabriel waved his hand. "Neither do most of the people who work *in* national politics."

It was a small joke that went nowhere.

"Professor," continued Gabriel, "just to get you up to speed, I've read the case file on Michael Fayne as well as the transcripts of your subsequent testimony."

Swann nodded. He gripped the armrests of the chair.

Gabriel cocked his head to one side. "I know that Dr. Feldman called you regarding the incident in Los Angeles."

"Yes, but I don't know much about…"

"There's been another."

The statement, those three little words, slapped Swann to a shocked silence.

"In fact," continued the Chief of Staff, "there have been three additional incidents.

"In L.A.—?"

"No. One in Chicago, one in St. Martinville, Louisiana, and the most recent in Providence, Rhode Island."

"My…*God*. All like Fayne…?"

Instead of answering, Gabriel asked, "How much do you know about the Los Angeles case?"

Swann cleared his throat. "Next to nothing. I tried to get some information, I even flew out there, but the police stonewalled me."

"What *do* you know?"

"That there was another…another…"

Gabriel gave him a hard, cold smile of encouragement. "I think we're past the point where we should be afraid of saying the world, professor. I think we all have to accept that what we are dealing with here are vampires."

Even now, even after everything, it was hard for Swann to hear that word without flinching. However he nodded and repeated it. "Vampires. God."

"Los Angeles," prompted the Chief of Staff.

"Oh…the papers said that there were four murders, but I might not even have noticed it if not for Dr. Feldman's call. She said that a woman who was in a coma apparently woke up, went crazy and killed some people. As far as I know the police haven't caught the woman yet." He paused. "The papers all said that the victims were drained of blood. That their throats were torn out and their bodies mutilated. After that reporter, Miss Nitobe, broke the whole Michael Fayne thing, the L.A. papers grabbed it and said that it was the same thing. Dr. Feldman believes it is, too."

"And you?"

"I don't know. People tend to sensationalize. I mean, have you seen the papers? Everything's vampire, vampire, vampire. Some people are talking werewolves and zombies, too. It's insane."

Gabriel pursed his lips. "Here are the facts," he said. "The subject of this case is one Anelia Stoeva, fifty-seven years old, unmarried. She worked for a company that cleaned office buildings. Forty-four days ago she called into work sick and was driving to a pharmacy to pick up a prescription for antibiotics when she was involved in a very bad three-car accident on Sepulveda Boulevard. One driver was killed in the accident, and Ms. Stoeva and the third driver were hospitalized. The third driver, by the way, was treated and released. He's since been re-admitted, this time to a military hospital, and is under observation."

"Observation? Is he…?"

"So far he's merely a very confused and frightened citizen, but he'll remain our guest for now. As for Ms. Stoeva, she remained in the hospital for over a month following the accident. In a coma, apparently. She was close to clinical brain death and as she had no relatives the hospital administrators were seeking court approval to remove her from life support. However…four days ago Anelia Stoeva went missing from the hospital. The duty nurse was found dead in the patient's room. And, yes, the papers were that much right in that her throat was torn out and her blood drained."

"All of it?"

"Enough of it. Forensic examinations concluded that there was saliva in the wounds and DNA testing makes it a positive match to Ms. Stoeva. The same is true of the other victims."

"The papers said that other victims had nothing in common?"

"So it seems. A real estate agent from Burbank, a UPS driver, and a little girl in a playground. There are no known connections, so it appears that Ms. Stoeva is killing out of need and opportunity rather than according to any agenda."

"And they haven't found her?"

"Not so far."

Gabriel leaned forward. "Professor Swann, this was a woman who was very nearly killed in a traffic accident. She had multiple broken bones and internal injuries, not to mention head trauma. Granted, her bones were knitting and they'd done what they could in surgery, but in short she was a step away from being declared dead. She was meat. Even if she woke up, there's no workable scenario to explain how she would have the physical strength to attack and kill four people. The UPS driver was a big man, six-two and two-twenty. Served a tour in Iraq early in the war. She ripped him apart. I mean that, Professor Swann… that brain dead, crippled woman tore his arms out of their sockets and nearly ripped his head off. A professional offensive tackle for the Cowboys couldn't do that." He leaned back. "So…we would like you to explain that to us."

"I—can't."

Gabriel smiled. He was in his early sixties, with iron-gray hair and a precisely trimmed mustache. "Try," he said.

Swann chewed a crumb of skin off of his thumb. He looked at the wall, at the ceiling. Gabriel waited him out. Finally he took a breath and turned to face the Chief of Staff.

"First…tell me about the others," he said. "How similar are they to Swann and this woman—"

"Stoeva," provided Gabriel.

"Stoeva. How similar are the other attacks? Have you managed to arrest any of the, um, perpetrators."

"No, to that last question, though I am assured that we are close to making an arrest in two cases. Rhode Island and Chicago. As for the others, we don't even have I.D.s on the killers. All we have are victims."

"All the same? Dismembered and drained of blood?"

"Actually, no." Gabriel flipped open the folder, selected high-resolution digital photo and handed it over.

Swann almost dropped it.

"Jesus Christ," he gasped. The picture was horror show stuff. The *thing* displayed in the image could only vaguely be described as a human being. He could barely stand to look at the lumps of torn flesh and the ends of jagged bone. Swann handed the photo back, happy to be rid of it. "That's not like Fayne's victims. That looks like an animal attacked it."

"Not far off," admitted Gabriel, his face grim. "The body was mauled and partially devoured. Forensics tells me that the amount of blood at the scene closely approximates what you'd expect to find in a teenage girl."

"That…that was a teenage girl?"

Gabriel showed him a second picture. A lovely face, clearly Native American, with straight black hair and almost Asian eyes. "A Navajo girl, age eighteen, named Madeline Tsotse. She worked at a burger stand in a fairly remote corner of the reservation. She went missing five days ago and was found yesterday morning."

"Five days? That means it happened before Los Angeles…"

"Yes. That's part of the problem, Professor Swann, we're beginning to put together a pattern of attacks that span the country. The earliest known attacks are Michael Fayne's first victims. However, the Chicago killings began only four days after Fayne's first kill."

"How come that's not on the news?"

Gabriel nodded, approving of the question. He removed another picture. This one was a morgue photo that showed a disheveled and filthy man with long tangled hair and a ragged beard lying on a slab, a sheet pulled down to reveal his torn throat.

"We have five victims like this in Chicago," said Gabriel. "All street people. The chief medical examiner made the connection between the murders because of similar reports that crossed his desk from five different hospitals. Chicago P.D. are working with our task force to keep this as far off the radar as possible."

Swann looked up sharply. "Task force?"

"That's why you're here, professor. At the direction of the president Homeland Security has begun assembling a team to handle this crisis. And…we think it *is* a crisis. Even though there are differences in most of the cases, there are also very disturbing similarities."

"What similarities? And how does this all involve me? I was brought in to interview Fayne and advise the New York police, but…I'm out of it now." He paused. "Right?"

Gabriel said, "We'll get to that in a moment. First, here are pictures of the Rhode Island victims."

These were the worst of all. Six pictures of children. Or, at least Swann thought they were children. They wore the kinds of pajamas or night gowns parents put on children. On toddlers. Three wore diapers. They were in small beds, they each had stuffed toys. But every single one of the six bodies was as withered and desiccated as a mummy. Far more than blood had been taken from them.

If Gabriel hadn't darted out a hand the pictures would have fallen from Swann's numb fingers. The Chief of Staff stood and crossed quickly to a sideboard, poured water into a glass and pressed the glass into Swann's hands.

"I'm sorry to drop all this on you, professor," said Gabriel. "I really am…but as I'm sure you can understand, we're all a bit lost here."

Swann sipped the water, choked and coughed, sipped again and set the glass down.

"You said…you said there were similarities. What did you mean? None of these look the same as what I saw."

Gabriel removed another sheet from the folder. Swann took it with great reluctance, but this time there were no horrific images. It was a lab report. Much of the information was technical, written in the obscure language of true medical professionals. But one line from the lab technicians summary leapt out.

Saliva from all of the samples provided demonstrates the presence of the I1V1 pathogen.

Swann raised his eyes from the paper to meet the hard eyes of the Chief of Staff.

"The Ice Virus?"

"Yes," Gabriel said slowly. "Your theory that vampires were—or perhaps *are*—a genetic branch of the human evolutionary tree is being taken seriously. Our best geneticists are at this very minute studying the DNA samples we've collected. They're trying to knock down your theory that the genetic potential for vampirism, if it exists at all, might reside within junk DNA. But...so far it looks like you might have hit the bull's-eye with your first shot. The leading theory is that the Ice Virus somehow triggered or activated some dormant genes. The genes that were once responsible for the phenomenon we've come to believe is the myth of the vampire. Your theory is being given serious study, professor."

"Hey, it's not like I *want* to be right about this..."

"Professor, I think we can both agree that it would be better for everyone if this is something genetic rather than things that go bump in the night. We can't very well react or respond to the supernatural, can we?"

"No," Swann said softly. "But...does that mean that everyone who was infected with the Ice Virus is going to...?"

"To become a vampire?" said Gabriel. "We had all better pray that this is only a rare occurrence. Very rare. Considering that each of these cases involves multiple murders, the math is deeply frightening. And, by the way, that's why Homeland is spear-heading this rather than the FBI or local law enforcement."

"Why? I thought Homeland only dealt with terrorists?"

Gabriel said, "We are dealing with an outbreak of vampirism, Professor Swann. Can you think of a situation more aptly suited to the word 'terror'?"

Swann could feel the blood drain from his face. He used his fingers to wipe sweat from his eyes. "But...why bring me here? How can *I* help?"

Gabriel nodded again. "I have scientists and science geeks of every stripe. I have city, state and federal cops, I have the military. What I *don't* have is someone who understands what we're facing. I don't have a vampire expert."

"Okay, sure, but everything I know about the subject is from folklore. From legend and myth."

Gabriel held up the photos of the dead children. "A myth isn't responsible for this, professor. It may be that we all—every single person on the planet—may have to adjust our thinking about what belongs in fairy stories and what's out there walking the streets of our cities."

Swann turned his face away from the pictures.

"Ice Virus," he murmured.

"Ice Virus," agreed Gabriel, "though now I think we may have to come up with a new name for it. Perhaps something starting with a V."

"STALKING ANNA LEI" PT.1

🕷

James A. Moore

–1–

The rain came down in sheets and made looking at anything even harder than the darkness had already managed. The problem was, I needed to see what was inside the building across the alley from me and between me and that building there were around fifteen cops and enough cars to bring them all to the Stansford Arms Apartments.

Sometimes a vampire can't catch a break.

The winds were blasting the hell out of the brick wall I was leaning against, and the water was dripping in my ear and half blinding me. I settled my claws for a few more seconds, said a very quick prayer, and then I jumped, hurtling the forty-five feet between buildings and praying very, very hard that I didn't miss.

Ah, lightning. It's great stuff for atmosphere, isn't it? It's also very bright and the thunder that follows it when it's close enough to blind you is absolutely deafening. I was reaching for the wet stonewall when the flash went off, and sure enough, I was looking in the right direction got get flashed right and proper.

Claws. Remember that part? Yes, I have claws. They're a fairly new thing for me, but I have them and they saved me from an embarrassing and messy ending.

The stones were rough, not smooth, and that helped, too. But mostly it was the claws that cut into the mortar between the stones that stopped me from dropping several stores and landing on either a squad car or a couple of cops. I'm pretty sure I called for my mother, or just possibly for God. I'm not too proud to admit I wanted to wet myself, not that anyone would have noticed in the downpour.

A few more moments of muttered curses and I was on the roof of the building. There was nowhere to hide from the rain, but at least there were a couple of air conditioning units up there to help me duck the cops I hadn't expected to be on the lookout. I guess when it comes to the murder of a prominent political figure's son, nothing gets over-looked. There were two uniforms up there, both of them looking as wet and unhappy as I felt. Getting past them wasn't very hard. I'm stealthy these days. You know, when I'm not almost falling to my death.

The stairwell was a different story. There were no officers to see, but there was definitely nowhere to hide, so I had to move as quickly as I could while trying to stay quiet.

I made it a whole two flights down before the first uniform saw me. He was looking at something in the corner of the narrow landing between flights, his flashlight lighting the area a good deal more than anything around it. You know how spies always look cool in black, in all those action flicks? Turns out they wear it for a reason. The pants were black, the shirt was black, my waterproof duster was black—and soaked through, thanks—but the buckles on my boots? Those were sil-ver and shiny. He saw them as I was coming down the stairs and the next thing I know, he's shining the light in my face.

A second after that, he was screaming. In his defense, I've seen what I look like when I'm working. I'd have screamed too.

Did I mention that I'm a vampire? I am. Only I'm not even sure if that's the proper term here.

Whatever the case, he had his service pistol aimed at my face before he'd finished screaming.

I looked down the barrel of that pistol and I screamed, too

–2–

A little bit of background information might be necessary. Look, it's my story and I'll tell it the way I want. I'll get back to the action, but I guess as some point I have to tell you why I was out in the middle of a massive storm and what would make me want to go and take on a small army of Chicago's Finest.

By now you've heard all about the vampires, right? I mean, about Michael Fayne, the doctors working on him and how there are other people who are coming down with the same sort of problem? Well, I'm one of them. My name is John Lei. I was born and raised in San Francisco's Chinatown. I'm fourth generation American, but that's where I was born. I'm not pure Chinese, I'm not pure anything, but I am a mutt and very proud of it. Got some Caucasian somewhere along the way, according to my grandfather, but I also have Korean, Japanese and, of course, Chinese in my background. Why do I bring that up? Because apparently what happens to you when you get hit by the V-Virus—that's Vampire Virus. Somebody actually tried to make "Vampirus" into the go-to word, but it didn't work. You know how Yuki Nitobe is kind of like the reporter authority on what's happening? Yeah. The guy that came up with Vampirus isn't. If you want to come up with a catch phrase and it doesn't work? Let it go. It might save your career—anyway, what happens to you when you catch the virus is apparently affected by your genetic history. Junk DNA, who knew it would have ethnic attitude? Well, if there is any good, old-fashioned European in my family, it wasn't enough to let me get all romantically handsome or even all sparkly in the daylight.

Anyways....

I'm minding my own business, doing a little work for one of the locals at home and before I can actually finish—let's just say I was debt collecting and leave it at that, shall we?—before I can finish collecting, I dropped like a stone. If I hadn't had a couple of friends along for the ride, I might have not made if back from that particular trip. Tommy and Rio have been my buddies since we were in the fifth grade. They called the ambulance and then made sure the paramedics knew where to find me before they ran back to report everything to our employers.

Me? I wound up in the hospital with a fever that broke records—in excess of one hundred and fifteen degrees—and then I wound up in a coma for three days. I don't remember a single bit of that. I was too busy having some mighty strange dreams. Maybe we'll get to those another time.

I recovered from the fever. That's the important thing, right? I got better. There were a few changes, of course, but I'm getting used to them. First big change was the color of my hair. I point this out because even after generations in the US there are a lot of superstitious people in Chinatown. Why is that important? Because when I got out of the hospital every hair on my body was white as snow. Not gray, not a little faded, white. Lot of people looked at it and maybe thought I was making a statement, like when I was fifteen and dyed my hair bright red (And THAT particular adventure ended with my father shaving my head.). Not this time. I just have white hair. Most everybody seemed fine with that, but a couple of the older neighbors took one look at me and got the hell off the street. Turns out having your hair go white is a sign of evil for some people. Me? I had no idea. I do now.

Let me explain something here. I'm not superstitious. I'm even very religious, but I think I get it. According to the news—Go, Yuki!—the genetic stew that causes this change might have caused problems in the past. There's a few people and a couple of doctors out there who believe that the vampire legends from around the world are maybe an indication that this virus existed before and maybe even affected people in the past. Ever hear of a hopping ghost? Well, as near as I can figure it out, if the legends are accurate and these things existed before—and throwing away all the stuff that our ancestors might have made up to explain the insanity—I am one. Not because my hair went white. Not because I'm a vampire. Not even because I was basically so deep in a coma that I might as well have been dead for three days. Nope. It's the rigor mortis that did made me decide.

For three days after I get out of the hospital my joints are aching and my legs are sore as hell and I'm too tired to do any stretches and then go to sleep same as I always have and when I woke up the pain was so bad I screamed. Every tendon in my body got stiff while I was sleeping. All of them. My legs, my arms, my back and my hips, all shot to hell in an instant. I couldn't move without being in agony. You know who helped me out? My little sister, Anna. Unlike me, Anna's a health nut. She's into yoga, does the whole Tai Chi thing, eats right and, just to add insult to injury, she's a straight A student. But it was her that figured out that I needed to stretch, and her that helped me stretch even while I was cursing her out and threatening to kill her a dozen times over.

There are acids that build up in the bodies of athletes. Turns out my body generates a lot of those acids, or something like them. It's a side effect of my condition. I either stretch every day and a lot, or I get to be crippled. I've learned to stretch. A lot.

We'll get back to that. Let's talk about the cop, shall we?

– 3 –

The cop started screaming for me to freeze, and I have to admit I might have panicked a little. I tried running away. Hey, it's what I did when I was younger and it's what I went to when I saw that gun.

Here's the thing: I can run very, very fast these days. I was back up on the roof before I knew what was happening, only by the time I got up there the cop had not only started following me, he'd also radioed to everyone else in the building that he was following a suspect. And everyone on the building, too. So those two guys I'd snuck past before? They were heading in my direction and there was nowhere I could hope to go to avoid dealing with at least three armed professionals who wanted to know what the hell I was doing at their crime scene.

Listen, I'm a lot of things, and not all of them are nice. I make my living by dubious methods, and I tend to like the better things in life, so I make my living doing a lot of dubious things for very dubious people. You get me? Good. I don't like to say some things straight out. What I do not do, however, is kill people. It's not my thing. I've hurt a lot of people in my time and I've gone to bed feeling bad about it more than once, but they always mended from what I did. You don't mend from death, so I don't deal in it.

Guess what? Guns kill people. I don't carry one for that reason. The men chasing my narrow ass did not see it the same way. They were looking for a killer with superhuman abilities and between my funky looks and the fact that I'd just sprinted two flights of stairs in something like seven big steps, I was fitting the bill. So I had maybe three choices and all of two seconds to figure out which one it was going to be. Choice number one, I could surrender. I have to say, that really wasn't an option. Why? Because I had my monster on at the time, and the guys with the guns? They might be the sort who shot the bejesus out of vampires and then worried about whether or not they were guilty. I really couldn't take that chance, especially since they were looking for a vampire already and that one was a killer. My second choice was I could go through these guys and I didn't much like that one, either. I've done a few unofficial tests. I'm much stronger than I used to be, I'm a lot faster,

271

and I'm pretty damned tough. Under the right circumstances, I can take a beating and get back up without any problem. But I'm not bulletproof, or if I am, I haven't exactly tested that theory yet.

That left me with one option. I took it. I ran. Right off the side of the building.

Actually, I ran to the edge and then I dropped. And while I was dropping, I let out a few girly screams and clawed at the windowsills and screamed a bit more. Four stories down I caught a window ledge and stopped my fall. About two seconds later I was breaking through the window and not the least bit worried about waking up the inhabitants. I crouched on the windowsill for maybe two seconds, saw that I wasn't actually going to land on someone and that I hadn't shredded anyone with the glass from the broken window, and then I ran. The room was dark. I didn't care. That's another neat little side effect of my new life. Anna tells me I have "Cat eyes" when I go all monster-face. All I know is I can see just as well in a dark room as I can in a lit one. I made it out of that bedroom and into the hallway and from there I hit the living room and the front door of the apartment. I got very lucky and no one was home.

Out the front door I took a few seconds to look around and then I went straight for the stairs again. There wasn't really an option. I had to get to the fifth floor, which was three down from where I was, and I had to check out the scene below. Once I was there I wouldn't have to wait around for long. I knew what I was looking for and if I found it, I could get gone a minute or so later. I hit the stairs running and I didn't stop. And I maybe could have, but if I had, the cop that I was running into would have had the time to draw and fire on me.

I'd be lying if I said everything slowed down. I've heard people say that it happens, but it never has for me. I started moving and the cop on the stairs had enough time to see that I was coming before I hit him in the chest and moved on past. I didn't look back to check on him, but I heard him hit the wall and bounce. Around to the landing and I didn't have time to really do the human thing, so I caught some wall and ran along it for a couple of seconds. Then I was down to the next flight and bounding down the stairs. The door to the stair well was just opening. I slammed it shut as hard as I could, which meant I saw the metal frame bend a bit and felt the steel door buckle. No cops from the sixth floor, but thanks for playing.

On the fifth floor everything got messy. There was no choice about it, that was where the crime scene was, and that was where I needed to be. That also meant that most of the police were already there, and even with the alarm called and back up demanded, most of them weren't moving. They had a crime scene to watch, right? I'm running through the door from the stairs and all I can think to myself is that I'm handling this the wrong way. Vampires are new on the scene.

No one has really decided what's to be done about this "epidemic," and here I am making it worse for any decisions, because I'm tainting a crime scene. I'm screwing up whatever evidence there is, and in the process, I'm probably leaving all sorts of evidence about myself, because I'm too fucking stupid to wear gloves. I have a record, okay? I'm not exactly a saint. And the troubles I'm making for vampire kind? I have no doubt they'll come back to haunt me.

But I don't exactly have a choice, do I? See, the monster that's out there killing people? I've been chasing it since San Francisco, hunting the damned thing down, because it took my sister from me and no one in the world means more to me than Anna.

–4–

Not long after I fell sick and came home, I discovered the unpleasant truth about my condition. Oh, I'd heard all about the vampires by then, but there were only a few of them when I got sick, and by the time I got out of the hospital no one was even considering the word "epidemic." Well, not true. Maggie Ruiz was. I only know that because she called my house and asked if she could speak to me. She found out about my case exactly too late to stop me from leaving the hospital. She was perfectly willing to pay for me to come see her, or, barring that, she was willing to come see me. I told her I'd think about it. I thought she was off her rocker.

Then the hunger hit me. Listen, I still eat food. I like food. I would even go so far as to say that Big Mac is one of my favorite friends and I love him even more when he brings his cousin, Large Fries along to visit. But the hunger doesn't have anything to do with food. I know, because I tried feeding myself for two days, desperate to stop that painful emptiness inside of me. I ate like it was Thanksgiving and it never touched the hunger. I've never been addicted to anything. I don't even smoke cigarettes and everyone I know smokes cigarettes. Seriously. But all I can say is I guess the hunger is like withdrawal symptoms from some of the heavy stuff. I was shaking, I was sweating, I was having trouble seeing straight.

I guess maybe it was instinct that let me survive. I guess maybe instinct has kept a lot of vampires alive, only in my case, I guess maybe I was luckier than a lot of them. I didn't go for blood. A lot of vampires apparently do. Some go for meat, some go for blood. I went for something less substantial. Call it what you want. I prefer to call it life force. I went for the energy inside instead of the wet, juicy stuff. Sound weird? I'll try to explain. I was having cravings, only I didn't know what they were for. Like I said, food wasn't doing it. I was getting close to trying my luck with one of the other vices, crank or coke or even something worse because I was feeling as low as I ever have and the doctors said there was nothing wrong with me. No fever, no nothing. I was just feeling that ravenous hunger and it wasn't leaving me alone.

And it was Anna to the rescue. She came into my room and looked at me for a moment, her face as calm as ever, and worried her lower lip before she nodded to herself and left again. By that point I was having trouble doing anything at all. Seriously. It was bad, and I was sweating and shivering and clawing at the sheets. And yes, I tore my bed linens to shreds because I didn't see the claws that came out of my fingers and even if I had, I wasn't in a state of mind to notice.

Anna came back with a dog. I'd seen the animal around the block a few times; it was a stray, I think. A pudgy, well fed stray that all the locals liked well enough. Anna brought the animal into my bedroom and closed the door. She looked at me on the bed and the dog sniffed around for a few seconds before starting a low rumble in its throat. It didn't like me. This animal that had always been friendly in the past— and had often gotten a few of my French fries when Big Mac came to visit—suddenly didn't like me very much.

Anna didn't say anything. But she looked at me in silence and then closed the door and left me alone with the dog. It tried to get out. It scratched at the door and it whined and it turned and looked at me and it growled, and it whined some more.

And I lunged for it, the hunger burning so brightly I thought I'd scream.

The dog screamed instead. Have you ever heard a dog scream? I wish I could say I'd never heard that sound.

When the screaming stopped, I could hear the sound of Anna crying in the other room and the hunger was gone, and the lifeless body of that silly mutt was in my hands. There were no wounds on the poor thing's body, but it was dead.

Vampire. There was no blood involved, but I still had a special hunger and it needed to be fed if I wanted to live.

I asked Anna how she knew what to do. My little sister, the scholar, the good one who made mom and dad proud. And she looked at me and shook her head. "I read the newspapers, Johnny. I'm not stupid. You had your monster-face going and I knew, so I did it."

My monster-face. That was her term for it. I guess maybe I just like that one better than Vampirus. It stuck. So it turns out when I decide to use my abilities my body goes through a physical change. I get my monster-face. My fingers get a little longer, I can see that one easily enough. If I go at it too long I start to grow fur on my body. Yes, fur. Long white fur to match up with my long white hair. I dye the hair, by the way. It's black these days. Stops the old ladies on the block from freaking out too much. My teeth grow longer, and they get round. My face changes. I had to practice for a while, but I finally figured out how to make the monster-face happen. If I had to say I look like anything in particular when I change, I'd have to go with cat. I get a feline muzzle, my eyes get bigger and rounder, and the color goes green and the pupils get all cat-like and slitted, my ears also get pointy. It's a little unsettling. Okay, it freaks my ass out. But it's a part of what I am now. And the longer I wear the monster-face, the more progressive the change becomes. The more I look like a cat and the less I look like John Lei. It's actually sort of helpful in some cases, like when I'm facing off against a room full of pissed off police officers.

–5–

Did I mention the angry cops? Yeah. Thought so.

There's no two ways to this. I had to get in, get out and stop long enough to look for clues along the way. And all I had to do was dodge all of the police officers in the place. Cops who had already been alerted to an intruder and were investigating the sort of murder that was going to make their lives miserable already. Was it my best move ever? I'm gonna have to go with no. Still, sometimes you have to do things you don't want to do. I can only imagine what went through their heads, really. I mean, I know what I looked like: big, white, wet, pissed off cat in people clothes. I ran into the room and looked around as fast as I could. Living room, nothing of importance, aside from several cops. I wasn't looking to get into a fight, just to get evidence. I started for the hallway and one of the cops did the police thing and stepped in the way, reaching for the gun. I hit her in the face. Yes, her. Yes, the face. No, I am not proud of that moment, but it was all I could do. Given a choice between hitting a woman—even a cop—and saving my sister, there is no choice. I did the right thing.

She smacked into the wall hard enough to crack the plaster. I kept going and ducked down, praying really, really hard to avoid getting a bullet in the back. Something stung across my left buttock and a second after that I felt the heat. I guess sometimes God or whatever has a sense of humor, because I sort of got my wish. I got grazed instead of dead.

Three doors, and two of them were closed. The only one that was open had three uniforms coming out of it, and unlike the one I pushed past, these already had the guns out. I let out a scream and they sort of half jumped from their skin. Did I mention I don't sound quite right when I'm doing the monster-face thing? According to Anna, I have a deeper voice. I also have a scream that sounds like a teakettle on steroids. I still don't quite know what to make of that, but it freaks people out a bit. Poor Anna almost wet herself the first time I did it. In my defense, she'd just slammed the car door on my fingers. That shit hurt.

You know what the difference is between a highly trained officer of the law and the average loser with a gun? Training. What? It's not a trick question. A lot of people maybe freak out when they hear my scream. The cops? They got a little jumpy, and then they opened fire on the monster that had just taken down one of theirs. How could they know if she was alive or dead? I didn't know myself, and I was the one that hit her. So they opened fire. And I ran at them even faster. I can't dodge bullets. I can't run so fast I break the sound barrier—seriously though, how cool would that be?—and I am not bullet proof. The only real chance I had was that they could only shoot me if I was far enough away to let them shoot without killing themselves in the process. I cleared the distance between me and them fast enough that they only managed one shot each. The first bullet ripped past my ear and left it ringing. The second bullet caught my coat and took a chunk of the fabric. The third bullet fired caught me in the stomach. That one hurt a lot. I didn't have time to stop and complain about it, or to really check what sort of damage got done. I kept running. And I hit the three of them like a bowling ball hits pins. I moved on through and they went sailing.

And as soon as I cleared the three cops at the threshold I was in the room and falling on my face. Like I said, I'm not bullet proof. And momentum only takes you so far. The pain hit me even harder as I fell into the master bedroom and took out a chair that was situated in front of the adjoining bathroom. The place was luxurious, but I didn't have a lot of time to check that out. I was bleeding, I was hurting, I was desperately in need of getting away from the cops in the room and the ones I'd just knocked halfway across the room, too.

There were too many scents: I could smell the cops, I could smell their individual odors, from sweat to cologne to hairspray, the cigarettes a couple of them indulged in when they weren't at an active crime scene, and I could smell the corpse that was still sprawled across the bed.

Edward Blevins was a partier. He liked to have a good time, and I bet under different circumstances I might have even gotten to like him. According to the people I talked to on the way to his place, the son of the Sixth District's state representative was generous when it came to sharing his cash and his drugs alike. He was quick witted, liked to share the wealth and had a thing for Asian girls. So, you know, we had a lot in common once upon a time. Of course, the fact that the girl he was with that night was my sister might have put a damper on things.

I was too late, as evidenced by the cops everywhere. I knew that when I showed up, but he was the only lead I had, so I had to press forward. Blevins was dead, of course. He'd been torn apart, same as the last victim, and there were parts of him missing, same as the last time. It's possible he was handsome when he was alive, but the flesh had been taken from his face, and his eyes were chewed out. His tongue was gone. His heart was gone. If I had the time to check I'd have probably found out that his liver was gone, too, and his penis. Maybe a few other things, too, but all of the bodies had that much in common so far.

He was very dead. If it was like the last reported murders, he was alive when it started. The one before him had lasted almost ten minutes after the feeding began. The thing that was doing the killings liked to play with its food.

I got to my feet and threw a nightstand at the cop trying to tackle me. The furniture hit him square in his bulletproof vest. Turns out the things don't necessarily stop furniture. He fell flat on his back and didn't get back up. One sniff and I had it. The same smell, like salt and cinnamon and something that had gone just a little rancid. The exact same scent. And under that potent odor? I could smell Blevins, of course, and his insides, and his waste. And Anna. I could smell her, too. And I could smell her fear.

– 6 –

Listen, I didn't want this. I tried hard to adjust to my life with the changes that were taking place, and I tried to go about my life like nothing was different. I dyed my hair black. I cut it shorter, too, because it grows like there's no freaking tomorrow. I almost never had to shave before the coma, but afterwards, I started shaving like a hairy Greek man. Seriously, by four in the afternoon I start sporting a serious case of the fuzzies. And yes, the damn stuff grows in white. Anna started calling me her little Chia Pet. It was funny the first billion or so times, and after that, not so much.

I tried to get on with my life. I made adjustments. Faster, stronger, tougher, remember all of that? Didn't take long before the local heavy hitters decided it wouldn't hurt their feelings to have their very own pet vampire as an enforcer. I got a nice raise, and I got to start picking and choosing my hours. Hell, I even started going to school, because I had enough extra money to afford it. Anna was smart and got scholarships. I was a screw up and had to do it the old fashioned way. I was adjusting just fine.

And then the other one showed up. I would have been in deep shit, seriously deep shit, because while I wasn't exactly advertising my change in lifestyle, it wasn't like I was able to hide it completely, either. But I got lucky. I was getting checked out by Doctors Ethan Lebbon and by Maggie Ruiz at the same time that the first murder took place. And there were witnesses, so, you know, I got lucky twice over. While the good doctor was looking me over on behalf of Maggie Ruiz, something that was described as a "green, long-haired ape with tusks" attacked a bouncer at one of the local bars. That description? My granny used to tell us stories about the green ogres. They were beautiful people sometimes and they were monsters other times. And when they were monsters, they sort of had that same description. Ogres. Maybe it was another case like mine, you know recessive genes, viruses…And the next thing you know a guy is dead. The guy was just doing his job, and this thing came out of the alley where the bar let out and attacked him. People saw him try to fight the thing off. He hit it in the face four or five times and it took the blows like they were nothing. And then it grabbed him by one arm and dragged him back into the alley. As soon as he started screaming, I mean really screaming, the police were called in. Seems no one was quite brave enough to run down the dark alley and help him. I know I wouldn't have, not from what I heard about that thing. Whatever it was, it took all the same parts from the bouncer that it did from Edward Blevins. By the time the cops arrived, the thing had finished its work and made a run for it.

279

Ruiz was damn near attacked by the reporters when it happened. I don't even know how they knew she was in town. Guess what. I was with her when they found her. I don't know if they guessed I was a vampire, or if there really is a database somewhere that the reporters can access, but I got a microphone shoved n my face and got asked a lot of questions all at once. *How do you feel about the murder?* What murder are you talking about? Please get that thing out of my face. *The murder just took place, a man named Jared Bucksley was mutilated and parts of him were missing. What do you know about that?* I know exactly what you just told me. *How do you feel about it?* How the hell do you think I feel? It's disgusting. *So you don't eat your victims? Do you drink blood?* I don't have victims. I don't drink blood and I eat food. You know, the stuff you buy in stores.

The questions could have gone on from there, but Ruiz cut off the interview and got me the hell out of there. Again, I don't know how they learned I was a vampire, but the good news was that none of them knew where I lived. I didn't get assaulted by cameras when I got home.

A lot of people were on the fence about the vampire thing then. A lot of people were already going on and on about how vampires are human beings who are afflicted and deserve the same rights as everyone else. Me? I'm all for it. A few less people were thinking that vampires were harmless by the time that little scenario hit the news. It's hardly the only crime that hit San Francisco that day, but it made the national news just the same and I remember very well that Illinois State Representative William Blevins was among the first ones to say that the vampires needed to be catalogued and assessed as potential threats before the situation got out of hand, if it hadn't already. William Blevins. Father of the late Edward Blevins.

I'm not a detective, but I caught that one quickly enough. And you want to know something? How's this sound for the sort of thing that can maybe make you wonder if there's a conspiracy going on? Blevins gets his son murdered for his comments. I had my sister stolen away from me. And between the two situations there were at least three more deaths, and each and every one of them was someone connected to the vampire situation. The second was a bishop who'd been throwing fits about how the vampires were actually demons and should be treated as such. I only heard about him because Rio heard about it on the news and let me know about it. Dude was in Eugene, Oregon, not exactly my home stomping grounds, but close enough to home that it seemed a like a good spot to check after Anna got snagged.

Anna disappeared two days after that interview. She called me on the phone and told me she was hearing someone outside our apartment. I was out doing a little work for my employers, and I wasn't even far away. But by the time I got home she was gone and the front door had been destroyed. My folks weren't home. They were actually away on vacation. I think that's a good thing. The green ape thing took Anna, but I don't think it would have taken more than one hostage.

Here's my favorite part: it left a note for me in Cantonese. Not just words, but the Chinese symbols. I don't even read Chinese. I had to go down the street and get the thing translated by Rio's mom. Rio's my hero right now, him and his mom both. They've been the ones who've kept me up to date on everything. I freaked out when I heard that Anna was gone. I also knew I'd be going after her. I called Rio because I needed that translation and his mom took one look at the paper and told me what it said.

" 'Your sister is mine. You called me "Disgusting." Stay out of this if you want to see her alive again.' " She looked at the paper for a long time and then looked at me and added, "It's signed with 'Blood-Suck Demon.' " Actually, she said "Hsi-Hsue-Kuei," but I'm translating here. It means the same thing.

I could see that Rio wanted to say something about that. Probably he thought that was about as cool as any name he'd ever seen signed on anything. Rio's big into anime and loves a good monster story. He kind of freaked out a bit when I got the virus. And then he kept asking if I knew how I got it. I figured it was because he wanted to get the virus himself, like there weren't already a lot of people who'd gotten sick off the vampire virus without changing.

Some things haven't changed in a very long time. I'm not saying there's no such thing as police in Chinatown. There are. But for some stuff you don't call the police. I knew there wasn't going to be a ransom note. I knew there wasn't going to be communications between me and the thing that took my sister. It wanted to make sure I left it alone. I didn't trust that it wasn't going to hurt my sister. I went back to the apartment and caught the thing's scent. I even found a little evidence in the form of a thick strand of coarse green hair. The stuff is thick and heavy and dark green. It isn't dyed. I memorized the scent and then I started looking. I probably hit half of San Francisco while trying to track down that scent before Rio told me about the attack on the bishop in Oregon. I never found a fresh trail, but the thing got around. Its trail moved all over the damn place. I recognized the smell when I got to Oregon and when I moved on from there, too.

–7–

So Blevins was dead. My sister had been there, and likely used as bait again, and now she was gone and so was the green thing. I looked at the cops, they looked at me. I went out the window again, screeching and screaming and praying I didn't break my leg when I hit the ground.

You know how cats always land on their feet? Not me. I landed on my backside and dented the crap out of squad car when I hit it. Windshield got trashed, windows got trashed. The lights stopped flashing and the siren started screeching and I bounced off the thing, crawled to my hands and knees and limped away as fast as I could. I was very, very grateful for the rain before it was all said and done.

Edward Blevins was a waste of my time. Nothing personal against the guy, but as leads went, not such a good time for me. But that didn't mean I was done in Chicago. See, Edward Blevins was dead, but I was thinking he was just a means to an end. It wasn't Ed that made the comments about vampires being identified and tracked and I was thinking that was the real reason for the guy getting targeted. His father was a powerful man, a political figure with some clout. That bishop that died was the same way. So was the lady who got herself killed by the thing

I was chasing when it stopped in Colorado. She was a country singer or something like that and she'd made several comments about the vampires being a blight against God. After I heard that that I didn't pay her any attention, but somebody else did. It wasn't much to go on, I admit that, but it was all I had. Three of the six people who'd been killed by the damn thing were all connected with the very fast growing anti-vampire sentiment the media was giving air time every day. I think the bouncer was just a meal, honestly. I think maybe the poor bastard was just there when this thing got hungry the first time, like I got hungry. Or maybe there was a different reason that I was missing altogether. All I knew about him was a name and that he'd died in my hometown.

And after that, Anna got attacked. And then the bishop. And then the country singer. And then there was the guy in Des Moines, Iowa, a Chinese American named Leonard Hong. I heard about him because Rio knew who he was. Hong was kind of into the same sort of shady business as my bosses. By shady I mean illegal, and by illegal I might be talking about drug trade. Allegedly.

Anyhow, Hong got killed. I figured the same basic scenario: My sister is a good looking girl. If she wasn't my sister I might be able to say that with more ease, but she is my sister. I don't think of her that way, but Rio had made a few comments back in the day before I threatened to kick his ass. And Tommy still made them regularly. I couldn't really threaten to kick Tommy's ass though, because he's a black belt in something I can't even pronounce and the one who taught me about how to fight. Anyhow, Anna is a looker. I figured the green ape was using her as bait and then doing a good job of taking out his enemies. I know that Hong was robbed when he got killed. He apparently had a lot of cash on him. So far my sister was being useful and that meant she got to stay around. I prayed she'd stay useful until I could reach her.

In the meantime, I went looking for William Blevins.

Okay, that's a lie.

I crawled away from the crime scene I'd made a mess of, I made it to the cheap motel where I was staying, which was almost two miles away, hiding and using back streets, and then I went to sleep for a few hours, aching and whimpering.

Like I said before, I'm not bullet proof.

I was bleeding, and I had to check the wound. I stripped out of my clothes, and looked at the hole in my stomach. It wasn't very big and it was healing nicely. I got lucky, I guess, because the bullet went clean through. Two bullet holes. Three if you counted the one in my ass, which I didn't because it was mostly healed by the time I got to the hotel. I stayed in my monster-face and I went to sleep. When the sun rose, I was back to being my usual self, and I was wound free.

I tried standing up and fell on my face, and screamed against my arm as the pain tore at my legs and hips and back.

I forgot to do my stretches.

Hopping Ghost. I hopped all the way to the bathroom, ate four Tylenol and then did my stretches for almost an hour before I could walk without feeling like my legs were being torn apart. It sucks, but I have to look at it as a fair enough trade, I guess. I mean, come on, I took two bullets, fought off a dozen cops, almost managed to leap forty-five feet through the air and survived a five story fall to the ground below and in return I had some painful moments when I forgot to stretch. There are a few benefits to go with the pain.

Of course, if none of this was going on, another vampire maybe wouldn't have taken my sister from me. It's hard to say for sure.

After stretching and cleaning up, I turned on the television and watched the local news while I called Rio to see what was happening on the home front.

"Dude, where the hell are you hiding?" Rio's voice sounded stressed. More than usual, I mean, because Rio always sounds like the world is ending.

"I'm in Chicago. Where else would I be?"

"You need to lay low for a while, John. Seriously."

"Why? What's up?" I moved over to the sink outside of the bathroom and turned on the courtesy coffee brewer with one pack of instant coffee and one pack of decaf. I figured if I played my cards right I could brew up something that was sort of like real coffee before I had to head out into the world again.

"What's up?" His voice broke and jumped a couple of octaves. "What's up? Are you crazy?"

"Rio. I'm in Chicago and I just got out of bed. I don't know anything. Tell me without the drama, okay?"

I expected to hear him tell me that Blevins was dead. I expected, maybe, to even hear that Blevins' dad was dead. Instead he surprised me. "Chow Liu is what's happening. Your green monster killed Chow Liu."

I could tell by the urgency in his voice that I was supposed to be surprised and maybe even worried, but the name meant nothing to me. "Dude, who the fuck is Chow Liu?"

"Seriously, John, do you ever pay attention when we're working?"

To be fair, the answer is no. I don't need to know who is who; I just need to know who to collect from. The job is kind of a no-brainer for me.

"No, Rio. You know that. I'm normally thinking about other things." Okay, to be fair I'm normally thinking about women. I've had a ridiculous libido ever since I changed.

"Chow Liu is the big shit of Chicago's Chinatown, dude. Or he was. Your green monster just killed him. They're already saying you did it. Even though it did to him what it did to the others."

My ears started ringing and I managed to get to the bed before I would have landed on my ass. "Oh. That Chow Liu."

"You work for Kang, man. And you're known. And you've been spotted in Chicago. I don't know who or how, but you got spotted, John. Liu's guys are looking for payback and what Kang said is that they're looking for you."

Screw the coffee. I was wide-awake just that fast. Like I said before, I'm not bulletproof. You know who has more guns than the entire Chicago Police Department? Chow Liu's people.

And they wanted me, dead or alive.

— 8 —

I spent about ten minutes showering and getting dressed and then I got the hell out of that hotel, because I'd been dumb enough to register under my real name and that meant I was probably going to get visitors sooner or later. I didn't want visitors. I wanted to find my sister and get her home. Only now there were complications. Bad complications. And I didn't have a whole lot of allies here. I needed to get out of Chicago and I needed to get back home and there was no way to do that without making arrangements.

First thing I had to do after I left the hotel was call Kang. I had no desire to do that, but I also needed to make sure we were straight, because if there's one thing worse than pissing off the leader of a rival triad it's pissing if the leader of your own triad.

Kang was, well, Kang was interested to hear from me.

"You left town without telling me." His voice was cold, strictly business. Then again, his voice is always that way.

"Did Rio explain?" I was really, really hoping that Rio explained.

"Yeah. He did. You find your sister?"

"Not yet." I looked around the area and climbed into the junker I'd picked up in Colorado. It was a piece of crap, but it was cheap and so far it hadn't broken down. I live in San Francisco. I don't normally drive and when I do I'm driving my folks' car and they'd taken that with them when they went to L.A. So, you know, I had to improvise.

"You're in deep shit, John. Not with me, but you're in deep shit."

"I swear, I didn't do anything to anyone, man. I'm just tracking the green thing that took my sister."

He muttered something in Chinese. I couldn't make it out because it was too soft and I realized he was talking to himself, which he normally reserved for when he was very agitated. "I can't send anyone to help you, John. I do, it looks like I'm involved in this. I don't like it, but I can't help you."

"I'm cool with that, Kang." Actually, I kind of wanted to cry. I wasn't at all cool with it, but what can you do? I wasn't going to cry in front of the man who paid my bills, or even over the phone in front of him. "I just needed to make sure you and me are okay before things get bad." I corrected myself. "I mean if they get bad."

"They're going to get bad. I already got three calls from Liu's boys. They want blood."

"Why mine?"

"You've got a reputation, John. You're a known name."

"What? Since when?" What the hell was he talking about? I asked him as much.

"Around the same time you got white hair and fangs, man. The only reason I'm not sweating this a lot more is because they're worried. They don't know what you can do, and I'm not volunteering anything." I wish I could say that comforted me.

"Listen. I have to go. I have to work out some plans."

"You didn't do this. I know that." Him saying those words? That actually made me breathe a little easier. "Find your sister and come home."

I had to find the green ogre. I had to find it and I had to get rid of it. I might even have to kill the damned thing and I didn't want that. But if

I needed to hand over a head to the Chicago triad to make sure that I got out of this in one piece, it wasn't going to do me much good to hand them mine. I still needed it. I'd never killed anyone in my life, and when it came to my feedings, I only killed when I had to. I'd taught myself tricks for feeding off a lot of people at once, so they got a little tired and I got fed without killing anyone or anything. I mean, seriously, most times I just go to one of the local pet stores and when I leave the only problem is the dogs and cats are a little less noisy than when I came in.

I had to find the green ogre. I had to find my sister. I had to stop the green thing from killing anyone else. I had to stop the local triad from killing me. I had to clear my name. I had to maybe stop the ogre from killing a politician with too much of an opinion about vampires, before somebody else made the connections that I'd made and the press decided to declare a war on vampires. Listen I wasn't alive when the whole country was going bugshit over Communism and wanting to crush the Red Scourge, but I had heard stories about the troubles back in the day and I wanted no part of that stuff. I just wanted to go to school and make a little money on the side.

I just wanted the same thing everyone else wants, really. I wanted to have an ordinary life.

Not a chance in hell.

⌘

"THE BALLAD OF BIG CHARLIE" PT.2

Keith R.A. DeCandido

— 8 —

Mia Fitzsimons sat in the press area for the debate between Mickey
Solano and Hugues Charles. Normally, this sort of event would have a
press section of about a dozen seats, and Mia would have had her
choice of them, as maybe half would be filled.

But thanks to the Reverend Mann and his sermon—which Mia had
now heard exactly two hundred times, she'd been counting for no
good reason except perhaps so she could have a proper measurement
for her suffering—the size of the press area was tripled and it was
packed. She was squeezed between Josh, an overweight reporter from
an Iowa paper ("Our readers want to know who the reverend was talking about—and hey, I'll take the free trip to the Big Apple"), and an
overweight blogger whose name she never got who'd been writing
about I1V1. She had no idea how the latter managed to score press
credentials.

And that was just journalists—camera operators were all over the
place, with lights blinding anyone who looked anywhere near an aisle.

To her annoyance, Jack Napolitano—now working for RSN—had
been chosen to moderate. To her surprise, they didn't provide an extra
chair for his ego.

The debate had been going well, and the Iowa reporter was getting
cranky at the lack of a mention of Reverend Mann.

"The next question," Jack read off an index card (this was still the Bronx, and a teleprompter wasn't in the budget), "is about the death penalty. Mr. Solano, you're in favor of reinstating it in New York State, and Mr. Charles, you've been very much set against it. Mr. Solano, can you explain your position?"

Solano smiled. He was dressed in a dark maroon suit. "Be happy to. When the Court of Appeals declared the death penalty law unconstitutional, they took a bullet out of every prosecutor's gun. The death penalty is absolutely a last resort, one that should be reserved for the most heinous of crimes—but it needs to be available for those. Now, Mr. Charles has never called for the death penalty, even though he had opportunities to do so while the law was still on the books. And you know what? *I agree with him.* There weren't any cases that came up in the Bronx during that time that called for the death penalty."

Points for Solano on that one. Mia jotted down a few notes.

"But I maintain," he continued, "that to rob prosecutors of that as a possible sentence robs them of the ability to do their job, and I have continued to lobby the Court of Appeals to reverse its decision. Having said that, if I am elected, I will, of course, abide by the law."

Mia snorted. *Stuck the landing, there, Mick…*

Jack looked over at Big Charlie, wearing a tailored charcoal pin-striped suit. "Mr. Charles?"

"There are no cases where the death penalty is called for."

And there's the sound bite. Mia jotted down the line in her notebook.

"Yes, you may provide historic examples like Adolf Hitler and Osama bin Laden, but these are not people who would ever be prosecuted at the Bronx County courthouse. But of all the arguments to be made against the death penalty, none are more compelling than the simple fact that innocent people have been found guilty of capital crimes. It is bad enough when the state condemns one of its citizens to death, but it is unconscionable that the state would do so to an innocent person. As for Mr. Solano's argument—prosecutors have dozens of options of punishments that fit the crime. The idea that the death penalty would cripple prosecutors in their jobs when Mr. Solano himself admits that it would not be used very often if at all, is ludicrous."

And there's the other sound bite. This time there were cheers. Jack whirled around to glare at the audience, as if their cheers were a personal affront. Then he read the next question off the index cards. "The Reverend Josiah Mann recently said during one of his sermons that Mr. Charles should not be permitted to live due to his suffering from I1V1. Mr. Charles, how do you respond to such a threat to your life?"

Next to Mia, Josh sat up in his chair, fingers hovering over his laptop.

"I do not believe any threat to my life was made. Reverend Mann is a devout, dedicated man of God, and I do not wish him any ill will. But he has said many things I disagreed with before last Sunday, and I daresay he will say more things I disagree with after this. He is welcome to his opinion, as are his followers. Since very few of them reside in the Bronx, I am confident that they will not be voting in September or in November, so my concern for his effect upon my chances are minimal."

"Oooooh," Josh muttered. "Burn."

"Well, he's right," Mia said.

"Oh, not complaining. Mann's poison, and I can't wait to tell my grandkids that I was there when he got put in his place by a werewolf."

"Mr. Solano?" Jack prompted.

"Mr. Charles is far more generous to Reverend Mann than I am. Yes, there are people out there suffering from I1V1 who are causing harm, and yes, those people are dangerous. But not everyone has decided to channel Count Dracula and suck people's blood. Some of them—most of them—are just people who are trying to go on with their lives. Mr. Charles is one of them, and he should be respected for that, not condemned. And anyone who does condemn him for that isn't a man of any God that I'm familiar with. Reverend Mann is a rabble-rouser and a scumbucket, and if he ever does come to the Bronx, he'll find out how we treat those kinds of people."

More cheers followed that, and Josh grinned. "My grandkids are gonna get a *great* story once they exist."

Again Jack impatiently waited for the cheers to die down. "The next question is for Mr. Solano. Are you concerned that your opponent has publicly stated that he is a werewolf, and is part of why you're running against him to prevent a self-described monster from running the prosecutions of this county?"

Solano actually rolled his eyes. "Let me ask you something—if Mr. Charles had had come out as a homosexual, would you even ask that question? I'm running for Bronx District Attorney because I think that it's time for new blood in that office after twelve years. I think that it's time for Mr. Charles to step down and give way to a different vision, one that can build on what he's accomplished. I think that the D.A.'s office has become ossified and that I'm the man to apply the rust-off. That has nothing to do with whether or not my friend over there has a disease that allows him to change into a *loup garou*."

Mia shook her head. It almost didn't matter what Big Charlie said in response. Solano just had to support him before tearing him down. It made him seem noble, but she didn't think that was going to be enough.

The blogger to her right was just muttering, "Awesome, totally fucking awesome" to himself as he made notes on his tablet.

–9–

Transcript of "On the Street" segment of Good Morning NYC

GOOD MORNING NYC: Today's "On the Street" asks the people of New York the question: Should Big Charlie be elected Bronx D.A. even though he's one of the many people suffering from I1V1?

PERSON #1: All's I know is, I can walk home at night without feelin' like I'm getting jumped by no crazy man, and it's been that way since he been D.A. I don't care what he turns into, he's gettin' my vote for damn sure.

PERSON #2: You kiddin' me? The guy's a freakin' werewolf. I ain't voted for him before, but I sure as hell'm votin' for him now! That's who I want a murderer lookin' at inna courtroom, know what I mean?

PERSON #3: God, no. Never. I mean, I don't vote or anything, but if I did, I would never vote for one of those people. Not ever.

PERSON #4: Not only am I not voting for him, I've given money to Solano—and I can't stand Solano. But seriously, the man is no longer even human. How can he enforce human laws when they no longer even apply to him? Christ knows I have no respect for that Mann guy, but he was right on the nose with that one. He ain't Big Charlie anymore, he's a monster, and he needs to be put down.

PERSON #5: You know he's the best BLEEPin' D.A. this town's seen, yo. He ain't even turned into no werewolf that nobody saw. So hell with that—I be votin' for him soon's I register, an' BLEEP.

PERSON #6: I admire him for coming out and telling the truth. God, I wish more politicians would do that. They spend so much time saying nothing that they don't say anything. This is a guy who came out and told everyone what happened to him. He didn't wait for a reporter or an Internet video or a police investigation to say, "Oh, yeah, didn't I mention that I snort coke off call girls?" or whatever. He probably could've gone the whole year without telling nobody, but he did the right thing. For that alone, I'd vote for the guy. But it's gotta wait until November, 'cause I'm an independent.

— 10 —

Oddly, Mia's second time on Helen Lashmar's show made her a lot more nervous than her first.

The first time was so last-minute, she didn't have the chance to get nervous. Now, though, she had the Bronx Zoo's entire butterfly conservatory in her stomach as she sat through makeup.

Next to her was Hannah LeBoeuf, a commanding African-American woman who was one of the ACLU's lawyers. "You'll be fine," Hannah was saying. "You're good on camera."

Mia shrugged, which earned her a glare from the young man doing her makeup. "I appreciate that. I'm just worried about Mann's guy." Tim Markinson, the public information officer for the Blessed Church of Enlightenment, was on the panel as well. "They've just been…" She trailed off, unable to form words to do justice to her annoyance at the shitstorm Mann's sermon had caused for Big Charlie.

"I'll take care of Markinson. He's an empty suit that does whatever he has to make sure the donations keep comin'."

"Thanks." The fourth panelist was Senator Alex Kapsis, whom Mia had met several times. *So that's two friendly faces, at least.*

Within a few minutes, they were seated around the table, cameras all around, lights shining brightly in her face. On the monitors in front of her, the closing credits from the previous show were running. The host had yet to arrive, but the other three panelists were present. Markinson wore a light blue suit that made him look like he was taking someone to the prom in 1952. Senator Kapsis looked like a college professor in his tweed jacket, and was on his cell phone.

"One minute to air!" somebody bellowed, and the butterflies started flapping their wings so hard in Mia's stomach she was sure they were changing history so the dinosaurs didn't die.

Last time, a PA had yelled at John Generico for talking on his cell phone in the studio, but he was an asshole and Kapsis was a U.S. senator, so the rules were probably different.

But when Helen Lashmar stormed in, staring intently at her smartphone as she walked, she said, "Okay, let's get this party started," which was apparently what she always said before the show began.

"In five—four—three—" The assistant director then held up two fingers, then one, then pointed to Helen. "Good morning. We start with our roundtable segment, where a panel will tackle the news of the day. Joining me today are Mia Fitzsimmons of the New York *Daily News*, Timothy Markinson, the public information officer for the Blessed Church of Enlightenment, ACLU lawyer Hannah LeBoeuf, and Senator Alex Kapsis of New York. I1V1 has been all over the news lately, with the Reverend Mann of the Blessed Church of Enlightenment calling for the death of Bronx District Attorney Hugues Charles, better known as 'Big Charlie,' and the discovery that murdered Chicago talk-show host Danika Dubov also suffered from I1V1." She shook her head and smiled. "A werewolf running for public office and a vampire hosting a tabloid talk show."

Helen was about to start a question when Markinson interrupted in a low, nasal tone. "I'd like to object to your characterization of the Reverend Mann's words, please, Helen."

"Of course, Tim, you—"

Markinson barreled forward as if Helen hadn't spoken. "The Reverend Mann did *not* call for the death of Mr. Charles. The Reverend Mann is a firm believer in the word of God, and the very words of God as handed down to Moses were that people should not commit murder. The words of Exodus 22 state that one should not suffer a creature of magic to live among us. A good analogy would be what King Saul did in the First Book of Samuel, driving all necromancers and magicians from the Kingdom of Israel."

It required all of Mia's self-control not to let out an interjection on the air that RSN's Broadcast Standards and Practices would not have been happy with. She had an entire bit on 1 Samuel ready to go, and this blue-suited Jesus freak just stole her thunder.

"When Saul contradicted his own order by consulting the Witch of Endor, he was condemned, and his army was soon defeated, leading to Saul's suicide."

Mia's words all but exploded from her mouth. "So what're you saying, Tim, that we should kick Big Charlie out of New York and send him, where, exactly?"

"He can no longer be in the community of God, and he must be removed from it as Saul did the magicians and necromancers."

The senator jumped in before Mia could respond. "Interesting, Mr. Markinson, so now you're saying that the Bronx is part of the community of God? Because I recall the reverend saying more than once—including after the September 11 attacks—that God had abandoned New York City. Given that, the Bronx would be the ideal place for someone you want to condemn to the same fate as the Witch of Endor."

Unable to help herself, Mia smiled.

Markinson looked nonplussed. "All of America is part of the community of God, Senator. What the Reverend Mann did in 2001 was express a *fear* that God had abandoned the city of New York."

Now Mia rolled her eyes. "So is this is what you do, Mr. Markinson? The reverend says something inflammatory and crazy, and you go on TV and tell people he didn't really *mean* that, what he *really* meant was *this*."

"That's not at all fair, Mia," Markinson said in his most condescending tone. *And you're "Tim" from now on, you self-righteous prick.* "The Reverend Mann's words are often taken out of context by a biased media and as public information officer, it's my job to clarify and explain when people misunderstand the reverend's words."

Hannah said, "I can't speak for Mia here, but I've read the reverend's words, Tim, every single one of them. Not once did he ever say 'cast out' or 'remove from God's community' or any of the other phrases that you've been using nonstop since the video of his sermon hit YouTube. He was calling for Big Charlie's death."

"Are you saying that the Reverend Mann doesn't have the right to speak his mind?" Markinson's condescension actually got worse, which Mia wouldn't have credited as possible a few seconds ago. "Because I would find that a *fascinating* position for a lawyer from the ACLU to take.

"Oh, I've got *no* problem with Mann speaking his mind, and I would defend his right to say it in court. But unless I *am* the one defending him, then I've got the right to say that he's full of it, and that he's calling for the death of a good man."

"Of course," Senator Kapsis said, "that raises the question of whether or not D.A. Charles still *is* that—a man, that is. Danika Dubov wasn't exactly what you'd call a paragon of journalism, but she wasn't a sadistic torturer, either—at least until this virus got her and turned her into some kind of vampire. The Chicago police found dozens of people she'd been literally feeding off of for weeks. With all due respect to Mr. Markinson and the Reverend Mann, concerns about whether or not D.A. Charles is part of God's community is of less immediacy than his place in the human community."

Hannah shrugged. "Well, the human community in his home city seems fine with him. His poll numbers have gone up since he announced that he was a *loup garou*. And that's the point, this is a local election for a small part of one city. If that small group of people are okay with him, then I don't see the problem."

"Now hold on a minute, Hannah," Kapsis said, "we're not talking about a rural town with a few hundred people electing a sheriff. The Bronx has a population that is the same as that of the state of Alaska. And it's one-fifth of one of the most important cities in the entire world."

"With all due respect, Senator" Mia said, "I don't see what difference that makes. If it *was* a little town upstate, or if it is the Bronx—which, by the way, has *twice* the population of Alaska—the point is, it's up to those of us who live there to decide. It doesn't matter what we say or what some televangelist says. It's up to the people. And *that's* what matters."

"The Rev—" Markinson started, but Helen interrupted.

"I have to cut you off, Tim—"

Markinson interrupted right back. "The Reverend Mann is *not* a 'televangelist,' which is a term we find quite offensi—"

Sternly, Helen said, "Tim, *please*, we have to take a break. When we come back, a look at the president's new proposed budget."

Mia let out a long breath after the PA said, "And we're out."

"Nice job," Hannah said with a smile.

Looking over at Markinson, who looked like he'd eaten an entire lemon, Mia smiled and said, "Thanks."

– 11 –

Detective Hector Trujillo winced when he saw Mia Fitzsimmons from the *News* approach the crime scene.

At the moment she, like all the other reporters outside the Upper West Side apartment building where Senator Alex Kapsis had a co-op, was behind the yellow crime-scene tape. Two other *News* reporters were already there, reporting on the senator's murder, so Trujillo wasn't entirely sure what Fitzsimons was doing there.

Fitzsimmons was talking animatedly to Officer Nugent at the tape. Nugent looked like he wanted to haul off and belt the reporter, and Fitzsimmons looked like she wanted to do likewise.

"S'okay, Nugent," Trujillo said. "Let her through."

Nugent gave the detective a dubious expression, but waved her through. She ducked under the yellow tape and approached Trujillo.

"Saw you on TV, Fitzsimmons," he said as she walked up to him. "Lookin' good."

"Thanks so much, Detective. God, it's been, what, two years?"

"Sounds about right," Trujillo said neutrally.

"When I gave you that witness that let you close the Rojas case?"

Again, Trujillo said, "Sounds about right." He didn't want to commit to anything until the reporter laid her cards on the table.

"Of course," she said with a smile, "I could've just sat on the witness and wrote the story, but no, I helped you out. You got promoted to second-grade after that, didn't you, Detective?"

So she was calling in the favor. "Can you stop fucking around and get to it, Fitzsimmons?"

"I thought you'd never ask." She took out her digital recorder.

Trujillo held up a hand. "Hold up—I ain't sayin' *nothin'* on the record…"

"Fine." She dropped the recorder back in her purse. "But can you tell me on the record that the senator was murdered?"

"The M.E. ain't made it official—but the bastard was ripped to pieces by teeth. Looked as bad as Bellevue."

Fitzsimmons nodded. Trujillo shuddered just from mentioning it.

He'd gone to the Academy with Detective Jerry Schmidt, and had attended his funeral after he was ripped to pieces by Michael Fayne, the first vampire, at Bellevue Hospital.

The reports he'd read of what happened when Jerry was killed were frighteningly similar to what the senator's living room looked like right now.

But he wasn't about to share that with Fitzsimmons. He finally realized what she was doing here—she was on the Big Charlie beat, and when he last saw her on television, she was on with Senator Kapsis talking about the D.A.

"Okay, look, we got a guy runnin' from the scene in custody now. The senator's nephew."

"Nate."

Trujillo nodded. It wasn't exactly a secret that Nathan Kapsis was a bad seed who had failed to appear for his day in court after he beat up his famous uncle. "He's FTA for the assault charge last year. Senator's wife said they ain't even heard from the fucker in a year."

"And he's got I1V1?"

"Looks like. Luther Swann said he's a—"

"*Vrykolatios*?"

"Gensundheit." Trujillo attempted a smile, but it didn't entirely work. "And yeah, I guess that's how you pronounce it. I got it in a text from Swann."

"It makes sense—cannibalistic, Greek."

Trujillo didn't care about any of that, he just wanted to close the case with a minimum of fuss. As far as he was concerned, this was a dunker—the nephew did it.

The only problem was the press angle, especially with the primary tomorrow. But at least now he had a way to repay Fitzsimmons.

A paddy wagon had pulled up, and two of the uniforms were leading a handcuffed Nate Kapsis to it. He was a skinny kid, with the muscle tone of a string bean.

Trujillo stared down at Fitzsimons. "We done here?"

"You said the senator was torn to pieces?" After Trujillo nodded, Fitzsimmons went on: "So how'd that little guy manage that?"

Shrugging, Trujillo said, "He's a vampire. Thought they was all super-strong and shit."

Fitzsimmons shook her head. "Not a *vyrkolatios*. They feast off family—"

"What, like that TV bitch in Chicago?"

"Yeah." Fitzsimmons let out a breath. "It's possible that Nate came at the senator and chowed down, but he doesn't have the strength to—"

Trujillo held up both hands. "I don't wanna hear it. I got me a dunker here, and you ain't fuckin' it up for me. The nephew did it—he's got the vamp disease, he's got a grudge against his uncle, and he's already a fugitive. It fits, and we ain't complicatin' this. Now we even for Rojas?"

"Sure." But Fitzsimmons barely seemed to pay attention to Trujillo. "It would need someone with a huge body mass to do something like that..." she muttered.

For his part, Trujillo didn't give a rat's ass. He had his killer in bracelets, he had a closed case to put under his name, and he no longer owed a reporter a favor. As far as he was concerned, it was a good night.

– 12 –

Transcript of "On the Street" segment of Good Morning NYC

GOOD MORNING NYC: Today's "On the Street" comes from last night's Democratic primary for Bronx D.A., as we asked people coming out of three different polling places in Riverdale, Morrisania, and Edenwald who they voted for, and why.

PERSON #1 (Riverdale): I'm sorry, but it's not any of your business that I voted for Big Charlie.

PERSON #2 (Morrisania): I ain't votin' for no werewolf, that's for damn sure. Solano all the way!

PERSON #3 (Edenwald): I grew up with Big Charlie. He's a good man—the best. I don't care if he turns into the Wicked Witch of the West, he's a good man. I vote for good men.

PERSON #4 (Riverdale): Oh, gosh, I just had to vote for Solano. I just don't trust Charles, y'know? The whole virus thing—it's just icky.

PERSON #5 (Morrisania): So he's a werewolf. So what? A woman turns into a monster from hell once a month, and I'd vote for a woman D.A., so why not vote for Big Charlie, know what I'm sayin'?

PERSON #6 (Edenwald): You only be carin' 'cause he be a *loup garou*. He ain't no *loup garou*, nobody'd even be givin' no BLEEP if he was just bein' Big Charlie runnin' for office again. I voted for him three times, and didn't nobody come out to be askin' me who I voted for with no news cameras then, now, did they?

–13–

Mia Fitzsimmons was sitting in the *Daily News* city room writing up her story on Big Charlie's victory. It wasn't official yet, but the early exit polls made it look like Hugues Charles would win the primary in a walk over Mickey Solano.

Bart Mosby, her editor, walked up to her. "Looks like your guy's gonna do it."

"He's not 'my guy,' Bart."

"Bullshit. Just make sure the big guy remembers how far up his ass your face was during this campaign."

Mia made a face. "Bart, seriously."

"I am serious. The vampire shit meant he was good copy, and now the D.A. owes one of my reporters a favor. And with Kapsis's murder, it makes even better copy. People're eating this vampire shit up."

"Yeah." Mia was looking over the M.E.'s initial report on Kapsis's murder—it was fast-tracked, since he was a U.S. senator, and Mia had a friend in the medical examiner's office—and frowning. "It's funny, I thought it might hurt Big Charlie, but it didn't."

"What would?" Bart asked.

"Hm? Oh, the murder. I mean, it was obvious that someone with I1V1 killed him."

"Yeah, the nephew."

Mia shook her head. "I don't think so. He's a *vyrkolatios*. They just feed, they don't murder—certainly not like that. He doesn't have the strength to tear him apart like that, and the M.E.'s report says there were both teeth and what looks like claw marks."

"Who gives a fuck?" Bart asked. "He's a vampire. They can do that shit. Whatever, I'm gonna go get a cigarette. Worst day in the history'a the world was when they—"

The rest of Bart's harangue was lost to distance—though Mia had heard his railing against the laws that prevented indoor smoking since her first day in the city room—but she wasn't paying much attention.

Nate Kapsis didn't have claws. Something here didn't add up.

On the TV, Big Charlie was being questioned about the senator's murder outside his campaign headquarters. "Nathan Kapsis has always been a very troubled man. His violent tendencies go back many years."

"Yes," one reporter was saying off-camera, "but he's never killed. Do you believe that contracting I1V1 made him—"

"As I said," and now Big Charlie was sounding testy, "he was always a troubled young man. I1V1 did not change that. Recall, if you will, that he had failed to appear before the court in answer to an assault charge on the senator."

"But Senator Kapsis wasn't exactly your best friend," said the same reporter, and Mia was wondering who it was, now.

"The senator and I were friends for many years."

Mia winced. That sounded rehearsed.

"But he threw you under the bus on Helen Lashmar's show the other day. Do you think—"

Judy Alejo stepped in at that point and cut the questions off.

Kapsis certainly hadn't sounded much like a friend to Big Charlie on Lashmar. *Could that have been seen as a betrayal?*

She finished writing up her notes—both for the piece that would be in tomorrow's *News* and for the story about Big Charlie that she was finding herself composing in light of the senator's murder—as the night wore on.

Eventually, Bart wandered by and said the news story was in the queue. Curious, Mia called it up on her laptop.

Big Charlie won sixty-three percent of the vote, and the turnout was seventy percent of the registered Democrats in the Bronx. Mia wasn't sure, but she was fairly certain those were both records.

"Now it's just the election," she muttered.

Bart laughed. "Right. Are the Republicans even runnin' anybody?"

"No," Mia said, "but Escobar's gonna be on the ticket."

"Who's that?"

"The Right-to-Life candidate. Hell, Big Charlie's gonna be on the Conservative ticket, along with Liberal and Green."

"Right, so the election's gonna matter." Bart snorted and walked off.

It will matter if Big Charlie can't run due to being in jail for murder. It was a crazy thought—Mia had spent most of the last four months around Hugues Charles, and he didn't have a murderous bone in his body.

But neither had Nate Kapsis. Hell, neither had Danika Dubov or Michael Fayne.

Maybe there's no story here, but I have to play out the string in case there is one.

300

Luckily, Bart wouldn't have any problem with her sticking close to the D.A.'s office moving forward.

– 14 –

Op-ed piece by Mia Fitzsimmons in the New York Daily News.

It started with Michael Fayne here in New York.

It's gotten far far worse.

In Los Angeles, a Laker Girl was attacked by an ape-like man who seemed to suck the very life out of her.

In Chicago, TV personality Danika Dubov kept victims in her home while Illinois State Representative William Blevins and his wife were horribly murdered.

In Paris, a massacre beneath the City of Light's very streets.

And here in New York, Anson Morris slaughtering his wife and best friend.

It's become impossible to turn on the news or read a paper like this one without there being some new vampire on the scene.

A year ago, Hugues Charles was sworn in to serve his fourth term as District Attorney of the Bronx. A year and a half ago, he won the Democratic Primary, as well as a virtually uncontested general election, despite having revealed himself to be a *loup garou*.

It would be hard to imagine Big Charlie succeeding in such an endeavor now. The lines are being drawn, human vs. vampire, and there's no real clear notion as to who will win.

Big Charlie knows which side he's on, though. In a press conference held on the first day of the Anson Morris trial, the Bronx D.A., he said, "It does not matter that I'm a *loup garou* for the same reason that it doesn't matter that I have dark skin or that my mother was born in Port-au-Prince. What matters is that I was elected by the people of this county to prosecute criminals. Anson Morris is a criminal. It also does not matter that he has claws and fangs that he did not have two years ago. What matters is that he committed a heinous crime, and he will be punished for that."

The surety in Big Charlie's voice makes him a lone voice in the wilderness these days. Violence committed by people with I1V1 has skyrocketed, and it's been followed by increased violence committed against them, what one pundit referred to as "preventative self-defense."

So far, Big Charlie has stayed above the fray. The question is, how long can he remain there?

His response when I asked him that very thing, was typically candid. "There is no fray to remain above. I am here to do my job. It is the same job I have done for twelve years, and I intend to do for another four, at least."

That surprised me, as I recalled lots of talk about this being his final term.

"I do not wish to make predictions. Four years ago, I could not have imagined the circumstances that we face now. My presence as a prosecutor in a major city might well be important for people to see. Those of us who suffer from this virus—those people that have been dubbed 'vampires'—we are all simply people. So many barriers against prejudice have been broken in the last fifty years. Civil rights, gay marriage, an African-American president. But now we have found another group of people to oppress."

Of course the big question is what Big Charlie will do if the proposed "Vampire Registration Act" currently on the Senate floor passes. One of the bill's sponsors is Senator Emily Krascznicki, who was appointed to serve out Senator Alex Kapsis's term after his murder.

"My job as District Attorney is to prosecute to the full extent of the law. I swore an oath to uphold the laws of the county of the Bronx, the city of New York, the state of New York, and the republic of the United States of America. If someone in my county is in violation of any of the laws under which we live, then they shall be prosecuted by my office."

More thorny is the death penalty, which has been off the books in New York State since 2004. There's talk in Albany of bringing it back solely for I1V1 cases.

"Again, my job as District Attorney is to prosecute to the full extent of the law. I can say that, personally, I am not comfortable with *any* legal decision that discriminates against a particular group of people. Imagine if the governor proposed a law that stated that only black people could receive the death penalty, or only Jews could. It would never even be considered."

But Big Charlie won't let ideology stand in the way of doing his job. "If it is put into law, then—if it's appropriate—I will prosecute with the death penalty in mind. But that decision will have little to do with the virus and everything to do with whether or not that punishment fits that crime."

Let's hope that the state legislature's object will be similarly all sublime.

— 15 —

Barel Grindberg honestly did not expect to ever be walking into Hugues Charles's office in the Bronx County Courthouse again.

Big Charlie was on the phone, but he gestured for her to take a seat in the guest seat while he spoke. It was a lot of legalese flying back and forth that Barel didn't even pretend to understand.

Finally, he said, "Thank you, Amelia" and hung up. "My apologies, Barel."

"No problem," Barel said neutrally.

"How are you doing?"

Small talk first, then. "Keeping busy. I've been doing some consulting and some writing. Actually, a bunch of publishers have been approaching me about writing a book about getting you re-elected. Just in general, that's enhanced my résumé."

"I am very glad to hear you say that, Barel, because I wish to hire you again."

Barel frowned. "The next D.A. race isn't for three years."

"Not for District Attorney. You are aware, of course, that Emily Krascznicki has declined to run for a full term, so Alex's seat is open. I would like to throw my hat into the ring, as it were, and I wish you to run my campaign."

Pulling her cardigan tightly around her chest, Barel took a deep breath in before replying. "Are you out of your *fucking mind*?"

Big Charlie recoiled as if he'd been slapped. "Not at all. I believe that, with my own profile increasing, this might be an ideal time to—"

"It is *not* an ideal time! It's the worst time in the history of the universe for you to be running for dog-catcher, much less U.S. senator! If you run, you will be absolutely destroyed. Remember what happened with Reverend Mann? Picture that *mishegoss* every single day. Public opinion on vamps is going down into the drain with every passing day, and if you try to run, you will be ruined. Hell, they'll probably force you to resign. People with I1V1 are getting *lynched* out there, Hugues!"

For several seconds, Big Charlie didn't say anything. His huge hands were folded together, elbows resting on his metal desk, staring at an indeterminate point to Barel's left.

"I appreciate your honesty, Barel. It is the quality of yours that I've always admired most."

"Thank you. So you won't do it?"

"I have not decided yet. In truth, I had not decided when I asked you. That you will not be willing to represent me—"

"I didn't say that." Barel spoke without thinking. She liked Big Charlie; she generally made it a rule not to like (or dislike) the people she worked for, but the prosecutor was such a teddy bear it was impossible to think ill of him. And she didn't want to disappoint him.

But after mulling it over for half a second, she realized she had to. "But I'm saying it now. It won't just be career suicide for you, it'll taint everyone who works for you. Don't do it."

There was some more small talk after that, and then Barel shook Big Charlie's enormous hand and left the office. She figured that would be the end of it. He had almost always taken her advice, and whenever he hadn't, he'd regretted it right afterward.

So she was stunned to hear the following as she watched *Good Morning NYC* over her morning tea: "Our top story on the hour: Big Charlie is running for Senate!"

"You have *got* to be fucking kidding me." Barel immediately opened up her laptop and started composing an e-mail to Big Charlie that boiled down to, "What the fuck is wrong with you, you *schmuck*?"

The man himself showed up on her screen as she frantically typed. "There has been an increasing call for more legislation against those of us who have contracted I1V1, and I believe that it is past time that those of us who have the virus had a say in how that legislation is crafted. Senator Kapsis lost his life to a family member who had the virus, and my announcement today is by way of reminding people that we are not monsters. We are people. Senator Kapsis's nephew was violent before he contracted the virus. And I was a District Attorney before I contracted the virus. I believe that I will be able to represent my home state in Washington regardless of whether or not I can alter my shape into a wolfen form."

"And faeries will come flying out of my ass," Barel muttered. Big Charlie's heart was in the right place, and nothing he said there was wrong. She made a mental note to send a well-done e-mail to Judy Alejo for that statement, as it was well put together.

But it wouldn't do a lick of good. Nobody was going to vote a vampire into office.

"State Comptroller Frank VanDerMeer has already announced that he will be running for the seat on the Republican side, but Big Charlie will have to survive a Democratic primary that already includes former New York City Mayor Aaron Barr, Manhattan Borough President Emma Jaffe, and State Senator Dianne Axisa. Oughtta be a fun race."

The one piece of good news was that no one on that list was going to scare anyone from running. Barr was far from the city's most popular mayor, a one-term wonder who created almost no impression, and Jaffe, Axisa, and VanDerMeer were bland career politicians who had almost no profile. Were it not for I1V1, Big Charlie could take the election in a walk.

As she was typing her poison pen letter to the D.A., she got a notification of a new e-mail. It was from Mickey Solano.

Barel frowned and clicked on the icon to open that mail.

Then she decided she was going to need another cup of tea. Possibly with some whiskey in it.

– 16 –

Transcript of a commercial paid for by
Citizens for Humanity.

By the people, for the people. This great country has always been about its people. But now it's in danger from creatures who may look like people, who may sometimes even appear to be people, but they aren't. Sadistic, brutal, vicious killers, with more of them every day.

And one of them is running for Senate. They call him "Big Charlie," but what they should be calling him is a monster. And he'll bring the monsters' agenda to Capitol Hill.

Don't let this happen. Let our country be for us, not the monsters who scare our children—who scare *us*. Make sure that when you vote for Senator, you *don't* vote for Hugues Charles.

Paid for by Citizens for Humanity.

– 17 –

Judy Alejo was on the phone with her sister when Helen Lashmar came on. So busy had she been with organizing interviews with Big Charlie that she hadn't even checked to see what she'd be doing, and she hadn't actually spoken to her sister in almost a month. Not that that was a bad thing from Judy's perspective, but now Perla was complaining to *mami* about it.

So Judy called her, and ignored the roundtable segment on Lashmar to listen to her carry on about how wonderful her two children were.

Just as she was about to bang her head into the desk, she caught Lashmar say, "—their candidate threw his hat into the ring: Mickey Solano, who was Big Charlie's opponent in his latest re-election as Bronx D.A. We've got—"

"Perla, I gotta go." Without waiting to hear her sister's objection, Judy hit end on her phone and dropped it on her couch while grabbing for the cable remote. Grateful for DVR technology, she rewound.

Lashmar was sitting at her desk with the I1V1 logo that RSN had been using for all their news stories on the "vamp sitch," as the vice president had insisted on calling it. "—ozens of Senate races starting to heat up, probably the one with the most heat is for junior senator of New York. The hottest of the hot-button issues is the vamp virus, I1V1, and the New York race has made it white-hot with the candidacy of Hugues Charles, an admitted vamp. Known as 'Big Charlie,' the current Bronx District Attorney has joined a wide field of Democratic candidates to replace Senator Emily Krascznicki. Today that race took a big turn when another candidate threw his hat into the ring: Mickey Solano, who was Big Charlie's opponent in his latest re-election as Bronx D.A."

Cursing, Judy leapt from the couch to find her laptop.

The camera angle changed to one that had Solano's smug face on a screen while Lashmar turned to look at him. "We've got him here via satellite to talk with us this morning. Thanks for coming on, Mickey."

"It's my pleasure, Helen."

Yeah, I'll bet it is. She found her laptop on her dining room table and opened it.

"This is your second run at Big Charlie in two years. What makes you think that this time will be different?"

I'm an even bigger asshole? Judy thought uncharitably as she impatiently waited for the laptop to start back up.

"It's only been a year, but the world has changed a lot in that year, Helen. The vampires are a real problem, and we can't just nod our heads and say they're just victims. It's time to get tough. Honestly, Charlie's doing great in the Bronx, and that's where he belongs. Let him stay in the community he's been such a big part of, and leave the legislation to the rest of us."

I was right, he is *a bigger asshole. He didn't used to be this patronizing.* Her laptop finally came back online and found her apartment's wireless network. She started a new e-mail message to Big Charlie.

"Now you've hired Barel Grindberg as your campaign manager, and she ran Big Charlie's winning campaign against you."

"What!?" Judy rewound the DVR again to make sure she heard that right.

"—ired Barel Grindberg as your campaign manager, and she ran Big Cha—"

"That *bitch*." Judy had always liked Barel, and couldn't believe she'd stab them in the back like that.

"Hey, I was just happy that she was available."

Solano droned on, and Judy got more and more livid. She knew that Barel had specifically advised Big Charlie against running again, and now she wondered if that sage advice had come before or after she'd been hired by Solano.

She finished composing the e-mail and then realized she needed to talk directly to Big Charlie.

Solano was droning on as she grabbed her phone. "—can't help but be an advocate for the vampires, and that's not what we need. We need objectivity. Charlie's been on the front lines of it, both as a victim and as a prosecutor. Hell, a third of the criminal trials in the Bronx in the last nine months have been vampire-related, and a quarter of the civil ones."

Judy shouted at the screen, "The D.A. doesn't handle civil cases, you dumb fuck!"

Big Charlie's voicemail came on. With a sigh, Judy waited for the beep. "It's Judy—call me back the *minute* you get this!"

"—not part of the machine. I *am* part of the community. Mayor Barr, Emma and Dianne—they're part of the system, and that system ain't workin'."

Oh, sweet Jesus, he is not pulling that shit, is he? Judy went back to her laptop to finish the e-mail in case Big Charlie checked that before his voicemail.

Solano went on: "Humanity's at war with itself right now, and we need people who can step up. I've always stepped up when it matters, when the people of New York have needed me, both as a lawyer and an activist. And honestly, what I said about Charlie applies to the others, too, in that they're too close. They're part of the problem, so they don't see the solution. I can bring fresh eyes, eyes that have seen the reality of what the world is turning into."

Judy hit send on the e-mail she'd composed before trying to call, and then leaned back on her couch. In truth, she had also been against Big Charlie running for senator. Before I1V1, she had figured he'd be gunning for it when a seat came open, but now? It was madness.

But she also believed that he could do some good, so it was worth the shot.

She just hoped that she wasn't fooling herself. Or him.

– 18 –

Mia Fitzsimmons thought that Jack Napolitano was going to crawl out of his own skin.

"Can you believe that snake-in-the-grass is the one moderating?" He shook his perfectly coiffed head. "This was *my* racket."

Mia tried to ignore him, all the while cursing whoever sat the two of them next to each other in the press area. The debate among Democratic candidates for senator was being held at Fordham University, and campus security had insisted on assigned seats for the press—and indeed for everyone else, as Big Charlie's presence on the dais led to some serious security concerns.

Jack had said that between every question, and Mia swore that the next time, she was going to kick him. Either that or ask how she qualified as a snake in the grass when *he* was the one who took her job when she was promoted?

The moderator he was complaining about was Yuki Nitobe, who had been asked to moderate by several of the candidates—though notably *not* Big Charlie. Mia figured they were hoping that having the journalist who broke the I1V1 story do the moderating would have people talking about vampires even more, thus focusing more animus on Big Charlie.

The sad thing was, it would probably work.

"Mayor Barr," Nitobe said, "the next question is for you. Do you feel that the most important legislative agenda before Congress in the coming months will be legislation against the I1V1 virus?"

"Absolutely," Barr said without hesitation. "This virus is producing people who are running roughshod over, not just laws, but morality." Barr started doing the cup-your-thumb-in-your-index-finger method of pointing that politicians kept doing because somebody told them it made them look forceful. Mia was looking forward to the day when someone figured out that whoever told them that was wrong. "Plus they have abilities that were never accounted for in current jurisprudence," Barr added. "Now I'm not saying people should be rounded up or anything crazy like that. I'm talking solely about the vampires who have committed crimes—we need to come up with different punishments and different methods for arresting, incarcerating, and prosecuting that small percentage of those who do commit crimes."

As with every question, that resulted in applause. Jack started to make a comment, but Mia just glared at him, and he clammed up.

Nitobe waited for the applause to die down. "The next question is for President Jaffe. What would be your response to a vampire who—"

Big Charlie then cut in, which was a breach in protocol. All the journalists around Mia sat up. "Excuse me, but I am afraid I must interrupt. This is the fifth question in a row that has dealt with I1V1. One would think that a United States Senator had little else to deal with in his or her day-to-day life than legislating against those of us who suffer from the virus."

Nitobe looked positively nonplussed, but before she could say anything, Emma Jaffe, the sitting Manhattan borough president, said, "Oh come on, Charlie, do you really think it's not an important issue? Vampires have been running rampant with no control, and it's been worse in the big cities. The world takes the lead from New York, and we need to provide that leadership."

Mia snorted, since that was probably Jaffe's already-prepared answer to that question.

Dianne Axisa, a state senator, jumped in. "I think Charlie raises a good point. There's a budget crisis, we don't have enough jobs or true national health care, there are serious allocation and tax issues facing this country—and we've spent all our time in this debate talking about one issue. Yes, it's an important issue, but it's hardly the only one."

Wow, two voices of reason. Mia jotted down notes. *One more than I was expecting.*

Solano got that annoying smile of his. "I gotta say, Charlie, I think it's kinda disingenuous for you to complain, since the only reason you're running is *because* you can turn yourself into a werewolf."

"My reasons for running are many, Mickey. But the primary one is to make sure that those of us who suffer from this virus are given a voice in government." He pointed at the two female candidates. "It was less than a hundred years ago that Dianne and Emma could not even vote for a state representative in Washington, much less attempt to become one. It took almost a century and a half for women to achieve that right—I fear that achieving similar rights for my own kind may take as long, and that is simply *not* acceptable."

A gasp passed through the room. Solano put voice to what everyone was suddenly thinking. "That sounded like a threat, Charlie. And having I1V1 doesn't exactly take away your right to vote."

Big Charlie was sounding more—intense? angry?—than Mia had ever heard him. His voice was tighter and tenser than usual. "I have spoken with many who have faced problems, especially those who have had their appearance changed by the virus. They no longer match the visage that appears on their driver's license or passport and are denied simple rights—and not just to vote. We do require new legislation, it is true, but Aaron's solution focuses far too much on the negative and not enough on the positive. We need to take charge of our own destiny, and not let it be defined by others."

The applause that generated was much more subdued and guarded than that of the previous candidates'.

—19—

Emma Jaffe lay in her bed. The television was on, and her laptop was open, but she wasn't paying particularly close attention to either one.

It had been an exhausting day, the latest in a series. Her staff was handling most of the day-to-day of running the borough of Manhattan, which was good, because this campaign was taking up all of her spare time. Any other time, a senate race wouldn't be this brutal, but D.A. Charles made it a huge story. She was spending more time on camera than she ever imagined she would.

On the other hand, it was publicity you couldn't buy. People all over the country were talking about her. Even if she didn't win the race, she had recognition now, and could parlay that into something much bigger. If senator didn't work, there was always mayor next year.

She looked to the empty half of the bed. *You coulda been part of this, Steve.* But then, her career had taken off since the divorce, so maybe he couldn't have been. Maybe he really had been holding her back.

The TV went to commercial, and a deep voice said, "Michael Fayne. Anson Morris. Nathan Kapsis. What do they all have in common? They're all New Yorkers, they're all vampires—and they're all *killers*."

She grabbed for the remote and turned the volume up. She and her staff had gone 'round and 'round over this ad. Even once they finally agreed to film it, finding the right voice had been hard. Her initial thought had been for a gentle female voice, but her campaign manager had convinced her that the deep, scratchy male voice was the way to go.

"Nathan Kapsis murdered his uncle, Senator Alex Kapsis—and now another killer *just like him* wants to take his seat. You wouldn't let the fox into then henhouse. So why should we let a vampire into Congress? Whatever you do next Tuesday—*don't* vote for Hugues Charles for Senate. Vote life, not death."

Then her own voice: "I'm Emma Jaffe and I approve this message."

The key, of course, was that last line in the ad. "Vote life, not death" was the point she'd be hammering home on the rest of her interviews for the next week. Fear was her best weapon right now.

A crack startled her, echoing throughout her apartment. "Hello?"

Steve had taken the dog with him when he left her, so the apartment was empty. She threw the covers aside, pulled her bathrobe tighter around her waist, and cautiously walked toward the doorway. She left the bedroom door open, generally.

A familiar *clack-clack* echoed through the apartment: paws on hardwood. But she hadn't heard it since Steve took Muttley.

Then the clacking got faster, and Emma's heartbeat did likewise. "Who's there?"

A shape formed in the darkness of the hallway, coalescing into a giant, four-legged, hairy creature, breathing heavily and moving toward her.

Her heart pounded into her ribs. She realized that using fear against Big Charlie was a weapon that worked both ways.

A second later, the shape leapt toward her, and she screamed.

– 20 –

Transcript of "On the Street" segment of Good Morning NYC

GOOD MORNING NYC: Today's "On the Street" is about the senate race currently playing out, as we went to Grand Central and asked commuters who they would be voting for.

PERSON #1: Yo, I'm actually *from* the Bronx, and I *voted* for Big Charlie every time he ran—but no way in hell I'm votin' for that mother-BLEEPer now!

PERSON #2: Honestly, I've gone to every candidate's web site and read over their platforms. VanDerMeer's right out—the man's living in the fifties, honestly. Barr never impressed me when he was mayor, and his campaign feels like a desperate attempt to remind everyone he's alive, y'know? Solano's just a scuzzball lawyer. Jaffe and Axisa are okay, I guess, but they don't seem to have much substance. I'll probably vote for one of them, honestly. The only candidate I find myself liking and agreeing with is Big Charlie—but of course, I can't vote for *that*. That'd be crazy.

PERSON #3: I'd sooner vote for the love child of Manson and the Son of Sam than I would the werewolf guy from the Bronx, I'll tell you *that* for free.

PERSON #4: I'm kinda torn between VanDerMeer and Big Charlie. VanDerMeer because he actually knows how to get BLEEP done, Big Charlie because it would just be awesome to have a real-live werewolf in Congress!

PERSON #5: Well, you can probably guess from my white hair and claws that I've got I1V1. I'm actually a registered Republican, so I can't vote in the Democratic primary—which is too bad, because I think it's great that Big Charlie is trying to represent us in Congress. It's about damn time, if you ask me.

PERSON #6: Solano, mostly because I wish I'd voted for him for D.A. last year. Jesus, the way Big Charlie's been—it's like he's a totally different person! Did you hear him in the debate? I didn't see it, but I read what people were saying about it afterward, and it's like he wants to lead a revolution or something. Definitely Solano. Shoulda paid attention to him before.

☾

"SPECIES GENOCIDE"

Jonathan Maberry

–1–
Congressional Subcommittee on the V Epidemic
Washington, DC
22 Days after the V-Event

"Let me get this straight," said the senator from Michigan, "there are different *kinds* of vampires?"

Luther Swann cleared his throat and leaned toward the microphone. "Um, that is correct, sir. In theory, at least. Or, I guess I should say, 'in legend.'"

His voice quavered a bit as he addressed the subcommittee. Swann had never visited the capital building before last week, and had never in his wildest dreams thought he'd be sitting at a table in front of a group of grim-faced senators. On TV those things always looked intimidating. In real life it was terrifying.

Almost as terrifying as what they were talking about.

"Please explain," said the senator. Every eye in the room was on Swann.

"I've spent the last few days going over all of the evidence collected at the different crimes scenes, and reviewing the medical test data from the subjects who have been arrested. Two of them bear strong resemblance to Fayne, in terms of what they did and what they appear capable of doing. But even then, 'strong' resemblance isn't the same thing as saying that they're from the same species."

"*'Species'*?" echoed the senator.

"Yes, sir," said Swann. "If we have to accept that vampires are real, then we have to be open to the possibility that there are several kinds."

"Why?" demanded the senator from Georgia. "I thought all vampires are the same. Fangs and capes and all that."

"All of 'that,' senator," said Swann, "is nonsense. It's the product of a century of Hollywood movies and two centuries of popular fiction. The version of the vampire we have in pop culture is in one way or another the by-product of Dracula, who was a fictional creation of Bram Stoker, and to a lesser degree *Carmilla*, created by Sheridan le Fanu, as well as the stage interpretations of Dracula and early silent films like *Nosferatu.* They took certain elements from European folklore and modified them for fiction. Every writer and screenwriter since has continued to tweak the model to suit their storytelling needs, and as a result there is virtually no resemblance—in either form or nature—between what you and everyone else view as a 'vampire' and the monsters of folklore. Vampires come in all shapes and sizes, from the stereo-typical pale-skinned reanimated corpse to fiery balls of light. Even the label 'vampire' is only commonly used because it's become a recognizable term—like calling all photocopiers 'Xerox machines' or facial tissues 'Kleenex.' They're radically different from country to country. Vampire legends are found among the earliest stories of the Assyrians, Hebrews, Romans and ancient Greeks and they don't resemble Eastern European noblemen in opera cloaks or sparkly teenagers with absurd hair."

A few of the senators smiled, but they were tight smiles.

"What are those differences?" asked the wizened old senator from Connecticut.

"I've written many books on—"

"Summarize for us," said the senator. "Other than drinking blood, what do we know about them?"

"Actually, let's start there. Vampirism isn't limited to the blood-drinkers. In fact barely a third of folkloric vampires are hematophageous—or, blood-suckers. I mean, sure, the blood-drinkers are the most famous of this group, but many vampires attack humans in order to feed off life essence, breath, or sexual essence. A few feed on emotions, others on faith, fidelity, and even knowledge. And quite a few vampires are necrophageous—flesh eaters."

"Good God," said the senator and several others in the room echoed his words.

"Also, we know that Michael Fayne and some of the other recent, um, *infected,* demonstrated incredible strength and speed, which is consistent with vampire legends. What we don't know is whether these infected will develop other powers, and specifically the powers and qualities of vampires from different countries."

"What kind of different powers?" asked the senator from Georgia.

"That varies. There are legends of vampires who can affect the weather, causing mists and storms. The Romanian *varcolaci* was reported to be able to cause eclipses, though this would involve forceful re-arranging of the solar system and would probably result in the destruction of the earth…so we can pretty much discount that as one of the taller tall-tales."

He looked around for more smiles, but no one was amused.

"Okay, let's look at a random sample of vampires," Swann said, ticking items off on his fingers. "The West African *asanbosam* grows iron teeth and iron hooks for feet so it can hang from trees and attack people. The *tlahuelpuchi* of the Mexican state of Tlaxcala separates itself from its legs and flies around as a carnivorous turkey who feeds only on the blood of infants. The Greek *vrykolakas* is a vampire who continually becomes more powerful as it feeds but which can only be killed on a Saturday. The *jigarkhwar* of India and the Russian *eretica* both possess lethal stares. Strangely, the *asuang* vampire of the Philippines is best defeated by engaging it in a staring contest and waiting until it backs down and slinks away. And, believe me, senators, I could go on and on. There are hundreds of species and thousands of variations. There are even vampires who, if they feed enough, become human again."

The senators looked at each other and then each pair of eyes returned to focus on Swann.

"Most of that has to be nonsense, right?" asked the senator from Maine.

"Probably," conceded Swann, "especially with the theriomorphs."

"The *what*?"

"Vampires who can shape-shift. Many vampires are reputed to be able to change shape at will. Oddly, changing into bats is incredibly rare in vampire legend. However, the *abchanchu* from Bolivia assumes the form of an old man who pretends to be lost and helpless, and when some kindly stranger comes along to help the old duffer home, out come the fangs and the bloodlust. The *adze* of Togo can transform into a mosquito. But, I agree…we aren't likely to see that. And even if these vampires *could* somehow change their physical shape, they would have to become something of equal mass. We may be stretching the boundaries of genetics here, but I don't think we'll actually dispense with the laws of physics."

No one spoke.

"Very well," said the senator from Georgia. "I guess the real question is…how do we kill them?"

–2–

Washington, DC

62 Days after the V Event

"What do you mean you won't help?" growled General May. "This isn't a favor we're asking…this is an order direct from the President of the United goddamned States. This is your country at stake here…"

Swann wheeled on the general. He wanted to hit this man. He wanted to punch the imperious sneer off the man's face and kick him down a flight of stairs; but he kept his balled fists down at his side. "Bullshit!" he snarled. "I agreed to help you by identifying the different species of vampires that are presenting during this crisis. I've done that, and I'm willing to continue doing that. But I will not help you slaughter every single person who—"

"They're not *people*, damn it," the general fired back. "They're monsters."

"They're people with a disease!"

"They are murderers. They're organizing out there." The general pointed at the window. "You've read the reports. There are *gangs* of them now. Gangs."

"Okay, so there are gangs. That's bad, that sucks, but you're acting as if they're terrorist cells."

"Yes, sir, that is exactly what we're doing because, from where I stand, it's the same damn thing."

"It's not the same thing from *street* level, general," said Swann with real heat. "Maybe you should talk to people rather than fondle your guns all day long."

"Now wait a fucking minute here—"

"No, you listen to me," said Swann, getting right up in the general's face. "We've had over three hundred new cases in the last month. Three hundred, and not even a tenth of the infected have killed people. That says something. That says that people are exerting control over this thing. Or, maybe it means that drive to hunt isn't overwhelming in all cases. Most importantly, it shows that we don't need to react with a blanket policy of kill 'em all and let God sort 'em out. That's Neanderthal thinking. These are still American citizens. They have rights."

"They have been deemed enemy combatants and threats to national security. This is from the Commander in Chief, professor, I'm not on the policy level. Nor, I believe, are *you.*"

Swann swung away from the general to keep from shoving the man through the window. Outside there were sirens and the air was filled with helicopters—news choppers and Army gunships. Down in the streets there was a rally. Thousands of people were down there, most of them storming the White House to protest the harsh treatment of the infected. Swann suspected that there were actual vampires seeded throughout the crowd. Maybe as rabble rousers or maybe as organizers of a protest to prevent greater harm. On both sides.

Even with the windows closed, they could both hear the chants and yells from the crowd.

Swann took a steadying breath and turned back to the general. "Please, listen to me," he said in a quieter but no less insistent tone, "we may be seeing the emergence of a new *race* of people. Or, the return of an older race. Either way, they are part of the overall *human* race. They are brothers or cousins. To destroy them all is tantamount to ethnic genocide."

"Oh, don't be absurd," sneered the general.

"I'm not. And I warn you now," said Swann, "if you proceed, I'll say as much to the world press."

The general got up in Swann's face. "That would be a mistake," he said quietly.

Swann nodded. "I know what you could do to me. I know what you probably *will* do to me. But, I won't stand by and watch my country do the kind of thing that we have fought *against* since we went to war against Hitler."

Before the general could reply, Swann turned and walked away, but he paused at the door. "And consider this, too," Swann added, "right now a lot of the infected are coming out and declaring themselves. They're seeking medical help, they're joining support groups. Right now most of them are not attacking us. But, if you go to war with them, then you will force them to fight back. Don't forget, general, that they are stronger than us, faster than us, and almost all of them look just like us. And we have no idea how many of them are out there. There could be millions. Hold that thought for a moment—*millions* of creatures who are higher on the food chain than we are. Is that really the war you want to fight?"

Before the general could answer, Swann turned and went out.

"STALKING ANNA LEI" PT.2

James A. Moore

—9—

So what do you do when you're a stranger in town and the cops want
to bust you and the crooks want to kill you?

What else? Go deal with politicians. In this case, I had to stake out
a certain congressman. I didn't much care one way or the other if
William Blevins continued to breathe, but if there was a chance that
watching him got me to my sister, I had to take it. It's not that hard to
find a person if you really want to. It's even easier if the person is a
celebrity. Even if they don't like to admit it, politicians are celebrities.
They have to be if they want to get re-elected. Okay, maybe that's not
true, but it sure seems that way to me whenever election time comes
around. In any event, the man had offices in the city and he went to
them. I don't know what I was expecting. I mean, I'd seen the guy a few
times on the TV and they kept showing the clips of him going on about
the horrors of vampires and how we should be controlled before we
became a problem. I guess I was expecting some kind of larger-than-
life type. But you know what I forgot? I forgot that the man I was trail-
ing was a father who had just lost his son. I barely recognized him when
he left his offices and got into the car that drove him back to his house.
He was a thin man, and his hair was even thinner, and even though he
was taller than me—not hard, I stand five feet, eight inches tall—he was
so hunched over in the cold air that he seemed shriveled. And yes, he

had a driver. Maybe he didn't normally have a driver, but with his son freshly murdered they weren't taking any chances.

I felt for him. I was trying to make sure my sister didn't join his son in the afterlife. For that reason I was going to follow him. But you want to know something? It's a lot harder to follow a man who has a police detail on him. The cop cars were all over the place. They didn't go crazy with the sirens, but they had blue lights going and he got where he was going in a damned big hurry. And unlike me, he was in a car. I couldn't trust my lemon to get me anywhere, so I had to stay on foot. Like I said, I'm really fast. I was also panting and wheezing by the time he reached his house.

His house, with the really big fence, and the nice, smooth lawn without any bushes. His house, out in the damned open, and me on the wrong side of the security.

There was good news. His neighbors had a lot of bushes and a few trees. I made it into a nice elm and recovered from the trip.

I thought about circling the perimeter a few times while I was bent over and catching my breath. Seriously, I watched all the vampire movies with my sister. She loved the sparkly guys. And okay, some of the girls were hot. But in those movies the vampires can do anything and they come out of it smelling like roses. I was stinking to high hell, my deodorant had died about five miles back, and I wasn't at all calm and cool. I thought my pulse alone was going to give me away. I waited outside until the sun set. Then I waited some more. The good news is, the cop cars vanished from sight eventually and started just checking the place out whenever they drove by. I guess maybe they were paroling the whole neighborhood. When I was pretty sure I had the routine figured out, I took a run at breaking into Blevins' place.

Really fast, really strong. Seriously useful stuff. So was the night vision. I was over the fence in one leap and I got up to the side of the house fast enough that even if I had screwed up the timing on the cop cars, I would have made it without being seen. I hadn't screwed up. The walls were brick and mortar, which looks great and is supposed to be all kinds of cool for saving money on heating and air conditioning. You know what the problem with brick is? It's not so easy to climb.

Unless you have claws, of course. I took off my boots and socks and started climbing. It wasn't easy and I had to take my time, which when you are considering how soon the next squad car is going to come around the corner, is not comforting, but it can be done. I made it to the second floor and to the balcony under what I guessed was the master bedroom before the police drove past. I don't think I've ever squatted that low or for that long in my entire life, but I waited it out as the car oozed along the road. I kept waiting for a searchlight, but I guess they were trying to be considerate of the people inside and I got lucky.

The door to the balcony was unlocked. Seriously. I figure if somebody had just killed my kid and I was worried that they might be coming for me, I probably wouldn't be at home. Even if I was, I would be locking every door and every window, because I'm paranoid like that. Of course, I'm not exactly the sort to run away, either. Need proof? I was breaking into a high profile government official's home and I was willing to do whatever had to be done because I was looking for my little sister. Not really the run-away-from-a-problem type, if you see my point.

There are a lot of old legends about vampires. One of the ones that never made sense to me is you need to invited into someone's place before you can enter. Know what I like best about that one? It's a lie. I moved into the place easily enough, crouching low and settling my feet carefully. I'd feel damned stupid if I snuck all the way into a place and then got busted because of a squeaky board. I found Blevins without any trouble. He was sleeping on the bed in the middle of the room. The woman next to him was probably his wife. I don't know if I ever saw a picture of her, but she was older, a little heavy and sleeping heavily. Not exactly the sort you expect a politician to cheat with, if you get what I'm saying. I didn't see any evidence, but the way they were resting I'd guess they'd both been hitting the sleeping pills.

So I was there and now all I had to do was hope that I was right and the damned green ogre was going to come for the old man and soon, because I didn't want to be waiting in the corner of the bedroom when the sun came up. It's a lot harder to hide in broad daylight and monster-face or not, I didn't much like the idea of trying to explain my presence to the police or to the nice politician who already felt I deserved to be locked away.

Used to know a cop when I was a little kid. He was a big guy, or at least I remember him that way and he was always hanging around the same restaurant when he did his paperwork. My uncle owned the restaurant and he kept me and Anna a lot of times when my parents were working. Anyway, the cop was always full of information. I think he just liked to listen to himself talk, but me and my little sister liked to hear him too, so it worked out pretty well. One of the things he told me that always stuck with me was that stakeouts are all about patience. You have to wait a lot, and then you have to wait some more. I guess maybe that's true. It felt like I was waiting for a few days, but the clock on the night stand said I waited about thirty minutes before the green ape showed itself.

I tried for subtle when I came in. Seriously. I was as quiet and fast as I could be. I was freaking brilliant. I wouldn't lie about that.

The ogre? Yeah, I'm guessing it jumped from the ground floor and just landed on the balcony because I felt the ground under me vibrate— and rouse me from my half-sleep, because apparently stakeouts require naps—and I carefully got myself back into a proper crouch as I waited for whatever would happen next.

What happened was Hsi-Hsue-Kuei. Blood-Suck Demon. I'd seen myself in the mirror, and I was kind of cool looking in a freaky way. But this thing? It was scary as hell. Seriously. The shape that came into the room was massive. I was about the same size as always when I changed. If that was true of this thing, I'm guess the biggest dude in the NFL got vamped when no one was looking. I guess if it had been standing up, it would have been close to seven feet tall, but it came in low and slumped over, arms nearly dragging the ground and head hunched until it was nearly between the two oversized shoulders. You ever see some of the pictures of Chinese monsters? Big, bulging eyes, mouths full of teeth too damned big and wide, ugly noses with flaring nostrils? Not far off from the reality, but not really quite as creepy as the reality, either. I'm guessing close to five hundred pounds of pissed off and ugly came into the room in a hurry, panting and grunting, with a thick black tongue poking out between the tusks on the sides of the mouth. Yes, tusks. Looked like somebody had mated a gorilla with a wild boar and only kept the ugliest of the offspring. The entire package was wrapped in long, stringy, green fur. The arms were too long, the legs were too short and the body was too damned thick with muscles. And looking at it hurt my eyes and my mind; it didn't fit with the real world. Oh, sure, the same could be said for me, but like I said, at least I'm sort of cat-faced and cool looking. This? It was a mess with uneven features.

The smell was the same though. No mistaking it. This was the thing that took my sister. Oh, and ate people when it was hungry. It looked at the bed for a second and I got ready to pounce. I had the element of surprise on my side and it was busy looking at Blevins and his wife on the bed. I have to be honest here, I was not happy about the idea of tackling something that was as big as three of me. But I was even less happy with the idea of my sister being kept against her will.

I took my chance and leaped for the thing, claws sliding out on my fingers, teeth bared, and my monster-face showing in all its glory.

And that big, lumbering ape of a monster turned and snapped me out of the air, grabbed me in its hands and smiled at me with the meanest expression I have ever seen.

— 10 —

"I was wondering when I'd see you," it said to me. When it threw me against the wall I heard the plaster crack and the board behind it, too. Or maybe that was my ribs. It was hard to tell past the way everything went sort of gray and I forgot how to breathe. I've been hit plenty of times. You don't do the sort of work I do if you don't get used to being slapped around now and again. But damn, I have never been hit that hard before. I pushed off the wall and reached for that green face, fully intending to give as good as I got. The ogre had a different idea and hit me in the face with a fist almost as big as my head.

After that, I stopped fighting. Unfortunately, the damned thing didn't seem to feel the fight was over just yet.

— 11 —

I woke up maybe twenty minutes later, at least according to the clock. It was hard to say past the blood that was coating the alarm's face.

That woke me right the hell up. I sat up fast and then waited for the room to stop spinning. The ogre was gone, but the Blevins' were both still there and very, very dead. I guess it got hungry. What can I say; maybe mutilation is the sort of work that builds up an appetite. I couldn't tell where one body began and the other ended. I made it to my feet and looked away before I could puke, because while I wasn't feeling my best, I didn't feel leaving my last meal on the floor of a crime scene would exonerate me. I raised my hand to wipe at my face and felt a wet slick across my lips. One look and I could see that I'd been smeared with blood. I'm betting it belonged to both of them. I'd just been framed. Or at least I would have been if I'd stayed around. If I didn't heal quickly enough there's every reason to believe that the police would find me on the premises covered in the blood of the victims. Doesn't take a genius to figure out how that would work out, does it? I'd just been set up by six hundred pounds of ugly, fast and smarter than it looked. Not my best moment.

I didn't dare touch anything. I looked in the mirror and saw that there was blood on my face, but not on my hands, except where I'd put it when I wiped at my mouth. That meant the ogre hadn't thought to use my fingerprints, at least. Take what you can get and call yourself lucky. I went out to the porch, crouching the entire time, and I looked carefully at the lawn and surroundings. Nothing. No cops, no green King Kong waiting to kick the crap out of me again. I dropped down to the lawn and landed in a squat. My head was throbbing and my ribs still felt like someone had twisted me into a new shape, but at least I landed on my feet. What can I say? I guess I'm more graceful when I'm deliberately dropping twenty feet as opposed to falling sixty or so. I was still barefoot, so maybe the cops wouldn't notice the spot where I landed. On the other hand, I could see where the ogre had hit the ground and it looked like two small craters where those feet hit the grass.

I reminded myself that there was no time to panic. I had to remind myself a lot, because I really, really wanted to panic right then, and I grabbed my shoes and socks. No time to put them on. Stronger, faster. Works great until you've had the shit knocked out of you. I still made it back over the fence and into the bushes just before the cop car came around the corner. This time the lights were flashing and the siren was screaming loud enough to wake the dead. Well, maybe not the Blevins family, but you get the idea. Does that sound callous? Maybe it is, but the man had already stated he didn't much like my kind, so I have a little trouble feeling too guilty.

I waited until the first dozen or so cop cars had pulled in. No doubt about it, I was set up by that ugly ape-thing. It tried to frame me. I didn't have the time to worry about what sort of evidence I might have left behind. I didn't study the bodies too carefully but I knew that certain mutilations had probably occurred and that made it easier for me. No matter if I left a fingerprint or a hair or what have you, the Hsi-Hsue-Kuei had definitely left behind more. It had been hoping to frame me by me being there. That didn't work.

The socks and boots went on and I checked my face as best I could, cleaning away the blood smears. Yes, I licked. Yes, as much as it disgusts me, the blood tasted sweet. I have to be honest here. I liked the taste. I could see where the appeal was. I just wasn't going to let myself feed that way. I couldn't. My parents would never forgive me. Anna would never forgive me.

Anna. I had to find my sister. I was running out of possible leads. The damned ogre kept killing them. I needed help on this. The only problem was there wasn't any help to be had. Well, okay, that wasn't completely true. I knew at least a couple of people in Chicago I could maybe turn to. It's a smaller world these days than it used to be. The Internet saw to that. But knowing I could turn to them didn't mean they didn't have loyalties elsewhere, if you see my point. I knew them, yes, and I could maybe even trust them, but if they also knew the local gangs and that some of the gangs wanted me dead? Where were their loyalties going to fall?

It came back to Anna in the long run. Even if they knew me and knew the locals, Anna was a different situation. Anna was a good person and she was in a bad situation. And a lot of the same people that knew me knew her and liked her. It was all I had to go on, so I went with that while I made my choices.

Twenty minutes later I was well away from the latest crime scene and I made my phone call.

I guess you could say I got lucky. First, Lisa answered the phone and second, she didn't hang up right away. Ten minutes after that, I was on my way to her apartment. I stopped once, when I coughed up a clot of blood and decided it was time to fix the problem. Remember when I said I'm not a bloodsucker? It's true. I also try to avoid killing animals whenever I can. But you have to draw the line somewhere, don't you? I'm okay with killing if it has to be done. In this case I looked around and leaned against a tree that looked like maybe it had been around when Lincoln was elected president. I don't drink blood. I consume life force. That means I can take from any living thing. Some life forces are small, some are bigger. I hoped the tree would live through me feeding, but there was no guarantee.

I touched the tree and let instinct take over. I felt the energies drain from the tree, pull from the ground around it and from the manicured lawn it where it rested. Sometimes I have to wonder if there's a limit. I drank deep, but I swear I think I could have kept drinking and taking and maybe never had enough. I made myself stop when the hunger faded down and my chest stopped hurting. I'll heal either way. I can be starving or I can be well-fed and I'll heal from almost anything, so far at least. But if my batteries are full I heal faster and better.

When I let go of the tree I was feeling a lot better. The tree was looking about the same as before, but there was a spot where I'd touched it that was discolored. If it went like it usually does, that would be all. But a few times, I've walked away and come back a day or so later and the tree has been dead or that mark has spread across the whole thing and I know it's already dying. Some things you can't fix. And a guy's gotta eat.

– 12 –

A little information about Lisa Kresswell. She's a street tough, She went to school in San Francisco with me and Anna at PS #132. She moved around a lot and she got stuck with us. Before that her family lived in Alabama and before that they were in Boston. And the list goes on. But back in the day she told me she was from outside of Chicago originally and I guess she had the need to go home. That meant I got lucky.

Being street smart doesn't mean being part of that community, and that's a good thing sometimes. I mean, yeah, I have my job and all that stuff, but that's not the same thing. Anna is street tough, but she stays out of that crap because she knows better. I'm just too stupid to follow my own common sense.

Lisa wasn't hard to find, and like I said, she was good enough not to throw a rock at me as soon as she heard my name. We have history. Nothing serious, but it could have been if things had turned out differently. Biggest problems were the same stuff that always matters in high school. She was white and I wasn't, and she was moving away with her family and I was staying behind. We both promised we'd stay in touch. We both lied. Okay, me more than her, yeah, but it was both of us that did the lying.

Last time I saw her she was dyeing her brown hair a different shade of purple almost every day, her hips were narrow, her chest was small and she was dressing in clothes that hugged her body. This time around her hair was its natural color, her chest was decidedly bigger and I couldn't see her hips past the baby she was growing in her belly. I know

I must have stared like a monkey, and the entire time she gave me her usual no-nonsense look with a half-smile on her pretty face.

"What the fuck is that?" I stared hard at her belly, which was really a lot larger than the last time I'd seen it. I mean I stared hard, because, honestly, I never thought I'd see Lisa pregnant in a million years.

"It's called a baby. Don't believe that shit about storks. This is where they come from." Lisa pointed to the appropriate spot on her body. I think I must have blushed because she laughed at me and punched me in the shoulder.

I looked past her at the rest of the place, trying to spot the baby's daddy. Last thing I needed was a pissed-off future dad who decided to take his frustrations out on me.

She shook her head. "It's just me. Long story and none of your business."

I stepped inside when she gestured and I kept my mouth shut. I knew Lisa well enough to understand that if she wanted to tell me about what happened between her and some guy, she'd tell me. The apartment was decent sized and it was obvious that at least a couple of people lived there, because it was too big for Lisa alone. There were three doors that were all closed and looking down the hallway I could see the bathroom door was open. Even if one of those rooms was a closet, the other was probably a second bedroom. Also, I could smell the different odors of different people. And I could smell their colognes, their cigarettes and a strong odor of coffee. I wasn't about to point out that any of that stuff was bad for the baby. Not my life, not my kid.

"So what's going on with Anna?" Straight to business. Even when we were tight, Lisa never played around with being patient. We sat down and I told her everything I knew, even the part about me being a vampire. That part had her shaking her head. That was fair. I still shook my head about it a lot myself.

"That's all there is to say." I shrugged my shoulders. "I'm at a loss here, Lisa. I don't know what to do. I know I've got a lot of people after me, and I know I've got to find Anna." I must have looked as miserable as I felt, because she got up from the chair where she'd settled while I talked and she moved next to me on the couch. A moment later we were hugging. Nothing passionate or anything, just hugging and it was nice to do that. You really can't be caught hugging on a lot of people when you're working as an enforcer, if you see my point.

"Anna called here the other day, John." Lisa's voice was soft, reluctant.

"What?" I sat up and pulled away from the embrace. She should have told me that earlier.

"She told me she was being hunted. She said she was coming to Chicago and asked if she could stay here. I said yes, but that was the last I heard." Lisa's face was open and honest, same as always. Thing about Lisa was, she didn't like to lie. She might avoid a subject if she didn't want to hurt someone's feelings, but she didn't like to lie.

"Why didn't you tell me before?"

"I'm telling you now." She shrugged.

"Lisa, damn it. You know what I mean."

Lisa looked away from me and stared at the carpet on the floor. It was just a standard apartment shag, not exactly exciting stuff to give a close inspection. "She said she was running from you, John. She said you were the one chasing her."

"That's crazy." It took an effort not to yell. It wasn't her fault and I knew that. Still, I was stunned. "I'd never chase after Anna. She's my little sister. She's my responsibility." She always had been. When we were growing up, Anna was left in my care as often as not while the folks went to work and made a good living for us. That's just the way it was, the way it always had been.

"I know. That's why I'm telling you." She put her hand on my shoulder and I looked at her. We were close once, and it hurt me a little to think about her, about how much she had changed in just a few years. Christ, she was about to have a kid! "I know you'd never hurt Anna. I told her that, too, but she said you'd changed."

I felt shame right then. I was blushing and looking away from Lisa and I clenched my teeth and tried not to feel that cold spin of self-loathing, but let's be honest here, we all do things from time to time that we regret. I always regretted working for the mob, but I could justify it. Maybe that was the problem. Maybe Anna couldn't. And then there was the vampire thing. Anna was the one who helped me get through it, but that didn't mean she enjoyed it. I remembered her crying after I killed that damned stray. And the shame bloomed like a floral explosion in my chest.

"She got taken, Lisa." I looked at my friend and stared hard. "She got grabbed by the damned ogre. I saw the thing. Hell, I got my ass kicked by it just a little while ago." Why would my sister say such things about me? The shame was back again, and repulsion. Was I really that horrible? The one person I always looked out for was so sickened by me that she lied about me and wanted to run away from home to get away from me?

Lisa shook her head. "I don't get it, either, John. I haven't heard from either of you in a long time and now you're both calling me." I opened my mouth to say something and she stopped me. "I'm not pointing fingers, I'm just saying I haven't been around you guys in a long time and I don't know all of the details."

We could have maybe gone on like that, with me lost in guilt and self-loathing and Lisa maybe not making things better or worse so much as reminding me of how much my world had changed in the last few months. We might have gone on that way, but then my cell phone rang and when I looked at the caller ID I saw Anna Lei. My sister. I'd tried her cell a dozen times and it always went straight to voice mail. I figured the damn ape-thing had crushed the phone or Anna left it somewhere and the charge died. So the last thing I expected was that call.

Of course I answered it. What the hell else was I going to do?

"Anna?"

"John! You have to get out of here. It's coming for you. It wants you dead, you hear me?" My heart soared hearing her voice. I wasn't even aware of how much of me was sure she was already dead until I heard her speak. I could have cried, even with the words she was saying.

"Where are you? Tell me. I'll come get you."

"Run, John! Just run!" She sounded so worried, so desperate.

"Where are you?" I was screaming now, and there wasn't much choice. My head was aching with my pulse and all I could think about was getting Anna safely away from that thing. And as it yelled for me to tell me where she was I heard the sounds of a struggle come through the phone. A second later the call ended and I was left staring at the screen on my phone that told me the connection had been lost.

Know what the problem with being an over-protective big brother is? You go a little crazy when something happens to your little sister. I started pacing and I clutched my phone so hard I heard the case crack a bit. I was smart enough to put it back in my pocket after that. Lisa watched me for several seconds without saying anything. When she finally asked me about the call, I told her word for word what Anna had said.

And when I was done and I'd calmed down a little, Lisa shook her head and sighed. She got up and walked as best she could to the kitchen. She took her time in there and I knew that was a sign that she was thinking of what she had to say to me. When she came back a minute later, it was with a glass of beer for me and a bottle of water for her. After I'd taken a couple of gulps from the beer she shook her head and said what was on her mind. "You should listen to her, John."

"What? Leave her with that thing?"

"Yeah." She was looking me in the eyes and I knew she was completely serious, but it was hard for me to accept that idea. "John, I don't think you're seeing the whole picture here. You're too close to it."

"What do you mean?" Lisa was direct enough, but I guess I was feeling particularly thick. In my defense, it had been a hard day.

"First, she's still got her phone. That means she's been carrying the phone the entire time she's been gone. Second, she only just called you after you had a run in with the green thing. Unless the green thing is telling her what's going on and what to say, she has no reason to suddenly call you. Maybe it makes sense to you, but it doesn't make sense to me." She shrugged her shoulders. "Why would she wait over a week to tell you to run unless she had a good reason?"

"Maybe it told her what to say."

"Maybe it did." She kept staring at me, and I started to understand what she was trying not to say.

"You think that Anna is working with this thing?"

"I don't think anything. But it's a little strange that your sister calls you after you have a run in with that monster and after it leaves you alive to take the fall for what it's been doing. Seems to me like the thing doesn't want to kill you but wants you out of the way. You said you change shape when you're fighting. Maybe it does the same thing. Maybe it can hide in plain sight, same as you can."

"I have to work at it."

She gave me that look that told me I was being stupid. She was really, really good at giving me that look. Maybe that was one of the other reasons we never got too serious. The truth can be unpleasant to face. "So you have to dye your hair and shave. Maybe it has to do the same thing. Maybe it doesn't even have to do that much. No one knows, because you're both different. I mean, have you really paid attention to the V-Virus stuff, John? There's some weird ass shit going on and you aren't even close to the top of that list. Seriously."

Honestly? I hadn't much paid attention. I never had the time for the news. Even when I found out what was going on with me, I was too busy doing other things. What can I say? I hate studying.

"You think maybe she's working with this other vampire?"

Lisa shrugged again and shook her head. "I don't know. I just know that something weird is going on. Maybe she made a deal with it. Maybe she's trying to protect you by leaving with it. Maybe she's dating the damn thing. Who knows?"

"Okay, there's no way my sister is dating that thing."

"Why?"

"It's a green gorilla!"

"You're a big white cat with bad joints. What's your point?" Again with the *you're-being-stupid* look. "For all you know the damn thing is Brad Pitt when it's not a green monkey."

Outside a police car went screaming by with sirens wailing and lights flashing and I froze for a moment. It was easy to relax around Lisa, but I wasn't about to forget that I was in a serious situation here. I wasn't really guilty of anything, but the police were on the lookout for my monster-faced self and it was possible that someone working with Maggie Ruiz might make the connection and report me. I didn't know if there were others like me or not. I wasn't exactly in the loop when it came to vampire statistics.

I stood up and shook my head. Big mistake. The room tried swimming a bit. I thought I'd had a big enough snack earlier to fix the trauma from earlier, but maybe I was just damned tired. I had been on the move for several days.

"You okay?"

I looked at Lisa and stepped back from her. She was pregnant. If my body decided to do something instinctual about feeding, I didn't want to take a chance on her or her baby getting hurt. "I think I better leave. I don't feel good."

"Maybe you should sit down, John." She looked worried.

"I can't take any chances. You and the baby. You can't be around me if things go wrong."

She looked like she'd been slapped in the face when I said that.

Remember how I said Lisa doesn't like to lie? She's not good at it. She gets this guilty expression on her face that causes her no end of

331

troubles. She not only doesn't like to lie, she sucks at it. She got that guilty expression on her face as she looked at me.

"John. I'm so sorry."

"What?" The room shifted on me, started tilting hard to the right and I had trouble focusing on her. Until that moment I thought I was just tired. It never once crossed my mind that I might be drugged. The beer in a glass. I should have known. Lisa was like me, much more likely to offer a bottle or a can than to pour it.

"I had to, John. They said they'd hurt the baby." She was crying. Damn it, she was crying, there were tears in her eyes and her hands moved up to cover her mouth as I reached for her and missed.

I didn't miss the table though. I caught the coffee table with my chin as I fell toward the ground. Didn't miss the ground either. I hit it nice and hard with my face.

$$-13-$$

I woke up eventually. I don't know how much time had passed, but I had a nasty headache and my jaw was sore. I was stripped down to my jeans, my feet were bare, my chest was bare. I was also hanging by my arms, and had been up there for a while judging by the pain in my shoulders. I couldn't have told you where I was on a bet, but there was a smell of old blood and meat and it was cold. The building was brick and wood and had seen better days. Maybe it was an old slaughter-house, they had a lot of those back in the day in Chicago. I remember that from high school at least. See my point? Not really a lot to go on. Oh, except for the small army of Chinese guys around me. They were a good hint. Chow Liu. It only took me a second to do the math on that one. His people were probably really, really pissed off about how their boss died. And really, one vampire is probably as good as the next when it comes to the blame game.

The dude that came over to give me the stink eye was all lean muscle and tattoos. A lot of tattoos. Looking at his arms, I wished I could read Mandarin because there were a lot of symbols and words and they maybe could have told me a little about the guy carrying the long knife in his left hand.

"I didn't kill Chow Liu." What else could I say?

He looked me in the eyes, careful to stay just out of range from where my feet could have kicked him. As I was hanging by the arms, this was maybe a good idea, or maybe a very generous belief in how athletic I was. Because I wasn't really sure myself, I tried moving my legs and winced. I'd been out for a while and my old friend rigor mortis had come to visit. I could barely even start to bend my legs without wanting to scream.

Finally the man spoke to me. "We know."

"Then why am I here?" He had me at a loss. I expected to be in trouble because their boss was dead, but if I wasn't getting blamed, there had to be another reason.

"New boss wants you here, man." He was maybe twenty-five years old, and on second glance I could also see that he was covered with scars under his tattoos. I didn't know who he was, but the term badass motherfucker came to mind. Seriously, you don't get scars like those unless you've been in a lot of fights and I'm guessing he won most of them.

"Who's the new boss?"

"Hsi-Hsue-Kuei." He smiled when he said it. Then he stepped around me, doing a slow circle. I was very aware of the really big knife in his hand as he moved behind me. I heal well. That might not mean as much if he stabbed me in the kidneys, or if he put that blade through my heart. Seriously, it was a big knife. The kind hunters use to make a clean kill and then to skin whatever they just finished gakking. "You really a hopping ghost?"

I shook my head. "Not a ghost, man. I'm just a guy."

"Naw." He was back in front of me and shaking his head. "You ain't just a guy. You're one of them. You're a *jiangshi*."

"You see me hopping anywhere?"

"I bet I can make you hop." He sneered at me. I sneered back. Now and then you have to play at tough, even when you don't feel it. I swung my legs a couple of times and he stepped back. While he was watching, I raised my legs to chest height—and I even did it without screaming. It hurt. That's all I can say. My arms were already blood deprived from being suspended for so long and they weren't happy with me after that. Felt like both of my legs were breaking and there were a lot of popping noises to go along with that thought. But when I put my legs back down the worst of the tendon problems were at least manageable. I wasn't going to be running anywhere without doing some stretches, but I'd be able to stand at least.

"I can maybe hop on my own." I looked above me at the rope that was holding my wrists. It had been tied to a wooden rafter two stories above me. "Want to see?"

I heard the deep voice that called out coming from behind me and felt the hairs on my neck rise in protest. I hadn't smelled it, hadn't heard it, but the green ape was there. "Stop beating your chest and get to this." The words weren't for me. I am convinced of that.

"Get to what?" I didn't like the sound of this, not one little bit.

"Boss says I cut your heart out, it proves I'm loyal." The guy smiled at me. "I got no problem with cutting your heart out. Nothing personal, just what I have to do."

I nodded my head. I could see his point. Maybe if I didn't have my sister and my family to think about, I could be as cold as him, but I hoped not.

Here's the thing; I'm not a gymnast, and I'm not even all that flexible, but I am a changed man. I'm a vampire, whatever that really means. Here's the parts that matter: faster, stronger, tougher. Get me?

I shifted my hands so I was holding onto the ropes above me, and then I pulled with all my strength. I didn't hop so much as I launched myself toward the sky. My legs weren't a hundred percent, my arms were screaming at me, but I was up and out of range of the dude's knife for a moment. Long enough. I twisted my body and landed on the rafter. My arms weren't fast enough, but my legs caught on. Next thing I know, I'm hanging upside down, fifteen feet off the ground, and doing my best not to cry like a baby because everything hurts so much. The rope was still around my wrists. I didn't have the time to work my arms until I felt the blood flowing properly again. If I'd had that sort of time, I could have probably snapped the ropes after a couple of minutes. We're talking nylon and the stuff was meant to hold a lot of weight, but like I said, I'm strong these days. Also like I said, no time, so I went all monster-face and did the next best thing. I tore the ropes apart with my teeth. They tasted like crap, but I wasn't there for a meal. I was there to get free.

They were all screaming after that, the tattooed guy, his friends and the green ape. I tore my hands free, spit out the pieces of rope that weren't wedged between my teeth, and shook my arms to get the blood where it needed to be, all the while hanging upside down and praying my legs would hold me.

A couple of the toughs were screaming about how they had a clear shot, but Tattoo wasn't having any of that. I knew the score, of course. He had to prove himself. I don't know exactly what went down in the town, but I could do the basic math. The ogre wanted to take over. Tattoo was cool with that, he might have even helped the ogre get to Chow Liu, but he still had to prove himself to the new boss if he wanted to be the second in command. Anyone else helping would make him lose face in front of the new boss. Guess what? That's not the sort of thing you do if you want to show how tough you are in the Triads.

So he had to take me out all by himself, or he maybe had to die trying. Guess which one I preferred.

I was so busy looking at him that I didn't even look for the green ogre. I mean, I'd just heard it, right? How far could it go?

Of course, it had jumped to the second floor balcony earlier. I should have remembered that. I heard someone let out a shocked scream and as I was looking toward the screamer, I felt the beam I was on shudder. Then the green paw was on me and yanking my leg away from the rafter. It could have killed me right then—it could have killed me earlier, too—but instead it let me fall. I landed on my feet again, and tried to bend my knees to take in the impact. Only my legs still weren't a hundred percent and instead of taking in the impact, my legs just gave out under me and I hit the ground.

The pain was gigantic. Listen, the big green thing had busted me up earlier and I'd gotten back up and run away before the cops could get to me. But I'd done my stretching and I'd been prepared then and now my legs were already in pain and I had probably ripped a few tendons when I tried landing. I fell flat and screamed, a hard screech that echoes off the walls around me and had half the men in the room covering their ears. My scream isn't normal anymore; it's loud and unsettling. Not everyone freaked out, but a lot of them did.

Tattoo was not among them. While his friends were freaking out and I was trying to recover from the pain tearing through me, he moved in fast and hard and kicked me in the face. I said he looked hard, but I didn't know the half of it. Listen, I'm not bragging but even before the change I'd have placed good money on me holding my own against almost anyone. This is a fact: before the change, he'd have killed me with that first kick. And the sad part? That wasn't even his best shot. While I was falling backward and trying to recover from what felt like a mule bucking its hooves into my face, he came around fast and drove the damned big knife of his into my stomach. I felt it slice through muscles, cut into my internal organs, and I grabbed his arm because I could see him tensing. He was about to pull upward and disembowel me. That's all there is to it. He was about to kill me. The pain I was feeling went away, lost in a tide of adrenaline that let me keep going when I should have been falling down.

I locked my hands onto his wrist and squeezed as hard as I could and it was his turn to scream. I felt the muscles moving like putty under my fingers and the bones beneath those muscles creaking and then he was kneeing me in the side of my face, his knee bashing my eyebrow and my eye. I didn't mean to let go of his hands, but I did it anyway. It's hard to keep your grip when you can't think straight and I couldn't do much of anything after that kick. Stronger, faster, tougher and getting my ass kicked.

I have to go ahead and say it. I should be dead right now. He had me. I can lie and tell you how I fought back from the edge of disaster, but I didn't. He whupped my ass. When he was done kneeing me in the face, he punched me in the throat. While I was trying to figure out how to breathe, he ripped the knife out of my guts and danced back out of my range, probably content to watch me die. And I would have died right then and there. I believe that.

But, again, vampire. Instinct took over. I lashed out, I felt the hunger flare like a miniature sun in my chest and it demanded satisfaction. I was aiming for Tattoo but he wasn't where he had been a second before. Instead some poor bastard who'd been cheering him on took the brunt of my body's demands. I feed on life force. I said that already, I know, but I try to feed on different sources, because after what I did to that dog? I never want to hear that sort of scream again and I never want to feel that kind of guilt again.

Whatever it was that made him a living, breathing man left his body in one gigantic wave that slammed into me and knocked me down. I felt like I was strapped to a generator, and it was going overtime. I felt like I'd been dying of thirst and was suddenly filled with sweet, cool water. I could use a million more examples, but I'll leave you with just one more. In that instant I understood why people can get hooked on drugs. I was satisfied, I was sated. I was full to overflowing with energy and with every part of me felt perfect. The wound in my stomach? Gone. Healed. My jaw? It was fine. My eye and the socket around it that

I think was probably shattered? All just fine. The man that I ripped that life force from?

He died screaming, his body shivering and shaking and the hair on his head smoldered. His eyes were gone, burst from his head by whatever it was that I did to him. He was dead.

And I felt better than I ever had before.

That feeling? It was better than sex.

And the green ogre stepped forward and clapped its hairy paws together.

I looked toward the thing and felt myself coming down from that incredible high. I still felt nearly invincible. I was looking at the Hsi-Hsue-Kuei and wondering why I'd ever been afraid. In that moment I was pretty sure I could break the damned thing over my knee without even trying.

And that thing looked at me and smiled.

Tattoo came at me again, his face determined, and the green ogre held up a hand and stopped him. That was good. I was feeling like I could eat again, and I was betting my little buddy with the knife would taste about as sweet as anything ever could. The worst part? I was horrified by that feeling and at the same time I didn't much care. I wanted this. I wanted to feel him die and to steal that vitality for myself.

"Are you getting it now, Johnny?" I looked at the ogre as it spoke. I was looking while the shape changed, growing smaller before my eyes. Anna called the way I looked right then wearing my monster-face. I never guessed that she had one of her own. My sister looked at me, her body naked before a dozen men, and she did so without any shyness.

I knew she was my sister. There isn't an expression she can make that I haven't seen at least a few times. There isn't a mark on her face or a scar on her arms, no matter how small, that I am not familiar with. I was there when she got those scrapes. I was there to bandage them and make her feel better. I knew she was my sister.

And at that moment? I didn't know her at all.

−14

"Say something, Johnny."

"What the hell?" I stared at her and she came closer, her face as familiar and alien as could be. She was my sister, yes, but my sister could never, ever have done the things that the green ogre had done.

She couldn't possibly be a killer. She couldn't mutilate living people and feast on their bodies. She was my sister! Impossible.

"I had to make you see. I had to make you understand what it feels like." She put her hand on my shoulder and I twitched. Part of me wanted to run from her. Part of me still wanted to protect her. There had to be some sort of insane mistake.

"Make me see what?" I was yelling, I admit it.

"You starve yourself. You don't let your body get what it needs. This is what we're supposed to be." She was so calm. I couldn't really understand that. How could she be so calm when the world was falling apart? What would our parents say? What would anyone say?

"You killed a lot of people, Anna. We can get help though. We can find a good lawyer." I was trying to explain it all to her, to make her understand. This didn't have to be the end of everything. If she would just come home with me, we could make it all work out.

"Don't be stupid. I know what I did. I did it on purpose." My ears were ringing. I could hear her, but I didn't want to. Her words didn't make any sense. "This is what we need. This is why we were chosen, We're going to rule here, Johnny. You can rule with me. We can run everything." She looked into my eyes and stared hard, reading me as easily as I thought I could read her, and then she looked away, shaking her head. "You don't get it. You don't want to get it."

"Don't get what? That you're a killer?"

"So are you!" Anna pointed to the man I'd killed. His body looked wrong. I couldn't have said exactly why, except that he was dead. But there was more to it. I'd done something to him, something so intense that it screwed up his corpse, too. "You killed him and you liked it!"

"No!" I was lying. I had liked it. I'd never felt better. I was still feeling it. But the difference is, I never wanted to feel that way again. I was already sickened by what had happened.

Anna turned away from me, her face showing her contempt. Then she turned back and took a swing. By the time her fist connected with my jaw, she'd changed again. The blow felt like a wrecking ball slapping me senseless. Tattoo might have skills, but Anna had raw power and speed. She was tougher than me. My little sister, the one I'd always protected, was tougher than me. Stronger than I ever imagined. Before I could recover she hit me again and then a third time. Each blow staggered me. I tried to defend myself, I did. I mean that. But she was too fast. Too strong. Too damned tough. When the last blow dropped me to the ground she stepped back and waved her men away from me.

She had me dead to rights. I couldn't make myself attack her.

Anna looked down at me. 'This is done. Stay away from me. Go home to San Francisco. Stay away from Chicago, or I'll kill your little girlfriend and her baby. You understand me? You stay away and they are safe. You come back and I kill them." The problem was simple: Anna knew me too well. She knew I cared about Lisa. She'd known all along. When she went to Chicago, she knew that I'd contact Lisa sooner or later. Just like she knew I'd follow her if she left San Francisco.

"Anna, why are you doing this?" It was all I had. I couldn't beg. She wouldn't listen. I could tell that already. Whatever changes had taken place in her when the vampire virus got to her, they'd warped my sister's brain somewhere along the way.

She moved closer to me, leaned down until her bestial face was inches from mine. Her eyes met mine and she stared. Both forms were completely different. Her eyes were not the same, and yet I found myself wondering how it was I didn't realize before then that she was the Hsi-Hsue-Kuei. "Because I'm tired of being Johnny Lei's little sister. Because I'm tired of being our father's daughter. Because I'm me. And now everyone will know that I'm somebody, too."

And then she left and I let her go.

I had to, because I knew exactly what she meant. She'd said it before and I'd always ignored it. The world is changing. It's getting smaller all the time. There are countries in the Middle East where women are finally getting rights. There are places in China and Hong Kong where women are allowed certain rights, too. But in San Francisco? In Chinatown? It never occurred to me to see if my sister wanted my protection. It never crossed my mind that she might want to be more than the smart sister who got the good grades. I don't know if it's because I was working for the Triad or simply because she wanted to prove herself in a place where girls were never really allowed a chance. But there was no denying that she was stronger than the guys she was surrounding herself with. Hell, aside from her and a few of those guys, there was no one who didn't believe that I was responsible for killing Chow Liu. I maybe dodged the bullet on Blevins—time would tell—but there was no way anyone was going to doubt that I had something to do with wiping out the head of the Chinese mob in Chicago. That might be great for street creds, but not so much for increasing my life-expectancy.

Anna was grown up. Anna wanted to show the world that she could do it her way. Maybe that would have been a cute coming-of-age story in a lot of cases, but Anna, my little sister, was no longer the girl she'd been.

I left Chicago that night. I didn't stop in to tell Lisa everything was cool between us, because it wasn't. I didn't try to talk my sister out of the path she'd chosen, because I knew I couldn't. Instead I headed for home. Back to San Francisco and my school classes, my parents and my job. I don't think I'll be able to quit that any time soon, whether or not I want to. I need to keep tabs on my sister, you see, and that's about the best way to do it. No one in the Triads so much as sneezes without someone else hearing about it.

I'll be keeping her secret for now. I haven't even figured out what to tell them when I get home yet, but I'll think of something.

And in the meantime, I'm going to convince myself that the rush I got feeding on that poor bastard was just my imagination. See, it felt too good. I knew a guy once that refused to get high because he said it felt too good. I didn't understand that until now. I feed on plants and take a sampling here and there and I can live just fine. I start feeding on people, and there's going to be a big problem. Anything that feels that good has got to be bad for you and even if it isn't bad for me, it's murder on the people around me.

So I'll be telling myself it wasn't all that great. And I'll do my best to convince myself while I head for home. And you know what? I'll make it work because if I don't, if I can't handle the desire for more, I could find myself in Chicago again. Anna wasn't kidding about her offer. She'd let me work with her. All I'd have to do is feed like her and the rest would be easy.

There's only one problem with that idea, really. Monster-face or not, I still have to look myself in the mirror every day.

⌘

"THE BALLAD OF BIG CHARLIE" PT.3

Keith R.A. DeCandido

−21−

Mia was surprised to see Detective Trujillo calling her. She never figured to hear from the detective again after he helped her out with the senator's murder.

"Hello, Detec—"

"Look, Fitzsimmons, we never had this conversation, okay?"

She frowned. "Uh, okay. What conver—"

"I caught the Jaffe murder, okay? And it's *seriously* fucked up. We're talkin' the exact same thing that happened to Kapsis."

Mia recalled that the borough president's apartment wasn't far from that of the senator—and both in the 24th Precinct. So it wasn't a surprise that the same detective caught both. "So what's the problem?"

"The *problem* is that this time we got footage. Jaffe had video surveillance on her place. Everywhere but the bathroom and bedroom's covered, and this was a fuckin' *wolf*."

Her heart leapt into her throat. "Big Charlie?"

"Nah, he's alibi'd. After that ad she ran? He was second on our list after her ex. But nah, he was in his office all night. Got footage'a *that* too. God bless security cameras, right?"

"So why're you—"

341

"'Cause somethin' ain't right. Look, Kapsis is closed, and it's stayin' closed. You don't reopen a senator's murder case if you wanna keep your job, so fuck that shit, but you? You ain't got nothin' to lose, and this ain't sittin' right with me. Come by the two-four when you get a chance—I got a DVD'a Jaffe's security footage for ya. Maybe you can use it."

Mia smiled. "I guess I owe you one now, huh, Detective?"

"Damn fuckin' right."

With that, he ended the call, and Mia's smile fell. If it was a wolf-like creature who killed both Senator Kapsis—who'd just criticized Big Charlie on the air—and President Jaffe—who'd just started a nasty ad campaign against Big Charlie—then things did not look particularly good for the Bronx D.A.

The next morning, first thing, she took the bus to the #2 train, taking that to 96th Street in Manhattan, from which it was a short walk to the 24th Precinct. Sure enough, a padded envelope with a rewritable DVD was waiting for her at the sergeant's desk. Not wanting to wait, she went to a Dunkin' Donuts on Broadway and opened up her laptop, putting the DVD in the tray.

Then she pulled out her phone and called her editor.

"Bart, I may have something. And I need to run it by you to make sure I'm not crazy."

"Okay," Bart said nonchalantly. He'd had reporters do this to him all the time.

"I got my hands on the security footage of Emma Jaffe's apartment."

"What?" Bart was less nonchalant now. "How'd you—"

"Never mind. The point is, I'm looking at what attacked her. It's a wolf."

"Shit."

"Yeah, and it gets better. Big Charlie isn't the only vampire out there who changes shape. You've got other *loup garou*, you've got *tlahuelpuchi*, *vârcolac*, *abchanchu*—"

"Get to the point," Bart said impatiently.

"Sorry." She'd been doing a lot of research lately, and she sometimes forgot that most people didn't care as much as she did. "Anyhow, the one thing that's constant with all the shapechangers is that they keep the same mass."

"Meaning?"

"Big Charlie is about 275 pounds. When he turns into a wolf, he's still 275 pounds. The wolf I'm looking at on this DVD is less than 200 pounds."

"You sure?" Before Mia could answer, Bart said, "Of course you're sure, you're quoting Eastern European vampire names at me off the top of your head."

"Actually, only the *vârcolac* is Eastern European. The others are—"

"I could give a shit. Look, Mia, where you goin' with this?"

She hesitated. "I don't know yet. But it isn't Big Charlie killing these people."

"What?" Bart's voice got distant.

"Bart?"

"Oh, fuck. All right, get Castro over there." His voice grew louder again. "Gotta go, Mia. And so do you—your guy's house just got torched."

– 22 –

Partial transcript of Special Primary Day Coverage *on Channel 12*

CHANNEL 12: With ninety percent of the precincts now reporting in statewide, it appears that the race for senator is in a dead heat between Mickey Solano and the late Manhattan Borough President Emma Jaffe. The tremendous support for Jaffe coming after her brutal murder only a few nights ago is impressive. Even more impressive is that the less than one percent of the vote received so far by Bronx District Attorney Hugues Charles. Indeed, some reports are that Big Charlie—a self-confessed vampire—has received less than a hundred votes statewide, a historically low number. Quite a turnaround from his landslide victory in the Bronx D.A. race lasts year.

Speaking of Big Charlie, we have a breaking story in the Bronx. Nishanda Henry is on the scene. Nishanda?

NISHANDA HENRY: I'm at the home of Bronx District Attorney

Hugues Charles—or, at least, what's left of it. The house, located on De Reimer Avenue in the Bronx, caught fire an hour ago. Firefighters have gotten the blaze under control. Although several members of the press and dozens of protestors have been present at Big Charlie's house fairly consistently since Manhattan Borough President Emma Jaffe's murder last week, no injuries have been reported yet.

I have to emphasize that "yet," because so far there are three people missing, and two of them are Big Charlie and his mother, Marie Charles. The third is Jack Kearns, a former NYPD detective who has been serving as the head of Big Charlie's security detail during the primary race. The lead firefighter on the scene, Lieutenant Eamon Mahony, had this to say.

LIEUTENANT EAMON MAHONY: We been through the entirety'a the wreckage'a the house, and we not only haven't found any bodies, we haven't found any evidence'a bodies. No blood, nothing. This was a slow burn, not the kinda thing that burns bodies so badly there's nothin' left. We responded in more'n sufficient time. It's a preliminary judgment, but I'd say that nobody was home when the fire was set.

HENRY: According to NYPD spokeswoman Jane Amundson, police have put out an all-points for all three missing occupants of the house, saying that they are wanted for questioning in the presumed arson. While NYPD has categorically stated that Big Charlie was not a suspect in the murder of Emma Jaffe, protestors have remained camped outside his house since that murder, with the threat of violence always there. It is unknown if one of them started the fire or not.

For Channel 12, I'm Nishanda Henry.

– 23 –

Judy Alejo sat in her office staring into space, biting the right side of her lip.

She had turned her phone off, and couldn't bear to look at her e-mail. Her laptop was open to news stories about the late Emma Jaffe's victory and the disappearance of Big Charlie following the firebombing of his house.

Someone knocked on her door. Probably her assistant. She ignored it.

"Judy, I'm sorry, but Mia Fitzsimmons is here to see you?"

She sighed. Had it been anyone other than her former high school classmate, she would have called security.

"Come on in," Judy said after a long sigh.

"You look like crap," Mia said without preamble.

That prompted a bark of laughter. "Yeah, well, the next time I walk out of this courthouse will prob'ly be the last. Ain't no way I'm keepin' my job. My boss has gone missing, and even if he didn't actually kill nobody, everyone *thinks* he did." She glanced over at her laptop. "Every op-ed in the city's about how innocent people don't run, and even if he didn't kill Jaffe and Kapsis, he prob'ly got one of his *loup garou* buddies to do it for him." She shook her head. "Christ, he didn't even *know* any other *loup garou*!"

"Well, he knew one." Mia sat down in Judy's guest chair.

Judy frowned. "Excuse me? I knew everyone he knew, and—"

"You knew her, too." Mia took a deep breath. "Okay, I don't have much by way of actual proof of this, but—did you ever see Charlie transform?"

"Well—" Judy hesitated. It was funny, with everything they'd discussed, both among themselves and with the press and other politicians and lawyers, she hadn't even realized that she never saw the transformation. She'd been calling her boss a *loup garou* for over a year now without any empirical proof. "No, I didn't. But so what, he—"

"I don't think he actually *has* I1V1."

"That's crazy."

"Remember when he announced that he had it?" Mia was flipping through a note pad now. "He said he would provide records of his doctor visit."

"Yeah, so?"

"Judy, I never got those health records. Nobody did. We all kinda forgot about it in the mess of the race, and besides, it wasn't that big a deal. I mean, why would anyone lie about something like that, right?"

"He didn't lie!" Judy stood up, pacing her small office. "Jesus, Mia, do you really think he'd do something that crazy? Charlie's the sanest person I know, and he'd never open himself up to all that bullshit—"

"Unless he wanted to protect someone he loved."

Judy whirled on the reporter. "Excuse me?"

"The cops are keeping it quiet, but the evidence points to the same killer for both Jaffe and Kapsis."

"I thought it was the nephew who got Kapsis."

Mia shook her head. "There's no way Nathan did it, he's a *vrykolatios*. He doesn't have the strength. I'll bet real money that his lawyer uses that when he finally goes to trial."

Shaking her head, Judy said, "I don't get it, Mia, what—"

"It's his mother. Marie Charles is the *loup garou*."

For several seconds, Judy just stared at Mia.

Then she burst out laughing.

"Nice one, Mia. Marie's a *loup garou* and I'm the queen of fucking England. Now I remember why I didn't like you in high school. I'm calling security to haul your bony white ass outta here."

Mia stood up as Judy reached for her phone. "Please, Judy, hear me out. I don't like this either, but *it fits*. Marie doesn't actually have an alibi for either killing, and the wolf that killed Jaffe weighs about the same as she does."

Judy stared at her. "That's all you got?"

"I told you I didn't have anything solid. But I know him—and so do you. Look at what we do have, and think about how he feels about his *maman*. You really think he wouldn't do all this for her?"

Instinctively, Judy wanted to say no. But she couldn't. The woman sailed to New York from a violent country while eight months pregnant to save her son. And Big Charlie had always been one to repay his debts.

He'd try to avoid her being subject to the nightmare of press coverage of being the vampire mother of a politician. And he'd also try to fix it so that things were better for others of her kind.

"No wonder he wanted to run for senate so bad," Judy whispered. "Jesus, he kept insisting, no matter how many people told him it was stupid. And it never made sense. But now—" She looked at Mia. "How sure are you?"

Mia just stared back. "How sure are you?"

Neither woman said anything in response.

—24—

Op-ed piece by Mia Fitzsimmons in the New York Daily News.

"Ladies and gentlemen, the Bronx is burning."

That was the thought that went through my head as I stood in front of Hugues Charles' burning house two months ago. I had been on an errand in Manhattan when my editor told me that his house was on fire. I immediately hopped in a cab and high-tailed it to De Reimer Avenue only to watch Big Charlie's home go up in flames.

Back in 1977, Howard Cosell said those words when he saw the South Bronx on fire from Yankee Stadium. A young Hugues Charles heard them and swore he would protect the Bronx to keep it from burning.

On a Tuesday night in September, he officially failed. The Reverend Josiah Mann—a so-called religious leader who has never set foot in New York City as far as I know—called for his head, and TV commercials called him a monster and a menace. The day before her tragic murder, Emma Jaffe, one of his opponents, aired a commercial that called a vote for him to be a vote for death.

All of them missed the point. Big Charlie was just trying to protect the people of the city he called home from burning down.

It's been two months since that night that the Bronx burned, and while it was just one house on De Reimer Avenue, it was as devastating as those multiple fires were in October 1977. Big Charlie is still missing, with no sign of him or his maman. We can only assume that Marie Charles and her son are in hiding. We can only assume they're okay.

Today, Mickey Solano is the new junior senator for New York State. When he is sworn in early next year, he will be expected to vote on legislation against the very virus that gave him his job. After all, if not for I1V1, Alex Kapsis would have finished his term and likely been re-elected, opposed only by the same Frank VanDerMeer who only managed 30% of the vote against Solano. If not for I1V1, Big Charlie would probably have not been opposed by Solano in the Bronx D.A. race, which raised his profile.

Now the Bronx will have an inferior D.A, New York has an inferior senator, and a good man whose only mistake was that he was powerless against a virus he couldn't help contracting, has disappeared, leaving only ashes in his place. Worse, those who have I1V1, who had put their hopes in at last having representation in Congress, have gone even further underground, vilified even more by the Reverend Manns and Mickey Solanos of the world.

Ladies and gentlemen, the Bronx is *still* burning.

☾

"EMBEDDED"

Jonathan Maberry

Near Harrowgate Park
Kensington, Philadelphia
142 Days after the V-Event

Luther Swann ran hunched over through the rotor wash, following the ten-man SpecOps strike team. He was one of two civilians with the team. The other was a televsion reporter, Baird Lang from Chicago, selected by lottery to accompany V-Team Eight on this mission.

It was Swann's fifth raid.

He thought that by now he'd have become hardened to it, but it seemed that every time he deployed from a Black Hawk it was like tearing the scab off of a wound.

Swann knew this would be bad.

Behind him the Black Hawk dusted off and swung high and wide until the thwop-thwop-thwop of its blades faded to nothing. The soldiers of V-Team Eight—nicknamed V-8 by the press—came up to a row of burned-out cars and knelt. The last man on the team guided Swann and the reporter, Lang, to a safe spot behind an overturned UPS truck.

Beyond the row of cars was a no-man's land of debris. This whole neighborhood was in ruins. Most of the blue-collar row homes were burned-out shells. The nearby Tioga elevated train station was in rubble, the train tracks twisted down to the ground. There had been five major clashes here in the last month. Two wins on either side, and one stalemate that had only ended when the vampires had slipped away under cover of darkness.

These vamps were part of the New Red Coalition. They were the kind of threat General May had predicted. Organized, armed, and highly dangerous, working like a terrorist cell. In the last several months New Red teams had made successful strikes against key targets. They'd destroyed over forty major railways and blown up nineteen bridges across the country. Nobody had yet counted how many miles of electrical and phone lines they'd torn down.

Baird Lang, sporting a fresh five-hundred-dollar haircut, had interviewed one of their organizers, a vampire who called himself "Orlok." Cute, Swann thought, the name inspired by the silent film, *Nosferatu*. Many "out" vampires were taking so-called "V-names" from pop culture, like they were DJs. There was even one whose Twitter handle was "Count Chockula." On good days, Swann thought that was amusing.

On days like today…not so much.

In the interview, Lang had asked Orlok what Swann felt was the most significant question anyone in the media had posed so far: "Do you speak for all vampires?"

Orlock laughed. "Yes, even though too many of my red brothers and sisters have not yet shaken off the chains of human domination. The New Red Coalition is small, we admit that, but like the heart which is only a small part of the body, so we are to our people. Small, but vital. Without us, our people will die. Without us, the humans will hunt us to extinction…as they did in the Dark Ages. We will not let that happen."

Then Cooper asked, "Homeland has designated you as terrorists. What is your reaction to that?"

"We are not terrorists," said Orlock, his tone hot with bitter rage, "we are people fighting for our lives."

"But you've made many strikes against non-military targets."

"Sure…how else are we going to get people to listen?"

Public opinion was split on the matter, and every time one of the major pollsters posted numbers, Swann saw how the non-infected were swaying. At first they were dead set against the vampires, then they swung the other way based on Swann's appearances on *Anderson Cooper 360*, the *Daily Show*, and forty-two other shows. Now, with the New Red Coalition bombing trains and disrupting cell and cable service, the public was turning against the vampires.

Tomorrow it might be different.

And the day after that it might all change again.

Today, though…

Today, the public wanted blood. Knocking down telephone poles interrupted cable lines, and you don't mess with cable. The public doesn't forgive transgressions like that.

Swann crouched down and watched the soldiers of V-8 lock and load. He knew that a fleet of gunships armed with mini-guns and rocket pods were in a schoolyard four blocks away. The vampires in the row house across the street were all going to die.

It was just one cell. One of who knew how many, but from the pre-strike briefing, Swann knew what kind of message this was going to send.

General May had been crystal clear: "We're not looking to take prisoners. Once you determine that there are no non-infected in that house, then by God it's open season."

The soldiers had cheered.

The reporter looked excited. This was ratings gold.

Swann felt his heart sink. There was no way to win this kind of war. No way in hell.

The team commander yelled, "Go!"

And hell is what it became.

They breached the door with a heavy weight swung by two burly men. The frame splintered and the door flew inward. The men with the weights faded back and the V-8 shooters rushed inside. Hard-faced soldiers in black BDUs, with Kevlar padding and ballistic shields. M4s, combat shotguns and Glocks. Swann wore a full set of body armor. So did the reporter.

They'd been shot at before.

Swann had taken a round in the chest once, but as he ran to follow the team he could not remember where it had happened. Trenton? Newark? Or the raid at Coney Island?

The bullet had been a Teflon-coated cop-killer round. Swann couldn't remember the fight but he could remember that bullet. It had earned its name by punching through the bodyarmor worn by SWAT team member. It had killed the cop and passed entirely through him and though it lacked lethal force by the time it struck Swann, it still carried enough force to crack two ribs. And to paint his face with the officer's blood.

Swann waited for the bullets to fly, for them to swarm through the dusty air of the small house, for them to sting. To wound. To kill.

But the vampires did not fire.

Not a single gun.

Not a single shot.

They were getting smarter than that.

Swann had warned of this.

He had warned them.

The lead V-8 shooter made it all the way through the living room and into the kitchen before the first bombs went off.

&

"VULPES" PT.2

Gregory Frost

−12−

In the dream she was scaling the wall of ice. Harry Gordon and John Bail were climbing alongside her. Harry had something like twenty axes on his belt. She looked up, and the wall ran up for miles. As soon as she saw that, her joints began to ache, shoulders and elbows as she struck, caught, struck, caught. She went up the sheer face of it like a spider. Nothing was going to stop her, not even exhaustion. She would not be left trapped on this climb.

Harry said, "There's nothing wrong with you, nothing at all." He sounded like Vincent. She paused and looked over at him. John Bail was right beside her, and he'd transformed. He had silvery irises, like movie special-effect eyes, and his hands had become claws. She scrambled up faster, but he stayed beside her. He wasn't even climbing, just floating against the ice. "John, stop it!" He laughed. "Harry!" she cried. Harry had been her de facto protector over the four months. Looking after her had provided a sort of safe intimacy for him. Now he swung beside Bail and sized her up with the same silvery eyes. He said, "What's a little poison in your blood?" Then he soared up the ice, leaving John alone beside her.

"Well, I don't know about you, but I'm starving." He reached over and wrenched her left arm, pulling the ice axe free. He tried to bite her wrist but she tore loose from his grasp. She dangled from one axe, kicking with her crampons to find purchase, but they only scraped and scraped as if the ice had turned to stone. He cackled with delight and reached for the other arm. She swung her left and buried her axe in the side of his head. Bail didn't bleed at all and seemed only mildly surprised. He looked her in the eye. "That won't help," he told her, and then lunged. She let go of the other axe, tipped away from the ice wall and plummeted toward the black sea below. Zipper fall, she thought. She could not survive it.

At the point of impact she awoke. The bed was bouncing beneath her as if she had floated up to the ceiling and then dropped. She hadn't had a falling dream since she was a teenager.

It was daylight. The apartment was silent. Either her grandfather was still abed after the late night, or else he was gone and she'd been so deeply asleep she hadn't heard. She lay there until she had shaken the dream off. Then she got up.

Miraculously, she felt fine, even strangely energized, like an echo of how she'd felt after making love with Costin. She could have put on a track suit and gone running. Maybe she'd been so exhausted that she had finally overcome her jet lag, which didn't really make much sense.

On the way to the kitchen she glanced in the mirror to be certain her dark hair hadn't turned completely white. It was still the same spade shape. Maybe there was a tiny fleck more. Her cheek, on the other hand, was purplish and yellow, swollen and wincingly tender.

Her grandfather had left her laptop on the kitchen table where she sat. He had been in her computer? That was unusual.

She opened it. The screen came to life with the front page of Agentia de Investigata Media, and its one word headline: VAMPIRI!

Why ever did he want her to see this? She lit a burner for hot water, then sat down to read. According to the thumbnail column, the so-called vampire plague was spreading. Cases had been reported not only in New York but all across North America. She clicked to see the full article. Halfway through, it quoted a Dr. Margaret Ruiz, an epidemiologist. She was convinced that some form of infectious agent was responsible, and in the following paragraph speculated that the cause could even be an old bacteria or virus "possibly reintroduced as a result of global warming, released into soil, water, or air through melting glacial ice."

Ruksana sat back, repelled by the words on the screen. Melting ice. Decebal had read the same article while eating his honey and bread and must have seen the same implication as she: that she had been infected in Antarctica, and it had turned her into one of these so-called vampiri. If she believed that, then she must turn herself in to some authorities somewhere. Not the police. They couldn't possibly comprehend.

The team...If she was infected, then so were the others—at the very least Harry and Vincent and John. Maybe Kwasi. He had handled the samples.

The tea kettle began to shriek. Abruptly she found herself at the stove, lifting the kettle from the burner. She'd moved—how had she done that? Her thoughts had been elsewhere, but she had no memory of jumping up, could not find the memory.

She needed to calm down. All that pent-up energy—it had her bouncing in place. She needed to do something. She just didn't know what. For the moment she poured water into her tea pot.

Someone rang the buzzer and pounded on the door at the same time. The muffled voice of Costin called, "Ruksana! Are you there? Open up, please! Ruksana!"

She flung back the door.

He rushed to her, wrapped his arms around her. "Oh, my God. You're all right? Tell me you're all right—oh, look at your face. Does it hurt? My sweetheart." He kissed her other cheek, then stepped back and sized her up in her nightgown. The moment held a strange frisson of déjà vu, and she thought, I'm having too many of these—Costin and Decebal both. It's something wrong.

"I'm all right," she said without much enthusiasm.

Her hyper-energy seemed contagious. Costin came past her and went to the table. He shrugged off his leather messenger bag and coat, glanced at her laptop then back at her. "I was in the cybercafé, trying to repair my hangover, and there was a report on the TV about the dog attack at the university and they showed your car. I've been trying to call you for an hour."

Her phone. It couldn't be in the bedroom or she would have heard it. No one could sleep through *Ride of the Valkyries*. Her black coat was hanging on its peg in the entryway beside her. She lifted the nearest sleeve, noticing the brownish stain along it that she'd seen last night in the hospital. She dug her hand into the pocket. It was empty.

So were the others. The phone hadn't come home with her. She had no idea if it had been in the car or had ended up on the pavement or the lawn.

She explained as best she could what had happened after she stopped to get her mail.

At the end Costin said, "So the bastard got ripped by the dogs. I think I'll start giving them kibble. He didn't hurt you, then? Didn't—"

"No, he hit me once. That was all, before the dogs, I guess." That was more than enough.

"The police will have your phone. We should get it back—I'll go with you."

"Maybe in awhile. I need to eat breakfast, have my tea. I need to calm down, not get crazy." She gestured at the teapot. "Do you want a cup?"

"Sure," he said. "Fine." He grabbed her around the waist again and pressed his head to her belly. "I'm just so glad you weren't hurt."

She understood what he meant. After that, perhaps in a gesture of trying to help calm her, he talked about the orchestra group and how they had taken their revelry to another bar, but she hardly heard. Despite her best efforts her thoughts kept drifting back to the laptop. Finally she turned it and launched her email program.

"Oh, I tried you there, too."

Among the dozen messages were two from him with the subject "Where Are You?" She had intended to send an email to Harry, but her attention was caught by the flagged email above it, a message from Kwasi Nkrumha with the subject "URGENT!"

The message was brief: "Samples show mitochondrial activity. NSF wants to contact team members immediately. Call in!" He'd listed three international phone numbers. They looked to be from the US, probably government numbers.

"What is it?" Costin asked. She pushed the laptop to him. He stared at it, perplexed. "This is English," he said. She remembered that he didn't read English very well. She told him. "I don't understand. Mitochondrial activity?"

"Mitochondria. They have their own distinct genome. Anthropologists use mitochondria DNA to distinguish evolutionary traits. At least that's what I remember from university."

"I still don't see."

"We brought back samples from the ice a few days before I came home. He is saying that, despite being in the ice for tens of thousands of years, the samples contain a living agency." She thought of what the epidemiologist in the news had speculated, although she couldn't comprehend how vampires formed an evolutionary trait. But if she had turned into one last night…

"Ruksana."

Costin's worried gaze met hers. She said, "I may have been exposed to something, and no one knows what the effects might be. And if I have, probably you have, too. And Decebal. Anyone I've come in contact with." Already she was imagining the ripple effect of so many flights across so many international boundaries. Who had sat next to her on those flights? Or behind her or in front of her? And where had they flown? Who had she brushed up against in the terminals? And what if that were true for the whole team, all going home?

My God, it's too late.

"But exposed to what?"

"I don't know. He doesn't know, either. It could be nothing, just some ancient rotting seaweed or plankton. Just, they want me to contact them right away. All of us on the team that came home—we're to call." She could almost hear his thoughts as he tried to fold this information in with what had happened last night—how did a contaminant in Antarctica connect to an attack in a parking lot in Bucureşti?

The door buzzer went off. Costin started to get up, but she said, "No, stay. Let me. In fact, would you go into the front room so whoever it is doesn't see you here?" She was thinking, given the news coverage, that it might be a reporter, and if so, she had no intention of letting him in or of finding out more about her or of waylaying Costin when he tried to leave.

The buzzer sounded again. She squinted through the peephole and was astonished to see the police detective from last night. As she unlatched the door, she thought *Well, at least this won't feel like déjà vu.*

Opening the door, she said, "Inspector, what are you doing here?" Then before he could answer, adding, "Should I call you inspector principal or is just inspector acceptable? I don't know the etiquette. I'm ashamed also to say I don't remember your name. I know you said it."

"Not surprising under the circumstances. It's Marin Lucescu, and inspector is perfectly acceptable, Miss Vulpes." He gestured past her. "May I come in?" Under his other arm he had a large padded brown envelope.

She stepped aside and allowed him to pass her. Instinct directed her, kept her from hesitating, from appearing guilty, even if she couldn't explain what she might be guilty of. "To the right," she said, ushering him into the room with Costin.

The front room served as a library for her and Decebal, although the majority of the books belonged to him. Ruksana snatched a robe from her bedroom door before going in herself.

She introduced Costin to the inspector. She explained that he had just shown up because she wasn't answering her phone, which she'd only now discovered was not in her possession.

Lucescu chuckled and handed the thick envelope he'd been carrying to Ruksana. "We were having a similar problem, until someone noticed that this phone collected among the evidence went off every time we tried to call you."

She opened the envelope, seeing inside her phone and the mail that she had picked up before the attack.

"All of your mail was on the floor of your car. Most of it escaped contamination."

At the word, she twitched. "Contamination?"

"Blood spatter. That there isn't much on the mail or the passenger seat tells us a good deal about where the more savage part of the attack took place. It is almost all his blood of course, very little belonging to you, and that's mostly smeared on the seat and the mail, probably from when he struck your face. Again, consistent with what you remembered."

Costin said, "But the news, they said it was a pack of dogs attacked him."

Lucescu nodded unhappily. "We would like it to be dogs. Last night that seemed the obvious explanation."

Ruksana swallowed. "Now it's not?"

"Unfortunately, there's no evidence of a dog pack. Feral dogs running through that much blood would have left prints all over the parking lot. We have his prints of course, and a few of yours, Miss Vulpes, that indicate he dragged you onto your feet, out of the car. I was wondering if by chance you remembered anything more of what happened. Often the amnesia from a trauma is temporary, and we're looking at some confusing data."

"I'm sorry, no. I did have a nightmare last night but it was about falling."

"A dream of helplessness—very common post-traumatic nightmare. Next time, see if you have enough control to turn it into a dream of flying. They say that's healthier." A moment of uncomfortable silence followed, and then Lucescu turned to Costin. "Since you're here, Mr. Stelea, I would like to get a statement from you, just as a matter of record, to corroborate hers."

"Certainly." He glanced worriedly at Ruksana. "But I want to know, if it wasn't dogs, what was it?"

"No idea. None." Then he half-smiled. "One of the officers even suggested it was these vampires that are in the news. That's how in the dark we are."

Ruksana drew in her breath. Costin and she traded worried glances. The headline on her computer, the exposure—he had reached the same conclusion as she.

Lucescu observed their demeanors and laughed. "Really, you shouldn't concern yourselves terribly, unless these new vampires are incredibly wasteful. No blood went missing from what we can tell. Neither of you was bitten." He sighed. "Honestly, we may never figure it out. No one cares much about a dead rapist except that he's dead."

She stood clutching her phone and the envelope, and willed Costin to ask no more questions. Just standing here she could be infecting Lucescu.

No one moved or spoke. Finally, she couldn't stand it. "Well, I'm going to go charge my phone and put on some clothes. You can conduct your interview in here if you like."

Costin replied, "Actually, I should like to get some more coffee. Could we do it at a coffee bar?"

Thank you, she broadcast silently to him.

"Certainly," replied the inspector. "I could use a mid-morning snack myself. We'll leave you, then, Miss Vulpes. Oh, and I expect you'll have your car back tomorrow. As I said, we've completed our spatter analysis, and that's really all there was for us there." He turned away, then paused, his head bowed. "Actually, there is one more thing. I just want to confirm. I know I asked you last night. But—you don't own a dog and never had a dog in your car the past few months. Is that correct?"

"That's right."

"No fur coat?"

"Never. I'm opposed to them. And anyway, I was doing research in Antarctica since November. The car was in storage."

"Storage, eh? Could someone have taken it out? Your grandfather, for instance."

"He doesn't drive. All I can tell you is, I took it out for the first time last night, and I had no sense that anyone had touched it."

He nodded in disappointment, and continued on into the entryway, followed by Costin, who ducked into the kitchen to grab his coat and laptop bag.

Ruksana followed Lucescu. "What's so significant about my having a dog in the car? You said it isn't dogs."

He turned. "Not a pack of dogs, no. But there is fur, some white hairs both in your car under where you were lying on the driver's seat, and on the victim, in the blood around him. Our lab is having a lot of trouble identifying it. It's not synthetic, but we're thinking maybe an exotic pet? There were also a couple of prints, smeared of course and so we can't be sure what they are. They might even be your toes if he was supporting your weight, but that scenario is inconsistent with other evidence. As I said, nothing about this is clear. It's almost as if some avatar came into being to protect you and then vanished into thin air." He glanced at Costin behind her. "Probably what I should be asking is if you worship any ancient gods." He gave her a resigned smile and opened the door.

Costin didn't kiss her. He whispered, "I'll call you," as he passed.

That was the moment she realized that he might have wanted to get out of there not to protect her so much as out of fear of her.

She sat at her kitchen table beside her cold tea. She quit the browser page to get rid of the awful headline, and closed the laptop. It wasn't until a sob burst from her that she realized she was crying.

— 13 —

A short time later, with the phone starting to charge, she sorted through her calls: Three from Costin followed by two texts insisting she call him; a half dozen more from a city number she didn't know but that was probably the police trying to contact her. Sandwiched in the middle of those lay a quick text from Vincent: *Kwasi contacted. Team arriving Paris ASAP incl Harry. U must come 2. Special body convening. Need your samples. Blood. Will send details. Vincent.*

It had arrived last night. It didn't surprise her that they were moving fast to contain and identify this, whatever it was. This was the side of Vincent she'd seen when they had first been thrown together: smart and efficient. Whatever bad blood lay between them, he obviously was putting it aside in this emergency. They were all going to be lab rats despite his best efforts to bury the matter. How much did anyone know? If they were convening a special inquiry, what did they know? More than she did, certainly. She texted back. *I'm here. Ruksana.*

She took the time now to do a search on her laptop and read as many of the articles on the new vampires as she could. Two named an individual in New York, a Michael Fayne. He seemed to be the first of them—but that had occurred in October!

She could find no relation between him and NSF nor any Antarctic team at all. Had some previous scientific expedition inadvertently carried the same contamination back with them? Or was any of this even related? She had only the flimsiest of evidence that what infected her had anything to do with these so-called vampires. That was Decebal and his folklore forging links without any evidence. They could as easily have encountered a previously unknown strain of streptococcus for all anyone was saying.

She chided herself for not sticking to facts, to scientific analysis— what she knew, not what she supposed. Periglacial rock was easily identifiable, the processes working on it observable, recordable—ice in the facies splitting immense boulders again and again to form the rubble. Conclusion based on observation, the scientific method.

But the events of last night were not a known quantity. It all might have been an anomaly. It might have been dogs, regardless of what evidence the police had found. And her position relative to it was entirely subjective. She was part of the events, not the clinical observer. What could she know for certain?

Ruksana closed her eyes and tried to see it all again—the car door flung open, the terrible pain of being struck as she turned, then flashes of light and the pain overwhelming her, followed by the coarse face of the man above her, big as the supermoon in the sky as he pulled at her clothes, trying to drag her out, and there was that claw, reaching up to slash his mouth and face—reaching up from where she lay. Her arm, her hand, however transformed. Black claws and white fur. Not a hallucination after all, not—

Wagner's *Valkyrie* blared out of her phone, startling her so much she nearly dropped it. The call, she saw, was from the hospital where she'd been treated last night.

The woman on the other end identified herself as a lab technician. There was a problem with the blood they'd drawn from her. Something had corrupted the sample, and they needed to draw another. Could she spare some time today to stop into their lab?

Ruksana said she would try, then ended the call. Now there could be no question of whether the exposure had affected her. Of course nothing had corrupted the sample. It was already corrupted. Her blood was corrupted. If she showed up at the hospital and allowed them to draw more blood, they would soon enough realize it, too, and she would find herself tagged as Romania's patient zero. She must get away, get to this organized response in Paris immediately. If NSF was assembling a team, that's where she needed to be. If she was destined to be a lab rat, better to be one in a lab that actually understood what it was facing.

She was about to shut off the phone but saw that she had another unread text message.

This one was from Harry Gordon. *Booked flight 4 U, Alitalia, through Milan. In your name. Departs 2:10. Arrives Paris tonight 10:05. Can U travel by day? Please confirm.*

Harry, always the thoughtful, responsible one. And there was the question: "Can you travel by day?" Surely that could mean just one thing.

She replied with *Yes, on my way now*, and then scrambled to throw a few things in her travel bag—changes of underwear, cosmetics, nightgown, an extra sweater and top. She threw in her passport. She would need to take a taxi to the airport if she wanted to make that flight—no time to ride trolleys today. Decebal would be confused, but she would make him understand. Undoubtedly, Harry and the others had expected her to see the message earlier. They had no way of knowing the police had possession of her phone.

She pulled on her black coat and a multi-colored scarf and headed down to the street. If he found out, would Lucescu think she was running away? And was she? How long would she be gone? She really had no idea what she was going to find at the other end. She was infected with something. Maybe the whole team had been. Certainly they didn't need her on hand as a scientist. Only as a subject. How could that possibly resolve?

She went to the bank and withdrew enough money to cover a short stay abroad, then hurried to the airport, where she barely had time to check in and get her ticket before her flight began boarding. She tried to call Decebal, and got no answer. He would be teaching or on his way home. Next she tried Costin, but then changed her mind and cut off the call after one ring. There was no time for anything she needed to say there—and what could she say? Instead she sent her grandfather a quick text to keep him from worrying when he got home: *I am gone, will call explain later.*

By the time the flight took off and she had put her phone in air travel mode, her grandfather had not replied. She wondered how late in the day he was teaching this semester, realized that she hadn't asked anything at all about his teaching since she got home. She had been so self-absorbed, which was not like her. Most of the talk had been of her affair with Vincent, and how Costin might respond if he found out, which now seemed so utterly irrelevant.

She imagined that any investigation into the matter of exposure and contamination would require a list of who she'd been in contact with—especially who had been intimate with her. Maybe she didn't give off contagion by breathing, but sexual transmission seemed indisputably likely—transmission by bodily fluids seemed like an inescapable conclusion. The next time Costin and she met, he might not be very happy to see her.

In Milan, she had a layover of hours and used the time to try to reach her grandfather again. This time Decebal answered after the first ring. He was at home and must have been holding the phone. When she explained where she was calling from, he said in a voice that left no room for hedging, "Tell me."

She explained that whatever she had been exposed to in Antarctica—virus or bacteria—she was now almost certain that it had triggered a transformation in her the night before. There had been no dogs. There had been only Ruksana and the rapist. She described for him the image of her transformed arm. The latest communiques from Paris indicated that her entire team had potentially been exposed to the same substance. She was going because she feared that prolonged contact with her would prove dangerous. Even now Costin might be at risk. To help him as well as herself, she needed data, not supposition, which was all she would get if she stayed in București. Neither the police nor the hospital had the means to deal with this. Their only option would be to isolate her, lock her away. It was for everyone's protection that she had to go, even though she didn't know what awaited her of if they would ever let her come home. And it was still possible that they would come for Decebal and Costin. There could be no guarantees with so much unknown.

By the end, tears were sliding down her cheeks, and she had to move off to a corner of the terminal in order not to draw attention. She had only now admitted to herself the possibility of permanent estrangement.

Her grandfather remained silent for so long afterward that she said, softly, "Bunicul?"

"Fată drăguţă," he said, "you have not become a vampire." He spoke with absolute certainty. How could he have such assurance when for her the ground was shifting like quicksand, pulling her into a pit of doubt? She opened her mouth to ask him.

The phone started to beep. She looked at it. The low battery warning message flashed at her. There hadn't been time to let it charge at home. And if anything went wrong, she would need it when she landed in Paris.

"Bunicul," she said, "I have to go, my phone's dying. Let me charge it and call you again."

"Listen to me, my girl," he said. "You are not vampiri. You cannot be, do you see? You're the very *scourge* of vampiri. It's in your—"

The call disconnected. The phone had drained. She cursed it and put her head down on her knees. Then she raised her head. There were shops across the way, and back in the terminal as well.

Still with plenty of time left before the Paris flight, she shouldered her bag, got up and headed off into the bowels of Malpensa Airport in search of a universal power adapter. Someone must have one for sale.

–14–

At De Gaulle Airport, she was met by a man she had never seen before. He held a sign with her name emblazoned on it. He wore a black suit and black-framed glasses, and didn't smile. He was pale, like someone who spent all their days in front of a computer and never went outside. She wasn't sure what she had expected—something resembling a lab team led by someone who could explain what was going on. The lack of such a reception made her wonder if maybe the NSF had already established the contamination was not particularly communicable. Would Harry have put her on a flight in the first place if she was spreading contagion? It seemed unlikely, but there was so much she didn't know yet, and what her grandfather had claimed to know in her final call to him from Milan only confused matters further. She desperately wanted him to be wrong, despite that his interpretation, as bizarre as it was, thus far explained everything.

The driver took her bag and ushered her through the airport. The central corridor of the airport with its overhead gridwork of struts made her feel as if she was walking inside of a giant dirigible or some alien spacecraft.

The car was a gray Mercedes. He held the door for her to get into the back seat. No one else was in the car. They pulled into traffic and headed toward the city. It was all deadly formal, a driver discharging his duties with disinterest. Being in close quarters with him made her uncomfortable in a way she couldn't explain. She edged to the opposite side of the car and pressed her face to the window.

The moon, still yellow and large, was just off being full. Would that matter? Awhile she watched it flick between buildings, then glanced again at the driver. "How many have arrived?" she asked.

"Some," he answered.

"Harry Gordon?"

"Yes."

"John Bail?"

"Don't know the name. Like you, they're all here at the pleasure of M. Dusault."

It was a moment before she realized who he meant. "*Vincent* is in charge?"

The driver gestured at the Parisian landscape ahead of them. "It is his city, after all. His idea to coordinate, collaborate." He finally had the courtesy to glance at her, though there was nothing friendly in the gaze. "He was quite insistent on your participation, mademoiselle. There are situations where certain individuals are born for the moment. M. Dusault is the man for this time." He said it with pride.

She sat silently after that. The conversation was entirely wrong. No one would put Vincent in charge of a program dealing with disease vectors. He was a geologist, a mountaineer. What he knew of human biology couldn't amount to more than a vague understanding of cell division. Kwasi in charge—that she would have understood. In fact...

She took out her cell phone and as surreptitiously as possible texted him: *In Paris. Vincent in charge NSF inquiry? Please explain what U know.*

Glancing up, she saw that the driver was watching her in the mirror. He had no doubt seen the glow of the phone. "Just checking on my grandfather," she explained.

The driver said nothing. He circled Paris and then from the Boulevard Périphérique turned back toward the city. They came up to a large hospital complex—she glimpsed a sign, *St. Anne*—but kept going, finally turning onto Boulevard St. Jacques. It was a split road, and almost immediately they entered a wooded stretch. A moment later, the driver pulled over and stopped. He got out.

She peered over the seats. There seemed to be nothing to see. Oncoming headlights flickered through the trees, but there were no obvious buildings or landmarks anywhere near them.

The driver opened the door and held out a hand. When she climbed out, he said, "You go in here. Someone will be waiting to take you down. Don't want to use the tourists' arrete, now, do we?"

None of that made any sense to her, but she took her bag and walked away from the car into the chill Paris night. Her breath steamed. Around her, the woods smelled of wet humus, as if it had just rained on the old, rotting leaves. She found a path and walked along it, hearing the car start up behind her and drive off. Oddly, the darkness became less pervasive as she went deeper in, details weirdly visible as if it was a painted landscape bathed in ultraviolet light.

Her phone vibrated. She stopped. She had a message from Kwasi: *Urgent NSF still wants hear from U. Paris? Maybe WHO. Not us. Will inquire. Kwasi*

She stopped. Vincent had lied. Kwasi hadn't been contacted at all, knew nothing about this, which lent some credence to Decebal's interpretation of events. And her eyes, the way she could see in the darkness, like a superhero with magical powers. She could even see the tree roots ahead of her. Was Harry even here? She had to know.

The path led to a structure shaped like a chess piece rook. Someone in a long coat stood beside it, still, seemingly unaffected by the cold. Nearing him, she had the same frisson as with the driver, an inherent repulsion. He said nothing, but pointed to a metal door in the side of the tower. Both it and the tower had been sprayed extensively with graffiti.

Inside, an old metal staircase corkscrewed down into more dimness. The space smelled of ancient wet stone and rot, and another stink beneath that, which she identified as human bowels: a sewer.

She was halfway down when Harry Gordon stepped into view below. He wore slacks, and an open windbreaker over his belly. "Hey, Rooksie," he said. "You know, Vinnie wasn't convinced you were coming, but I knew." He opened his arms and embraced her in a bear-like hug. He smelled vaguely unpleasant, like a cheese that had gone off.

For an instant she experienced the same repulsion, and reacted by stepping away from him. He gave her a strange look, as if he wanted to see deep inside her, and the repulsion was replaced by an inexplicable desire to kiss him. He seemed to be fully aware of her emotional sea change, and broke into a lewd grin, which revealed a mouthful of needle-like teeth.

Ruksana gasped. "Harry."

"Oh." He put a hand over his mouth, pretending embarrassment. "It's my Celtic roots come to the fore." He dropped the hand and laughed. "I really haven't worked this all out yet you know?" He made a self-deprecating smile. "You wouldn't have realized it, but I was planning to kill myself when I got home. I mean, Linn's dead, they were gonna split me open like a lobster to clean out my arteries, and NOAA was ready to retire me. So, what the fuck? And I got home and this happened, almost immediately. It was weird, you know? I knew and I didn't know what was going on, all at the same time. Like the old me was still in complete denial about this. Vincent figured it out, though. Hell, he called me, told me to get over here before NSF nabbed me. Our old pal, Kwasi, had them all scrambling."

He inspected her teeth. "I see you don't have any obvious fangs. Then again, what I don't know about Romanian vampires would be everything. I do like the hair, though. That's very sexy on you." He squeezed her arm. "Come on, let's go see Vinnie. He's back in the Crawl with a few snacks. Saved you one. He's still a prick, though."

As he led her through the old stone tunnel, Harry played tour guide. "If you went back the other way, you'd find the ossuaries and the tourists. That's the 1786 part of the catacombs, when Paris decided to stuff the diseased corpses down underground in these old Roman quarry tunnels. You watch the limestone walls closely, you'll see some fossils in them—should appeal to the geologist in you. Go down this way farther, you'll hit water. You'd think the Phantom of the Opera was going to sail by."

The sharp tang of the place lay on the back of her tongue like a paste of chalky salt. Ahead somewhere, a man yelled, but stopped almost immediately. She became aware of a soft guttural sound nearby, like a muted growling.

Harry gave her an approving glance. "Getting hungry, are you?"

Startled, she realized that the noise had been coming from her. Covering her shock, she asked, "Is John here, too?"

His alluring gaze faltered. "No," he said. "John didn't make it. Best we can figure, he turned in the middle of the flight home from Rio, while he was asleep. Woke up remade and attacked the passenger next to him on instinct, took a major bite out of the guy's arm before other passengers and crew wrestled him down. Some military ex-commando was on board, and pretty much dislocated one of his arms. They strapped him into an isolated seat, but then the sun came up, and he couldn't move. Wasn't like me. Broiled him where he sat. Poor bastard never had time to adjust to the change." He shook his head. "But Deb's here with us, and Childs—he's off down the tunnels somewhere, hunting cataphiles."

"Cataphiles?"

"Yeah, teenagers, twenty-somethings from Britain and Germany, places like that, they break in and sneak down here. There are about a million places to do that, too. Cataphiles go exploring, spend days down here without surfacing. On top of them, you got all kinds of squatters. Childs likes to work solo, enjoys the adventure of the hunt and culling the herd. I'm not sure what kind he is, but he shares some of my talents. Look him in the eye, he'll give you an orgasm."

They arrived at an opening in the wall. Kerosene camping lanterns turned low stood on the floor to either side.

"Go on in," said Harry. "You're expected." He grinned at her, and again she felt that allurement. It reminded her of her grandfather's stories of faeries and how they could beguile those they desired. The changes weren't imagined. They were real. It was all real. Those folktales had been handed down from a time when such things were possible; and now, somehow, they were possible again.

She stepped into The Crawl. It seemed to be a series of interconnected chambers. The first one was strewn with debris: wrappers from power bars, crushed soda cans, broken glass bottles. More graffiti and bright murals decorated the walls. A skinny man who looked like a drug addict lay on a filthy sleeping bag in one corner. He looked up at her. His eyes were bloodshot. He smiled just to show her his fangs.

"Vincent!" called Harry. He was answered by loud animal sounds, like from a pack feeding hyenas. To Ruksana, he said, "Let's go in here," and led her through another doorway.

The corridor was narrow and low. It emptied into a large room with a rough uneven floor and sides that had been carved out to form makeshift benches.

"Look at this," he said. He stood beside another carving. Someone had taken the time to carve a miniature castle out of the rock. There were crenelated towers on both sides of the main entrance, which needed only a drawbridge. The central keep stood shoulder high beside Harry. "Amazing, isn't it? Somebody had a lot of time on their hands."

In the center of the room hung a wide circular chandelier that seemed to have come from such a medieval castle. Four thick candles burned on its rim. Despite the size of the room the ceiling was so low that even she would have had to duck to get under the chandelier. A sense of claustrophobia had already taken root in her and now swelled by the moment. She thought of the moon outside, thought of its light. She grew increasingly terrified that without that light she was helpless.

Behind her, someone shuffled into the narrow corridor, and she turned around.

A tall slender figure emerged. He was dressed all in black: slacks and turtleneck. The sweater shone wetly from the dark stream that had run down from his mouth over his chin. In the dim light, it looked for a moment as if the whole lower part of his jaw was gone, instead of merely hidden behind a pennant of blood. She gasped as he stepped into the candlelight.

Vincent was more obviously altered than Harry. His eyes were dark and sunken, like holes in his face. His skin had gone gray. The handsome libertine had transformed into a ghoul. "I'm so glad you came," he said. His teeth were all sharp, too, but spade-like, not the needles between Harry's lips. He sniffed the air as if trying to get the scent of her perfume. "I can smell the change in you. I was worried you hadn't come over. McCabe didn't—did he tell you? We called him. Martin knew what had happened to John and was already turning himself in to some CDC office in the U.S. But he hadn't changed, not one bit. Don't understand any of that, do we, Harry?"

He came closer. Behind him, Deb Arliss came into the room. She looked surprisingly like herself, although with two fangs glinting, and blood on her lips and spattered down the front of her coat. Behind her two more, who hadn't been members of the team. They looked plump, well fed, their faces flushed. They held between them a naked teenager. He was bleeding from multiple wounds but was still alive. Vincent glanced around at them and then back at her. "That's right, the word's gotten out that we're down here in the hypogea. I know you were thinking it has to be that biofilm that got on us—maybe so, but these people had already turned before I came home. Ahead of all of us. How is that possible, can you imagine? Did some earlier ice sail into the Gulf Stream and melt, do you think? Or maybe a flock of procellariids scooped some up and shat it out over Notre Dame and New York."

He chuckled. "These fellows were so confused, directionless. Trying to hide what they were, and starving for it. Whereas I, the moment I changed, I knew I needed to be underground. I experienced the most terrible cramps, I can tell you. I thought it was airline food—which might in some sense be true. I'm afraid I'd feasted on a stewardess before I knew what I was doing. I had invited her to spend the night with the least honorable of intentions, but, well, I ate her instead. It turns out I'm anthropophagous, so I'm not like the others here. Except perhaps for you since we don't know what you are." He paused for a moment as if listening for something no one else could hear. Then he said, "Harry, here, can go outside in the daylight. Doesn't bother him in the slightest. He's a—what did you call it?"

"*Dearg Due,*" Harry replied.

He waved at the name dismissively. "Means something to him, not to me. I and the others are terrified at the thought of sunlight, like victims of porphyria. Deb even sleeps in a crypt. But you are like Harry, too. You can travel in the light without ill effect. We need more with that skill to bring in the meals." He had quietly moved closer all the while he was talking, and now he grabbed her wrist, his fingers like talons. "What kind are you exactly, hmm, Ruksana? And where are your teeth?" His breath was so cloacal that she grimaced and tried to yank her hand away. Instead he pulled her closer. "Far too squeamish, that much we know." The vampires behind him laughed.

The chamber seemed to crackle, as if an electrical charge had begun circling it. She was suddenly hot, drenched in sweat, and she wrestled one arm free of him and frantically tugged off her coat. Decebal had advised to get her shoes off, too. She kicked them loose.

"Yes," said Vincent, letting go of her. The others crowded closer, even Deb, leering as if she was undressing for their entertainment. "Let's see what you are."

Ruksana threw the coat aside, but still panted. She leaned her hands on her thighs and tried to regain control. The coat wasn't enough—she continued overheating.

Panic attack, she thought and pulled her sweater over her head, dropped it upon the coat. She pressed her hands to her face—only they weren't her hands any longer. The palms were rough brown pads, the fingers white with fur. The nails were growing as she watched, curving into black claws around the tips of her fingers. Decebal had told her not to fight the change when it came, but to embrace it, as if it was something she might master. He had been sure it would come. How had he known?

She clutched at her furred belly, but the cramps weren't cramps—the pain radiated from a core point out into her joints like rays of sunlight. She threw back her head and howled. Her slacks became loose as her hips shifted, slimmed. But her thighs swelled with muscle and the fabric of her slacks tore. She could feel her lips pulling back from her teeth, feel the blunt snout of her nose, hear the whuff of her breath.

"What in hell?" Vincent said. "What kind of hairy vampires do they raise in Romania?" He grabbed for her again and she slashed over his arm and across his torso. Astonished, he stumbled back, staring at himself. "What?"

Deb had scrambled aside. The other two with her dropped the naked victim they'd been carrying. An instant before they could move to escape, Ruksana sprang. Her legs felt like steel springs. She caught the nearest one's throat in her jaws, while her nails dug into his back and split him open. Violently she shook her head, throwing off jets of blood, ripping through muscle and gristle, relishing the kill. His partner fled down the narrow corridor.

A fierce shout from behind Ruksana made her whirl with her vampire victim still in her grip. Deb Arliss's grabbing fingers plunged into him instead of her. Ruksana let the body go, leaving Deb to try to get free of it. She curled her left hand over Deb's head, claws hooking deep beneath the jaw. For just that second she experienced something like lust in anticipation. Deb opened her mouth in a wail of combined terror and hate, and madly disentangled one arm and prepared to strike. With her other hand, Ruksana caught Deb by the hair, and the hand under her jaw yanked up. Bone snapped and skin ripped apart, black blood sprayed the low ceiling. Deb's wail ceased.

She flung Deb's and the other body aside. Only Vincent remained in the room. Harry was gone. He had to have fled through another doorway, deeper into The Crawl.

Vincent had stumbled over to the miniature castle. One hand pressed tight against his belly, trying to hold himself in. "This is how you thank me?" he said, and slid down until he was sitting. "By turning out to be a fucking werewolf?" He hissed in pain. "I had plans."

She turned and bolted deeper into the maze of The Crawl. Harry was in here somewhere, loose and dangerous; but he must have been swift as well, because she found no trace of him by the time she had circled through all the rooms and come out where they had been feasting. It looked like that chamber had been a makeshift youth hostelry for a dozen cataphiles—their cooking supplies, foodstuffs, a case of bottled water, sleeping bags, and packs were still there. She found four corpses, drained, bitten or chewed upon, and the freshly denuded skeleton of a woman—that would have been Vincent's handiwork.

She circled back to where the teenager lay in the doorway. She lifted him. He whimpered in fear. She tried to tell him she wouldn't hurt him,

372

but found she couldn't form any words. She was neither wolf nor woman now.

She supported the naked boy, but had to turn sideways and edge through the narrow corridor. Vincent's helpless cry of agony and rage echoed from behind her. Another instance of déjà vu; she thought of the cry she'd heard as Harry had led her down the passage.

She took him back to the room with the bodies, and then helped him put on clothes and a parka. Whether they were his or not, she didn't ask. It was enough that they covered him.

Back out between the lanterns, she went left toward where Harry had told her there was water and, presumably, a way out other than the stairs into the woods, where the driver might be waiting for her.

They crept along for perhaps ten minutes, at one point passing an old rusting white sign in German: *Rauchen Verboten!* Something yowled in the distance, but the sound could have come from almost any direction. The passage finally opened up onto a wide expanse of arches over what looked to be an underground river. The floor protruded out in one spot, like a small jetty for Charon. Across from it there was a metal ladder.

She helped the youth start up the ladder, but this last leg of the journey he was going to have to make alone. She found that in this shape she could not climb at all.

At the top was some kind of grate that he managed to push aside. The last she saw of him was his legs disappearing out into the night.

With him gone, she walked out onto the small jetty over the black water. She looked down, hoping to see her own reflection, what she'd become. But while her vision was sharp in the darkness, there was no light source reflecting her upon the waters. She might have been a ghost hovering there, formless, attached to nothing. It seemed strange that she hadn't changed back. Was her body warning her that it wasn't over yet?

Keenly, she stretched her senses out for any errant detail. She heard the slosh of water as it pushed around her and dripped from a pipe far off to the right. And then finally there came the softest scuff of a step from the creature that was attempting to sneak up on her.

She turned slowly, expecting to face Harry.

Brian Childs stood a dozen feet away, as still as a statue, hoping perhaps that in the darkness she would not sense him. He wouldn't know that she could see. Ribbons of blood covered his shirt front, suggesting that imitating a statue had proved successful with the hapless cata-philes he had hunted down. She lowered her head, still watching him, and growled.

He shifted his pose, and now waves of enchantment poured from him. She had always thought him attractive, but he appeared now stunningly handsome, his jaw sharpening, becoming curiously like Vincent's, as if that image had been plucked from her thoughts. Hooks of desire tried to find purchase in her, but slid around her ineffectually. She imagined that any unprepared prey would fall immediate victim to his charms. He was like a closing flytrap. Such power he had. Where did it come from? All varieties of plants and animals used chemical lures and defenses. But pheromones came from fatty tissues, and generating them expended energy. Generating so much that victims swooned—that had to be exhausting. He would need to feast again to make up for it; and in her case, all that effort was wasted, although he didn't—couldn't—know.

Tentatively, she reached out one hand as if imploring him to take it, take her. She leaned back her head, offering her throat. Brian, or what he had become, closed the distance. Behind his glamour, she could make out the true—and more repulsive—image of him. That image, ghostly, flicked its tongue back and forth between two prominent fangs at the corners of its mouth. He hovered over her smaller form. With a gesture almost affectionate, he tilted his head toward her to feed. His eyes rolled up in anticipation.

Her fingers closed around his throat. The black claws punctured his jugular. He stared at her, wide-eyed, betrayed. The glamouring fell away, revealing skin rough as tree bark. A moment longer she held her fingers pressed tightly to his neck. Then she opened her grip and the blood sprayed out of him. In an instant he was nearly unconscious, his head rolling. She let go completely. He collapsed at her feet.

She left him and returned to The Crawl. All the while she listened but there was still no sign of Harry Gordon, no sound or scent of him. He had fled. Vincent had said unlike most of them he could go out into daylight. What was it, made him different? Made them all different? Brian was not like Vincent or Deb. He shared traits with Harry but wasn't the same, either. As Decebal had told Ruksana while she sat in Malpensa Airport, she was their scourge, their natural predator. She still didn't know how he knew this, but he had predicted she would transform in their presence exactly as she had done.

In the chamber where most of the bodies lay, she tore open the plastic sealing the case of bottled water. The bottles were difficult to hold, but she slit them open and poured the contents over herself, rinsing away the blood in her fur. The horror of what she'd done would not be so easy to wash away.

She opened the packs and collected clothing from them, stuffing everything into one of the cleaner rucksacks. Then she returned to the castle room to retrieve her own coat and the bag with her passport and money.

Vincent lay there on his side. He had finally lost the strength to hold himself together, and his intestines were pushing out through his black turtleneck. His eyes glittered in the light of the fat chandelier candles. He watched but didn't move more than his lips. Only pink froth bubbled out through his horrible teeth. Tradition dictated staking vampires or cutting off their heads. She didn't see the necessity of that. Vincent was not going to recover.

Navigating the metal stairs up proved the most challenging. Her strange feet slid, skittered, and she could not hold onto the railing, the coat and the rucksack. What was it going to take to change her back now? Why wasn't this like the first time? She would have been happy to forget all that had happened this evening, to erase the emerging part that had thrilled at slaying them all as she had forgotten the rapist she had slaughtered.

At the door she paused to listen beyond it and, hearing nothing, opened it and left the catacombs. No one was outside nor lurking in the woods. In this form, she thought, it would be impossible for someone to sneak up on her. No sign of the driver or Harry, not even his scent on the wind.

She stepped out from the stone tower and into a patch of moonlight through the bare branches overhead. The moonlight stung. Unprepared for the sharp pain, she stumbled and pitched forward onto her knees. Her joints burned. She tried to twist away from an agony that was inside her, impossible to escape. Terrible light exploded in her head.

When it was over, she lay curled into a ball on the cold ground. Her arms, hands, her body was hers again. The pain was something distant, as if it had happened years before. Naked, she rolled onto her hands

375

and knees, and let her head loll for a minute before she tried to get to her feet. But the energy was there, that same strange energy that had come to her in the aftermath of the first attack.

Ruksana shivered in the cold, alive and tight as a steel spring, but finally dug into the rucksack for clothes. They weren't terribly fresh but at least they were warm. She put on her coat, sat on the concrete step and put on her shoes. Her own bag she stuffed into the rucksack, which she hoisted onto her shoulders.

She walked back through the woods dividing the highway. As she did, a half dozen police vehicles, sirens screaming, zipped past her. She turned and walked the other way on the shoulder of the road, facing the oncoming traffic.

Shortly she saw a sign for Pl Denfert-Rochereau a half kilometer ahead. It bore the symbol for a metro station, an M in a circle. She was ravenously hungry now, so instead of going straight to the airport, she took the Metro to St. Michel, and went up to find a restaurant. She hoped it wasn't too late. She wanted something hot.

– 15 –

The story broke before her AirFrance flight boarded.

A suspended television screen between gates flashed the word "Vampires!" over the head of the news anchors.

A slaughter had taken place in the catacombs below Paris and all further tourism there was suspended indefinitely. The prim newswoman announced, "We have confirmation from the government this morning that the plague of new vampires that has swept North America is with us in Paris. Like warring street gangs, it seems that different factions of these blood-suckers are fighting for dominance. This latest battle left only a single human survivor, whose identity is being withheld at this time, but who provided police with a description of one of the monsters."

Possibly the strangest Identikit drawing in history filled the screen. She knew it must be a portrait of her, although nowhere in the fierce eyes, elongated snout and sharp elflike ears could she find a hint of herself.

"Strangest of all, according to the survivor's statement, this creature defended him against others and led him out of the tunnels to safety. So far there's been no trace of it anywhere, although the remains of four so-called vampires and seven humans have thus far been located in the tunnels. The commissioner of police assures the public…"

Ruksana moved away from the screen, retreating to the nearest restroom in the terminal. She sat in a stall for perhaps half an hour, so paralyzed by the enormity of it all that she couldn't manage to stand up and leave. She had killed them eagerly. If Harry hadn't escaped, she would have hunted him down, too, though he had been her good friend. Deb Arliss had roomed with her. Why was there no guilt, no shock as there had been the first time?

Finally she heard the announcement that her flight was boarding, and she made herself stand, heft the rucksack and unlock the stall door. In front of the sinks she paused to splash water on her face. She stared deep into her own eyes as if she might find her soul in them, and made a particular point of not looking at her silvery mane of hair.

−16−

"Nine hundred years ago," explained Decebal, "our Wallachian ancestors, yours and mine, were tasked with guarding the living from vampires. I suspect we had been doing this for many centuries before this was written down. We were considered to be werewolves, just as the revenants were classified all as vampiri. The specifics are lost now beneath layers of superstition and folklore, just as Pausanius conflated the real story of Damarchus the Parrhasian, our ostensible ancestor, with Lycaon, a king who in myth was turned into a wolf by Zeus for serving the god a dish of human flesh. Even Pausanius confessed he doubted the connection, but he gave us no more of Damarchus than that. The truth is all lost, save that our kind existed in 400 B.C., and so, we must assume, did our enemy."

Seated across from him at the kitchen table, Ruksana pushed back her white hair. "Then where did they all go?" she asked.

"I don't know. The Church moved across Europe and wherever they landed, they cursed our kind as demons in league with the devil, just as they did every witch that they ever encountered. There was no white magic. There was their good and everyone else's evil, period. That drove us into hiding, but it doesn't account for our eradication.

"I think we were already fading away then, as were the last of the vampiri. Sometime before the 13th century, we vanished altogether, consigned to legend, to stories that scared children—the Red Riding

Hoods and the clever foxes. We were a genetic dead end, Neanderthals. Believe me, I have looked into every written text to try to find evidence of us, and there's so little. The Church had usurped our position in the society as they did those Night Walkers of the Friuli that I've told you about. There could only be one force for good in any village, and by Christ it was going to be the Church. So when we truly died out, we had already been consigned to the shadows."

"So I am a throwback to an earlier form? A genetic freak?"

He sat awhile, thinking of how to explain it.

She had arrived home almost twenty-four hours after arriving in Paris. On the flight she'd been unable to sleep, but once home could barely make it up the stairs to the apartment while hanging on him. Decebal had carried her to her bed, and she'd slept the clock around. He had made her a fritata and she had eaten every speck of it and drunk an alarming amount of wine, which seemed thus far not to affect her.

He said, "When I saw that white spot in your hair, I wondered. That— the mark of the white wolf—is in the literature. Of course in the stories, werewolves are just wolves. What I told you I suspected when you called me back from Malpensa Airport is true. And what I read while you faced them in Paris makes me think that we have had this inside us all this time, waiting for their return. Now because of some unexplained agency it's come to life again. The nature of that agency interests me only a little. What interests me utterly is that at a time when the vampiri resurrect in our midst, you have become what our people used to be. That is too great a coincidence." He smiled slightly. "Also, I am glad to have removed your shoes."

She smiled, too, though not sure whether she was persuaded by his folkloric endeavors or not. He had shown her a piece circulating on the internet, penned by an internationally renowned folklorist named Swann that came to not dissimilar conclusions about the vampires themselves. Decebal was even now trying to contact this man. But she was tired of the discussion.

She reached over and fumbled with her phone. "I need to call Costin," she said.

Her grandfather gently placed his hand over hers and the phone. She met his gaze, full of portent. "You cannot," he said.

"Bunicul, don't terrify me anymore. What's wrong?"

"You cannot see Costin ever again."

"Why, because of what I am? I know, I'll have to make him understand that there's a very real risk being with me—"

"It's too late for you to make him understand. The risk was the risk. He…he turned while you were in Paris. The police have him. Or they did."

"What?" Then she shook her head and smiled. "But that's good, he's already infected, we won't have to worry, will we? He's—"

"Little Flower, Costin is not of our people."

She sought in his eyes for any meaning but the one he intended. "No," she said, "it's not right. How did I do this to him?" She glanced desperately around the apartment as though it was a trap, a cage, and there had to be an escape, a way to put things back where they should be. "I have to get out of here, away, anywhere. I can't stay here."

His hand upon hers squeezed, bringing her attention back to him. Her eyes welled with tears, and so did his. "No, it's not right," he told her, "nor is it your fault. It is a thing that happened to you, to him. To us. If you go near him now, you'll kill him. There won't be a choice, it will be instinct. What you described, the thirst in the catacombs—that will befall you again. He is the enemy now through no fault of his or yours. I'm so sorry."

She wiped at her eyes. "Don't you see, this is why I can't stay here. Listen to me, bunicul, if I'm carrying this disease, this plague, then I'll contaminate you. I might have already."

"You might. And I can only hope that you do. Look at me, child. See how I'm wearing out. It's all I can do to climb the stairs in the evening now. My finger joints are knots of pain, and soon my hands won't be any good for anything. I have to pay attention just to hold the handle of a pan. Another year and it'll be a fork that I can't hold. I live in books, in my mind. That's what I'm reduced to. And here you have this energy that you can harness.

"I want to feel what that's like. I want to run in the night the way our people did once through the mountains of Wallachia. Even one time before I die, that would be enough."

"Oh, bunicul."

"Hush. There's more you must consider. These polyphyletic creatures know that you're the enemy now. They know that you are out here in the world, a threat to them. But they don't know about me."

"About you?"

He lowered his gaze and stared hard at his hand upon hers. She looked too, as a tremor shook his hand. He gritted his tobacco-stained teeth, but would not stop.

Slowly, his fingers straightened, thickened, and a soft white fur sprouted along the backs of them and all the way to his wrist. His fingernails began to lengthen. He broke off then, collapsing back in his chair, his breathing labored.

"Grandfather, stop." She leaned across the table to him.

He pressed his hand to his perspiring forehead. It was his normal old hand again, liver-spotted, etched with blue veins. His hair, she only realized now, was whiter than she remembered.

"Whatever comes," he told her softly, "we will hunt it together."

"EPIPHANY" PT.2

Yvonne Navarro

— 11 —

The first time she kills another human being, all she can think afterward is that it was nothing like the rabbit.

It is the first week of December and some of the people in town, most likely the ones with kids, are already starting to put out Christmas decorations. Mooney is a week away from completing her first semester of college, and although she's technically four months pregnant, she looks like she's a lot farther along, six months at least. She hasn't gone back to see Dr. Guarin, but she isn't feeling good anymore, either. She's eating fairly decently—her belly isn't affecting her ability to catch small animals at all—and she's not nauseous, exactly, but she's…*something*. It's a feeling that's in her head and her heart; it grows a little day by day and nothing she can think about will shake it off.

Then she wakes at a quarter to four in the morning with the complete certainty that if she doesn't change how things are going, the child inside her is going to die.

When she looks back on it later, there was never any question about what she needs to do. Months ago she mastered the art of moving silently without even trying; the trailer is in total darkness but she slips on some clothes and is out the door without so much as making the old floor creak. There is a three-quarter moon outside but the changes in her DNA have enhanced her night vision; it's as if God Himself has flipped a light switch on the desert. She sees everything, in every direction, from the peeling paint on the wood siding on the north end of the trailer to the faint movement of the scrub grass up the road and to the right that signals a scavenging coyote. In fact, even though it's at least three hundred feet away, she can smell it—it has blood on its muzzle from something it killed and ate, probably a pack rat, only a few minutes before.

But the coyote holds no interest for Mooney tonight. She has gone beyond that.

Driven by need and guided by instinct, she moves into the cold desert night, circling behind Mother Gaso's trailer and heading southwest. The Mexican border is only slightly over twenty miles away but she feels no fear as she eases through the winter-dead grasses, slipping from mesquite tree to mesquite tree, passing like a shadow despite her size. It takes twenty minutes at the most and then she catches the scent of humans. It drifts on the still, chilled air simply because it is so out of place to creatures, like her, who can pick up such things. There are two of them, and they are heavy with the smells of unwashed flesh, dirty clothes, and cheap snacks, the kind that can be carried easily but in reality give no nourishment to a weary body and only serve to drive a man's thirst to maddening proportions. Mooney lifts her head and inhales more deeply—they have run out of food and water, and now they are sluggish with the cold, surprised by the elevated climate that drops the nighttime temperature to only a few degrees above freezing.

When Mooney strikes, she goes for the male.

It is not a loss of control, of something that happens out of desperation and the body overriding everything else in order to feed itself, as happened with the rabbit. She knows what she is going to do before she makes her move. She even plans it, choosing the male because the female is more likely to run rather than try to come to his aid. Her hair and teeth are not the only thing that has evolved more and more with the passage of time; in the last couple of weeks she discovered it was no longer necessary for her to break her prey's neck to disable it because her bite could do exactly that—once her teeth sink into something's neck, it's pretty much all over. It's a handy new skill and one she appreciates, reminiscent of the disabling effects of a Mojave rattlesnake's neurotoxin, even if she is a little disconcerted at the thought of how much venom must be going into her meal in order to so quickly incapacitate it. However much it is, it's spontaneous—no conscious thought, no evaluation, no preparation, and she herself is immune to it. Strike, feed, and it's over.

Just like with the man who is her first human casualty.

Mooney is fast enough to be little more than a blur coming at the two Mexicans. One moment she's watching them from thirty feet away, the next she shoves them apart hard enough to send the female tumbling ass over head into the grass. Mooney snaps her mouth closed on the male's neck and her fangs hook instantly into his carotid She feels a hard pulse from somewhere beneath her cheekbones and the fist the guy is sending toward her head stalls in midair as he goes first rigid, then limp in her arms.

A few feet away the woman is screaming but Mooney isn't sure if it's because her companion is being attacked or because she's landed nearly on top of a sprawling prickly pear cactus, the kind with two-inch purple spines; they are buried deeply into one side of the illegal's flesh from shoulder to hip, and every time the woman tries to free herself, they just push deeper. Mooney would be annoyed at the constant bawling except that this is her first human meal—

—and it is *exquisite.*

The man's blood fills her mouth and coats her tongue, and it's like everything good she's ever eaten rolled into one fantastic flavor. She has no idea if it's because this is her first time or if it's because she didn't realize until now, this very moment, that despite her ingestion of animal blood, or maybe *because* of it, she and her unborn child were slowly starving. She can also taste *him*, what he is in his very core—refried beans and pork tamales, corn tortillas, roasted poblano peppers and homemade *mole* sauce, the fiery salsa that he has always loved.

He will never taste it again.

It seems like only moments before Mooney is finished and the man's body is motionless in her arms. She lowers him easily to the ground and studies his face, which is as still and waxen as the high, bright moon above her. His mouth is slack and his eyes, slitted open a quarter of an inch, stare at the sky. Does he see something now that she knows nothing about? Perhaps someday she'll know, when her own time comes; for now, Mooney leans over and draws her hand down the front of his face to close his eyelids just to make sure he isn't looking at her. She feels guilty but in a distanced sort of way, like the way someone feels a twinge of regret when they see the soft, gentle gaze of a cow but sit down to a bowl of beef stew at dinner that evening. For her, the distance between the two is just a lot less. She wipes her mouth with the back of her hand but her skin comes away clean—there is no telltale red stain, and certainly nothing resembling the gore depicted on television or all the famous vampire tales. Good; she would hate to be so stereotypical.

The woman's screams have faded to miserable sobs interspersed with a high-pitched wheeze every time she tries to move. Mooney walks over and looks down at her, sees the way the barbed spines of the cactus have embedded themselves deeply into her body. The woman has her eyes squeezed shut as if she can't bear to see any more than she already has, or perhaps she believes she is about to die and doesn't want to stare death in the face. She is wrong on both accounts; Mooney is satiated and has no desire or need to harm this pathetic Mexican woman—she's really more of a girl closer to Mooney's own age. Mooney circles her, studying the tangled mess of cactus pads, but she can't see any way to get the woman free without puncturing her own skin in hundreds of places.

"I'm sorry," she says at last. "There's nothing I can do. If I had gloves…" She doesn't finish because the woman obviously doesn't understand her and the sound of Mooney's voice is only making her more panicked. Even if she did understand English, she would never believe she wasn't slated to end up just like her dead partner. Pulling her from the massive cactus trap would probably cause her enough pain to make her go insane, and then what? She would flee into the desert and die anyway.

Ultimately, Mooney walks away and leaves the woman to whatever nature and the desert night have planned for her.

–12–

Her face fills out and she gains eight pounds overnight. When she looks in the mirror before class the next morning, her skin is glowing with health. She feels as good as she did after the first time she vomited at school, but this time she's not hungry. She has come to think of herself as the counterpart to the snake god that so many ancient Native Americans revered; maybe, like that powerful, dangerous entity, she only needs to fully feed every so often. The people of Sells have no idea how lucky they are as the days pass and Mooney remains full and peaceful, content to go to her classes and stay in her bed in the deepest, darkness hours of the night.

Ten days before Christmas, she knows it's time to feed again.

She sees the Chief of Police's car go screaming past on Highway 86 in the morning before her first class, hears more sirens somewhere south of town as she heads into the classroom. With no tall buildings or trees to break it up, sounds—a dog's bark, a coyote's yipping, the scream of a hawk as it dives for its prey—carries for miles out here. Her fellow students in geology and micro economics grow more distracted as the morning progresses, sneaking peaks at their cell phones and texting until the economics teacher orders them all turned off. When class is over, Mooney gathers her books and thinks about going to sit in the sun, intent on taking a nap until her business management class starts at one o'clock. There are only five other students in her current class and the one-word comment that a dark-skinned girl whispers in her direction as she and her friend push past Mooney is as clear as though it were announced over a loudspeaker.

"Parasite."

Instead of being angry, the name-calling actually makes Mooney stop and think. Is she just that? A parasite—a creature that takes from a host and gives nothing in return, has absolutely no value? She thinks about this as she goes outside and finds her place in the sun, pulls out the combs in her hair to let it fall around her shoulders and back like a protective, snake-patterned blanket. But what about the people of this town? Those who are so much like Mother Gaso, who takes the state's money to support Mooney but gives her charge almost nothing in return. Used clothes from the thrift stores, little to no spending money, and barely a place to sleep and decent food to eat. She knows the state funding isn't much so all that would be okay, except there was no attention or affection either, those things so abundantly free and available. Yeah, her and all Mooney's other relatives who had turned their backs on her when her parents died. And why? Because of a generation gap, a rift in the ability to understand. It is true that she herself has taken, but only from one person and only because it was necessary for survival in the way of nature and the food web—the predator and the prey, natural selection and may the strongest survive. So who were the *real* parasites?

She is still thinking vaguely about this concept throughout her afternoon class as the hunger pangs begin to grow in her belly and bleed away her ability to focus. Of all her classes, this one has the fewest students—only three besides her—but they all sit as far away from her as they can. Mooney is not insulted. In fact, she prefers it that

way, especially when she realizes that there is a point at which her appetite begins to veer toward the feral, where her need for sustenance begins an insidious attempt to exert power over reason. She doesn't want to be like the raving creatures in the sensationalistic photos that are being splayed more and more frequently on the nightly newscasts—surely there must be others like her, who still have logic and intelligence, *reasoning*, about how their new lives will play out, the paths waiting for them in the future. Right now, with emptiness twisting in her belly and the baby undulating in her womb like some kind of multi-limbed Kali godlet, she can literally smell the blood of each of the other people in her class. The fat boy at the end of the row is showing false bravado by sitting only three desks away from her; she can tell from here that he has cats in his family and his mother uses baby powder-scented dryer sheets when she does laundry. The two girls huddling in the back corner are barely out of their teens and beneath cheap, girly cologne, they smell mostly like Mother Gaso and almost all the other people in this town, the instructor included—tepary beans, pork, the oil that is soaked up by the fry bread that is a staple of their diets. They really should eat better.

Finally the class is over and she can get the hell out of here and unbind her hair. But her relief is unfortunately temporary, abruptly cut off when she rounds the corner of the building and finds Chief Delgado standing in her way. "Red Moon, I need to talk to you."

Mooney stops and waits. She has an idea—a very good one, in fact— what this is about. "All right."

"Border Patrol found a couple of bodies outside of town this morning," he says. His voice is even but his heart is beating faster than it should—he's afraid of her. He continues anyway, doing a fairly good job of keeping his voice steady and authoritative. "A man and a woman. Know anything about them?"

Mooney doesn't flinch. "Why would I?"

"They were illegals," he tells her. "A man and a woman. One of them was bit in the neck. Maybe a snakebite." He reaches up and takes off his sunglasses, fixing his oil-dark gaze on her without flinching. "But I'm thinking it's probably something else. And because they're not sure, they're going to do an autopsy and find out." When she doesn't say anything, he continues. "The woman somehow got herself all wrapped up in a bad cactus patch. I guess she couldn't get herself free. Probably died of exposure. The man's looking pretty dried up, if you get my meaning."

"And what does this have to do with me?"

He stares at her. "I'm wondering if you've gone a step farther in this vampire thing," he says bluntly. "Maybe you thought you'd try something new, so you chased him down."

Mooney laughs. "Seriously?"

His expression folds itself into a scowl. "Yes, Red Moon. There is nothing funny about murdering someone."

"Have you looked at me lately, Chief?" she demands. "Really *looked* at me?" When he blinks because he doesn't know what she's talking about, Mooney drops her book bag on the ground then uses her hands to mold the oversized peasant blouse she's wearing around her belly. "It's been a few months since you came by the house," she says. She lets her tone of voice make it clear she thinks he is a fool. "Do I look like I can chase someone down?"

The look he gives her is one of half embarrassment, half horror. "You're pregnant?"

"I think the answer to that is pretty obvious."

"Who's the father?"

Now it's Mooney's turn to be surprised. "That's my business." It's an automatic answer, but even if she were able to declare something other than *one of the three Mexicans who raped me that day in the desert*, she wouldn't have. It takes only an instant for her to follow his line of reasoning, but she doesn't say anything more.

Delgado's face darkens and he folds his arms across his chest. "Word around town is there's a boy on the north side who has the virus, too."

"No one talks to me, so I haven't heard anything about it. If there is, I don't know him."

"I don't guess you have to." His jaw is set with anger. "That kid you bit went to school and probably kissed his girlfriend, who spread it to her mom, who gave it to the toddler at home and then sent him to day-care the next morning." He lets out a breath. "Hell, you did the same damned thing, didn't you? No telling how far it's gone now."

She shrugs. "What do you want me to say, Chief? It's not like it was on purpose—I had no idea anything was wrong. A virus spreads and there's not much anyone can do about it. It's why we can't get rid of the common cold."

"This is a whole lot more serious than a cold, Red Moon."

"But not nearly as bad."

His head jerks. "How do you figure that?" he demands. "People die because of this. Themselves, and they kill others. We've all seen the news, read the papers. And now you brought it here."

"People die because of a lot of things," she snaps back at him. "In case you aren't keeping up with your own department, that would be DUIs, drug use, and hey, let's not forget all the crap—drugs, weapons, people—being smuggled in by the Mexican cartels. Maybe you ought to re-order your *To Do* list and put me at the bottom instead of the top. Besides, the virus would have gotten here eventually on its own. All the scientists say it's already spread around the world. Only a very few change because of it, and not all of those end up dying or going crazy or whatever. The doctors aren't even close to understanding it. There are probably shitloads of vampires out there going about their lives and no one even knows what they are." Too late she realizes that's the worst thing she can say, but like so many things in life—the wrong words, rejection, hatred, the taking of someone's life—it can't be undone or forgotten.

"I'm going to suggest again that you leave," Chief Delgado tells her stiffly. "Everyone's already jacked up about the murders this morn-ing—"

"Murders?" Mooney puts her hands on her hips, intentionally emphasizing her belly. "You said the guy was snake bit and the woman died from exposure. How does that equate to murder?"

He steps close to her. "You think tying your hair back makes that rattler pattern invisible, girl? Not hardly—everyone's seen it. And I still remember those fangs you showed me in the trailer." Mooney back-steps, knowing he will think it's because she's intimidated. The truth is he, like her fellow students, just smells like food. "If someone gets a hair up their ass and decides it's you who killed those Mexicans, I won't be able to protect you."

She tilts her head knowingly. "Won't be able to? Or just *won't*?"

"Don't go there," he snaps. He jams his hat harder onto his head, even though there's no breeze to work it loose. "You know how it is around here, Red Moon. Everyone is related to everyone else, even if they have to go back generations to find it. It's a small pool of shared DNA. People marry closer than they probably should and there's not much new blood. People know that, and they aren't happy to find out you brought in something that might change them."

"Don't talk to me about how everyone is related to everyone else," she says acidly. "When my parents were killed and I needed help, suddenly no one in Sells counted me as family even though I'm blood relations to probably half of them, all because my parents thought differently and taught me early to realize I don't need the Tohono O'odham to dictate every part of my life. Now as far as anyone here is concerned, I'm just a little monthly cash that helps Mother Gaso pay her bills. Maybe they should have gotten the hell out of this nowhere little desert town a hundred years ago and spread their Tohono O'odham joy a little farther." It's her turn to step toward the Chief of Police, boldly encroaching into his personal area, pushing her face forward until it's only an inch from his. Something about her expression makes him stumble backward this time. "Did you ever consider that the change is a *good* thing, Chief Delgado? That it's something the Tohono O'odham people *need*? Everything should evolve, including humans. Adaptation is the key to continuing existence. The scientists talk about how this is ancient stuff in our DNA coming back to life, but I wonder if it's not just God looking to fix his own screw-ups.

"Maybe I'm the wake-up call the people around here have needed for centuries."

–13–

The mountains to the west are too far to see, so it's a long time until nightfall. Hunger twists in her gut and the child moves with it, pushing restlessly at the walls of her womb. With Mother Gaso watching her never-ending television shows inside, Mooney sits on a battered lawn chair in the bare ground area at the back of the trailer, ignoring the textbook on her lap and instead watching the sun sink like a ball of liquid yellow fire in the washed-out western sky. This is the time when the sun is at its strongest and she soaks in the heat greedily, pulling her blouse up to expose the stretched skin of her belly and warming herself like a snake on a rock. The baby rolls and moves almost constantly, and she's amused by the tiny bulges that rise and fall along the otherwise smooth and round surface. The movement increases as the light gives way to dusk and finally darkness, tiny fists and feet lightly battering her insides as though the infant is showing its frustration at her food-deprived stomach. Or is the baby itself hungry? She thinks the answer is yes on both accounts.

Mooney rises and walks into the desert. She needs no preparation, no weapons or water. Above her is another three-quarter moon, waning just as it was the last time she fed; she thinks this is pretty funny—no doubt someone will make this connection and start blathering about werewolves, and someone else will act like an "expert" and point out that werewolves only come out during the full moon. If there's a reason at all to the timing, it's far more likely that the moonlight enables her to hunt more easily.

And so that her prey can see her more easily, she has not changed from the bright yellow peasant blouse she slipped on this morning. She is a splotch of unexpected color in the night, luminous in the moonlight as she weaves a path between the mesquite and acacia trees, the cholla and prickly pear. The brittle grasses nip at her ankles but she makes no sound as she moves across the rock-strewn ground and works her way steadily through the sparse knee-high scrub. She heads southwest and walks for nearly three hours before she finds what she wants, and she locates them long before she allows them to see her.

Three silhouettes of men, dark-skinned Mexicans who have no right to be in her country. They have found a reasonably deep dry wash sheltered by older mesquite trees and used it to conceal the tiny fire they've built to try and hold off the bitter desert cold. Mooney can smell the rabbit they've caught and spitted above the fire, its bloody pelt carelessly tossed aside for the insects and scavengers. She moves closer, still not making a sound, and breathes deeply...

Oh, yes.

She wouldn't have been able to do this, to know what she does, had it not been for her New York trip and the gift that Michael Frayne bestowed upon her that day in Starbucks. Now, however, her world is entirely different—*she* is different. Their scents swirl inside her nose and fill her with memories, none of which are good: the beating, the pain, the rape, their mocking, triumphant laughter. Even so, she is oddly calm, ruled not by anger but by cold logic and need. She must feed, and in doing that, she will also have justice. How fitting.

Mooney steps from the shadows of a nearby mesquite tree and stands in the moonlight.

The first one jerks as he sees the bright yellow of her blouse, then he shouts and runs toward her. His companions do the same—no hesitation, no stopping to think or question the presence of a brightly-dressed woman so far into the emptiness of a nighttime desert. It is only when she doesn't run that they slow and circle her warily, like a trio of coyotes measuring a larger animal before their attack. One has some kind of club, another a small machete, the third nothing but his bare hands. They jabber away in Spanish but Mooney cannot understand them—she knows only a few basic words in Spanish because what little second language she has is Tohono O'odham. What she does comprehend, however, is the universal sound of their cruel merriment. The tallest one, unarmed, is the boldest and he reaches to grab her arm, then his face goes rigid with shock as he recognizes her. There is something in her face that makes him yank his hand aside as his laugh sputters away. Her black eyes reflect the moonlight and look like slits of silver. The other two glance from him, their leader, to her and back again; recognition slides across their features and suddenly they, too, realize that something here is terribly, terribly wrong.

"Do you remember?" Mooney whispers.

She has no idea if they know what she is saying, but their size, number, and weapons are simply no match for her. She lunges at the one with the knife first, catching the wrist of the other man before the downswing of his club can connect. She snaps the bones as though they are kindling at the same time her teeth plunge into her target's shoulder. She feels that same semi-pleasurable pulse in her jaw and he reels away from her, his dirt-encrusted knife dropping forgotten to the ground. The first Mexican is screaming at the night sky, his voice raw and loud and shattering the desert's tranquility; his club had tumbled away when she crushed his wrist and now she wrenches him forward and bites him, too. His wails change to a strangled sound and he topples to the side, rolling into a ball and spasming in the spiky weeds next to the other one. Instinctively Mooney knows they are beyond saving and will die whether or not anyone arrives to help them. Had she realized this, she would have bitten that woman last month, given her a mercy kill before leaving her to die in the agonizing grip of the prickly pear cactus. Live and learn.

The leader of the trio is not as brazen as his companions. He snatches up the machete and backs away to what he thinks is a safe distance, holding the blade in an easy grip that speaks of experience. His gaze skips away from her face to focus on her belly, and Mooney can *feel* his bewilderment as he dares to try to meet her eyes again. Does he wonder how she can defeat them in her condition? Or does he wonder about something else? She decides to enlighten him.

"*Tu*," she says and points to him. Then she points at her stomach. "*Padre.*"

The expression on his face is, as has been said in a thousand television commercials, priceless.

He shakes his head vehemently. "No," he says. "*Yo no soy el padre.*"

Mooney just smiles and nods.

And leaps for him.

It is over almost too quickly to be satisfying. As fast as he is with the machete, it is nowhere near fast enough—the blade never even comes close. The thing that saves her from complete disappointment is the feeding; he is larger than the man she killed last month, and she is hungrier. She drinks deeply and slowly, her lips pressed intimately against the artery just below the man's jaw, enjoying the warmth, flavor and spiciness of his blood and feeling the excitement of her baby ease to satiation as her stomach fills and the nutrients flow from her to it. The sensation is almost orgasmic, fueled as it is not only by hunger but revenge—how fitting that this child should be nourished by the blood of its father. By the time she is finished and she drops his corpse unceremoniously on the dirt, his companions are also dead, the toxins from her bite having sent her retribution through their bloodstream.

Mooney leaves their bodies in the red dirt of the desert and, because it's exactly what they deserve, hopes that its creatures will tear them apart.

−14−

They come for her in the early morning, on the last day of the year. She stands on the front steps and watches Delgado's blue and white police car turn into the dirt driveway, followed by two green and white Border

Patrol vehicles, one an oversized SUV, the other one of those super-fast Chargers all the cops are driving around in these days. There are a handful of additional cars behind those—two rattling pick-up trucks and three dirty old sedans, all of which she's often seen around town. She wonders why they need all these vehicles, and in particular the police SUV. Perhaps they think she is too big to sit in the back seat of one of the regular cars, although any such speculation is probably due to her last, uncomfortable-looking appearance in town on the final day of the semester, only the day after her triple killing in the desert. She dismisses the idea as quickly as it runs through her mind; that they would ever be concerned with how she feels is ludicrous. Whether they are or aren't is irrelevant anyway; a lot has happened since two weeks ago, and she is not the same Red Moon Lopez she once was.

393

Mooney finds the fact that Chief Delgado has brought the Border Patrol as backup insulting, their very presence as contradictory as her own modern day existence as a Native American. Everyone pounds their fists for equality and fair treatment in the white man's world, but at the same time they put labels on themselves and borders on their land and scream at the first idea of integrating into the rest of the country. Instead of being American, Mooney is Native American; instead of being Tohono O'odham, Mooney is an outcast; instead of being human, she is a vampire. Each layer of classification results in more separation, uncompromising and isolating. Where is the equality for her in this situation? Or for those like her? It is, she thinks, the ultimate hypocrisy: the oppressed Native Americans turn on her and, if the men coming toward her home are any indication, single her out for elimination, or at the very least, imprisonment. Assuming they plan to let her survive the next hour, would they someday walk her and the others who emerge as a new species of human along their own Trail of Tears?

Instead of pulling in close to the trailer, all the cars stop a hundred or so feet away. One by one the engines shut off but no one gets out until Chief Delgado finally opens his door and heaves his bulky frame into the eye-blistering morning sunlight. He must be the catalyst for everyone else to act courageous, because more doors open and men spill forth like bad examples of vigilantism, hips swaggering under the weight of gun belts, a couple of others armed with hunting rifles, their holds careless and loose as they try their best to fake their bravery. They stand and stare in her direction, as if willing her to simply walk down the steps and hold out her wrists for a set of handcuffs. She can feel their uncertainty from here, can smell the fear seeping from their sweat glands, even from this distance. At last Chief Delgado starts toward the trailer with the others lagging behind; the sight of Delgado's "backup" makes the phrase *I got your back* run through Mooney's mind with a new and mocking definition. Such loyalty.

Mooney watches as they approach, but she is not afraid. She never was. She is, however, infused with a different emotion, although pinpointing it is difficult. Pride comes to mind, but that applies to something other than herself. She lifts her face to the morning sun and her snake-patterned hair cascades down her back, protecting her body from the elements, camouflaging her when she needs it. Her deep inhalation pulls in a chilly morning breeze that is slowly warming and the smell of the creatures heading toward her who don't realize they are little more than a convenient food source. That makes her grin, and suddenly she knows exactly what she is feeling.

Power, and...

Superiority.

Mooney knows then, instinctively, that they will not, they *cannot*, hurt her. Even with weapons, they aren't good enough, strong enough, or fast enough. She has been busy these past couple of days, and she is hungry already, ready to eat again in a much shorter time than previously.

And she is not alone.

Her changed DNA had accelerated her pregnancy, but there was even more of a reason her belly grew so large and so quickly. Dr. Guarin had gotten a hint of it during her last examination, but since she had not returned and had refused an ultrasound, he'd never had the opportunity to recognize the echo as the heartbeat of a second fetus. The birth of her twins the day before yesterday was both bloody and painful, but already she is healed, trim and lithe, and far stronger than she has ever been. Now, inside the trailer, her son and daughter suckle contentedly at either side of Mother Gaso's throat; Mooney has already decided she will not see them feed on the blood `of the Sonoran desert's small, scrawny animals as she once had to.

Her morning visitors are closer now, within fifty feet, and now the desert breeze carries their scents to her as individuals. Each is unique, the young, the old, the well-fed, the almost alcoholic. The first time she admitted to Chief Delgado that she was a vampire, she'd told him she would not bite him, but reality will apparently necessitate she break that promise. Her mouth waters and a delicate line of saliva slips out of the corner of her lips. She wipes it away and smiles at the men, being very careful not to show her teeth.

Not long ago she was a woman who felt she had no identity, born in a land stolen by the white man from her forefathers, then herself made into an outcast by those same kinsmen even before she was raped and cast aside like unwanted trash by invaders from a neighboring country. If her DNA is to be believed, the people headed her way are not the rightful owners of this land. The rightful owners, the *true* First People, were Mooney's own long-ago ancestors, the ancient forefathers whose powerful DNA had come before them and then gone dormant…

But had resurrected itself within her and the few chosen like her.

And, of course, in her offspring.

Tomorrow marks the start of a brand new year, a new age. Mooney is moving forward, transforming herself into that which the future demands in order that she survive. And in doing so, she has also regressed to the time of her first *real* ancestors. For the first time in her life, she finally knows who she is:

In this re-emergence of America's natural selection, this re-evolution, she is truly the first of the First People.

– 15 –

Six Months Later

There are three vehicles coming across the border, matching black SUVs with thick, oversized tires and reinforced bodies lifted high enough to clear most of the brush and cacti. The tires are probably filled with some kind of semi-solid sealant to withstand the cactus spines, but the SUVs are still going slowly, driving around the mesquite and acacia. Mooney grins because ironically, their back and forth movement reminds her of a snake sliding across the ground.

She climbs into her own vehicle, a battered and dusty Toyota 4-Runner that looks like it has seen better years. When she starts the engine, it thrums with nearly silent power, proof that the work done by the Border Patrol mechanics is spot on. The interior is clean and comfortable, outfitted with a radio and GPS, air conditioning for the summer and heat for the winter. She's been driving the truck for over five months;

when she needs to, she uses the radio to call in but has never turned on anything else. She doesn't even know if the other stuff works. There are spotlights across the roof, but she only uses these to help the Border Patrol clean up.

What's in the SUVs the drug mules are driving? Marijuana? Cocaine? Black tar heroin?

People?

No illegals, that's certain. Those are generally relegated to bigger vehicles, the kind that can transport anywhere from a couple of dozen to a hundred at a time, and they're never like the fine rides crawling across the unforgiving dessert a half mile away. Probably just drugs, but you never knew when a cartel might decide to transport some trusted workers to the U.S. side in an effort to set up a good way station.

Mooney angles across the terrain without using the headlights, her natural night vision picking out the easiest and fastest route to intercept the small fleet. Pedro Conde is about thirty-five miles to the southwest, but it's doubtful they crossed the mountains. More likely they'd driven the dirt roads that ran around the southeastern end, then crossed the board by veering onto natural terrain toward the southwest, searching for a place that ICE and Border Patrol agents won't be watching.

But there is one special ICE HSI agent who *is* watching. Very closely.

Mooney picks a spot about a hundred feet in front of the oncoming entourage, stops the truck and turns on the headlights. The cones of light thrown by the lead vehicle's bright lights dip sharply as the driver slams on the brakes and stops. The rear two SUVs do the same, and the first SUV and Mooney's 4-Runner face each other in some kind of cold, mechanical stand-off. Other than the engines, the only noises come from the desert, insects and night creatures testing the air, a slight breeze that makes the driest mesquite branches shiver and rattle. After a silent thirty seconds, she opens the door and steps outside, leaving her badge and the bullet-proof vest she has never worn on the passenger seat. There is no overhead light to let them see her face or anything else about her before she gently closes the driver's side door. She could be a man or woman.

Or something they've never even considered.

Doors open in all three vehicles and men climb out, two from each SUV. Mooney hears the ratcheting of metal as slides are pulled back on weapons; with her empty hands hanging by her sides, she steps in front of the 4-Runner's headlights, giving them a very female silhouette. Although they can make out only her outline, she can see every detail in front of her, their dark hair and skin, jeans, dirty T-shirts, boots. And guns, of course. Always guns.

"*Hola, amigos,*" she calls in a sweet voice. "*¿Cómo estás?*"

They are already starting toward her. The man in front, probably the leader, lowers his gun slightly. "*¿Quién eres tú?*" he demands. *Who are you?*

But Mooney has already disappeared into the night before he so much as finishes his question.

She is a blur in the darkness as she takes them out one by one, always coming from whatever direction they aren't facing. A cry of surprise, a quick death, then on to the next; bullets start spewing from their weapons when the second man falls, but they are useless streaks of yellow fire into the desert. Her work is over so quickly—literally in less than a minute—that there isn't even time for her to enjoy it. When the killing is done she feeds, taking her time and sampling from each, being careful not to get blood on her clothes. After she is filled, she goes back to the 4-Runner and takes two clean half-gallon jars from the back. She chooses the body that had the purest blood, slices his throat open with the swipe of a single fingernail, then hoists him up with one hand and lets gravity do the rest, filling both jars to take home to the twins. They're growing at an amazing pace and the meal won't hold them for long, but the inviting empty land leading to Route 85 and the fenceless span of border between Mexico and the United States insure an unending supply of retribution-free food.

When her task is complete, Mooney wipes down the jars and dumps an oversized glob of hand sanitizer onto her palm to cover the blood smell. She radios her position to headquarters, then leans against the truck door to wait, popping a mint into her mouth and remembering how life always seems to bring the biggest surprise when you think you know what you're facing.

Mooney already knows that she will be behind the back of the trailer before the first shot is fired, but suddenly Chief Delgado does the one thing she least expects.

He leans over and lays his rifle on the ground.

As she stares, the others do the same—pistols, rifles, a couple of old shotguns, all splayed on the dirt like a display at some ratty western gun swap. Even the two Border Patrol agents who bring up the rear are now unarmed as they move past the fidgety townsmen and take a spot on either side of Chief Delgado.

"I'm not looking for a war, Red Moon," Delgado says. "No one wants the wrong people to die."

The wrong people? She raises one eyebrow but says nothing.

The younger of the Border Patrol agents lifts his chin. "We have a proposal for you, Ms. Lopez." He glances at the other agent, who's clearly older and his supervisor. Even at this distance, Mooney can see that his name tag reads Silva. Moving slowly, Silva walks to the bottom of the stairs and holds a business card out to her. She takes it and sees the Immigration and Customs Enforcement logo.

"On the back of that card is the name of an ICE special agent recruiter," Lopez tells her. He folds his arms and looks at her steadily. "He'd like to meet with you about becoming an ICE Homeland Security Investigations agent."

It's taken eighteen years and a genetic modification, but finally Mooney has found her place in this world.

"LAST BITES"

Jonathan Maberry

Washington, DC
188 Days after the V-Event

Luther Swann sat as straight as the stitches and bandages would allow. He tried to follow everything the senator from Georgia was saying but there was a constant ringing in his ears. The doctors said it should go away in time. Like the cuts and broken bones. All of it would heal in time.

At least he hadn't lost his leg, like the V-8 team leader; or been blinded like the TV reporter from Chicago. All Swann had were sixty-seven stitches and eight broken bones. The thigh was the worst, but in this war, that was getting off light.

"Tell us about the vampires in Scranton," asked the senator, repeating his question louder.

Swann said, "Most of the vampires killed in the raid on the New Red Coalition headquarters in Scranton were too badly burned or mangled for us to classify them. However, of the twenty-eight prisoners taken there and the four scouts arrested later that day, we have members of nine separate vampires species, including another *kathakano* and two more of the German *alps*. There was also one previously unrecorded species."

"Unrecorded at all, or—?"

"No, unrecorded in this conflict. Henry Periot of Albany demonstrated qualities consistent with a *craqueuhhe*, a kind of necrophageous vampire from France. Mr. Periot's physical strength was far greater than most other species of vampire and even though he was shot four times he did not sustain life-threatening injuries. Dr. Feldman can speak to that, but apparently his body's wound-repair system is working at a super-normal level."

"How many species does that make so far?" asked the senator from Maine.

"Twenty-seven," he said. "But if we count those species who have played no part in the hostilities, then the number jumps to eighty-nine. And that includes a few species from the non-hostile population that we haven't yet labeled and which, apparently, are not mentioned in the literature of world myth."

The senators studied him.

"How many reported cases of infection?" asked the senator from Maryland.

Swann rubbed his eyes. "In the United States? Just under eighteen hundred. Worldwide, just over five thousand."

"Do you have a guess as to why America has a disproportionate number of cases based on world population?"

"I have a few opinions," said Swann. "The first is that America is a melting pot. It's in our tourist brochures. We have an incredibly wide and deep genetic pool here. That accounts for a lot of it, and because of so many people with mixed heritage, it's obvious why we're seeing so many of the most dramatic variations on the classic ethnic vampire model."

The Maryland senator cocked an eyebrow, "But...?"

"But overall, I think the math is wrong."

"Wrong...how?"

"The numbers are low. Way too low. It's almost two hundred days since the first outbreak, since Michael Fayne. We know that the I1V1 virus has had a chance to spread everywhere. The ease of international travel and the movement of so many people every minute of every day has spread the disease everywhere. And our scientists are still insisting that it's in the atmosphere, that it's being released every day by the melting of the polar ice. Taking all of that into account, and given that everyone on earth carries the dormant gene for vampirism, then there is no argument to support why there aren't many more cases of active infection."

"Many more? How many more would you like?" asked the senator, grinning at his own bad joke.

Swann gave him a flat stare. "It's not a matter of what I would *like*, senator, it's a matter of what makes sense. There should be tens of thousands of infected by now. Maybe hundreds of thousands. Here and abroad."

The senator from Maine leaned forward. "Do you have any explanation for why there aren't more infected? I mean, if you're correct, there should be vampires everywhere."

Swann was a long time in answering. He looked into eyes of the men and women who sat at the long table across from him.

"Senator, I think there *are* more infected. Many more."

The senators said nothing. Not all of them looked shocked. Swann studied the faces of those who did *not* look at all surprised.

"After the first wave of the infection, what did we do?" asked Swann. "We went to war with them. Immediately. No pause, no hesitation. By the fifth reported case we were labeling the infected as terrorists. Granted, some of them attacked first, but when we pushed back we pushed back very hard. Perhaps too hard. I warned General May about this. Perhaps we pushed back so hard that the vampires learned a valuable lesson."

"What lesson is that?" asked the senator from Georgia.

"They learned to wait. They learned to watch. They learned that to survive, they have to hide from us."

"So, you think that there *are* more of them out there?"

"Yes, sir, I do."

"What are they waiting for? To attack when we're not looking? To blindside us?"

"I would think, senator," said Swann, "that they're studying us. They *know* that we are their enemies. We've taught them that. Just as we've taught them to fear us and hate us."

"That goes both ways," said the senator from Maine.

"It does, in some cases," admitted Swann. "But I've been saying all along that we need to look at the numbers, to consider the percentage of the vampires who have been openly aggressive toward us. Even now, even after all this conflict, we're still only talking about a small percentage of that population. Two percent, maybe. But now…after what we've done, after Scranton and Philadelphia and the other major offensives, what do you think is going through the minds of that other ninety-eight percent? What do you think is going through the minds of all of the vampires who are still hidden? The vampires who are to blend in? What do you think they're thinking about us?"

The senators were quiet for a moment, then the senator from Louisiana spoke. She had been quiet for most of the hearing. "I have two additional questions."

Swann nodded.

"Do you truly and unreservedly believe that there is a large population of undeclared infected hidden within the human population?"

"Yes, senator, I do."

"And…do you believe that this war is over?"

"As long as both sides react with fear and aggression, then no, senator, I do not." Swann gave her a small smile. "Do you?"

The senator paused for just a moment before replying. "No, I do not."

Swann cocked his head to one side. "Then I hope we make better choices tomorrow than we did today, because if this escalates into another full-blown open conflict, I don't think either side can win. Or, to put it another way, I think both sides would lose. Wouldn't you agree with that, senator?"

The senator from Louisiana gave him the smallest of smiles in return. "Yes, Professor Swann, I believe I would."

V-WARS CORRESPONDENTS

KEITH R.A. DECANDIDO is the author of almost 50 novels, at which point he gets a gold watch. Or something. He's written a butt-load of novels, short stories, and comic books in a variety of media universes, from TV shows (*Star Trek, Supernatural, Buffy the Vampire Slayer*) to videogames (*World of Warcraft, StarCraft, Dungeons & Dragons)* to movies *(Cars, Kung Fu Panda, Serenity)* to comic books (*Spider-Man, Hulk, X-Men*), and much more. In 2009, he was granted a Lifetime Achievement Award by the International Association of Media Tie-in Writers, which means he never needs to achieve anything ever again. He's currently working on a Leverage novel, *The Zoo Job*, based on the hit TNT series. His original fiction includes the high fantasy police procedurals *Dragon Precinct, Unicorn Precinct*, and *Goblin Precinct*; and the SCPD novel series about cops in a city filled with superheroes, including *The Case of the Claw* and the forthcoming *Avenging Amethyst*.

He's involved in two other shared-world projects: "Tales from the Scattered Earth," which includes his novels *Guilt in Innocence*, and the upcoming *Innocence in Guilt*, as well as a series of short stories; and *Viral*, a series of thriller novellas created by Steven Savile, for which he wrote the opening story, "-30-." In case "The Ballad of Big Charlie" didn't make it obvious, Keith was born, raised, educated, and still lives in the Bronx. Keith is a member of The Liars Club. Find out less at his mediocre web site at DeCandido.net, read his inane bloggy ramblings at kradical.livejournal.com, or follow him on Facebook (facebook.com/kradec) or Twitter (@KRADeC).

JOHN EVERSON is a former newspaper journalist and the Bram Stoker Award-winning author of the novels *Covenant, Sacrifice, The 13th, Siren* and *The Pumpkin Man*. He has also penned several short fiction collections including *Needles & Sins, Vigilantes of Love* and *Cage of Bones & Other Deadly Obsessions*. Over the past twenty years, his short stories have appeared in more than 75 magazines and anthologies. His work been translated into Polish, Italian, Turkish and French, and optioned for potential film production. For information on his fiction, art and music, visit John Everson: Dark Arts at www.johneverson.com.

GREGORY FROST is a writer of best-selling fantasy, supernatural thrillers and science fiction. He has been a finalist for every major fantasy, SF, and horror fiction award. His latest novel-length work is the YA crossover duology, *Shadowbridge* and *Lord Tophet*, which was voted "one of the four best fantasy novels of the year" by the American Library Association; it was also a finalist for the James Tiptree Jr. Award in 2009, receiving starred reviews from Booklist and Publishers Weekly. His previous novel, the historical thriller, *Fitcher's Brides*, was a finalist for both the World Fantasy and International Horror Guild Awards for Best Novel. He is the current fiction workshop director at Swarthmore College in Swarthmore, PA. Gregory is also co-founder of The Liars Club.

NANCY HOLDER is the *New York Times* bestselling and multiple award-winning author of the *Wicked, Crusade*, and *Wolf Springs Chronicles* series. She's written tie-in projects for "universes" including *Teen Wolf, Buffy the Vampire Slayer, Angel, Hellboy, Saving Grace, Zorro*, and *Kolchak*. Her latest novel, *On Fire: Teen Wolf*, will be out in June. She also writes comic books and pulp fiction and teaches in the Stonecoast MFA program at the University of Southern Maine. She and her daughter, Belle, are published co-authors, and spend every dime they make together at Disneyland. Visit Nancy at www.nancyholder.com, and on Facebook and Twitter.

JONATHAN MABERRY is a *New York Times* bestselling author, multiple Bram Stoker Award winner, and Marvel Comics writer. He's the author of many novels including *Assassin's Code*, *The Wolfman*, *Dead of Night*, *Patient Zero*, *Ghost Road Blues*, *Rot & Ruin* and others. His nonfiction books on topics ranging from martial arts to zombie pop culture. His comics for Marvel include *Captain America: Hail Hydra*, *Punisher: Naked Kills* and the *Marvel Universe vs.* franchise. Since 1978 he has sold more than 1200 magazine feature articles, 3000 columns, two plays, greeting cards, song lyrics, poetry, and textbooks. Jonathan continues to teach the celebrated Experimental Writing for Teens class, which he created. He founded the Writers Coffeehouse and co-founded The Liars Club; and is a frequent speaker at schools and libraries, as well as a keynote speaker and guest of honor at major writers and genre conferences. Jonathan lives in Bucks County, Pennsylvania with his wife, Sara. Visit him online at www.jonathanmaberry. com and on Twitter (@jonathanmaberry) and Facebook.

JAMES A. MOORE is the award winning author of over 20 novels, thrillers, dark fantasy and horror alike, including the critically acclaimed *Fireworks*, *Under The Overtree*, *Blood Red*, the *Serenity Falls Trilogy* (featuring his recurring anti-hero, Jonathan Crowley) and his most recent novels, *Cherry Hill* and *Smile No More*. He has also recently ventured into the realm of Young Adult novels, with his new series *Subject Seven*. In addition to writing multiple short stories, he has also edited, with Christopher Golden and Tim Lebbon, the *British Invasion* anthology for Cemetery Dance Publications. The author cut his teeth in the industry writing for Marvel Comics and authoring over 20 role-playing supplements for White Wolf Games, including *Berlin by Night*, *Land of 1,000,000 Dreams* and the Get of Fenris tribe book for *Vampire: The Masquerade* and *Werewolf: The Apocalypse*, among others. He also penned the White Wolf novels *Vampire: House of Secrets* and *Werewolf: Hellstorm*. Moore's first short story collection, *Slices*, sold out before ever seeing print. He recently finished his latest novels, *Blind Shadows* and *Run: A Subject Seven Novel*. He is currently at work on several additional projects.

YVONNE NAVARRO lives in southern Arizona, where by day she works on historic Fort Huachuca. She is the author of 22 published novels and well over a hundred short stories, and has written about everything from vampires to psychologically disturbed husbands to the end of the world. Her work has won the HWA's Bram Stoker Award plus a number of other writing awards. Visit her at www.yvonnenavarro.com or www.facebook.com/yvonne.navarro.001 to keep up with slices of a crazy life that includes her husband, author Weston Ochse, three Great Danes (Goblin, Ghost and Ghoulie), a people-loving parakeet named BirdZilla, painting, and lots of ice cream, Smarties, and white zinfandel. Her most recent work is *Concrete Savior*, the second book in the *Dark Redemption Series*.

SCOTT NICHOLSON is the international bestselling author of more than 25 books, including the thrillers *Liquid Fear, Chronic Fear, The Red Church*, and *Disintegration*. He has also written four children's books, four comics series, and six screenplays, as well as 80 short stories. His website is www.hauntedcomputer.com.